ALL THE DARK SECRETS

When terrible tragedy strikes at the local colliery, the residents of Fairley Terrace's ten houses suffer more than one loss and for Maggie Donovan the world turns upside down. Turning for comfort to the one man she can trust, she finds a sudden and undeniable passion instead. But any future with Josh Withers seems a betrayal of her past, and Maggie realises the only way to survive is to conceal a very dark secret of her own . . .

ALL THE DARK SECRETS

JENNIE FELTON

LARGE PRINT

First published in Great Britain 2014
by
Headline Publishing Group

1 885664 21

First Isis Edition
published 2015
by arrangement with
Headline Publishing Group

A catalogue record for this book is available
from the British Library.

ISBN 978–1–78541–036–9 (hb)
ISBN 978–1–78541–037–6 (pb)

Published by
F. A. Thorpe (Publishing)
Anstey, Leicestershire

Set by Words & Graphics Ltd.
Anstey, Leicestershire
Printed and bound in Great Britain by
T. J. International Ltd., Padstow, Cornwall

This book is printed on acid-free paper

For my darling husband Terry
1936–2013

Acknowledgements

When I'm writing a book there is always some new avenue to explore about which I know nothing! This time it was the making of stained-glass windows. And I couldn't have done it without the help of a dear friend, Richard Jones. Richard's father did actually make a stained-glass window for a cathedral in New York in the 1920s, which gave me the idea. As a hobby Richard followed in his father's footsteps. He explained the process to me, showed me round his workshop, and loaned me a manual which had belonged to his father. Due to ill health, he was unable to check what I had written and sadly has since passed away, so while I hope I have not made any blunders, if I have they are entirely down to me. RIP, dear Richard.

So many people play a part in bringing a book to publication that listing them all would be a bit like an overlong Oscar acceptance speech, so I'll simply say a huge thank-you to everyone at Headline. I must make special mention, though, of my lovely editor, Kate Byrne. And many thanks too to Sheila Crowley, my agent, and her assistant Rebecca Ritchie, who is never more than a phone call or an email away.

Last but not least, my heartfelt thanks to my wonderful family and friends who have been there for me throughout a very difficult year. I love you all.

Historical Note

"In this grave are deposited the remains of the twelve undermentioned sufferers all of whom were killed at Wells Way Coal Works on 8th November 1839 by snapping of the rope as they were on the point of descending into the pit. The rope was generally believed to have been maliciously cut."

So reads the inscription on a gravestone in a churchyard in the Somerset coalfield near to my home, and it provided the inspiration for the terrible accident which is the catalyst for my story.

Though of course what I have written is all fiction, this disaster was all too real.

I have, however, used a certain amount of poetic license in my story, which begins in 1895. By this time the hemp rope hudges had long been replaced by four-deck cages. However, I have explained that the owner of Shepton Fields, my fictional pit, was a penny-pinching coal master who did not want to invest in his mine. I hope readers will bear with me on this — and enjoy the story!

Don't go down in the mine, Dad
Dreams very often come true

Robert Donnelly and Will Geddes

Prologue

Something terrible was going to happen. Maggie knew it. One minute she was walking hand in hand with Jack in the dew-fresh meadow, watching the grey morning sky streak pink above the dark skyline, listening to the dawn chorus of the birds and loving the scents of summer; the next she was so afraid she could scarcely breathe. The feeling of oppression and dread was all around her in a suffocating cloud, and inside her too, tightening her chest and chilling her to the marrow. Her fingers tightened on Jack's, but when she turned towards him, looking for comfort, she saw that it wasn't Jack at all, but her father, Paddy. And Frank Rogers, who lived a few doors away from them, was there too, taking her other hand. Frank Rogers? Why was Frank here? She didn't understand. It made no sense, and the confusion added to the terrible feeling of foreboding, bringing her to the edge of panic.

Maggie's footsteps faltered and she came to an abrupt halt, but the hands holding hers pulled her on.

"Come on, my girl, we'll be late."

"No! Dad — no! Stop! Please . . . You mustn't . . ."

But it was no good. Her father ignored her pleas, dragging her on along the path worn by many feet through the knee-deep grass.

1

"No, Dad, no!"

And then, quite suddenly, the ground was giving way beneath her, and she was falling. No, not falling, plummeting into inky blackness. She tried to scream, but no sound came; it was trapped somewhere deep inside her. There was a sharp, fetid smell in her nostrils and a rush of cold air against her hot cheeks, but she couldn't breathe. Every vestige of breath was being forced out of her lungs, and terror was coursing through her in an icy tide. Falling, falling, faster, faster; dear God, would it never stop?

It was the violence of the jolt that woke her. For a moment, Maggie lay motionless, feeling the rapid beating of her heart beneath her ribs and staring into the darkness until her breath came easier and the terror began to recede a little.

A dream. That was all it had been. A dream — well, a nightmare really. But it had been so real! And the horror of it was with her still, binding her tightly like a fly caught in a spider's web. She sat up, swinging her legs over the edge of the bed. She didn't want to risk going back to sleep in case the dream began again. She padded across her tiny bedroom and drew back the curtains, letting moonlight flood in. Outside, it was illuminating the very fields she had been walking through in her dream, and beyond them, the great black carbuncle that was the colliery waste tip — the batch, as they called it. Though it was a warm summer night, Maggie shivered, and the shiver was not just because she was suddenly cold, but because the terrible sense of oppression was still enveloping her, just as it had in the dream.

All very well to try and tell herself it was nothing, just a shadow of something that hadn't been real. All very well to scoff and pretend it meant nothing. Maggie didn't like it when she got a feeling such as this one, different from normal apprehension because there was no solid reason for it. Almost inevitably it was the precursor of something bad. Ever since she was a little girl she'd known that. A sick feeling in her stomach at the thought of going to school and there'd almost certainly be trouble of some kind; childish trouble, maybe, but something to upset her day. One summer, she hadn't wanted to ride on the back of the hay wagon as she usually loved to do; she'd felt that awful shadow of dread as Ewart and Walter, her older brothers, had pulled her up on to the bales of hay. And sure enough, the wagon had rolled into a rut in the ground, and two or three bales broke free and fell, taking the children with them. Walter had broken his leg, and walked with a limp to this day. So it had gone on over the years: not a frequent occurrence but one that was reliable enough to alarm her when the dark foreboding overcame her.

Maggie had never told anyone about it; she didn't even want to acknowledge that somehow she could foresee the future. In any case, she wasn't seeing, exactly, just feeling a distress that wasn't yet justified. But this . . . this was far worse than anything she had ever experienced before. It wasn't just the terror of the dream, though, that was still making her shudder, even though she was now wide awake. It was the dense black

3

fog that had closed in around her, and the dreadful weight inside her, making her feel sick with dread. As she stood at the window, the moon disappeared behind a cloud and the whole vista before her went dark, as if a light had gone out. Maggie shivered again. Should she tell someone this time? But tell them what? That she'd dreamed she was falling? Nothing too unusual in that. That Jack had turned into her father and Frank Rogers had been there too? Nothing unusual in that either. Everyone knew that dreams made no sense. No, it was this weight of oppression that was really frightening her, but if she told anyone about that, they'd just say it was left over from the nightmare, and perhaps they would be right.

Reluctantly Maggie dragged herself back to bed and pulled the woollen blanket of crocheted squares up to her chin. But it was a long while before she could bring herself to close her eyes, and even longer before she fell into a fitful doze. She didn't dream any more that night, but when she woke next morning, the feeling of foreboding was still with her.

She must forget about it, she told herself. It was nothing but the aftermath of a horrible dream. And even if it wasn't, there wasn't a thing she could do to avert whatever it was that was going to happen.

CHAPTER
ONE

June 1895

"Hey, look, it's the rag man! Billy the rag-and-bone man!"

"Where'd you get yer coat, Billy? Off Farmer Barton's scarecrow?"

The jeering youths were squatting collier fashion against the rough stone wall of the outbuildings that backed Fairley Terrace — or, as it was known locally — the Ten Houses. Billy Donovan had seen them there as soon as he came out of the back door of number six, and his heart had plummeted in his skinny chest.

His tormentors were the bigger — and older — lads who worked with him at Shepton Fields Colliery — fourteen and fifteen to his twelve. As far as they were concerned, he was fair game; they called him a sissy because he still worked on the screens in the pit yard whilst they were "carting boys" underground, and they looked down on him for being one of the Donovans, the poorest family in the rank and, in their eyes, nothing but scum. Billy wished he didn't have to walk right past them, but there was no way he could avoid it, not unless he wanted a good hiding from his father. He glared resentfully at the quart jug in his hand. Paddy

5

Donovan had told him to take it down to the snug of the Prince of Wales and get it filled with best bitter. And when he wanted a drink, Paddy Donovan was not a man to cross.

"Hey, Billy! Billy the Didiky!"

Billy lowered his head, staring at the ground and plodding on. It wasn't the first time he'd been called a didicoy, as the locals referred to gypsies. He longed to yell at the lads that he wasn't a didicoy, that his father was Irish and had only come over to England because there was no work to be had in Dublin, but he knew better. It would only make things worse if they saw they were getting to him. Fury rose like bile in his throat. How he hated them! Not that that would worry them much. But one day — one day he'd get his own back. Just let them wait — he'd show them!

"Hey, look, Billy's off to the boozer!" That was Frank Rogers, who lived at number two, a big, thickset lad with a puggy nose and a loud, jeering voice. "Gonna make you big and strong, is it, Billy? That'll be the day!"

"Naw, it's for old Paddy to get tipsy again. He oughta get you a decent pair of trousers afore he spends it on beer." That was Charlie Oglethorpe, at fifteen, the oldest of the lads.

"Shut up!" Billy muttered.

"What's that you said?" Charlie snarled.

A hobnailed boot shot out right in front of Billy, and he cannoned forward, landing with a sickening thud on his hands and knees, the quart jug shooting from his hand as he tried to save himself.

6

"Have a good trip, Billy," Frank Rogers laughed.

The jug had rolled towards the youths; they leapt to their feet, and Dick Riddle, who fancied himself as a footballer, got a steel-capped toe underneath it and gave it a nifty flick.

"To you, Frank!"

To Billy's horror, the youths began kicking the jug one to the other. He scrambled to his feet. His hands were grazed and bleeding and his neck hurt, but he scarcely noticed. If the beer jug got dented, he'd be for the high jump and no mistake!

"Give it here! Hey, don't do that! Give it here!" he begged.

His tormentors ignored him, kicking the jug about enthusiastically. Then Frank Rogers dived to pick it up, waving it in front of Billy's face, taunting him.

"Want yer jug, Billy? Come and get it, then!"

Billy threw himself at Frank, skinny arms flailing wildly; Frank twisted away. Billy made a grab at Frank's shirt, and the thin fabric ripped thread from thread beneath his skinny fingers.

"You tore me shirt, you little bugger!" Frank threw the jug down, diving for Billy instead. They went down in a heap, Frank pounding the smaller boy furiously, Billy scrabbling helplessly. Charlie and Dick stood by, yelling encouragement.

"Give him a good hiding, Frank!"

"Kick his brains out — if he's got any!"

Frank was sitting on top of him now, his full weight pressing down on Billy's stomach, whilst he banged the smaller boy's head on the hard ground. Billy was seeing stars, and he could scarcely breathe. If he thought at all, it was that his last moment had come.

The commotion of the fight carried clearly through the open door into the little scullery of number six, where Maggie Donovan was blacking her boots ready for work next day. Maggie always blacked her boots on a Sunday evening — the rest of the week they had to make do with a lick and a promise, just a quick wipe over with a duster to keep them looking respectable enough to meet the high standards of Mrs Augusta Freeman, owner of the drapery shop in High Compton where Maggie was a sales assistant.

"I expect my girls to be smart at all times," Mrs Freeman had said when she had taken Maggie on as an apprentice. "A slovenly appearance is the outward sign of a slovenly mind, and will not be tolerated."

Her small, beady eyes had gleamed behind her wire-rimmed spectacles as they swept critically over Maggie, seeking the shortcomings she had expected in a Donovan, and finding none. Maggie's high-necked blouse was as pristine white as only a blue bag in the washing water could make it, and perfectly pressed, her dark skirt the very picture of modesty, and the tiny posy of silky rosebuds pinned on the waistband showed style and imagination, both qualities that would prove an advantage in a draper's assistant. But all the same . . .

"I also expect a willingness to work hard, an ability to learn, and, most importantly of all, courtesy to the customers," Augusta said sternly. "The customer is always right, no matter how much you think they might be inconveniencing you."

"I know," Maggie had said. "I won't let you down, Mrs Freeman, I promise."

That had been five years ago. Now Maggie was a fully fledged assistant in the drapery shop, and was even helping to train up Cathy Small, the newest apprentice. She'd done very well for herself — for a Donovan — everyone agreed.

Maggie paused now in the cleaning of her boots, blue eyes narrowing as she heard the commotion. A fight — there was no mistaking it. And Billy had just this minute gone out to fetch her father's beer.

She dumped shoe brush and boot on the oilcloth-covered cupboard that served as a worktop and hurried to the door, looking along the rank. Yes, it was a fight, and as she had feared, Billy was involved. She couldn't see much of him because that great galumphing Frank Rogers was sitting astride him, but she'd know his carroty hair anywhere. And it was plain he was getting the worst of it, as usual. Why did those bullies have to pick on him all the time?

Maggie shook her head in disgust and set off up the rank to intervene. It wouldn't help Billy in the long run, but she couldn't stand by and watch her little brother taking a beating from those thugs.

"Hoi!" she yelled loudly as she approached them. "What d'you think you're doing?"

For answer, Frank Rogers banged Billy's head on the ground again.

The Irish was up in Maggie now. Abandoning all pretence of dignity, she ran the last few yards to reach the fighting boys, grabbed hold of Frank's collar and gave it a hearty tug so that his shirt buttons popped all at once. His head jerked round, surprise and outrage written all over his rather red face.

"Stop that this minute!" Maggie ordered furiously. "Leave our Billy alone and pick on someone your own size, you bully."

For a moment she thought he was going to defy her and let into Billy again. Then he thought better of it. He'd had his fun, and there would be plenty of other times to knock seven bells out of Billy when his sister wasn't there standing over them like an avenging angel. He gave the boy one last punch, just to show he wasn't really afraid of Maggie, and let him go.

"Bloody Donovans!" he muttered as he got to his feet, trying to button his torn shirt, which was now also open to the waist.

Maggie was anxious that the boys might have really hurt her brother, but she knew if she showed concern it would only give them more ammunition to taunt him as a sissy. "Come on, our Billy, get up from there," she said sharply. "Look at the state of you! And isn't that our jug over there by the wall?"

None of the lads dared touch it again, right under Maggie's baleful eye. She might be a Donovan too, but they had a healthy respect for her sharp tongue, and anyway, she was a grown woman. As a rule, lads didn't give cheek to grown women — especially ones as pretty as Maggie. She rescued the jug and thrust it at Billy.

"You'd better go and get this filled up before our dad comes out and gives you what for," she told him. Then, turning to the other lads: "And if there's any more trouble from you lot tonight, you'll have me to answer to."

With that she turned and headed back towards number six.

"Billy the baby!" Frank hissed at Billy, who had started off in the direction of the Prince of Wales but had stopped to mop at his bloody nose with a rag that had once been the tail of a shirt but now did service as a handkerchief. "You won't always have your sister there to save your bacon. Next time . . . just you wait!"

Billy felt sick, not just from the beating, but from fear for the future. Frank was right — there would be plenty more episodes like this one. He lived in the same rank as his tormentors, worked at the same pit. There was no escaping them and there never would be.

Unless he could get away to Yorkshire, like his two older brothers, Ewart and Walter. Hope flared in him briefly, then flickered and died. Yorkshire was likely just as full of bullies as Somerset, and they'd pick on him too. Everybody picked on him and always had. Even his own father. Paddy had no time for him and wasn't afraid to show it.

Billy trudged painfully along the rank, fighting back tears. Resentment and hatred for his tormentors was like bitter bile in his mouth, mingling with the salty taste of his own blood. Oh, if only he could think of a way to get back at all of them. Just give him a chance and he'd show them he wasn't the useless lummox they all thought him. But how he'd ever get that chance he didn't as yet have the first idea.

"What's going on?"

Rose Donovan, Maggie's mother, was at the back door, peering out anxiously. Truth to tell, Rose's permanent expression was one of anxiety, and not without reason. Life had dealt her a bad hand. She had once been a pretty girl with a fine head of curly chestnut hair, which Maggie had inherited, and a neat figure, and she had caught the eye of plenty of lads who would have made her a far better husband than Paddy Donovan had. But from the moment he had arrived in High Compton in search of work, she had wanted no one but him. She had fallen head over heels for his swarthy good looks — dark hair, and eyes as blue as sapphires — his powerful physique, and the wonderful Irish brogue that was so different to the Somerset drawl she was accustomed to and sounded so much more romantic to her ears.

Rose had lost her head as well as her heart and allowed Paddy liberties no decent girl should allow a young man. But at least he had married her when she had found out that there was a baby on the way — well, wouldn't her father have taken the double-barrelled shotgun he used for shooting pigeons and rabbits to Paddy if he had not?

And then her troubles had started.

To begin with there was his gambling. Paddy fancied a bet on the horses and often passed a betting slip to the bookie's runner who hung around outside the

12

Prince of Wales pub, but though he was sure he was picking a winner, more often than not he lost. "The bookie always wins in the end," Rose's father used to say, and he was right.

Then there was his drinking. Rose had known that Paddy liked a drink, it had been part of his charm, but there was nothing charming about him when he got roaring drunk on a Saturday, spending half the wages that had been doled out to him before he even got it home. There was nothing charming about him when he yelled at her for not having a meal ready for him on the table, or a copper full of water hot enough for his liking when he wanted his bath. And there was certainly nothing charming about him when he turned on her and beat her.

The black eyes he gave her were the worst; she could hide the bruises on her arms under long sleeves and grit her teeth against the pain in her ribs so that nobody knew how much every breath hurt her. But the black eyes she could not hide, and no matter what stories she made up to excuse them, she knew the neighbours could see right through them to the shameful truth.

The first time Paddy had hit her was when Maggie was just a little girl, and truth to tell, Rose hadn't been able to find it in her to blame him. It was no more than she deserved, she'd thought, as she burned with guilt and shame for what she'd done. What husband wouldn't be driven to lash out under the circumstances? But after that first time, it had happened again and again, year after year, whenever he was angry with her, whenever he was drunk, whenever she fell foul of his quick temper and surly moods.

He didn't often hit her these days, and never when Maggie was about. He seemed to have a respect for his daughter that he never showed anyone else, certainly not Billy, and not even Ewart and Walter, his two elder sons. When they'd lived at home they'd tried to intervene too, but they had only been given a good hiding for their trouble. All Rose's sons took after her in build, and Paddy, who scorned them for it, could have beaten any of them senseless with a hand tied behind his back if they'd tried to take him on.

It was because of Paddy that Ewart and Walter had gone off to work in Yorkshire, Rose felt sure. They said it was because the work was easier there than in the narrow, faulted Somerset seams, but Rose knew that wasn't the real reason. They had wanted to get away from their violent father and the stigma that attached to them for being his sons. They had wanted to be able to bring home their wages and not have him take half off them to buy more drink, or back some "sure-fire winner". And Billy would do the same, she thought, just as soon as he was old enough. She couldn't blame them, but she did blame Paddy for depriving her of her children.

And not only her living children, either, but the ones she had lost for ever, too. Three miscarriages she had endured, one of them certainly because Paddy had punched her in the stomach when she was seven months gone. And then there was little Alice, dead of the fever. If they hadn't been so poor because of

14

Paddy's drinking and gambling, maybe she could have afforded the doctor's bills and Alice would be alive today. Ten years old she'd be now, but to Rose she would always be fourteen months, with a big gummy smile, toddling unsteadily on her plump little legs. The memory of Alice was an ache in Rose's heart that never went away.

Nowadays Rose was just a shadow of the girl she had once been. Her once pretty face was thin and lined, with a defeated look to it. The harshness of her life had taken its toll on her small frame, making her scrawny, and she was always exhausted. She took in washing to help make ends meet, so her hands were red and puffy, and in winter, long, painful cracks opened on her fingertips and never healed until summer came. Now, just to make things worse, she was pregnant again. She'd thought all that was behind her; the prospect of going through it again was a constant worry that weighed in her stomach just as the baby soon would.

She stood in the doorway now, arms wrapped around her sunken chest, fingers plucking nervously at the blouse that years of careful laundering had made thin as a bee's wing, as Maggie flounced back along the rank.

"What's going on? What's the matter now?"

"Oh, just those louts picking on our Billy again," Maggie said crossly. "I gave them a piece of my mind, but a fat lot of good that will do."

"What's that?" Paddy appeared in the scullery, on his way out to have a smoke while he waited for his jug of beer.

"Our Billy," Rose told him. "Them boys have been picking on him again."

Paddy grunted, surly and impatient as he always was where Billy was concerned. "It's time he learned to stand up for himself."

"That's easier said than done, Dad," Maggie retorted. "They're twice his size, all of them."

"And he's just a sissy!" Paddy said scornfully. "Our Ewart was no bigger at his age, but he could give as good as he got. He didn't get picked on, our Ewart, and woe betide the bugger who tried."

Maggie said nothing, but she knew he was right. Ewart had been like a little terrier, gouging and fighting dirty if needs be. But Billy wasn't Ewart, and never would be. As Rose had said to her once, Billy was different to the others.

"I've got to get these boots cleaned," she said, picking up the brush from where she'd left it. "Jack's calling for me later on, and I expect we shall go out for a walk."

"Oh, that's nice," Rose said automatically, but her heart sank a little.

Though it should have been no real surprise, since the two of them had been friends since childhood, she had a feeling things were getting serious between Maggie and Jack Withers, and the thought of her daughter leaving home if they should decide to get married was a depressing one. Maggie was the one ray of sunshine in her drab existence, and she was so good with Billy, too. With a new baby on the way, Rose didn't know how she would manage without her.

But these feelings were, she told herself, just her being selfish. She should be glad for Maggie — and she was. Jack was a lovely lad. She'd known him all his life, as the Withers family lived just four doors up the rank at number ten. He was quiet, and as decent as they came, unlike his brother Josh, who had a terrible wild streak. When he was younger, you always knew that if there was trouble, Josh would be at the centre of it, and later on, the police were at his door so often that it seemed certain he'd end up in prison. In the end his long-suffering parents had sent him off to Florrie Withers's brother and his family in Wales in the hope that they could knock some sense into him, but he was back now, and as far as Rose could see, as wild as ever. What was more, she had noticed the way he looked at Maggie and been a little alarmed. She, more than anyone, should know how easy it was to be bowled over by roguish charm, and though the two boys were like peas in a pod, both dark and good-looking, she worried that the very things that made Josh unsuitable were the same ones that might well make him attractive to a girl.

No, all things considered, she should just be grateful that it was Jack and not Josh that Maggie had taken up with. But she couldn't help hoping it would be a while yet before they decided to get married.

CHAPTER
TWO

Though both had plans for later, the two Withers brothers were enjoying an early-evening pint in the public bar at the Prince of Wales.

The inn was crowded, as it always was on a Sunday night. Most weekday evenings the miners who frequented it were too tired to socialise — by the time they'd had their bath and their tea, all they wanted to do was collapse into an easy chair and "snooge" till bedtime. And at this time of year, there were gardens and allotments to be tended, no matter how tired they were. But Sundays, when they'd had a day off, those that weren't out for a walk with the family or fussing with their racing pigeons liked to have a pint and a natter — "chewing the fat", they called it.

And tonight there was plenty of fat to chew.

"You know they'm talking again about closing down the pit, don't you?" said Archie Russell, one of the older men, wiping the beer foam off his chin with the back of his hand.

"And about time too!" Josh said forcefully. "The place is a death trap. Hasn't had any money spent on it in years."

The other men sitting around the table glared at him indignantly. All very well for Josh Withers to talk; he didn't work at Shepton Fields as they did. Since coming home from Wales, he'd got himself a job as a carpenter at Marston, one of the newest and best-equipped pits in the district — his uncle had taught him all about working with wood, apparently. Unlike the rest of them, Josh wouldn't find himself out of work if Shepton Fields closed, and many of them, Josh's own father included, would be lucky to get another job at their age.

"Let me tell you this, young 'un," George Parfitt said. "If we'd pressed for money to be spent on Shepton Fields, Sir Montague would have closed it down long ago. Not worth it, you see. Not for the coal that's left there."

Josh rocked his chair back on to its back legs, and shrugged his broad shoulders.

"Well, it's your funeral. But the ventilation down there is a disgrace. And you haven't even got a proper cage. That hudge should have been condemned years ago, and would have been if the authorities knew about it. Just a rope, for goodness' sake! I wouldn't go down on the bloody thing if you paid me."

"That's just it, though, in't it?" Archie Russell took another swig of beer. "We'm being *paid*. So long as Shepton Fields is open, we'm being *paid*. And that be a lot better than finishing up over at Catcombe in the workhouse, however you'd-a look at it."

"What have you got to say about it, my son?" George Parfitt swivelled on his stool to look at Jack, who was sitting quietly over his pint, not taking any part in the argument. "Are you going to let yer brother get away wi' talking like that? Shepton Fields is good enough for you and your father, so why bain't it good enough for he?"

Jack Withers sighed inwardly. Privately he agreed with Josh. Shepton Fields was a death trap, and if the authorities knew the half of it they'd have come down like a ton of bricks on Sir Montague Fairley, the owner, long ago. But as Archie had said, it was a living for so many of them, his father included. Jack wished with all his heart that he could leave and work in a better colliery, maybe even learn a trade as Josh had done. But he couldn't do that. Not while Gilby, his father, still needed work.

Although he was now almost twenty-two years old, Jack was still what was known as a carting boy. The seams here in the Somerset coalfield were too narrow and faulted for pit ponies, and so young men, crawling on their hands and knees, dragged the putts of coal from the face to the roadway, which was wide enough for tubs to run. It wasn't as easy nowadays to find lads willing to do that in an outdated pit like Shepton Fields, and Jack carted for Gilby. He'd once talked to Wilfred James, the manager, about leaving, and Wilfred had told him in no uncertain terms that if he went, he could take his father with him. So, against his will and better judgement, Jack stayed on. It would kill Gilby to lose his job at his age.

It wasn't in Jack's nature to get involved in arguments, though, and he didn't want to take Josh's part against men he had to work with. But neither did he want to pour scorn on his brother's assertions.

"I reckon our Josh is entitled to his opinion," he said peaceably.

"You'm too bloody soft!" George Parfitt said vehemently.

"If you say so, George."

Over Josh's shoulder, Jack could see through the open door to the snug beyond. Young Billy, Maggie's brother, was there, getting a jug filled up with beer — for his father, Jack guessed.

He shook his head, frowning. A pint with your mates was one thing; drinking alone as Paddy Donovan did was something else again. But at least seeing Billy there had given him an excuse to get away from the argument Josh had started, and he was keen to see Maggie anyway. He was madly in love with her, and the thought of being with her trumped a pint with his mates any day of the week.

"I'm going to love you and leave you." He drained his glass and stood up.

"Ah well, you've got better fish to fry, I dare say." George Parfitt winked at him. The other men guffawed. But none of them noticed that Josh wasn't laughing.

What was it, Josh wondered, that made him so soft when it came to Maggie? He'd known her all his life, from the time she'd been just a little girl in button-up boots and a smock, bowling a hoop along the rank, or pushing a rag doll in a crate on wheels that she pretended was a perambulator. Just another kid, and one of the Donovans at that, though Josh had never joined in the scornful jibes of his peers, who'd heard the disparaging remarks their parents made about the family and copied them in their own childish way. He hadn't even noticed her when he began taking an interest in girls. She was, after all, more than three years younger than he was, still no more than a skinny child, and there had been plenty of girls his own age coyly flicking their eyelashes at him and keen to show off their developing figures when he was around, a good-looking Jack the lad with a cheeky grin and an offhand manner that seemed to make them all the more eager to impress him.

But when he'd come home from Wales, where he'd been sent to live with his Uncle Fred and Aunt Eliza, it had been a different story. While he'd been away, Maggie had grown up. The first time he saw her, she'd taken his breath away, with her thick mane of chestnut hair, her wide laughing mouth and her sparkling blue eyes. He couldn't believe what a beauty that skinny little girl had become.

And it wasn't just the way she looked, either. There was something about Maggie that was special. Her soft voice, the way she carried herself, tall and proud, as if she was royalty, not a Donovan at all. And she was kind, yet not at all afraid to speak out when she thought it was called for — he'd heard her take the young toughs who lived in the rank to task more than once, such as when they'd been tormenting a mangy cat who'd come slinking along the terrace looking for scraps.

Maggie was special all right, but the trouble was, she was spoken for. She was walking out with Jack, his younger brother, and though Josh wouldn't have hesitated to try his luck if her beau had been anyone else, stealing his own brother's girlfriend was a step beyond the pale, even for a rascal like him. Even if he could have managed it — and he wasn't at all sure he could. She and Jack had been friends since childhood, and somewhere along the way that had developed into love. They seemed very close now. He'd seen the way she took his arm, smiling up at him so that they looked the perfect couple, and he knew Jack doted on her.

All the same . . . Josh still felt his heart miss a beat when he saw her. He couldn't help but regret that he hadn't been around when she'd blossomed from a skinny little waif into a lovely young woman — if he had been, he'd have made sure he beat Jack to it when it came to asking her out. And he'd never yet met any girl who could hold a candle to her in his opinion, though there was certainly no shortage of them lining up to vie for his attention.

And not just the single girls, either.

Josh checked his pocket watch. He'd said he'd see Peggy Bishop this evening if she could get away, and that was a welcome distraction from his feelings for Maggie.

He was playing with fire, of course. Peggy was a married woman now, though he'd known her back in the old days when they were both young, free and single. She was the first girl he had kissed, and it had been a thirteen-year-old Peggy who had first initiated

23

him into the mysteries of the female body, encouraging him to chase her round the haystacks or down to the river where the grass was long and sweet and a little wood met the meadow. He hadn't been the only one by a long chalk, he knew, but that hadn't mattered to him then, and it didn't matter now. Peggy was still as generous with her favours as she had always been, and that was a big attraction as far as Josh was concerned. Most of the girls he went out with turned coy when he tried to take things further than a kiss and a cuddle. They wanted a ring on their finger first, and a ring, and the commitment that went with it, was the last thing Josh wanted. He was nowhere near ready to settle down. No, much better to give Peggy a quick tumble, even though he suspected she'd begun to take their fun and games a little too seriously for his liking. He even enjoyed the thrill that came from living dangerously — Tom Bishop, the man Peggy had married, was known to have a filthy temper and wouldn't take kindly to being cuckolded. But that just added an extra frisson to the dalliance. And it took his mind off Maggie Donovan for a little while at least.

As the door swung shut after Jack, Josh stood up, jingling a handful of coins in his pocket.

"Right, lads," he said cheerfully. "I reckon I've got time to get another round in before I make tracks myself. Who's for another drink, courtesy of Marston, the best pit in the Somerset coalfield?"

As she finished polishing her boots, Maggie was keeping a sharp eye out for Billy. She didn't trust those louts not to waylay her brother on his way home, and if Dad's beer got spilled, there'd be hell to pay. He'd blame Billy, not his tormentors; might even take the strap to him.

They were in the alleyway behind the houses, kicking about a pig's bladder they'd got hold of to use as a football, not a bit ashamed of themselves. But they wouldn't be. For all that they were only carting boys themselves, they reckoned they were way above the Donovans in the pecking order.

Maggie sighed, and brushed a long strand of chestnut hair away from her face. It hadn't been easy growing up as a Donovan, but she reckoned she'd done pretty well for herself. She had a good job she enjoyed, and if she married Jack Withers — she had a feeling he was on the point of asking her — she would be joining a well-respected family. With any luck they would be able to get a little house well away from the Ten Houses and the folk who knew too much about the way her father carried on with his drinking and his gambling. And when her own children came along, at least they wouldn't have the cross of the Donovan name to bear.

Jack was a good man. They'd been friends since childhood, and she was very fond of him, though not as fond as he seemed to be of her. She just wished she felt a bit more excited at the idea of marrying him.

And a bit less worried about leaving her mother especially now, in her condition . . .

A worried frown creased Maggie's forehead and she glanced over her shoulder at Rose, who was cutting wedges of bread and cheese for the men's snap — with an early start in the morning, it was easier to prepare it overnight.

"Let me do that," she offered, but Rose only gave a tight little shake of her head.

"It's all right. I've nearly finished."

Maggie regarded her mother anxiously. "You should be taking things easier."

"Oh, don't talk silly. It's come to something if I can't cut up a bit of bread and cheese." Rose flourished the bread knife. "Go out and enjoy the sun while you can."

Reluctantly Maggie returned to the doorway, but she was still worried about Rose. She shouldn't be having more babies at her age — Maggie couldn't forget poor Annie Tremlett, a one-time neighbour, who'd had twins in her forties and never walked again, and she prayed nothing like that would happen to her mother.

It wasn't long before she saw Billy turn into the alleyway. To her surprise, Jack was with him. She went out to meet them, swishing her skirts past her father, who was sitting on the low bench outside the back door, smoking and hawking up globules of phlegm.

"What are you doing back this early, Jack?" she greeted him. "I wasn't expecting you for another half-hour."

"I'll go again then, shall I?" Jack teased.

Maggie smiled at him. "Get away with you!"

"I thought I'd better see young Billy home — make sure he didn't drink his father's beer on the way," Jack said, giving Billy a playful clip round the ear. "And it's a nice evening for a walk. Pity to waste it in the pub. I see you're making the most of it too, Mr Donovan."

Paddy grunted and hawked again, stretching out a hand to take his jug of beer from Billy.

"If you're taking our Maggie for a walk, just you behave yourself, d'you hear me?"

Colour rose in Maggie's cheeks. "Dad!"

"No, I know what it's like to be young. Don't you let him take advantage of you, my girl."

"What do you think I am?" Maggie retorted sharply.

"Too pretty for your own good. Just like your mother used to be." He wagged a finger at Jack. "You remember what I said, my boyo, or you'll have me to answer to."

Maggie turned away, embarrassed.

"I'll just fetch a shawl in case it gets cold later on."

"It's not going to," Jack said.

"All the same . . ." She flew into the house and emerged with a lacy white square. "I just wanted to wear it," she confessed to Jack as they walked along the alley. "It's new — I only got it yesterday. Mrs Freeman let me put it on one side, and I've been saving up for it for weeks. Isn't it the prettiest thing you ever saw?"

Jack smiled. He wanted to say that Maggie was the prettiest thing he ever saw, but fine words didn't come easily to him.

"I shouldn't have bought it really," Maggie confessed. "There's all sorts of more important things to spend my money on."

"If it makes you happy, then that is the most important thing," Jack said fondly.

It was the closest he could come to expressing his feelings.

At the end of the rank, the track broadened into a lane, bordered by shoulder-high hedges that were thick with meadow-sweet and cow parsley. Beyond the hedge on the right was a cornfield overlooked by the fronts of the houses in the rank; beyond that again was the colliery, Shepton Fields, its headgear towering above the pit yards, and the black mound of coal waste that they called "the batch" rising like a great dark carbuncle against the clear blue sky of the early summer evening. Maggie had never once stopped to think how odd it was that she could see both cornfields and coal dust from her bedroom window. She just accepted it for the way things were. Coal dust and cornfields, miners and farmhands, living and working side by side.

On the other side of the lane the hedges hid meadows that stretched all the way down the valley, steep and higgledy-piggledy, to a little wood with a river running through it. In winter it swelled to a torrent and sometimes flooded the lower reaches of the fields; at this time of year it was shallow and slow, muddied up by the herd of cows that trampled about in it to have a drink and cool themselves down when the sun was hot.

It had always been one of Maggie's favourite places. As a little girl she had often gone there, sitting on the bank with her knees drawn up to her chin, watching the darting dragonflies and the haze of gnats over the water, listening to the soft melodic gurgle as the brook ran over the stones and sucked at the bulrushes. Once she had seen a kingfisher, a flash of brilliant greeny blue. She'd gone back day after day looking for it, but she'd never seen it again.

At a gateway, Jack paused, "Shall we go across the fields?"

"If you like."

She knew why he wanted to go that way — he wanted a kiss and a cuddle, which was fine as long as it stopped there. When they'd first started walking out as a couple, rather than just the childhood friends they had always been, she'd quite enjoyed it. But lately he'd wanted to go further, and really she didn't like that at all. Of course, if he did ask her to marry him, and she accepted, as she probably would, she'd have to get used to that and more. But it wasn't something she wanted to think about, and when his hands strayed and she had to keep him in check, it made her horribly uncomfortable. A memory from long, long ago flashed unbidden to her mind. The kingfisher hadn't been the only thing she'd seen when she was daydreaming by the river as a child. Once, concealed in a hollow by the long grass and the overhanging branches of the trees, she'd seen Josh Withers and Peggy Bryant — Peggy Bishop as she was now — Peggy with the front of her blouse undone and her skirts rucked right up to her waist. Mortified as well as shocked, Maggie had curled herself into a ball, eyes tight shut, and stayed quiet as a mouse, praying they wouldn't notice her. If they did, she'd die of shame! But they hadn't seen her; when they'd gone again, she was able to creep home with no one the wiser, but the memory of it, of Peggy's giggles and Josh's low groans of appreciation that no amount of hiding could keep her from hearing, could still turn her cheeks scarlet and make her cringe with disgust. Silly, really. It was, after all, what men and women did, but they hadn't been men and women. They were Josh Withers and Peggy Bryant, just a few years older than her and nowhere near old enough to be behaving that way . . .

As soon as they were through the gateway and out of sight of the houses, Jack took Maggie's hand, and that felt so nice she wondered why she was so worried about other things It was nice when he pulled her into his arms and kissed her, too, but as his hand moved to her breast she felt the beginnings of the familiar panic. "Jack! Stop it! It's too steep for that here! We'll fall over!"

He gave her a sideways grin. "Doesn't matter, does it? The grass is nice and dry."

"It does matter! I don't want to fall over!" She tried to keep her voice light and playful as she said it, and that obviously must have given him the wrong idea, because before she knew it, his arm had slipped behind her knees, lifting her off her feet and depositing her on the sloping bank before dropping down beside her.

"Jack!" she protested, laughing. "What do you think you're doing?"

"I'll give you three guesses." His face was very close to hers, and as he kissed her again, his hand went to the buttons of her blouse, opening them stealthily.

She pulled away a little. "Jack — don't, please . . ."

"Come on, Maggie, where's the harm? I'd never hurt you, you know that." His breath was warm on her throat, just below her ear; his hand was inside her blouse now, his fingers slipping under her chemise.

She covered his hand with hers, holding it still. "Stop it now."

"There's nobody about."

"I don't care. You mustn't! Goodness knows where it will lead, and you should know I'm not that kind of girl."

"Oh, I know that well enough!" He rolled away, lying on his back beside her in the dry, scratchy grass, head turned to look at her. His eyes were dark with desire, but there was tenderness too in that look. "Your dad needn't worry his head about you."

"Whatever are you talking about?" Maggie asked teasingly. She knew very well, of course, and though she was relieved he was no longer trying to get her to do things she didn't want him to, she felt a little guilty, as if she were short-changing Jack, and also regretful that she didn't feel the way he did about taking their courtship a stage further.

She tucked her legs up beneath her skirts, plucking at a blade of grass, and Jack lay back against the bank, arms pillowed beneath his head. For a little while he was silent, then, out of the blue, he said: "What would you say if I asked you to marry me?"

Maggie came out of her reverie with a jolt, glancing down at him. He wasn't looking at her, rather staring up into the darkening blue of the sky, and his tone was deceptively casual. A wave of tenderness suffused her, both for the boy who had been her childhood friend and champion, and the man he had become. Oh, maybe he didn't excite the sort of feelings in her that took her breath away, but she'd always known this moment would come and been content with it. Jack was good and kind, honest and hard-working. He'd take care of her, provide for her and any family they might have. She felt safe with him. And she did love him . . . she did. She was glowing with it right now.

She tilted her head, tickled his cheek with the blade of grass.

"I expect I'd say yes," she said, echoing his light tone. "We'll just have to wait and see, won't we?" She scrambled to her feet, brushing the bits of grass out of her skirt and twisting a lock of hair that had come loose back into its pins. "Now, are we going for that walk or not?"

When he left the Prince of Wales, Josh cut across the fields, where herds of cows were grazing, making for the rickety wooden river bridge deep in the valley where he and Peggy had agreed to meet. It was a secluded spot, but within easy walking distance of the miners' cottages where Peggy and Tom lived. Just about safe, Josh reckoned.

There was no sign of Peggy when Josh arrived at the rendezvous, and after he'd been waiting for ten minutes or so, he began to doubt she was going to turn up. There had been a couple of occasions recently when she'd let him down because she couldn't get away, and Josh wondered if Tom might be getting suspicious. He hoped not. All very well for him to get a kick out of playing with fire, but it could turn nasty for Peggy. Josh didn't know Tom Bishop well — he worked at Northway, yet another of the rash of collieries that scarred the green Somerset valley — but from what he'd heard, the man was an evil-tempered devil. Perhaps it was time to call time on their clandestine meetings — no one could actually call it an affair — and look elsewhere for someone to take his mind off Maggie.

Just as he was thinking of giving up and heading for home, he saw Peggy coming down the path between the trees.

She'd put on a lot of weight in the last few years, he thought, but it rather suited her. Big breasts, big hips, the hint of a double chin . . . Maggie she wasn't, but what the hell? There was just all the more to get a hold of . . .

"You made it, then," he said, as he went to meet her.

She giggled, a little out of breath from hurrying.

"I told Tom I was going over to my sister's."

"And he believed you?"

"Didn't say a word. I've been a bit worried lately that he might have smelt a rat. He's been really funny with me whenever I've said I'm going out. But tonight he just said he was going down to the working men's club. I mustn't be too long, though. He might come home early, you never know." She looked up at Josh coquettishly through fair, stubby lashes. He thought of Maggie's thick dark ones, then pushed the image away and grabbed Peggy round the waist.

"We'd better not waste any time then, had we?"

33

"Oh Josh, you are a one!" She wound her arms around his neck, eager, as always, for his kisses, and he drew her towards the bushes.

"I reckon I'd better do a Sir Walter Raleigh, don't you?" He took off his jacket and spread it out on the grass. Then he sat down, pulling her down beside him and scooping up her skirts.

Peggy giggled, then placed a hand over his to stop him going further.

"You do really think something of me, don't you, Josh?" she asked, coyly. "I'm not just a bit of fun to you, am I?"

It was the same every time lately. She had to ask.

"'Course you're not just a bit of fun," he lied. "If you didn't already have a husband —"

"Hey! What the bloody hell do you think you're doing?" The yell of fury made Josh jump as if he had been shot. A short, thickset man was on the path above them — Tom Bishop. "You bloody bugger!" he roared. "What are you doing with my missus?"

Peggy gave a gasp of horror, hastily trying to cover her bare legs, and Josh scrambled to his feet. For once in his life he was speechless. Tom charged down the bank, grabbed Peggy and yanked her up so roughly she lost her balance and stumbled against him.

"It's a good job I followed you, you bloody cheating cow!" he snarled at her. "I knew you were up to something!"

"Calm down, mate," Josh said ineffectually.

"Calm down?" Tom was practically apoplectic. "I'll give her calm down when I get her home."

"Leave her alone, you great bully. If you want to take it out on someone, take it out on me."

Tom let go of Peggy's arm and whirled round. Expecting a punch to the jaw, Josh took a step backwards, readying himself. But Tom merely faced him furiously, his hands clenching and unclenching whilst a vein throbbed purple in his temple.

"Don't you worry, I bloody will!" he snarled between gritted teeth. "I know who you are. You're that Withers, aren't you? Work over to Shepton Fields."

It was clear Tom was confusing Josh with Jack, but Josh didn't bother to correct him. The first shock of being caught was wearing off, and with the rush of adrenalin when he'd thought Tom was going to start a fight hot in his blood, Josh was becoming aggressive himself, as he always did when he was up against it. Attack was the best means of defence in his book.

"If you were more of a man, your wife wouldn't have to go looking elsewhere," he said pugnaciously. "Look to yourself before you go blaming her."

Once again he thought Tom was going to charge at him like Farmer Barton's bull — and who could blame him? The man's features contorted with rage, a dark purplish flush suffusing his face and neck, and he came right up to Josh. But to Josh's amazement, Tom merely shook his fist under his nose.

"I've got your number, chum!" His voice was low, and shaking with fury and cold determination. "You'd better watch your back. Nobody messes about with my wife and gets away with it."

35

There was something almost comical in his stance, and Josh laughed shortly.

"Oh, you really bloody scare me."

"You'd do well to be bloody scared, mate. You can laugh now, but you don't know me. You better bloody watch out for yourself, that's all I'm saying." He turned to the trembling Peggy, grabbing her again by the arm. "Come on, you filthy bitch — home!"

"Hey — don't take it out on her!" Josh could feel his anger rising at the way Tom was manhandling Peggy up the bank. Goodness only knew what he would do when he got her on her own, and for a moment Josh almost went after them. But what good would that do? You didn't interfere between a husband and wife, and he couldn't protect Peggy when the front door closed after them. Anything he said or did might only make things worse for her.

But he didn't like the part he'd played in this. Yes, she'd thrown herself at him shamelessly, but he should have had the good sense to resist. Certainly he wasn't going to risk a repeat of this evening's fiasco. If Peggy came chasing after him again, he'd tell her so in no uncertain terms.

As he made his own way home, he wondered how she was faring. He hoped Tom wasn't giving her a hiding. But for all his nasty temper, that didn't really seem his style, unless, of course, he was more ready to use his fists on a woman than he had been on a grown man. Josh thought of the way he'd threatened him rather than punching him on the nose as he'd expected. It might just have been empty words, of course, but he could well imagine the man storing up his anger and resentment and waiting his chance to take his revenge in some cowardly way.

Oh well, if he did, Josh could deal with that. There wasn't much that worried him.

Except having to see his brother with Maggie Donovan. That was the one thing that really got to him, and he couldn't seem to do a thing about it.

Mam and Dad were arguing. Billy could hear their raised voices coming from the scullery, Dad growling, Mam shrill.

"It's the last thing I want! You should've been more careful, Paddy," he heard Mam say.

Billy thought he knew what the argument was about. Mam was going to have another baby. He'd heard her and Maggie talking about it, but when he'd questioned Maggie, she'd gone very red and told him it didn't concern him. Billy had been upset. For one thing, he didn't like being excluded; it made him feel as unimportant at home as he felt everywhere else. For another, the thought of Dad doing such things to Mam disgusted him.

The argument was getting worse.

"Aw, Jesus, Mary and Joseph! Will you stop keeping on, woman!"

"It's all very well for you . . . you're not the one that has to go through it . . ."

"I have to put up with your nagging day and night." Paddy was getting angrier by the minute — the beer was beginning to talk — and Billy decided to make himself scarce.

He picked up the dominoes he'd been idly shuffling through and stacked them back in their wooden box. Then he went out through the scullery. Mam was leaning against the oilcloth-covered cupboard, arms wrapped around herself, head bent. He thought she might be crying.

"Where d'you think you're going?" Paddy demanded as Billy tried to slip past him.

Billy's eyes skittered nervously. "Just out."

"Haven't you been in enough trouble tonight?"

Billy shrugged. He was always in trouble one way or another. He sidled between Rose and Paddy and out of the door.

The brightness was fading from the day, but the air was still warm. There was no sign now of his tormentors, thank goodness, but Billy hurried past the Rogers house anyway, half expecting them to suddenly appear and pounce on him again.

Up the track he went, without any clear idea of where he was headed. Perhaps he'd go across the fields and look for birds' nests. It was a good time of year for that. He might see Maggie and Jack. That would be a bit of fun, just as long as they didn't see him first. He quite fancied spying on them — he was curious to know what they got up to when they were alone. But there was no sign of them anywhere, and Billy opted to take the path that led along the side of the cornfield in the direction of the pit.

It was no novelty; it was the way he went to work every morning with his father and the other men. What was different was that tonight he was alone, and the pit yard was silent and deserted. No chimneys belching steam, no winding gear creaking, and the screens where he had toiled every working day, sorting the coal that came up from the depths, were still. With no queue of hauliers' carts waiting to be loaded and no busy coal-blackened men milling about, the yard looked big and strangely ghostly.

Wouldn't it be funny, he thought, if they were all dead and he was the only one left alive in the world? No more big lads bullying him, no more Gaffer Hawkins yelling at him to work harder, no more Dad taking his belt to him, or doing unspeakable things to Mam. Perhaps one day there'd be an explosion underground and they'd all be killed. But that wasn't very likely. Explosions were almost unheard of here in Somerset. The seams might be faulted and topsy-turvy, so that floor was roof and roof floor, but there was no gas. Firedamp was the only danger in that respect.

He didn't fancy going underground, all the same. The thought of the narrow dark passages so far beneath ground, where the sun never shone, frightened him — he hated confined spaces, always had. The other lads said it was all right. They talked — when they talked to him at all — about the mice that came creeping out for crumbs when they were eating their cognockers of bread and cheese, and they didn't seem to mind the guss and crook, the length of rope that went around their waists and between their legs so that they could

39

crawl along the passageways on hands and knees dragging the little putts of coal the colliers had hewed. He'd seen the ridges in the flesh of their backs where the rope cut into it. They said it didn't hurt once you got used to it, and the best way to harden the skin was to rub urine into it, but Billy thought it sounded awful.

No, working on the screens was bad enough; underground would be much, much worse. But he was going to have to face up to it soon. Some other young lad would be leaving school and taking his job, and he'd have to go down in that horrible hudge on the end of a long length of hemp rope with Frank Rogers and Charlie Oglethorpe and the others.

If it was still there.

He'd heard the men talking about it, saying it should have been replaced by a proper cage years ago, and that if the authorities knew it was still in use it would be condemned and Shepton Fields would close down, as like as not.

The thought gave him hope. A length of hemp rope couldn't last for ever. Perhaps it would give up the ghost before he had to descend to the bowels of the earth on the end of it.

Billy kicked a piece of coal that lay at his feet, and followed it across the pit yard.

CHAPTER
THREE

Maggie had been awake for much of the night, wondering whether Jack had really asked her to marry him and whether it meant they were now engaged, or if it had been a rhetorical question. Nothing more had been said about it — they'd gone for their walk, returned home, and parted just as they always did with a kiss in the shadow of the outhouses, though there was an unaccustomed awkwardness in the air between them. It was odd, she thought, but she hadn't wanted to broach the subject again in case she'd mistaken his meaning, and she wasn't sure whether she'd be glad or sorry if she had. In a funny sort of way the half-proposal had quite shocked her, though it was only what she'd expected would come eventually, and she'd tossed and turned, dozing only to wake again, until with the pearly grey light of dawn she realised it was almost time to get up.

Cockerels were crowing now in their pens in the back gardens along the rank, the first birds had started their dawn chorus, and she heard the creak of the stairs as her mother went down to start her day. Maggie pushed the bedclothes aside and got up.

Mam wasn't too well in the mornings these days; she'd better go down and help her. The fire had to be lit to heat the water for the men's tea, and they'd want some breakfast, too, before they left for work. Only a bit of bread and dripping, but someone had to make it.

She pulled on her clothes, laced her feet into her freshly polished boots and went downstairs.

Rose was on her knees in front of the grate, trying to get the fire going. She looked grey and pinched, and Maggie saw her heave.

"Let me do that, Mam," she said.

"No, you don't want to get yourself dirty. You've got to go to work."

"I won't get dirty," Maggie said, perhaps over-optimistically. She took the bellows from Rose, and Rose let her, covering her mouth with her hand to suppress the threatening nausea.

Maggie got the fire going and straightened up, looking at her mother anxiously.

"Have you seen the doctor, Mam?"

Rose managed a derisive snort. "And where would I get the money to pay doctor's bills, I'd like to know? What can the doctor do anyway? There's nothing wrong with me that another few months won't take care of."

"Well, have a word with Dolly Oglethorpe, anyway."

Dolly Oglethorpe acted as midwife for all the women in the rank, as well as being called on to lay out the dead.

"All in good time." Rose didn't add that she didn't want anyone knowing she was pregnant again until there was no hiding it. She was dreading being the subject of yet more gossip up and down the rank. Nothing was private here for long; the women talking outside their doors or over their washing lines made sure of that.

"We'd better get your dad and our Billy up," she said, changing the subject.

"I'll do it." Maggie clattered up the stairs and knocked loudly on the first door off the narrow landing. "Dad! Time to get up!"

A grunt from within told her Paddy was awake. She went on along the landing and pushed open the door to Billy's room.

Once it had been Ewart and Walter's room too, the three lads sharing the big double bed that took up most of the floor space. Now Billy had it to himself, and he was making the most of it, spread-eagled corner to corner.

"Come on, our Billy." Maggie went into the little room, squeezing past the bed to the window and drawing back the curtains to let in the first pale sunshine.

"Do I have to?" Billy groaned.

"Yes you do, if you don't want to be late for work." She tweaked the sheet to reveal his ginger mop and fair-skinned face flushed pink with sleep.

"Don't want to go to work," he mumbled.

"I don't suppose you do," Maggie said tartly. "But that's neither here nor there. If you can't keep time on the screens, they'll send you underground where our dad can keep an eye on you."

That did the trick, just as she'd known it would. Billy was out of bed and reaching for his rushy duck trousers in a moment.

Maggie shook her head, filled suddenly with tenderness for her little brother. She wished with all her heart that he was tougher, better able to stand up for himself, or that he was still young enough for her to be able to take care of him. But he was just at that in-between age when he was neither a child nor a man, and he wasn't finding it easy.

A shout from downstairs startled her, and she pushed past Billy and ran out on to the landing.

"Mam! What's the matter?"

She ran down the stairs and through the living room into the scullery. The back door was open and Rose was on the step, gesticulating wildly.

"It's a blooming dog!" Rose said over her shoulder. "A dog — come right into the house! Frightened the life of me, it did." She waved her fist again. "Go on — get away — go home!"

Maggie went to the door. The dog, squat and white, with a large head, small ears and one black-ringed eye, had retreated across the alley, but still stood there, tail wagging uncertainly.

"Go on home!" Rose shouted again, but the dog refused to move, looking at her with ears cocked, head on one side.

The bedroom window above them opened and Billy leaned out. "Hey, boy!"

Rose craned her neck to scowl up at her son.

"Don't encourage him, our Billy!" She glowered at the dog and turned to go back inside. "Make sure the door's shut, Maggie. We don't want him coming in again."

In the busy morning round, both Maggie and Rose soon forgot the dog. But Billy did not. When he had swilled his face and neck at the stone scullery sink, he collected his slice of bread and dripping and took it over to the window.

"He's still there. That dog. Do you think he's lost?"

"I shouldn't think so," Rose said shortly. "I expect the Bridges' bitch is on heat. Dogs will go miles if they get the scent."

"But he's not outside the Bridges' door," Billy argued. "He's outside ours. And he looks hungry. There's some old bacon rind, isn't there? Can't we give him that?"

"No we can't!" Rose snapped. "If you feed him, we'll never get rid of him."

Billy said nothing, but when he thought no one was looking, he slipped the remains of his bread and dripping into his pocket, wrapping it in his handkerchief. "I need the lav," he muttered, heading out of the back door.

The dog was still there. Billy took out the hunk of bread and dripping, and the dog's nose, cold and wet, nuzzled into his hand. Billy's heart swelled with pleasure. He'd be for it if his mam looked out of the window and saw that he had disobeyed her, but for once he didn't care.

He patted the dog, and it wagged its stumpy tail and licked his hand. Billy supposed it was because he could still smell lard on his palm. But he dared to hope not. For the first time in as long as he could remember, he felt as if he had found a friend.

Maggie was showing Cathy Small, the new apprentice, how to block a roll of cloth. Mondays were always quiet in the drapery shop, it being washing day, and the lack of customers provided a good opportunity for other things. Maggie had already changed the window display, a task she loved; she was very proud that Augusta had noticed her artistic streak and trusted her to arrange bonnets, gloves and silk floral sprays in a way that would attract the customers. Now she was engaged in training Cathy. But Cathy's attention wandered easily, especially if there were lads passing by outside, or if Horace, Mrs Freeman's husband, came into the shop. He was standing by the glass-fronted door now, thumbs tucked into the watch chain that stretched across his starched shirt front, casting surreptitious glances at the pretty new assistant, and Cathy was all fingers and thumbs.

"Oh Miss Donovan, I'll never get it right!" she groaned.

Maggie hid a secret smile. It amused her to be called Miss Donovan, something Mrs Freeman insisted on, since Cathy was her junior.

"Of course you will, Cathy. It's just a knack, that's all. But it's got to look neat, as if it's never been off the roll." She unwound the cloth once more and spread it out along the counter. "Now, try again."

Cathy's efforts improved when Horace Freeman left the shop to return to his own domain, the gents' outfitters next door. But it wasn't long before her concentration was wavering once more, this time due to a titbit of gossip her father had brought home with him from the working men's club the night before.

"It is Jack Withers you're walking out with, isn't it?" she said, a little hesitantly.

"Yes." Maggie was puzzled. "Why?"

Cathy caught her lip between her teeth, lowering her eyes as if wishing for once that she hadn't started this conversation. "Oh . . . nothing."

Then, as Maggie gazed at her questioningly, she went on, all of a rush: "I don't know whether I ought to say or not, but my dad told us that Tom Bishop came into the club last night in a proper temper, saying that he'd caught Jack Withers fooling around with his wife."

"What?" Maggie was astounded. "That's ridiculous! Jack wouldn't fool around with a married woman, especially not Peggy Bishop."

"I'm only repeating what he said." Cathy had turned rather pink. "That Jack Withers who works at Shepton Fields, that's what he said. And my dad reckoned he'd better watch out, because Tom Bishop can be really nasty, and he wouldn't want to be in Jack's shoes if Tom has got it in for him."

"It's nothing but a load of nonsense," Maggie said briskly, and at that moment Mrs Freeman came sweeping into the shop.

"There's a lot of chatter in here! Is any work being done?"

"We're just tidying the stock," Maggie said.

She pulled the roll of cloth towards her, blocking it herself quickly and neatly, but to her annoyance, her hands were trembling a little.

Where in the world had Cathy's father got such a story from? And men had the nerve to accuse the womenfolk of gossiping! Jack, carrying on with Peggy Bishop — ridiculous! Now if it had been Josh, she could have understood it . . .

Of course, that must be it, Maggie realised. People who didn't know them well often got Jack and Josh mixed up, and she supposed it was an easy enough mistake to make. They did look very alike, though there the resemblance ended, with Jack so quiet and Josh so wild. Trouble followed him around, her mother had always said. But for all that, there was something very attractive about him, with that breezy manner, the wicked twinkle in his eyes and the aura that might almost be danger that went with the hard muscles and the swagger. She could well imagine that Peggy Bishop might think it was a risk worth taking to go out with him on the sly. And for a moment she almost envied her — he'd put butterflies in *her* stomach the first time she'd seen him when he came home from Wales . . .

Maggie gave herself a little shake. All very well for Josh to get on the wrong side of Tom Bishop and not give a devil's cuss about it. But if Tom was mistaking Josh for Jack, then it was a different matter entirely. Suppose he got a gang of cronies together and waylaid

Jack in some dark lane? They wouldn't give Jack the opportunity to tell them they'd got the wrong man before giving him a good hiding. She'd have to have a word with him, warn him.

Though what he could do to avert such a disaster, she really didn't know.

When Billy got home from work that evening, he was surprised and delighted to find the dog lying in the shade of the outhouses, his head between his paws. The moment he saw Billy, he got up and trotted towards the boy, pushing his eager wet nose into his hand.

Billy hurried into the house, where Rose was bailing hot water into the tin tub in front of the fire for Paddy's bath.

"Mam, that dog's still here. Let me have those bacon rinds for him . . . *please*."

"Blinking thing!" Rose grumbled. Then she relented. "Oh, go on, then. They're in the bin. No . . . I'll get them. You go back outside. You're getting coal dust all over my clean floor."

Billy backed out hastily before she could change her mind, and a minute later she appeared in the doorway, with not only the bacon rinds but the knuckle bone from the piece of pork they would be finishing up cold for their tea.

"Here you are. Have this as well. I've cut the meat off of it, but I expect he'll find a few shreds if he's hungry enough."

"Oh, thanks, Mam!" Billy's face was wreathed in smiles.

"Just make sure he doesn't come in the house again," Rose admonished sternly.

She shouldn't be encouraging the darned dog, she thought. But it was good to see Billy happy and taking an interest in something. Just as long as he wasn't too upset when it wandered off again, as she was pretty sure it would.

A week later, however, the dog was still there, living on scraps and bones and sleeping on an old blanket in the corner of the outhouse. Though he disappeared a few times, once for a whole day and a night, he always came back.

Billy had given him a name — Bullseye, since he had a black patch around one eye in his otherwise snow-white face. It seemed to suit him. What was more, Billy felt they were two of a kind, both of them outcasts in their own way, and the thought was strangely comforting.

In that short space of time, Bullseye had become his dog, and the focus of his world.

CHAPTER
FOUR

"I've got something to tell you, Maggie."

Jack was trying very hard to keep his face straight, but there was no mistaking the smile that was trying to break out. It lifted the corners of his mouth and twinkled in his eyes.

It was another warm evening. Though it was still early in the year, summer had come early and the air was heavy with the scent of new-mown hay wafting across the terrace from the field beyond. The farmer and as many men as he could muster had been busy all day, harvesting the crop before the spell of good weather broke, and Maggie had been watching from her bedroom window as the heavy horse pulled the threshing machine up the field and back again and the sweating hands loaded the hay on to carts. Now she was at the back door, called down by Rose when Jack had come knocking.

"What's that, then?" she asked, curious to know what he was looking so pleased about.

"Come over here." He drew her to the far side of the track, out of earshot of the houses, and the beam he had been trying to suppress escaped, lighting up his face. "You know I asked you to marry me the other night? Well, I went to see the manager today, and we can have a house." He hesitated, the smile wavering a little. "That is . . . if you haven't changed your mind."

Maggie was quite taken aback. Since that night nothing more had been said, and she'd come to the conclusion that she'd taken what was a casual question for a proposal. Now she was not only startled but a bit overwhelmed, and for a moment she was speechless.

Jack's face fell.

"You have thought better of it."

"No . . . no . . . but when you didn't mention it again, I thought . . . Well, I thought you couldn't have meant it."

Jack laughed self-consciously. "I think I frightened myself, Maggie, and I shouldn't have asked before I had something to offer you. But I meant it all right. There's nothing in the world I want more. Suppose I were to ask you again, properly? I don't think I can go down on one knee here, right outside your back door, but . . . I hope you'd still say yes."

"Oh Jack!" The little niggling doubts were still there, had never really gone away, but she'd gone mushy inside. She did love him — she did — even if the earth didn't move for her the way it did in fairy stories. And he'd gone so far as to approach the colliery manager about a house for them to live in; that showed how serious he was about this, and must have taken a good deal of courage.

"Of course I'd still say yes," she said. "But you should have talked to me again about it. You've given me quite a shock."

"I know. I'm sorry. The thing is, I heard about this house coming vacant and I didn't want to lose the chance of it. Adge Scrivens is off to south Wales with his family — he's got a job in one of the pits down there. And it's a really nice house — one of those cottages down on the main road. Well, it's ours if we want it. It's only got the two rooms up and two down, but it'll suit us fine. We can go down and have a look at it any evening, Adge said . . ." He broke off. "I'm sorry, Maggie, I'm rushing you. But I was just over the moon when Wilfred James agreed that we could have it. You are pleased, aren't you?"

"Yes, of course I am," Maggie said faintly, but her head was spinning.

"Oh Maggie, you've made me so proud and happy." Jack was beaming from ear to ear. "I can't wait to tell the world you're going to be my wife!"

"Hang on, we must tell my mam and dad first, and your parents too," Maggie said sternly. "We don't want them hearing about it from anybody but us, and Wilfred James already knows, by the sound of it."

Jack grinned, a little shamefaced.

"I suppose by rights I should ask your dad for his permission. Shall I do that now?"

Once again Maggie experienced the scary feeling that she was riding in a carriage pulled by a runaway horse. Everything was happening so fast. But . . .

"You might as well, I suppose," she said, swallowing her apprehension. "He's in the kitchen."

"Don't look so worried," Jack urged her, but he looked apprehensive too. "The worst he can do is throw me out on my ear."

"Oh Jack, I'm sure he won't do that." Maggie laughed, and immediately felt better. "Come on, let's get it over with."

She took his hand and led him into the house.

"Well that's lovely news!" Rose said, hugging Maggie.

Jack and Paddy had disappeared into the parlour, leaving the women in the kitchen, but, of course, the moment the door had closed after them, Maggie had told her mother what it was that Jack wanted to talk to Paddy about — as if Rose hadn't already guessed.

"I couldn't be more pleased," Rose went on. "Jack's a lovely lad, you couldn't wish for a better. And that's more than can be said for some you've looked at in the past."

Maggie threw her a quizzical look, and Rose huffed.

"You know very well who I'm talking about. That Reuben Hillman that works in the gents' outfitters."

"Oh, him!" Maggie laughed. "There was never anything in that. Once was quite enough."

"And I was very glad about that." Rose sniffed loudly. "I've never liked that lad. I couldn't say what it is, but there's something about him . . ."

"He's harmless enough," Maggie said, but she knew what her mother meant. There was something about Reuben Hillman that made her cringe inwardly too.

54

Reuben worked as an assistant to Horace Freeman in his gents' outfitters next door, and when Maggie had started as an apprentice in the drapery, he'd taken a shine to her.

Truth to tell, in the beginning Maggie had been quite flattered. Reuben's father was a clerk at the office of the local solicitor, his mother was one of the most respected women in town, and his grandmother ran a dame school in a cottage in the high street. Though scarcely gentry, the family was certainly "a cut above", as the saying went, thoroughly respectable, and not one of them a miner. When Reuben asked her to walk out with him she'd tried to put to one side the fact that she really didn't find him in the least attractive. It was uncharitable, she'd thought, to hold it against him that he was rather stout, with podgy hands, a soft mouth and beady little eyes. You couldn't judge a book by its cover, and he might turn out to be really nice.

But it wasn't long before she knew she'd made a terrible mistake. Nice or not, when he'd taken hold of her hand it was all she could do not to snatch it away; when he'd tried to kiss her, she'd curled up inside with revulsion.

"Reuben, behave yourself!" she'd reprimanded him, trying to pull away.

But he wasn't to be put off so easily.

"Come on, Maggie. Just a little kiss."

"No — stop it this minute!"

One of his hands had been about her waist, holding her fast, the other . . . oh, she must have imagined it, surely! Not even Reuben Hillman would dare to touch her breast — would he?

She'd tensed, twisting away, wriggling out of his grasp, horrified, embarrassed and revolted by the imagined touch, the way his lips had felt, moist and flabby on hers, and the smell of him — carbolic soap on his skin, and something sweet and peppery in his breath. Even now Maggie couldn't smell carbolic soap without being reminded of that horrible encounter.

"It's time we went home," she'd said, desperate to escape but not wanting to mention the fact that she thought he had tried to touch her breast. After all, she couldn't be sure she wasn't mistaken, and it would be terrible to accuse him of something that might have been an accident.

"When can I see you again, Maggie?" He'd been like an eager puppy.

"Oh . . . I don't know. I'm not sure it's a good idea. Working together . . ."

"We don't," he'd argued. "You're in the drapery, I'm in the gents' outfitters."

"As good as."

"But I really like you!" To Maggie's horror, Reuben had looked as if he was about to burst into tears. His blubbery face had turned very pink and there was a wobble in his lip.

"I'm sorry," Maggie had said. "I really don't want to."

She'd thought that would be that, especially since she had started walking out with Jack not long afterwards, but she couldn't get rid of Reuben so easily.

He came through to the drapery shop on the flimsiest of excuses, staring at her like a moonstruck calf and smiling a soppy smile that made her dreadfully uncomfortable. If the gents' outfitters closed before the drapery, he would hang about outside for as long as he dared, in the hope of walking her home, she supposed, and if the shops closed at more or less the same time, he'd materialise as if by magic, grinning and trying to strike up a conversation.

"I'm glad it's you he fancies and not me!" said Beat Clements, her fellow assistant. "He's creepy!"

It was true, he was. There was something almost menacing about his obsession with her.

Well, now that she and Jack were going to be married, he'd surely realise there was no point in continuing with it, and leave her alone.

The front room door opened and Paddy and Jack emerged, Jack looking a little flushed and pleased with himself.

"Well, my girl, you can stop worrying yourself," Paddy said heartily. "Your chap here has asked me if he can marry you and I've said yes. Get the beer out, Rose, if there's any left. I reckon this calls for a drink, don't you?"

Maggie shook her head, smiling wryly.

What didn't call for a drink in her father's book? she would like to know.

Long after Paddy had finished the beer they had in the house and set out for the pub, Maggie and Jack sat outside in the warm evening air, making their plans.

Whereas in the days since he had first asked her to marry him Jack had avoided the subject completely, now he couldn't stop talking about it. He'd even gone home to tell his own parents the news whilst Maggie was helping Rose with making the men's snap ready for the morning, returning to tell her that they were delighted. Maggie wasn't sure that was quite true; though Gilby Withers was an accepting sort, she rather thought that Florrie would be none too pleased that her son was marrying a Donovan. But if so, she had kept it well hidden, for Jack was still barely able to contain his delight that his dearest wish was becoming reality.

"They asked if we'd set a date," he said now. "I said I expected it would be as soon as I can sort out any work that needs doing on the house we've been offered — but it's up to you, of course."

"That sounds fine," Maggie said. She still felt a little dazed, but Jack's enthusiasm was infectious, and getting married and setting up home was, after all, a great adventure.

"And Mam wanted to know where the wedding will be," he went on. "I think she's hoping it will be at the Methodist, but you're a Catholic, aren't you?"

"Not really," Maggie said. "Dad is — or was. He only ever goes to Mass at Christmas and Easter. And Mam was never in agreement with it, though she had to say she was when she married Dad. That's why we don't really go anywhere regularly." She considered. "Yes, I think we should definitely be married at the Methodist, seeing as how your mam is such a stalwart there."

"She'll be pleased about that," Jack said, sounding relieved. "And of course I shall ask our Josh to be my best man. He wasn't in when I told Mam and Dad or I'd have asked him already."

He took her hand, holding it between his and stroking her ring finger as if imagining he was slipping on the wedding band.

"What about you? Who will you have for your bridesmaids? It's a pity you haven't got a sister . . ."

"I think that sometimes too," Maggie said wistfully. It would be so nice to have someone to share all the excitement with. "But there you are, I haven't. Nor even any cousins. I suppose I could ask Beat and Cathy from the shop. But getting dresses for them would be an awful expense."

"Don't worry about that," Jack said. "I'll take care of it. I want you to have a day to remember."

"Oh Jack, thank you!" Tenderness suffused Maggie again. She was doing the right thing . . . she was! "But how can you afford it?"

"I'll find the money somehow," Jack said determinedly. "I've been putting a bit aside for some time now, just waiting to get up the courage to propose. It's not a lot, but I'm sure it can run to dresses for your bridesmaids . . ." He broke off. "Oh look, here's our Josh now. He's going to be surprised to hear our news and no mistake."

Maggie turned her head and saw the familiar tall, dark figure heading towards them along the track.

"Hey, Josh, come here!" Jack called as he neared. "What do you think? Maggie and I have just got engaged. How's that for a cause for celebration?"

Quite suddenly Maggie felt dreadfully flustered. How stupid was that? She'd have to get used to telling people about the engagement, and to being the centre of attention for a little while. But it wasn't just that. As she looked at Josh, she felt herself blushing and experiencing the same strange flutter in her stomach that she experienced whenever their paths crossed — strange, and unwelcome. Unsettled, she thrust her hand deeper into Jack's, taking comfort from the warm pressure of his fingers on hers.

For just a moment, it seemed to her, Josh's eyes darkened. Then he said heartily: "Well, well, I suppose congratulations are in order," and offered his brother a firm handshake, and if there was something forced in his smile, Maggie told herself afterwards that she'd imagined it.

"I was just saying to Maggie — I hope you'll be my best man when we tie the knot," Jack said.

Once again that shadow hovered in Josh's eyes; once again it was almost instantly gone.

"Well, I'd be pretty upset if you asked anyone else," he said lightly. "You're a lucky man, our Jack. I hope you know that."

"Oh, don't worry, I do!"

"Make her happy, all right?"

"If I don't, it won't be for the want of trying."

"That's all right, then."

And he was gone, walking along the track into the deepening evening shadows.

"I love you, Maggie," Jack said softly.

"And I love you," Maggie whispered back.

And almost managed to convince herself that it was the truth.

Next day, Bullseye followed Billy to work. The other boys threw stones, yelling at him to "Bugger off!" and Billy simmered with hatred, afraid they would hurt the dog, or frighten him away for good. But Bullseye seemed to think it was just a new game. He picked up one of the stones and ran after the lads, right into the pit yard.

"What's that dog doing here?" Gaffer Hawkins snarled. "He'd better keep out of the way or he'll end up in one of the coal sacks in the river."

But the threat did no more to deter Bullseye than the stones had done.

Halfway through the morning, Gaffer Hawkins, a short, stout man who perspired a lot, decided it had not been a good idea to wear his long-sleeved vest to work today. He stripped off his shirt and vest, put his shirt back on again, and hung his vest over an empty tub. And there it would have stayed had Bullseye not caught sight of it and decided it would make a good plaything. After sniffing it and tossing it about a bit, he began dragging it round the yard, trailing it in the coal dust that lay everywhere.

"Hoi!" bellowed Gaffer, furious when he saw what was going on. "That bloody dog's got my bloody vest!"

He began to chase it. Sensing even more fun to be had, Bullseye danced away from him and ran in a big excited circle.

"Billy Donovan! Get your bloody dog under control, can't you?" yelled Gaffer.

Billy called to Bullseye, who ignored him. He chased after him, to no avail. The more Billy tried to capture him, the more he was enjoying himself. And then, to add insult to injury, he retreated under a coal wagon, taking the vest with him.

Billy couldn't reach him; the only way he could think of to tempt him out was with food. Bullseye loved a bit of cheese more than anything. He untied the spotted kerchief that held his snap, got out the cheese and broke off a piece, holding it out to the dog.

"Here, Bullseye, see what I've got for you, boy!"

The dog inched forward on his belly, sensing a trap but unable to resist the aroma of good strong Cheddar. Billy caught him by the collar Jack had bought for him and dragged him out from beneath the wagon, then wriggled himself far enough under to reach the vest, which was now torn, filthy and wet from Bullseye's spittle.

"I got it, Mr Hawkins," he ventured hopefully.

"And look at the state of it!" Gaffer was steaming mad. "That was a bally good vest! Look at it!"

"I'm sorry," Billy said miserably. "He won't do it again."

"Too right he won't! You're nothing but trouble, Donovan, and you're big enough and ugly enough now to be underground with your father, where he can keep an eye on you. I'm going to see the manager right away and tell him to start you as a carting boy on Monday. Charlie Parfitt was telling me his boy Cliff is ready to leave school and looking for a job — I'll have him working here on the screens, and you can go bloody underground."

Billy felt his stomach fall away.

"But Mr Hawkins —"

"Don't talk back at me, you young whippersnapper. You're going underground out of my way and that's the end of it."

He stormed off in the direction of the manager's office and Billy could only stare after him, trembling, and helpless to do anything to change his mind.

"Oh Bullseye, look what you bin and gone and done now!" he muttered wretchedly.

He'd always known, of course, that it was only a matter of time before a new youngster was given his job on the screens and he was sent underground, but he hadn't thought it would come so soon, and the prospect terrified him. On Monday, barring a miracle, he was going to have to go down the pit in that horrible hudge.

In Billy's experience, miracles rarely happened.

When Josh left work at Marston Colliery the following evening, he was far from pleased to see Peggy Bishop waiting for him.

Josh had been in a black mood all day. The news that Jack and Maggie were to be married had come as a blow to him, and he'd realised that he'd been hoping all along that nothing would come of their romance. Now that hope had all but disappeared, and Josh had gone around as if the devil was in him, as his mother would say, snapping at everyone who spoke to him and letting out all his frustration and disappointment by attacking the wood so viciously that he had almost broken his saw. To see Peggy there, clearly set on waylaying him, was the last straw.

After the confrontation with Tom, he'd made up his mind that it had to be over, and he was sorely tempted to simply ignore her. But he owed her more than that, and in any case, he was still feeling guilty that she had probably had a hard time from Tom whilst he had escaped more or less scot free.

Josh slowed his step so he was lagging behind the other men, but there was no fooling them. He saw the nudges and winks and heard the low chuckles, and only hoped it wouldn't get back to Tom Bishop. But there was a pretty fair chance that it would. Though Tom worked at a different pit, everyone knew everyone else round here, and most were members of the working men's club.

"You all right, Peggy?" he greeted her.

She tossed her head and shrugged.

"What d'you think you're doing, waylaying me when I'm with my mates? I would have thought you'd have had more sense. We'll both be for it if Tom gets to hear about it."

Peggy stuck her nose in the air.

"Oh, I'm past caring about him."

"That's just bloody stupid," Josh said. "After what happened last time . . . He didn't give you a hiding, did he? If so . . ."

"What?" she asked, and he knew from the triumphant expression that crossed her face that she wanted to hear him say he'd give Tom a hiding back.

"I'm just asking. Did he?"

She pouted. "Not a hiding. But he's been hell to live with, and I've had enough. Truth to tell, I'm sick to death of him, so I'm leaving. My bag's packed, and I'm going to my sister's."

"You're *what*?" Josh was shocked. Plenty of couples had their ups and downs one way and another, but nobody actually left the family home. Nobody he knew, anyway.

Peggy smirked.

"That'll show him, won't it?"

Josh shook his head, bewildered and alarmed.

"He'll go crazy, Peg. You can't do that."

"Why not? He's made my life a misery ever since he caught us. I'm not putting up with it any longer. That's why I wanted to see you, so you'd know where to find me."

Josh swore inwardly. It would appear that Peggy thought that if she left Tom, the way would be clear for her to take up with him openly. And before long, she'd be expecting commitment from him just like every other single woman seemed to. The thought of being saddled with Peggy was not a pleasant one. What had seemed like a bit of fun was turning into a millstone round his neck, and he'd have to tell her in no uncertain terms that it was over.

The trouble was, he didn't feel up to the hassle here and now. She'd make a scene, he was fairly sure, and

65

that was the last thing he wanted with his mates within earshot and no doubt taking note of everything that was going on. Better, perhaps, to let her down gently.

"OK, so now I know," he said non-committally. "I've got to go now, though."

"But you will be in touch?" Peggy persisted.

"We'll see."

"Josh!" She caught hold of his arm, her beady little eyes raking his face. "You *will*, won't you?"

"Oh, I expect so. Come on now . . ." He shook his arm free. "We're making a show of ourselves. Just give it time, Peggy, all right?"

He could see she was far from satisfied, but for the moment she nodded, and Josh broke into a trot to catch up with the other men.

Blimey, he'd had a narrow escape there! Or had he? He still found it hard to believe that Peggy would actually leave Tom, but if she did, there'd be hell to pay. Tom wouldn't take something like that lying down. His wounded pride would make him mad as a hatter. So far there had been no evidence of him carrying out the threats he'd made the night he'd caught them together, but if he thought Peggy had left him for Josh, then he really would be gunning for him.

Oh well, no use worrying about that now. He'd just have to deal with it if it ever happened. And the chances were it never would.

"Our Billy's starting as a carting boy next week," Paddy said.

The family were having their tea — bacon, cabbage and potatoes moistened with the fat from the frying pan.

"He's what!" Rose was horrified. She dreaded the thought of her youngest son — her baby — going into the bowels of the earth and coming home with his waist rubbed raw by the rope that would be tied round it to drag the putts of coal. "Oh my Lord, I hoped it would be a bit yet!"

"He got on the wrong side of the gaffer today," Paddy said. "Hawkins won't have him on the screens any more, and I can't say I blame him."

He went on to relate the tale of Bullseye's prank.

"That darned dog!" Rose said. "I knew we shouldn't have encouraged him. Couldn't you have a word with Hawkins, Paddy? Try to get him to change his mind?"

Paddy snorted derisively. "As if he'd take notice of me! Anyway, it won't do the boy any harm to go underground. It might make a man of him. Now, are you going to eat that bacon, our Billy, or shall I finish it up?"

Without a word, Billy dumped the remains of his bacon on his father's plate. He had no appetite anyway. He felt sick with fright at the thought of what next week would bring. If he had to go down in that hudge, he'd just die. Oh, if only something would go wrong with it so they couldn't use it any more!

Terror exploded in Billy's heart, a terror so great it swamped him. He felt the chasm opening up beneath his feet as they tied him into the hudge, turning his stomach, making him dizzy, and the darkness closed in around him, the weight of all the tons of earth above him pressing down on his chest so he could scarcely breathe.

They couldn't make him do it! They couldn't!

But they would.

He grabbed the carving knife from the bread board in the middle of the table, brandishing it wildly.

"I won't go down the pit! Dad — please . . . don't make me!"

"Oh Billy!" Rose was alarmed by his white face and the crazed expression in his eyes. But Paddy merely tossed his head in disgust.

"Don't talk so daft, our Billy. And put that knife down before somebody gets hurt."

Billy stared at him, his breath coming in quick, shallow sobs. If he had been able to string two thoughts together, they would have been all about hatred for the father who had never once spoken up for him, who belittled and beat him and did unspeakable things to Mam. But Billy was beyond thinking. He only knew he had to get out of here before the terror swallowed him alive.

With another wrenching sob, he pushed back his chair so roughly that it overturned, and ran from the house.

It was late when Maggie left the shop that evening. Closing time was never strictly observed — if there were customers to be served, then served they must be. Mrs Freeman even refused to allow them to lock the door if anyone was so much as looking in the window.

And for some reason, the good people of High Compton seemed to have left it until the last moment to do their shopping today.

By the time Maggie was free to go, she was very tired. It had been a long day, and most of it spent on her feet, which felt hot and swollen inside her tightly laced boots. She'd be very glad to get home and take them off.

She and Beat Clements left together; Mrs Freeman had found a few more menial jobs to be done, and, as the new apprentice, they fell to Cathy, who was looking none too pleased about it. Maggie wondered, not for the first time, if she'd stay the course. She knew that Cathy had been hoping to get away in time to meet her latest admirer, Will Stevens, the baker's boy. She remembered only too well the days when she herself had been the one who had to stay behind tidying up so that shop and showroom reached Mrs Freeman's impeccable standards.

Maggie and Beat were so busy chatting that Maggie didn't see Reuben Hillman skulking in the doorway of the gents' outfitters, or notice him following as they made their way through the centre of town. It was only when she and Beat parted company at the crossroads that she heard hurrying footstes and turned to see Reuben behind her.

"Are you following me?" she asked accusingly.

"Don't be angry, Maggie." Reuben was a bit out of breath from the exertion of catching up with her; she was fit, and used to the walk, he was not. "I just wanted to speak to you, that's all."

"Surely if you had something to say you could have said it at work?" Maggie was feeling a little uneasy, for no reason that she could really explain except that she didn't like being alone on a quiet country lane with Reuben.

"Not really, no . . ." For a moment he seemed lost for words, then he launched into what sounded very much like a prepared speech.

"I've been wanting to ask you out again for ages. I shouldn't have tried to kiss you the first time, I know, and I'm sorry. I just couldn't help myself. But I won't do it again, I promise, if you don't want me to. Please, Maggie, won't you give me another chance?"

"Oh, Reuben . . ." Maggie groaned. *And are you sorry for trying to touch my breast too?* she wanted to say but didn't. She'd never mentioned it to a living soul and she wasn't going to now.

"Please, Maggie," he begged again.

"Don't you know I have a sweetheart?" she asked, exasperated. "In fact we're going to be married, Jack Withers and me."

"Oh, him!" Reuben's face darkened and he pursed his flabby lips in an expression of distaste. "You're far too good for him, Maggie. He's just a miner."

"And what's wrong with that, I'd like to know?" Maggie demanded, annoyed. "You're only a shop assistant yourself."

"But I won't always be." Reuben puffed himself up with importance. "I've got plans for the future, I'll have you know, and when I come into my inheritance I shall be able to start my own business. I could give you

70

plenty that a miner never could. I'd make sure you'd want for nothing."

"For goodness' sake, Reuben, aren't you rather putting the cart before the horse?" Maggie snapped.

Reuben reached out suddenly and gripped her arm, pulling her round to face him.

"I mean it. I'd do anything for you, Maggie. Anything!" He said it with an intensity that frightened her. Strange, she'd never thought of Reuben as frightening before — repulsive, yes, annoying, yes, but this . . . this persistence was bordering on obsession, and suddenly Maggie thought she glimpsed something almost sinister beneath that soft, chubby exterior.

"I'm very happy with Jack, thank you very much," she retorted, shaking herself free and trying to hide the panic that was beginning to threaten her.

She began walking away from him, hoping against hope that he wouldn't follow, and then, to her relief, she saw a figure she recognised coming in the opposite direction.

Jack! He did come to meet her sometimes when she was late leaving work; thank goodness tonight was one of those occasions! She hurried towards him. "Oh, am I pleased to see you!"

"What's wrong?" Jack asked. Maggie was visibly upset.

"That Reuben Hillman waylaid me and I just couldn't get rid of him." Maggie slipped her hand into Jack's. "Sometimes he really scares me."

"What did he say? He didn't hurt you, did he?" Jack asked, concerned.

"Oh, he just keeps asking me out and won't take no for an answer. I've told him we're engaged, though, so I hope that'll be the end of it." Now that she was with Jack, and Reuben was no longer a threat, Maggie thought it best to make light of the whole thing. She didn't want Jack confronting him; it would only make the situation more awkward than it already was.

"Well just let me know if he bothers you again, and I'll have a word with him," Jack said grimly.

"Don't worry about it — he's harmless enough. Just really annoying," Maggie said.

But as they set off up the road, she glanced apprehensively over her shoulder. Reuben was still where she'd left him, just staring after them. Even when he saw Maggie looking back at him, he didn't turn away, and though it was still warm, Maggie shivered suddenly. There was something unnerving about the way he was simply standing there, watching them go.

He was obsessed with her, she knew, and she was beginning to wonder just how far that obsession would lead him. He'd followed her tonight; he might do it again. And would it stop there? *I'd do anything for you, Maggie. Anything!* It hadn't sounded like a simple declaration of love; it had sounded almost threatening. Perhaps she'd been wrong to make light of it; perhaps she should tell Jack just how bad this had become, and ask him to come and meet her more often. But Maggie had never been one to play the helpless female. She was more than a match for Reuben Hillman, she told herself, squaring her shoulders. She'd deal with him herself.

"Let's hurry, Jack," she said, pushing her misgivings to one side. "My boots are killing me, and the sooner I can get them off and give my toes a good stretch, the happier I shall be."

It was dark before Billy came home. Rose — and Bullseye — were outside, looking for him.

"Oh, thank goodness, Billy! Where in the world have you been? I've been that worried!"

Billy's eyes were wide and staring. He did not even seem to notice when Bullseye pushed a wet nose into his hand.

Rose ushered him into the kitchen, where she poured strong stewed tea from the pot that stood on the hob.

"I suppose you've been off worrying yourself about having to go down the pit," she said, stirring sugar into his cup and handing it to him.

Billy mumbled something unintelligible.

"You know if there was anything I could do about it, I would," Rose said. "But I can't. You've got to go to work, and it's either down the pit or see if you can get a job as a farm lad. We could ask Farmer Barton if he needs any help, I suppose. But take it from me, farm work's no picnic, either. At least down the pit you get Sundays off."

Billy said nothing. He had placed his cup of tea on the mantelpiece and, for some reason known only to himself, picked up the clock key that lay there. Now he was repeatedly turning it over between his hands, putting it down, picking it up again, as if he was some kind of automaton.

"Is that what you'd like, then?" Rose asked. "For me to go and have a word with Farmer Barton — see if there's any chance he'd take you on? You're still on the screens till next week, aren't you? You're not due to go underground till then? If you really are so set against it, we'll see what we can do."

There was a long silence, then: "It's too late, Mam," Billy said flatly.

Rose sighed. She hated to see her youngest son so unhappy. But it was the way of the world. The Donovans were miners, like most of the folk who lived round here, and that was really all there was to it. She patted his hand.

"You'll get used to it, mark my words. This time next week you'll wonder what you were so worried about. Now, drink up your tea before it goes cold."

Just saying it comforted her, if not Billy. And she had no way of knowing that by this time next week, their lives would have changed for ever.

CHAPTER
FIVE

It began, that terrible, fateful day, like any other. Maggie and Rose were up with the dawn, working their way through their usual routine until it was time to rouse the men. When Maggie took out the ashes from the grate for riddling, the birds were singing and Bullseye, not yet ready to stir, regarded her lazily from his bed in the outhouse. It was going to be another fine, hot day.

When she went back indoors, Paddy was downstairs, a towel tucked around his neck as he attacked the day-old stubble on his chin with his cut-throat razor. He had been too tired last night to shave before going to bed as he usually did to save time in the morning. Of Billy there was no sign.

"You'd better give him another shout," Rose said. "He's gone back to sleep, I shouldn't be surprised. He had a late night."

"Bloody little layabout," Paddy muttered.

Maggie went upstairs. As she'd suspected, Billy was still in bed, the covers hiding all but a crest of bright ginger hair.

"Come on, our Billy, get up," she said, shaking him.

"Oh Maggie, no — I feel awful." He sounded awful too, his voice faint and slurred, and when she pulled the covers off him, she saw that his face was pale and puffy and he covered it with his hand to shut out the light. "I'm not going to work," he muttered.

"Don't talk so stupid, Billy! You've got to," Maggie told him.

"What for? Gaffer doesn't want me on the screens, so he won't care if I'm there or not. He can't sack me for it, anyway — he's done that already."

"They'll dock your wages."

"I don't care. Just leave me alone. My head's aching like billy-o, and I feel really sick too."

Billy pulled the bedspread back over his head and, defeated, Maggie went back downstairs.

"Billy says he's not going to work today. He's not well."

"I'll give him not well!" Paddy wiped the last of the soap from his face and flung down the towel. "He'll get up soon enough if I go up to him!"

"Leave him just for today, can't you?" Rose laid a restraining hand on her husband's arm. "He was ever so upset last night."

"He's always upset about something," Paddy retorted, but he didn't go storming up the stairs as he had intended. "Oh well, I suppose one day won't hurt. At least I won't have to look at his miserable face all the way to the pit. It's enough to turn the milk sour. Sure, I don't know what's the matter with the boy."

"You do too," Maggie said. "He's frightened to death of going underground. You know he doesn't like the dark. He never has."

"He'll just have to get used to it, then, won't he? Afraid of the bloody dark! He's just a big sissy." Paddy picked up his bottle of tea and the kerchief containing his cognocker of bread and cheese. "I'm off, then. Somebody from this house has to bring home a wage."

He went to the door, and Maggie followed him out.

"Dad, I know you've got no time for our Billy, but couldn't you try and do something for him? Gaffer just lost his temper, I expect. He'll have calmed down now, and he might give our Billy another chance if you had a word with him."

Paddy grunted impatiently. "He's got to go down the pit sooner or later, so it might just as well be sooner. He'll earn better money as a carting boy than he does on the screens, and we can do with that, seeing as we'll soon be a wage short here."

Maggie felt a flash of guilt. She knew what he was alluding to.

"I'm bound to get married sometime, Dad."

"Ah sure, and don't I know it." For just a moment there was regret on Paddy's florid features. Strange, a man always wanted sons, but Ewart and Walter had both left home as soon as they could, and as for Billy . . . well, the less said about Billy the better. But Maggie . . . he'd miss Maggie when she was no longer here.

The sound of a door banging up the rank, voices, and pit boots on the track, and Maggie looked round to see Jack swinging along, carrying his own cognocker and tea bottle, his father with him.

She flushed slightly, her hand flying to check that her hair was up neatly; she hadn't had time yet to tidy herself properly. But soon, she supposed, Jack really would see her as nature intended.

Gilby Withers, always a man of few words, nodded an acknowledgement, but Jack, full of the joys of spring, greeted them in cheerful imitation of Paddy's Irish brogue.

"Top o' the morning to you!"

He grabbed Maggie and stole a kiss so unashamedly it made her blush.

"Jack Withers! Will you behave yourself!"

"Not if I can help it." Jack winked at her. "See you tonight, sweetheart."

"Where's your Billy?" Gilby enquired mildly.

"Skiving," Paddy said shortly. "Making out he's not well. He's a waste of space, that one. Come on, lads, we'd best get a move on, or we'll be late."

The men walked off together along the rank. They were soon joined by Frank Rogers, running to catch them up, and, as they passed number three, by Charlie Oglethorpe and his father Ollie. The group would continue to grow as they neared the pit, all roads converging.

As she watched them go, a sudden sadness she could not explain twisted suddenly deep inside Maggie, so sharp that for a moment she felt she couldn't breathe. Then it was gone, leaving nothing but a small ache not unlike nostalgia or regret.

She gave herself a little shake. What on earth was wrong with her? She should be on top of the world too, just as Jack was. But the feeling of foreboding remained, nebulous but unmistakable, and all the brightness seemed to have gone out of the early-morning sunshine.

Peggy Bishop went to the back door of her little house and tried it for the dozenth time since Tom had left for work. No good. It still refused to budge.

She'd known it wouldn't, of course. She'd heard Tom turn his key in the lock when he left, and there was no way it could have miraculously undone itself. But she tried it again all the same, rattling it furiously as the panic and rage built up inside her. How dare he lock her in? She'd be stuck here all day in the stuffy, claustrophobic heat until he got home tonight. She had no key of her own; that had been lost long ago, and it had never worried her enough to go to all the trouble of getting another one cut. People didn't bother locking their doors until they went to bed at night, if then. Intruders were unheard of, and there was always someone about who would keep an eye open for dodgy pedlars or tramps.

Peggy knew she had no hope of climbing out of a window either. None of them opened wide enough. If she'd been ten years younger and a few stones lighter, it might have been a different story. As it was, she was very much afraid she'd get stuck, and even if she didn't, emerging head first into the peony bushes in full view of her neighbours was hardly dignified.

She attacked the door handle one last time, and exploded with frustration. How could Tom treat her like this, making a prisoner of her as if she was a common criminal? She wouldn't put up with it! She'd leave him the minute that door was opened, and go to her sister's. But of course, the reason he had locked her in was to stop her doing just that, though it was Josh he'd thought she intended running to. He'd locked her in last night, too, after the terrible row that must have been heard all the way to High Compton.

It was her own silly fault, of course. When she had got in after waylaying Josh, Tom had been waiting for her, his face like thunder. The bag she had packed earlier on in a fit of bravado had been dumped on the kitchen table — the evidence for the prosecution.

"What's this?" he had demanded, jabbing at it with a finger still black with coal dust.

Peggy had quailed inwardly, but managed to face him defiantly.

"What's it look like?"

"If you think you're going anywhere, my girl, you'm making a big mistake. I'm not having my wife make a fool out of me."

Peggy turned away. "You're a fool already," she muttered.

He heard her. "What did you say?"

She turned back. "Oh, just leave it."

"Leave it? And let you go off with that bloody Withers?" he spat. "Not bloody likely!"

"At least he doesn't shout and swear at me," Peggy said recklessly. "At least he knows how to treat a woman."

"Not by the time I've finished with him he won't!" Tom roared. "By the time I've finished with him he'll be good for nothing but pushing up the daisies."

Something in his face alarmed her, something cold and dangerous beneath the fury, but she wasn't going to let him see he was scaring her.

"Oh, don't talk so silly," she said dismissively.

"Silly, is it? My wife going with another man, making herself and me a laughing stock? Oh no, you're the one that's silly, Peg. And that bloody Withers too if he thinks he can get away it. Gadding about with my wife! Talking her into running off with him!"

"He hasn't —"

"No? What's this, then?"

He picked up her bag and threw it across the kitchen. It slammed into the plant stand that supported her precious aspidistra. The whole lot came crashing down, the china pot smashing and dirt scattering across the floor.

"Tom! Now look what you've done!" she cried, distressed.

Tom grabbed his coat from the back of a kitchen chair and marched to the door.

"Where are you going?" she demanded.

"To sort out that bloody Withers once and for all."

"Tom . . . wait! You've got it all wrong . . ."

He turned on her furiously. "I don't think so. Not after what I saw with me own eyes the other night. And you, my lady, can stay here. You won't be seeing him again."

He had stormed out. The key had turned in the lock and Peggy had spent a miserable evening incarcerated in her own home.

It was late when Tom came in, smelling of drink. Peggy had tried to talk to him, but he would have none of it. She lay tearful and unable to sleep while he snored beside her, and this morning when he left for work he had locked her in again.

She paced the floor, desperate to know what Tom had done last night, whether he'd gone after Josh and picked a fight, or whether what he'd said had been just a lot of empty threats. She was desperate too to see Josh — who had somehow come to mean a great deal more to her than just a quick tumble — and simply to get out of the house.

But she couldn't. Peggy covered her face with her hands and burst into tears.

"Where's our Billy, Mam?" Maggie asked, coming downstairs, dressed now for work.

Rose, who was retching over the stone sink in the scullery, looked up, wiping her face on the towel Paddy had used for shaving.

"Well — in bed, isn't he?"

"No, he's not," Maggie said. "His bed's empty."

"He must have come down while I was over in the privy," Rose said. "P'raps he's gone in the front room."

But she didn't think he had. She'd been in there herself only a minute ago, pulling back the curtains that were drawn religiously every night when it got dark, even though their front room, like everyone else's, was used only for special occasions — and as a last resting place for the dead whilst awaiting their funeral.

Maggie went to look anyway, but Billy was not there.

"He must have gone off somewhere with that darned dog," Rose said. "But I certainly didn't see him go. Oh, dear Lord, he worries me to death. You never know what he's going to do next. And if he's poorly . . ."

"He didn't want to go to work, that's all," Maggie said. "He'll be back when it's too late for that."

"Oh, you're probably right." Rose was fighting another bout of nausea. When it began to pass, she looked fondly at her daughter, who was drying the last of the breakfast things and stacking them away in the cupboard.

"I'm ever so glad you and Jack have made up your minds to get married. He's a good man, Maggie. He'll treat you right, no doubt about that. Though if it was his brother you'd gone for, I wouldn't be so sure. He's a wild one, is Josh. Trouble follows him around like night follows day. Always has. Well, that's why he got sent off to Wales, isn't it? To get him away from that awful crowd he was in with. And to give his uncle the chance to knock some sense into him. But you'll never get a tiger to change his stripes."

"A leopard to change his spots," Maggie said, laughing.

"What?"

"It's a leopard, not a tiger. And I think Josh *has* changed. He was just young and silly, that's all. He's grown up now."

"Hmm. If you say so." Rose looked unconvinced. "I still say you've got the best of it. I just hope it doesn't cause trouble between the two of them."

Maggie raised an eyebrow.

"Whatever do you mean? Why should it cause trouble?"

"Because I reckon Josh is sweet on you," Rose said shortly. "I've seen the way he looks at you, my girl, if you haven't."

Maggie huffed impatiently.

"Oh, get on with you, Mam! Don't talk so silly!" But she could feel faint pink colour rising in her cheeks.

It was nonsense, of course. Josh looked at every pretty girl that way. There was no denying he was a bit of a one. But all the same, she couldn't help remembering the shadow that had crossed his face when Jack had told him they were going to be married. And she couldn't forget the disconcerting tickle she felt deep inside whenever she saw him . . .

The unwelcome train of thought was interrupted suddenly. Something was going on outside along the rank, a man's voice shouting, doors banging.

"What on earth . . .?"

She ran to the door, the first sharp twists of alarm stirring in her stomach. Women were out all along the rank, converging on the figure of a boy who looked like Charlie Oglethorpe. *Charlie?* What in the world was he doing home? He should be at work. What was going on?

The sweet morning air was suddenly overlaid with menace, as if the sun had been obscured by a thundercloud, or a pleasant dream had taken on the aura of a nightmare.

Maggie's stomach clenched with terror. Something terrible had happened. But what? What?

She started along the track, and Charlie broke away from the stunned group of women and came panting up to her. His eyes were bulging, his cheeks flushed, yet around the edges of the blotches of high colour his face was paper white, and he was visibly shaking.

"What is it, Charlie?" Maggie gasped. "What's happened?"

At first he couldn't speak. His breath was coming hard. Then:

"Oh my God, Maggie," he managed. "It's the hudge. The hudge has gone down."

Maggie felt as if a chasm had opened up within her. The blood drained from her face and her knees went weak, but for a moment she couldn't grasp what Charlie was saying. It was too enormous. *The hudge has gone down*. But it went down every morning, several times, until all the men were underground. That wasn't what Charlie meant. It couldn't be. *The hudge has gone down*. Oh, dear God, surely it couldn't be *that . . . The hudge has gone down . . .* There had been some kind of terrible accident.

The group of women who had been frozen with shock a few moments ago had broken up, some disappearing into their houses, others running to the end of the rank, where the track joined the road leading to the pit. Maggie grabbed Charlie's sleeve.

"Is it bad?" Charlie nodded wordlessly. "Who?" she asked desperately, her voice little more than a whisper despite the clamour within her.

Charlie shook his head; whether in all the mayhem he really didn't know, or whether he didn't want to tell her, she couldn't be sure.

"I gotta let people know . . ." He shook his arm free of her grasp and ran on up the rank, knocking on the doors of those who had not come out to see what the commotion was all about.

For a stunned moment Maggie stood stock still, seeing in her mind's eye her father, Jack, and the others walking off along the track this morning, and feeling the icy waves of shock racing through her veins. Then she flew back into the house.

Rose was retching again over the scullery sink — the reason she had not followed Maggie outside to find out what was going on.

"Mam — there's been some kind of accident," Maggie said, trying to keep the tremble out of her voice.

Rose jerked upright, hand covering her mouth, eyes wide and frightened above it.

"An accident? What . . .? Who . . .?"

"I don't know." Maggie was desperate not to frighten Rose more than she could help. "I'm going to the pit now to find out."

"I'm coming too." Rose was wiping her face.

"No, Mam, you stay here. I can run faster than you. I'll be back the minute I know anything." Even as she said it, Maggie knew that her mother would follow her to the pit. Who could stay at home waiting for news at such a time? But she couldn't have borne to go at Rose's pace. She had to get there as fast as possible.

"Try not to worry, Mam," she added. "I don't expect it's any of ours involved."

But that, too, she knew was wasted breath. How could anyone not worry until they knew their loved ones were safe? The sick dread inside her was like a cloud of doom. As she ran along the lane, feet flying, heart pounding, each step, each heartbeat, was an echo of their names — Dad . . . Jack . . . Jack . . . Dad — and her lips moved silently with a garbled prayer. *Please God, let them be all right. Oh please, let them be all right.* She overtook other women who were less young and fit than she was, but she didn't stop to speak. The only thing that mattered was getting to the pit head.

In the yard, men in their pit clothes, though not yet blackened with coal dust, were milling about everywhere. Some huddled in shocked groups; others had gathered around the winding engine house. The single pulley wheel was still, and there was something ominous about that stillness in the midst of all the chaos.

Maggie stopped short, looking around wildly from one group to another, her sweat-misted eyes searching vainly for Jack and her father, then started to run again towards the group that were gathered around the headgear. A figure she recognised detached itself from the others — Ollie Oglethorpe, Charlie's father — and came towards her. He, too, looked totally unlike himself, his normally ruddy face ravaged and white with shock.

"Maggie, love, you don't want to go over there," he said awkwardly.

"But I've got to find Dad and Jack . . ." Her breath was coming in harsh, painful gasps.

Ollie went to put an arm round her heaving shoulders, then withdrew it awkwardly. Physical contact did not come easily to him, or any of these men.

"They bain't there, Maggie." His voice was low and distressed.

"Where are they, then?"

"Maggie . . ." Somehow he overcame his reticence and touched her arm. "Come over here, love, and sit down." He tried to steer her towards the low wall that surrounded the engine house, but Maggie shook herself free. Panic was choking her now.

"No — I've got to find them! Where are they, Mr Oglethorpe? Where are they?"

Ollie shook his head slowly, glancing away from the distressed girl for a moment as if to draw on hidden reserves. Dear Lord, that he should have to be the one to break the news! But better him than the manager, or the gaffer. Better someone she'd known since she was a little girl . . .

"There's been a terrible accident," he began awkwardly. "The rope broke. When they were winding down the hudge, the rope broke."

Although it was what she'd already gathered, she gasped, a short, sharp intake of breath, and her hand flew to her mouth as the full truth of it hit her. And yet she still couldn't take it in. Her thoughts were whirling like Ollie's racing pigeons when they were confined to their loft, a formless, ever-moving mass of fluttering feathers.

"Jack?" she whispered. "Dad?"

Ollie nodded grimly.

"And ten others. Young Frank Rogers, Ben Bridges —"

Maggie cut him short. She didn't care about Frank Rogers, or Ben Bridges, or anyone else but Jack and her dad.

"You mean they're down there and nobody can reach them?"

"They'm down there all right," Ollie muttered.

"But somebody must get to them! They'll be hurt!" she cried wildly. "How can they get down to them if the rope on the hudge is broken?"

Ollie gesticulated helplessly, wondering how to tell her the awful truth: that the rope had given way so soon after the hudge had begun its descent that it was almost certain no one could have survived.

"They'll go down from New Grove," he said awkwardly. New Grove, a mile and three-quarters away as the crow flew, was linked by its underground passages to Shepton Fields, providing ventilation of sorts, though the connecting tunnel was not big enough for regular traffic between the two pits. "A party's gone over there now to try to make a way through to them."

"That's where I should be, then!" Maggie was already turning away, urgency flooding her veins. "I must be there when they bring them up!"

Ollie caught her arm, stopping her. "Maggie . . . no."

She tried to shake herself free, eyes blazing.

"They'll need me, Mr Oglethorpe! I have to get over there!"

Ollie's stomach turned as he thought of the mangled bodies that would be brought out when the cage returned to the surface at New Grove. He couldn't let Maggie go there and see that. No one should have to see it — certainly not this young lass.

"You don't understand, love . . ." he began.

She pulled again against his restraining hand on her arm.

"Let me go, Mr Oglethorpe. I've got to —"

She broke off as a figure she knew well emerged from one of the doorways in the pumping house. Gilby Withers — Jack's father.

"There's Mr Withers!" she cried, and Ollie let go of her arm, all too glad to relinquish responsibility.

Maggie ran towards Jack's father, calling his name, but when he turned and saw her, she was shocked by the look of him. This was a very different Gilby from the placid, upright man she knew. His face was ravaged, his eyes red and staring; he was bent and old suddenly, and he moved like a man in a dream.

"Oh Maggie, Maggie . . ." His voice, full of despair, chilled her all over again. "I should have been on that damned hudge, not he!"

Tears of panic rose in Maggie's throat, almost choking her. She fought them down — and the dawning realisation of the awful truth along with them.

"I'm going over to New Grove," she said desperately. "Why don't you come too?"

Gilby shook his head slowly, unable for a moment to speak. Then, quite matter-of-factly, he said: "'Twouldn't do no good."

Still Maggie shied away, refusing to acknowledge the finality of what had happened.

"But they'll need us!"

"No," he said in the same almost unnaturally flat tone. "They won't need us, Maggie. They won't ever need us again."

And suddenly there was no escaping it, the terrible truth she had tried so hard to deny. They were dead. Jack and Dad and the others, whose names she hadn't even taken in. Twelve men and boys who had been on the hudge when it fell. But the others didn't matter. Only Jack and Dad mattered . . .

The sob broke in her throat and came out as a scream. "No!"

The roaring in her ears deafened her to everything else around her, yet the scream was there, echoing inside her head. "No! No! No!"

Maggie turned, fleeing she knew not where on legs that threatened to give way beneath her. Across the colliery yard she ran, dodging anyone in her way. Then, through the hot haze of tears, she saw Rose standing near the entrance with a knot of other women, arms wrapped around her thin frame, and still wearing her apron. The sight of her brought Maggie up short. She stopped, fighting to regain control of herself. Mam mustn't see her like this. Mam shouldn't be here at all in her condition.

For a moment panic threatened to overwhelm her at the prospect of having to break the news to Rose that Paddy was dead; then with almost startling suddenness she was the old, capable Maggie once more. Mam had to be looked after. Mam had to be told. And Maggie had to find the strength to do it.

Pushing her own grief aside, she went towards Rose and took her in her arms.

"Wherever has our Billy got to?" Rose asked distractedly. "He doesn't know what's happened. You'd better go out and look for him, Maggie."

It was mid afternoon and they were at home, drinking gallons of strong sweet tea, sitting in a daze at the kitchen table, trying to find things to do and then not being able to do them. Both were in such a state of shock that they had not yet been able to cry. The world had fallen in around them, yet in a way they were still in denial, discussing practicalities as if this were some minor domestic crisis, whilst their churning stomachs and shaking limbs told them it was much, much more.

"Don't worry about Billy, Mam," Maggie said. "He'll come home when he's ready."

"But it's not right he doesn't know," Rose insisted. "His dad's dead, and he doesn't know."

"Perhaps he does know," Maggie said.

Rose's eyes skittered round. "How do you mean?"

"Well . . . maybe he had a premonition. Maybe that's the reason he didn't want to go to work today."

But *she* hadn't had a premonition. She'd always thought she was the intuitive one in the family, and she hadn't for a moment imagined anything like this . . .

Then, with a sickening jolt, she remembered the nightmare she'd had a few weeks ago, when she'd seemed to be plummeting into the depths of the earth, just as the hudge would have plummeted this morning. And just before she fell, Jack and her father and Frank Rogers had been with her. Now they were all gone.

She'd known something terrible was going to happen, and she'd said nothing to anyone. Instead she'd pushed it to the back of her mind. But this morning, when she'd watched the men go off along the rank to work, an echo of it had come back to haunt her. She remembered the feeling of sadness that had overcome her suddenly as she saw them go. And still she'd said nothing. She should have trusted her own instincts, and recognised the warning for what it was. But what could she have done? They would never have listened to her, even if she'd run after them and begged them not to go.

Tears welled in her eyes and she pressed a hand against her mouth, fighting to hide the terrible rush of guilt and despair.

"I just wish our Billy was here," Rose said, desperately needing what was left of her family around her. Another thought struck her. "We'll have to let our Ewart and Walter know."

With an effort, Maggie pulled herself together. "Sir Montague said he'd take care of all that," she reminded her mother gently.

Sir Montague Fairley had arrived at the pit head at some point during the morning, and when word had come back from New Grove that everyone who had been on the hudge had indeed perished, he had spoken with all the grieving womenfolk. He had expressed sympathy, which they were too numb yet to feel resentful of, given the years of underinvestment in Shepton Fields; he had promised that no widow would be turned unceremoniously out of her home, and he had offered to arrange for relatives in far-flung parts to be notified of what had happened. They had listened to all he said in stunned silence, deferential still to this man whose pit had taken the lives of their husbands, sons and fathers.

"Oh, do go and see if you can find our Billy," Rose said. "I expect he's down across the fields. Bring him home, there's a good girl. He ought to be here."

Maggie got up, still moving as if in a dream, and went to the door. There was a deathly hush about the rank, and the day that had begun so brightly had clouded over, a thick grey canopy obscuring the sun. Dr Blackmore's horse and trap stood outside the door of number two — Frank Rogers' mother was in such a way that they'd called the doctor to her, Maggie guessed. She walked along the track in a fog of nightmarish unreality.

A small figure, running helter skelter, rounded the corner. Billy — with Bullseye at his heels. He pelted up to her, eyes wide, thin face tortured.

"Maggie! Maggie! Is it true? I met Charlie Oglethorpe, and he said . . ."

Maggie put an arm around the thin, shaking shoulders.

"Oh Billy! Yes, I'm afraid it is true. Dad's dead, and Jack, and a lot of others."

A shuddering sob escaped him.

"Billy, you've got to be brave," Maggie said. "Try not to upset Mam."

He stared at her as if all this was totally beyond his comprehension.

"Come on home," she said.

They went back along the alleyway, Bullseye following at a distance, as if he too realised that something terrible had happened and wanted no part of it.

Rain was falling by the time the broken bodies were brought to the surface, and the men who carried out the grisly task would never, for the rest of their lives, talk about the things they had seen.

"I want your dad home," Rose said. The years of ill-treatment were forgotten now; she remembered only the good times. She and Paddy had once been young and in love, and in spite of everything, she loved him still. "I want him home. Where is he?"

The remains had all been taken to the mortuary. Maggie knew that the only way Paddy would come home was in a coffin with the lid securely screwed down. His injuries, and those of the other men, were too terrible for the eyes of their loved ones.

Night had fallen early because of the thick cloud base. Lamps burned at the windows of cottages for men who would never come home, and tea stewed in pots on fireside hobs, the only sustenance for people with no appetite for solid food.

"Oh, what a day!" Rose said, an understatement that was typical of the stoical breed that was miners and their families. And then: "I'm so sorry, Maggie."

Maggie glanced at her, puzzled.

"Jack," Rose said. "All I've been able to think about is your dad. But Jack's gone too. And just when everything was working out so well for you."

Maggie turned away, unable to reply. All day she had refused to allow herself to think about Jack, for she knew that when she did, she would fall apart. She had tried to be strong for her mother, tried to be practical, but all the time the grief she was refusing to acknowledge had been there, gnawing at her insides, leaving her hollow, yet heavy as lead. Now it erupted, threatening to swamp her.

Jack was gone. She'd never again hear his voice, never touch him, never feel his hand, warm and sure, on hers. She would never stand beside him at the altar, never lie beside him, never make his tea and wash his pit clothes, never live with him in the little house he had been so delighted to be offered, never bear his children. Jack, her rock, her hope for the future, was no more, and she didn't know how she could bear it. And she certainly could not bear to think of what had happened today, or what it must have been like for him in those last moments as the hudge went crashing down into the bowels of the earth.

Why, oh why Jack? her heart wept. Why Jack, young, strong, honourable, kind? She hadn't deserved him. Now he had been taken from her and she had not even had the chance to say goodbye. Or to tell him that she loved him.

Guilt swamped her. She'd had her niggling little doubts about that. Had he known? Had she hurt him? Oh please, please no! The thought that she might have was unbearably painful. The tears that had been locked away inside all day spilled over, cascading in a hot tide down her crumpled face.

"Oh Mam," she whispered.

Rose's face crumpled too. For a long moment they merely looked at one another, sharing their grief and their loss. Then they went into each other's arms and clung together, weeping.

"I told you you wouldn't see that bloody Withers again, and I was right!" Tom Bishop said with something that might almost have been grim satisfaction. "He got his comeuppance all right! Trouble is, a lot of others had to go along with him."

"What are you on about?" Peggy asked distractedly. She had spent a terrible day locked in her cottage, but she had heard about the accident all the same. News of it had spread through the district like wildfire; when she had seen the neighbours gathered outside talking, she had opened the window as far as it would go and they had told her about it. But what Tom was saying made no sense at all.

"Your lover," he sneered. "He was one of them killed. And serve him bloody well right."

"Josh doesn't work at Shepton Fields," she said, puzzled

And then she realised: Tom had confused the two brothers.

"You bloody fool!" she shot at him. "Josh works at Marston. It's Jack at Shepton Fields. He's the one who's been killed."

It took a moment for Tom to take this in; he wasn't, and never would be, the sharpest knife in the box. Then his face changed, all manner of expressions she couldn't read distorting his puggy features before they were replaced by his usual belligerence.

"Well you'd better stay away from him then, hadn't you, if you don't want him to end up like his brother," he snarled.

The bar at the Prince of Wales was crowded for a weekday evening, for the men had felt the need to come together and talk about the tragedy with others of their kind who understood. But the atmosphere was subdued, and the familiar faces that were missing brought the events of the day home to those who were there as nothing else had done. Archie Russell was amongst those who had gone down with the hudge; the chair he usually occupied was empty, for no one else could bring themselves to sit in it.

"What a thing," George Parfitt said. "And to think we was only saying t'other night as how Shepton Fields weren't safe. Josh Withers was on about how that hudge was a bloody death-trap, and we were all pooh-poohing him. Now his own brother's dead."

"I don't understand it," said Jim Parker, another of the men. "That were a good thick rope, even if it were hemp and not wire. I can't understand how Hubie Britten didn't come to notice if it were getting frayed. He generally gives it a good check-over once a week or so." Hubie drove the winding engine.

"Well, he's getting on, coming up for retirement. P'raps his eyes bain't as good as they were. Or he's getting forgetful."

"Ah, p'raps that be it."

As the men shook their heads and supped their pints, none of them had any way of knowing of the serious discussion that was taking place at this very moment between Wilfred James, the colliery manager, and Sir Montague Fairley, the owner.

Sir Montague, very red in the face from all the brandy he had consumed throughout a long and difficult day, was pacing his drawing room, yet another glass in his hand.

"This is shocking, James — shocking! Are you absolutely sure of your facts?"

Wilfred James's face was drawn and, for once, almost as dirty as any miner's.

"There's no doubt," he said heavily. "No doubt at all. That was no accident that happened today. The rope didn't give through wear and tear. It was cut.

Somebody had severed it, strand by strand. Then, as soon as it had to take the weight . . ." He broke off, unable to finish.

"Good God! Then it's murder a dozen times over!" Sir Montague exploded. "But who would do such a thing? They must have realised the consequences!"

"Well, that'll be for the police to find out," Wilfred said. "I should have reported it to them straight away, but I thought it best to speak to you first."

"You did the right thing." Sir Montague refilled his glass from the crystal decanter that stood on a small pedestal table, then belatedly raised the decanter in Wilfred's direction. "Do you want one, James?"

"No thanks, Sir Montague," Wilfred said, though he could certainly have done with one. "In view of all I've still got to do, I think it's best I stay sober."

The implied criticism was lost on the pit owner, who was only glad his best cognac was not going to be wasted on his manager.

"Yes, I dare say you should." He took another healthy gulp. "Well, I suppose it's good news in a way."

Wilfred stared at him, frowning. "What do you mean? Twelve of my men and boys are dead — hardly good news, Sir Montague."

"No, no." Fairley waved his glass impatiently. "We could have been for the jolly old high jump, James. When they get over their shock, the men might well have been baying for our blood, not to mention what the authorities could have had to say about it. But if it was a deliberate act — well, we can hardly be blamed, can we? No one could foresee a vandal or a murderous madman severing the rope, now could they?"

"No, sir, I suppose they couldn't."

Wilfred James turned away, shocked and disgusted by Sir Montague's attitude. He wasn't going to say anything, though. He had his own job to think of — if job there still was. Doubtless Shepton Fields would be closed down now. He knew that Sir Montague had been considering doing just that for some time, but had been afraid that if he did, the miners at the rest of the collieries he owned might go on strike in sympathy. Well, this had done the job for him. No wonder he was taking it so well. Good God, he wouldn't put it past Sir Montague to be behind the severed rope himself.

"Are you going to call the police, or am I?" he asked coldly.

CHAPTER
SIX

Maggie was dressed and ready for work. She wasn't sure how she was going to manage to go out and face the world, but she knew she had to try. For one thing, she couldn't afford to lose another day's wages, especially now that they were going to be without the money Paddy brought home each Saturday, and for another, she was desperate for some sort of normality. She'd go crazy, she thought, if she had to stay at home all day, just going over and over the terrible events of yesterday with Rose and the neighbours, all of whom were in such total shock they could talk of nothing else. It would probably be the same at the shop, but at least she could keep busy, even if it was only to dust fixtures, roll lace and sort pins. Anything would be better than being cooped up in the hot, airless kitchen where grief and shock hung in a suffocating cloud. But she couldn't help worrying about leaving Rose with only Billy for company.

"Are you sure you'll be all right, Mam?" she asked, looking anxiously at her mother.

"Of course I'll be all right." Rose's voice was thin and shaky, but determined. "What's going to happen to me? I'm in my own home — for now, anyway. Till

Fairley decides he wants it for letting out to some other poor soul on his payroll."

"Oh Mam . . ." Maggie didn't know what to say. She couldn't yet begin to contemplate the consequences of what had happened. Dealing with the loss of Paddy, and Jack too, was more than enough. But Rose was right, of course. The pit owner was sure to want them out of his house before long.

"Go on, you get off or you'll be late," Rose insisted.

"Well, if you're sure . . ."

Maggie tossed her shawl around her shoulders and felt tears catch in her throat. Was it really only a few days ago that she'd worn it to go for a walk with Jack? It seemed like a different lifetime.

She needed her shawl this morning, though. The sun that had seemed to shine endlessly these last few weeks had disappeared behind an ocean of lowering grey cloud, and it was quite chilly. Or perhaps that was just her. Maggie didn't think she'd felt properly warm, or stopped trembling, since the terrible events of the previous day.

She walked quickly, hoping no one would emerge from any of the other houses in the terrace. She really didn't want to have to speak to anybody. But as yet, the doors were all firmly closed and it was eerily quiet. Maggie supposed the other pits would be operating normally, but almost everyone who lived in the Ten Houses worked at Shepton Fields, and it would be a long time, if ever, before coal was mined there again.

Soon she was out on the main road that led to High Compton, and this too was quiet. A horse and cart passed her with milk churns rattling; she saw it most mornings as it made its way from farm to farm, but the dairyman never called a greeting. He was a surly fellow, Maggie always thought, but today she was glad of it. As she rounded a bend in the road, she saw Farmer Barton driving his herd of cows across it on the way back to their field from the milking parlour. She slowed her step until they all disappeared from view behind the high hedges and Farmer Barton had closed the gate after them. Another encounter avoided. But it couldn't last much longer. As she approached the town, Maggie steeled herself and kept going at a brisk pace, hoping she wouldn't meet anyone she knew. To her relief, she managed it.

Freeman's, where she worked, was a big double-fronted shop on the corner of the high street, the drapery shop to one side of the main door and Horace Freeman's gentlemen's outfitters to the other. Maggie went around to the rear of the building as she always did and in through the back entrance, which opened directly into the showroom.

Augusta Freeman was there, unpacking hats from their boxes and selecting the ones that would go on the display stands. She looked up, surprised, as Maggie came in.

"Good gracious! Maggie! I didn't expect you to come to work today, my dear." Her tone was much kindlier than the brusquely efficient one Maggie was used to.

"I didn't know what else to do, Mrs Freeman." Maggie didn't take off her shawl; she just pulled it tighter around the high neck of the white blouse she wore for work, standing there in the doorway as if poised for flight.

"Oh Maggie, Maggie, I am so very sorry . . ." For once Augusta was lost for words.

"Thank you," Maggie said stiffly. She looked dreadful, Augusta thought, deathly pale, with huge dark circles beneath her eyes, which seemed strangely dead.

"Really, you shouldn't be here." Augusta set the bonnet she had been admiring on the counter. "You're in no fit state . . ."

"I need to keep busy, Mrs Freeman."

Augusta tried another tack. "But what about your mother? Shouldn't you be with her? She's had a terrible shock. Will she be all right alone?"

"She's not alone. Our Billy's there."

"Hmm." Augusta's lips tightened. She didn't know Billy well, but from what she did know of him, she wasn't impressed. "He's just a boy, though, isn't he? I'd have thought what your mother needs is another woman."

Maggie bit her lip, which had begun to wobble at the unexpected show of sympathy.

"Don't send me home, please, Mrs Freeman," she begged, and Augusta realised that what she needed most was a little normality, a respite from what must be the unrelenting atmosphere of doom and grief at home.

"Very well, Maggie. But I think it would be best if we found you something to do out here. You shouldn't be in the shop," she said, and this time it wasn't just kindness that was motivating her. First and foremost,

105

Augusta Freeman was a businesswoman, and she couldn't imagine that Maggie in her present state would be capable of serving the customers with the efficiency she demanded. Just seeing her there, looking so obviously distressed, might well deter them from coming into the shop at all. Unless, of course, they wanted to gawp at one of those affected by the tragedy, and Augusta didn't want that either.

"Before we do anything else, why don't you make us a nice cup of tea?" she suggested.

It was a long, awkward morning. Cathy didn't know what to say to Maggie, and avoided her as much as possible, while Beat was overly sympathetic, squeezing Maggie's arm whenever she passed and gazing at her with great mournful eyes that looked ready to spill tears. Maggie busied herself with the tasks Augusta set her: unpacking parcels from the wholesaler, dusting fixtures, and even arranging the bonnets on their display stands — a huge privilege, since that was something Augusta normally liked to do herself. But still she couldn't stop the trembling in her stomach that was making her feel queasy, and her mind kept wandering to terrible visions of what it must have been like for Jack, her father and the others in their last moments.

Unbeknown to Maggie, rumours that the tragedy had been no accident were already spreading like wildfire around the town. More than one customer who came into the shop mentioned it, and Cathy and Beat talked about it in whispers when they were alone —

gossip, even about something as momentous as this, was something Augusta would not tolerate.

"I can't believe anyone would do something so terrible!" Cathy said, shaking her head. "It's just downright wicked!"

"I expect it's a tale got up by Sir Montague to save his own skin," Beat opined. "He knew that rope should have been replaced donkey's years ago, and was too busy pinching his pennies to do anything about it. If he can shift the blame, he will."

But in the early afternoon, the rumour was confirmed.

Alice Love was married to the police sergeant in High Compton, and lived in the square, stone-built police station that had a small office at the front and three cells at the rear. The kitchen and living room were to one side of the building, but every sound carried up to the bedrooms, and nuisance though it was to be disturbed by the comings and goings of the two constables who shared the beat, or woken in the night by rowdy prisoners being brought in to be charged, or members of the public knocking on the door to report some crime or call for assistance, living on the premises had its advantages too. Alice was nosy by nature, and she also loved being the one in the know about what was going on. Even if Will, her long-suffering husband, had forbidden her to talk about what she'd seen or overheard, she was able to smile smugly when folk asked, tap her nose with a knowing look, and turn away revelling in her superior knowledge.

This time, though, there was no need for her to keep quiet. The police station had been a hive of activity all morning; Alfred Nicholls, the superintendent in charge of the division, had arrived from Bath, and investigations were already under way. Soon everyone would know that the rope on the hudge had been severed deliberately, and Alice was set on making sure that she was the one to pass on the news to as many people as possible.

The excuse she used for going into the drapery shop was that she needed a reel of black cotton to sew on a button that had come off Will's tunic, but Augusta was in no doubt it was just that — an excuse. She hovered like an avenging angel whilst Cathy served the obnoxious woman, her heart sinking as she listened with pretended indifference to what Alice was saying. Bad enough if the tragedy had been a terrible accident; this was even worse. How could the families of the victims cope with knowing their loved ones had been murdered? How could the town cope with it? The shadow of suspicion would turn neighbour against neighbour. Everyone would be looking over their shoulder for someone to blame. Augusta shuddered inwardly. She hoped Maggie had not overheard what was being said; she was in the showroom, but the door that separated it from the shop was far from soundproof. In any case, she would have to find out the truth sooner or later, and Augusta thought it would be better coming from her.

When Alice finally left with her reel of cotton and a self-satisfied smirk on her face, Augusta went into the showroom.

"Maggie, my dear, there's something I need to tell you," she said gently.

Billy was sitting on the bank of the river, scrawny knees drawn up to his chin, arms wrapped around them. Bullseye lay beside him, nose between paws, but his eyes kept flicking to his young master, and every so often he got up and went to him, nudging him gently.

"Oh, Bullseye, leave me alone," Billy snapped. For once he didn't want the dog's attention. He felt sick, his stomach turning over and over, and his mouth was so dry that he couldn't even moisten his lips.

It was his worst nightmare come true, the very thing he'd been so afraid of, hurtling down into the bowels of the earth with darkness all around. Helpless. Terrified. Being smashed to pieces . . . He pressed his hands into his eyes, but he couldn't shut out the awful pictures. He covered his ears, but he could still hear the screams in his head. And his heaving stomach felt the speed and the lurch of the fatal descent so vividly that he had to double over again, retching on to the bare earth between the tufts of lush grass.

Dead. All of them dead. It was too enormous a thing to take in. His dad . . . Jack Withers . . . Frank Rogers . . . He had hated Frank Rogers, and he had often thought he hated his father, too, but he would never have wished this on them. Not this. Never this. He didn't want to think about it, any of it, but he couldn't stop. Around and around it went until Billy thought he was going mad.

He covered his eyes with his hands again and began to cry, but no tears would come. It was as if every bit of moisture in his body had dried up. The sobs came all the same, racking his skinny body, tearing him apart. Billy thought they would never stop.

Bullseye was poking at him again with his nose, whining. He was restless, he wanted a game, and he didn't know what was wrong with his master. But something was, and Bullseye did what dogs do when they sense distress. He snuffled at Billy's face and began licking his ear and his neck.

At last Billy reached for him, grasping at the squat little body that had filled out now from all the scraps he was fed, and pulled him into the crook of his arm. There was comfort in the warm breath on his neck, the scratchy feel of the coarse hair under his fingers, and the steady beat of the dog's heart, and after a few minutes Billy's sobs quietened. But the ache was still there, deep inside him, and the blackness was still all around, closing in until he felt it had filled every corner of his mind and his body.

At least now he'd never now have to go down on the hudge, Billy thought. But given the enormity of what had happened, it was scant consolation.

It was Peggy Bishop's sister, Sarah, who told her the news about the rope having been cut deliberately. She lived on the other side of High Compton, but she had been into town shopping that afternoon, and made up her mind to go and see Peggy while she wasn't too far away. The last time they'd talked, Peggy had told her she was thinking of leaving Tom and asked if she could come and stay for a bit, but Sarah had heard nothing since, and she was worried about her sister and anxious to know what was going on.

Plenty of married couples had their ups and downs, of course, but leaving your husband was unheard of. Quite apart from the scandal it would cause, what would Peggy do? Sarah didn't want her sister staying with her for ever; though they got on well enough, Sarah's house was already overcrowded — she'd had five children so far, and given the ease with which she fell pregnant, there'd be more to follow before too long. (Funny, that, she sometimes thought: that she should have babies if she so much as *looked* at a man, whilst Peggy hadn't managed even one.) And how was Peggy going to live without Tom to support her? Sarah couldn't see her being able to contribute anything to the family budget, unless, of course, she found herself a job, but Peggy was lazy and always had been. She'd rather sit around all day than scrub floors for gentry or stitch gloves in the local factory. Really, Sarah couldn't afford another mouth to feed, even if that mouth was her own flesh and blood.

From what Peggy had told her, she'd gathered that her sister had ideas about setting up home with Josh Withers, but she couldn't see that happening in a hurry. Or even at all. Peggy was besotted with Josh, and Sarah could see the attraction — she'd fancied him herself when they'd all been young. But Josh was never going to be up for that. He was a Jack the lad, and he'd been taking advantage of Peggy, Sarah was sure. If she left

111

Tom, she wouldn't see Josh for dust. Sarah had warned her that that would be the end of it, but she wasn't sure Peggy had taken any notice. She was too moonstruck to think straight.

Sarah was determined, though, to have one more try at getting her sister to see sense before she did something she'd regret — and descended on Sarah for what might turn out to be a very long time indeed.

She tried the back door of Peggy's little house, relieved to see when it opened that Tom was no longer locking her sister in. She called "Coo-ee! It's only me!" but there was no response. Alarmed, Sarah called again — surely Peggy hadn't walked out already? She went through the scullery and into the living room, and there was her sister, fast asleep in one of the fireside chairs. She came to with a start, sitting up and wiping her mouth with the back of her hand.

"Sarah! Talk about frightening someone to death!"

"How can you go to sleep in the middle of the day?" Sarah demanded. "If you were Granny Dodds I could understand it, but at your age . . ."

"Oh, leave me be, our Sarah." Peggy struggled upright. "What are you doing here anyway? I don't usually see you in the middle of the week."

"I was in town and I thought I'd pop round. I'll go again if you want me to." But she sat down anyway in the chair opposite Peggy.

"I suppose you want a cup of tea now you're here," Peggy grumbled.

"I wouldn't say no . . ."

Peggy swung the trivet so the kettle was over the fire, then eased back into her chair again.

"The truth of the matter is I've been wondering how things are between you and Tom," Sarah said bluntly. "I've been half expecting you to turn up on my doorstep these last few days. You're worrying me to death, our Peg."

"There's no need for you to worry," Peggy said breezily. "I've been thinking things over, and I don't want to act too hastily."

"Well, thank goodness for that! I'm glad you've seen sense. Tom's your husband. You made your bed, my girl, you have to lie in it."

"Not for much longer, I hope." Peggy smiled smugly. "I just thought I'd let things quieten down for a bit. I don't want Tom chasing me over to your house — it's not fair on you. I reckon the best thing is to wait until I've got something fixed up with Josh. Tom'll think twice about knocking on our door and picking a fight. He knows Josh could beat him with one hand tied behind his back."

Sarah sighed. "If you want my opinion, it's never going to happen. Josh isn't interested in settling down with anyone, least of all you. You're living in cloud cuckoo land."

Peggy pursed her lips mutinously, and Sarah went on: "Besides, Tom might not pick a fight with Josh face to face, but he'd find a way of getting back at him. He's a dark horse, is Tom."

With a stab of discomfort, Peggy remembered the things Tom had said last night, and the callous way he'd talked about the terrible tragedy at Shepton Fields.

"Can we change the subject?" she said shortly. "What an awful thing that was, the accident at the pit yesterday. Twelve killed, they say. And all because Fairley wouldn't pay to put things right there, and the rope broke!"

"Oh Peg!" Sarah sat forward, hoisting her skirt clear of her ankles and resting her elbows on her knees. "You'll never believe this! I just heard. They're saying it wasn't an accident at all. That rope were cut! Cut, strand by strand. Can you believe it? Who in the world would do such a terrible thing?"

Peggy froze.

"The rope was cut?" she repeated incredulously. "You mean somebody did it on purpose so the hudge would go down?"

"That's what I heard. The police are on to it — the superintendent has come out from Bath to take charge of the investigation. They're questioning folk to try and find out if anybody saw anything suspicious, and if they know of anybody with a reason to want those poor blighters dead. I even heard talk that they might call in a detective from Scotland Yard . . ."

She chatted on, but Peggy was no longer listening. She had gone cold, as the most dreadful thought flashed unbidden into her mind.

Tom hadn't been just hard and callous last night when he'd talked about the tragedy. He'd seemed almost smug about it. Especially when he'd thought it was Josh who'd been killed. Busying herself with the kettle and teapot to cover the turmoil that was seething within her, she tried to remember exactly what he had said. *I told you you wouldn't see that bloody Withers again. He got his comeuppance all right. Trouble is, a lot of others had to go along with him.* She could hear his voice now, and she realised that he had sounded almost triumphant. Until he'd discovered it was Jack who had gone down with the hudge. That had put him out for a bit. *You'd better stay away from Josh if you don't want to end up like his brother.* That was what he'd said then. And it wasn't the first threat he'd made against Josh. What was it he'd said when he'd first found out for sure that she was seeing him? *He'll be fit for nothing but pushing up the daisies by the time I've finished with him.* Or something very like it.

Peggy's hand shook suddenly, and water splashed on to the hot trivet, where it sizzled and turned to steam.

"Hey, careful, our Peg!" Sarah warned. "Don't go scalding yourself!"

"Oh, I'm fine, Sarah," Peggy replied impatiently.

But she wasn't. She wasn't fine at all. She was suddenly very afraid that the person who had cut the rope and caused the hudge to go crashing down might have been a vengeful Tom.

As the day wore on, the anxiety Maggie had felt about leaving Rose alone with only Billy for company niggled more and more until she could think of nothing else.

By the time the hands on the showroom clock were showing five, she could stand it no longer.

"Mrs Freeman . . . do you think it would be all right if I went home?" she asked tentatively.

"My dear, you should never have come in today. I told you that this morning. Of course you can go." Augusta was actually relieved; Maggie had completed all the jobs she had managed to find for her away from the shop floor, and having her here looking like a ghost was beginning to take its toll on her. "Off you go. And I really think it might be best if you stayed at home tomorrow."

"Thank you, Mrs Freeman," Maggie said dutifully.

She collected her shawl and left by the rear door without saying goodbye to either of the other girls. Really, speaking at all was a tremendous effort.

As she reached the corner of the building, she caught sight of Reuben Hillman standing in the doorway of the gents' outfitters. It wasn't unusual for Horace or one of the assistants to step outside for a breath of fresh air if they had no customers, but she wished Reuben hadn't chosen this moment, and when he called her name she lowered her head and walked on, ignoring him. But just before crossing the road, she glanced over her shoulder and saw that he had taken a few steps along the pavement as if to follow her. Now he was staring after her with that sick puppy-dog expression that set her teeth on edge. Maggie turned her head quickly and crossed the road, but she had begun to shake, more upset than usual by his unwanted attention.

The pain of loss knifed through her again, bringing sudden tears to her eyes. She no longer had Jack to turn to if Reuben continued to be a nuisance. This was

116

something she was going to have to handle on her own. She had never felt more alone, more vulnerable.

Anxious to get home and make sure Mam was all right, Maggie walked quickly and purposefully, and before long she had reached the turning that led to the Ten Houses terrace. Whereas this morning the narrow lane had been deserted and quiet as the grave, now there were signs of life. Three small boys were kneeling on the road playing marbles, and little Lucy Day was pushing a rag doll in a packing case set on trucks, her pretend perambulator. A couple of men squatted against the wall, smoking and talking about the disaster, no doubt. They fell silent as Maggie passed, giving her the briefest of nods before hastily dropping their gaze. But thankfully there were no womenfolk to be seen — they would be indoors preparing the evening meal at this time of day — and Maggie made it to number six without having to talk to anyone.

Though the day had been warm and muggy once the first chill of morning had passed, the door was closed. As Maggie walked in, the oppressive heat of the kitchen, where the fire burned winter and summer, rushed out to meet her.

"Mam?" she called. "Mam, I'm home."

There was no reply. Maggie pushed the door wide open, kicking the doorstop into place to prevent it closing again. Usually at this time of day there would be signs of the meal Rose would be preparing — potatoes peeled and in the pot ready to go on the trivet over the fire, vegetables from the garden in a basket on the worktop. Not today. It was hardly to be wondered at really, but Maggie's anxiety twisted up a notch anyway, and she hurried through into the living room.

Rose was sitting in one of the fireside chairs, and to Maggie's astonishment, Bullseye was beside her, his misshapen head on her lap whilst Rose stroked his neck in a compulsive rhythm.

"Mam?" she said anxiously. "Are you all right?"

Rose seemed to come back from wherever it was she had been, snapping out of her trance.

"Oh, as right as I'll ever be, I expect," she said, with a little snort that Maggie guessed was an attempt at a laugh. "You're home early, Maggie. And I haven't even started on the tea." She pushed Bullseye out of the way and got up.

"Don't worry about that, Mam, I'm not hungry anyway. We'll get something presently. And I'm early because Mrs Freeman let me go. I think I've been more hindrance than help to her today." Maggie folded her shawl and put it over the back of one of the upright chairs. "Where's our Billy?"

"I don't know. I haven't seen him since dinner time. He's gone off somewhere, but he left the dog here — why, I don't know. He usually takes him everywhere." She sighed, shaking her head. "I'm worried about him, Maggie. He's taken this terrible hard."

"I expect he's all right, Mam," Maggie said. "He shouldn't have left you on your own, though."

Rose laughed shortly again. "Oh, I haven't been on my own. Folk have been popping in and out all day. Not that I want them to. I haven't felt like talking." She wrapped her thin arms around herself as if to ward off

118

unwelcome visitors, and the swelling mound of her stomach was clearly visible beneath her apron.

"All the same . . ." Maggie was wondering now how she was going to break the news about the rope of the hudge being cut deliberately. It was bound to upset her mother all over again. Unless she'd already been told, of course . . .

"Mam, I've heard something shocking," she began tentatively, but Rose wasn't listening.

"And it's not only the neighbours who've been here either," she went on as if Maggie hadn't spoken. "I've had Wilfred James here too."

"Wilfred James?" For a moment Maggie couldn't think who she meant.

"Wilfred James," Rose repeated with emphasis. "Manager at Shepton Fields. Came here to talk about burying your father, if you please. The cheek of it! And him one of the ones to blame for what's happened! I sent him away with a flea in his ear, I can tell you."

Maggie frowned, puzzled. They hadn't discussed Paddy's funeral yet, though it would have to be arranged sometime. But there was no rush; there would have to be an inquest before he could be buried, they'd been told.

"What's it got to do with Wilfred James?" she asked.

"Hmm!" Rose snorted. "That's what I'd like to know. Trying to soft-soap us, if you ask me. Fairley will arrange and pay for everything — that's what James said. If that's not his way of trying to keep us quiet, I don't know what is. He should have spent his money on

119

keeping his pit in good order before something like this happened. A fat lot of use it is now they've all gone."

Maggie hesitated, then took a deep breath.

"Mam — I heard today . . . the rope didn't give way on its own . . ." she said tentatively.

But to her surprise, Rose huffed with impatience.

"So they say. I don't know whether there's any truth in it or not. But if they'd put in a proper cable like they should have done, nobody could have cut it through like they're saying, could they?"

"That's true, I suppose," Maggie agreed.

"And now, to add insult to injury, they think they can walk in and take over the funeral," Rose went on indignantly.

Though it stuck in her craw too that someone other than the family should pay for Paddy's funeral, Maggie couldn't help thinking it wouldn't be such a bad thing. It had been one of the worries that had tormented her in the dark hours of the night. A funeral cost money — money they didn't have.

"Mam, I'm not sure we can afford to be proud," she said gently.

Rose turned on her furiously, the rage that had been simmering in her all day bubbling to the surface in a rush. "It's an insult and a disgrace. I can't have it! I won't!"

"Mam . . . I don't think you should be so hasty. If Sir Montague is willing to pay, then —"

"I haven't told you yet what he's suggested." Rose was trembling with anger. "A mass grave, in the churchyard at St Peter's. All of them in there together.

And just the one burial service. Your father was a Catholic, Maggie. He should have a Mass and a proper Catholic burial. He should be in the part of the churchyard that's reserved for Catholics, not stuck in a grave with all the others!"

"Oh Mam . . ." Maggie felt the ready tears pricking behind her eyes. Apart from Christmas and Easter, Paddy hadn't been near a church in years, but she supposed her mother thought it was what was required when it came down to it, the one last thing she could do for him. "Look, let's talk about this later. I don't suppose Dad would have minded very much one way or the other, but if it's what you want . . . we'll find the money somehow . . ."

She broke off. Someone was standing in the doorway that she had left open, a slight figure silhouetted against the light, late-afternoon sun turning the reddish hair the colour of burnished copper.

"Ewart?" she said wonderingly, hardly daring to believe it really was the brother she hadn't seen in several years.

"Maggie . . . Mam . . ." He came into the scullery, dumping his carpet bag on the floor beside the cupboard. And as Rose ran to him, taking him in her arms, Maggie felt as if an enormous weight was lifting from her shoulders.

Ewart was, and had always been, Mam's favourite. He would know what to do.

CHAPTER
SEVEN

"I'm going to go and have a word with Josh, see what the Withers family think about it," Ewart said, pushing back his chair.

Tea was over; when she'd got over the shock of seeing her beloved eldest son walking unannounced into her kitchen, Rose's first instinct was to feed him. "You must be famished, coming all that way," she'd said. "I don't suppose you've had anything proper to eat since you left Yorkshire."

"Don't worry about me, Mam. I had a pasty and a pint when the train got in, and the cart I got a lift on out of Bath was carrying a load of apples." Ewart was loosening the scarf tied around his neck and undoing the top button of his shirt.

"Apples? They won't be ripe yet, surely?"

"I reckon they were fallers, bound for feeding to the pigs," Ewart said ruefully.

Rose tutted, almost her old self.

"You'll get the belly ache, and you'll have nobody but yourself to blame. Give me a hand, Maggie, there's a good girl, and we'll get the tea on the go."

Between them, Maggie and Rose prepared potatoes and cabbage and fried bacon with the added luxury of an egg on the side — Lottie Weeks from next door, who kept hens in a pen in her garden, had brought half a dozen, still warm from the straw, when she'd looked in to commiserate earlier in the day.

By the time the meal was ready, Billy had put in an appearance — much to Rose's relief — but he looked every bit as wretched as he had when he'd gone out this morning. He ignored Bullseye, who was waiting hopefully for the rinds off the bacon, and barely spoke even to Ewart, though he hero-worshipped his older brother. As soon as he'd finished picking at his meal, he threw the scraps to Bullseye and clattered off upstairs.

"He's in an awful way about what's happened," Rose said, stacking the plates together. "Still, at least you're here now, Ewart. I reckon that'll help take his mind off losing his father."

"I didn't think they got on that well," Ewart, who sometimes spoke without thinking, said bluntly.

"He was still his father," Rose said, bristling. "Yours too. And Walter's. Is he going to be able to come down for the funeral?"

"He'll do his best." Ewart was drinking yet another cup of his mother's strong stewed tea, holding the mug between hands that were black-veined with coal dust that no amount of scrubbing could wash away. "It's not so easy for him, though, with a family to think of."

Though Ewart was the older of the two brothers, he was still free and single, whilst Walter had a wife, two children, and another on the way. He had met and married a Yorkshire lass soon after moving north; Rose, doing her sums, suspected the wedding had been what she would call "a rush job" — unless of course little Jimmy had come early, which she doubted. She'd seen her grandson only the once, when Walter had brought Connie and the baby to visit, and she'd never seen the newborn, Edie, at all. She wished with all her heart they were not so far away. But Walter seemed happy enough with his little family; he'd always been the quieter of her two elder sons, not given to racketing around as Ewart did.

There'd been a time when she'd worried about Ewart — he'd been a sight too friendly with Josh Withers and the rest of his wild crowd, and had earned a reputation as something of a scallywag himself. As a boy, he'd always been up to something; she wished she had a silver sovereign for every time a neighbour had come knocking on the door to complain that he had been scrumping apples, or playing that stupid game of leaving a parcel in the road with a long string attached, hiding nearby, and then jerking the string to make the parcel move when a passer-by tried to pick it up. Later, he and the crowd he'd picked up with were forever getting involved in fights, or coming home very late, or not until next morning, because they'd walked all the way in to Bath for a night out.

No, it was no small wonder to her that whilst Walter had settled down to family life, Ewart was still footloose and fancy free. But at least with him now living so far away, she didn't have to know about his carryings-on, and for all that she wished he'd meet a nice girl and settle down too, it was the rascal in Ewart that made him so lovable.

"So, we've got to talk about this funeral," he said, putting down his mug and pushing it back across the table.

It had been mentioned over tea, but since Rose was still so clearly upset at Sir Montague Fairley's suggestion, Maggie had insisted that any discussion should wait until they'd finished eating. Now Rose pushed back her chair and got up abruptly, heading for the teapot that was keeping the brew warm on the trivet over the fire.

"There's nothing to talk about. It's not right, Ewart. We've got to do things proper. A Catholic burial, and a grave that I can keep nice. I won't hear of anything else, so you might as well save your breath."

"But Mam . . ." Ewart sighed and bit his lip. He didn't want to say what he was thinking — that there might well be a grisly reason for the suggestion that all the victims should be buried in a mass grave. From his own experience, he knew only too well how far the hudge would have fallen, and what the terrible results of that might be.

"I know what you're going to say — that funerals cost money. Well, it's a bad job if we can't find it from somewhere so we can do the right thing by your father." Rose spun round, pointing the teapot at Ewart as if it were a weapon. "To tell the truth, I'd have thought you'd offer to chip in, our Ewart. You're earning good money now. I'd have thought you'd want to!"

"Well, of course I will, if that's what you're set on, Mam. But it might not be as simple as that . . ." Ewart broke off, still avoiding saying what was in his mind. Tact might not be his strongest point, but even he shrank from enlightening Rose about the possibility of bodies so mangled and broken it was impossible to separate one from another.

Rose, however, was not to be so easily put off.

"What do you mean, not that simple?" she demanded.

That was when Ewart pushed back his chair and got up. "I'm going to have a word with Josh, see what the Withers family think about it."

"I couldn't care less what the Withers family are going to do," Rose said disparagingly. "That's up to them. But I wouldn't have thought they'd want Jack stuck in with all the rest of them any more than I want it for your father. And I wouldn't have thought you'd want it either, Maggie."

"Well, I'm going to talk to them anyway," Ewart said, heading for the door.

Maggie got up.

"I'll come with you." She picked up the stack of dirty plates. "I'll put these in the scullery. Leave the washing-up until I got back, Mam."

There was a clatter of boots on the stairs and Billy appeared, his ginger hair sticking up in tufts as if he had been pulled through a bush backwards, as Rose might say, and his eyes red. He lowered his chin to his thin chest as he pushed past the others.

"Where are you going, our Billy?" Rose asked.

"Out." He disappeared, Bullseye at his heels.

126

"You see what I mean?" Rose said. "He's in an awful way."

"Leave him be, Mam," Ewart said. "Come on then, Maggie, if you're coming. Let's go and talk to Josh, and Mr and Mrs Withers."

It was Josh who answered the door of number ten, his wary expression turning to one of surprise when he saw his old friend on the doorstep.

"Ewart!"

"Josh." The two men shook hands, the double clasp the only indication of how close they had once been. "Look, mate, I don't know if this is a good time, but . . ." Ewart broke off; there was really no need to explain. There was no doubt why he and Maggie were here.

Josh stepped outside, pulling the door closed behind him.

"You want to have a word about Jack, and your father."

Ewart nodded.

"Will I do? I'm not sure Mam and Dad are up to it."

The door of the adjoining house opened and Hester Dallimore's head poked out.

"Oh, sorry, I thought that was somebody at my door . . ."

Josh glared at her; Hester was known for her nosiness, and he knew she hadn't thought any such thing. Seeing she was going to get short shrift, Hester withdrew, but left her door wide open. She'd be hiding behind it and listening, Josh guessed.

"Let's go down the garden," he suggested. "We can have a bit of privacy there."

He led the way across the track and around the corner of the block of privies and outhouses. Behind them, the gardens belonging to the Ten Houses stretched away at right angles to the terrace. Long and narrow, they boasted rows of potato haulms, cabbages, parsnips, carrots, and runner beans, with their pretty vermilion flowers growing up tall frameworks of long sticks harvested from the local thickets. Several of the gardens had runs where hens strutted and pecked at the dry soil; one had a pig pen, though it was thankfully right at the far end, so that the unpleasant smells that came from it didn't reach the houses unless the wind was in the wrong direction.

A tiny square of the Witherses' garden, just inside the entrance, had been laid to grass and bordered with hollyhocks, sweet William, and snapdragons. Florrie Withers loved her flowers, even though using the precious space for them was a luxury her neighbours thought she could ill afford, and Gilby had made a wooden bench out of an old piece of fallen tree so she could sit there on fine evenings and enjoy the blooms she tended so carefully. There was room for three on the bench, but Josh indicated that Ewart and Maggie should sit on it, and he squatted down on the grass in front of them. It would be easier to talk that way.

"Well, it's good to see you after all this time, but I wish it hadn't taken this to get you home," he said, rasping his fingers across his chin, where a dark shadow of stubble was beginning to show itself.

Ewart nodded, grimacing.

"It's a bugger."

"You're right there."

It was typical of the way the menfolk talked, hiding their true feelings, Maggie thought. She could see from the set of Josh's jaw and the bleakness in his eyes that he was feeling the loss of his brother as much as any of them, but he would never put his grief into words, and it was the same with Ewart. They put on a front that was as hard as the coal they hewed.

It wasn't so easy for her, though, and the fact that Josh looked so like his dead brother didn't help. Seen through a blur of tears, it might almost have been Jack sitting there on the grass. Maggie bit down hard on her lip and glanced away, unable to bear it.

But things were about to get even worse. As the men talked about the terrible events of the previous day, Maggie couldn't help but relive it in every nightmarish detail. So long as she'd kept busy she'd been able to banish the darkest of her thoughts to the corners of her mind, though they hung there in a thick, impenetrable fog through which no chink of light could find its way, but now she could no longer escape them.

The men's voices seemed to be coming from a long way off, and she heard only snippets of what they were saying. But when they got around to the subject of the funeral, she pulled herself back from the nightmarish no-man's-land where she had been wandering. This was important. She needed to hear what was being decided.

"Well, we're going to go along with what Fairley suggested," Josh was saying. "Truth to tell, Ewart, I don't think there's much option. It's going to have to be a mass grave, whether Fairley pays for it or not."

"That's what I thought," Ewart agreed. "Our mam is saying Dad's got to be buried as a Catholic, but she's not thinking straight. Trouble is, I don't fancy being the one to tell her why that's not going to happen."

Maggie frowned, puzzled. What was Ewart talking about? Then the explanation came to her in a blinding flash and she felt the blood leave her face in a rush.

Oh, dear God, it didn't bear thinking about. She wouldn't think of it. She couldn't!

"I've been to see Harry Rogers," Josh went on. "Young Frank was another of them that went down. And Fred Day, too. But I haven't seen Annie yet. I went along and knocked at her door, but nobody answered."

Fred Day, from number four. Maggie hadn't realised Fred was gone too. That made four dead from their rank of just ten houses. And Fred had a young family — two pretty little girls who always looked as if they'd just stepped out of a bandbox, in their freshly laundered smocks and with ribbons in their fair curly hair. Whatever would Annie do now? This wasn't just Maggie's tragedy. It had torn so many other lives apart too.

"I think I saw her brother going in as I was coming home," Ewart said. "If he's there with her, it might be a good chance to have a word. We've all got to stick together on this."

130

Josh nodded. "You're right there. And it's the inquest tomorrow — they're having it in the town hall. I'm going to go and see what they say. Why don't you come with me?"

"I'll do that. Knock the door on your way past." He got up. "Are you coming with me to see Fred's family, Maggie?"

Maggie didn't reply; she didn't even seem to have heard him. She was staring into space, tears misting her eyes. She was unaware of Josh shaking his head at Ewart, mouthing, "Leave her."

Ewart nodded, cottoning on.

"I'll come back and let you know what they say. And if they're going to the inquest too." He touched his sister's shoulder, squeezing it gently. "I'll be back in a minute, Maggie."

She came out of her reverie with a start.

"Oh — I've got to get home, Ewart. I've got to help Mam with the washing-up."

She started to get up, but Josh scrambled to his feet, taking Ewart's place on the bench and pulling her down again.

"I'm sure there's no rush, Maggie. You look as if you could do with a bit of time to yourself. Stay here with me and wait till Ewart comes back."

For once in her life, Maggie did as she was told.

"Don't upset yourself, Maggie," Josh said when Ewart had gone.

The minute the words were out, he realised it was a stupid thing to say, but in all honesty, he was at a total loss for words. It broke his heart to see Maggie like this, so white and drawn, as if all the life had been sucked out of her. But what did he expect? She'd lost her father and her fiancé in the most terrible way. Being Maggie, though, she would be steeling herself to be strong for her mother and Billy, pushing her own grief to one side for their sake whilst all the time it was tearing her apart.

"Now that your Ewart's home, he'll take care of everything," he went on awkwardly.

"He can't bring them back, though, can he?" Maggie's voice was bleak and a little bitter.

"No, you're right there." Again he thought it wasn't the right thing to say, but words weren't Josh's strong point any more than they had been Jack's.

"Oh Josh, I'm sorry." Maggie drew her fingers across her cheeks, wiping away the traces of her tears, though he could see they were already seeping out again. "How can I be so selfish? You've lost your brother too."

A lump rose suddenly in Josh's throat. He glanced away for a moment, choking it down. When he turned back, only the hard set of his jaw revealed the momentary weakness.

"That's true enough. I wish to God it had been me, not him."

Maggie reached out and covered his hand with hers.

"Don't say that, Josh. Don't even think it."

"It's true, though. I do. Our Jack was a good man. Never did anybody a moment's harm. A good son, too, always looking out for Mam and Dad, while I've caused them nothing but trouble. The rotten apple, that's me.

Always have been. Ask anybody. No, I should be the one that's gone, not him."

He fumbled in his pocket for cigarettes and matches, lighting one and drawing on it hard, his eyes narrowed against the curling smoke.

"You and Jack were different, that's all," Maggie said, her own grief forgotten for the moment. "That doesn't make you worth any less, and you mustn't think for a moment that it does."

Josh's lips curled round his cigarette in a wry smile. It was nice of Maggie to say so, but he couldn't believe she meant it.

"Well, it's no use wishing things were different," he said at last. "It won't bring our Jack back any more than your Ewart being here can. No, all I can do is make sure I look out for Mam and Dad like he would have done. It won't be the same, I'll never be him, but I'll do my best."

"I know you will, Josh," Maggie said. "And so will I. They would have been my mam and dad too before long, remember."

Josh took another hard pull on his cigarette, thinking that where Maggie was concerned, at least, Jack had been a very lucky man. Her beauty didn't just go skin-deep, like some.

"If it's any consolation to you, I can tell you that you made Jack very happy when you agreed to marry him," he said awkwardly. "Happy — and proud, too. He was over the moon to think you were going to be his wife. That's one thing I'm really glad about." He grinned sadly. "I told him he'd drive me mad if he didn't stop whistling 'A Little of What You Fancy Does You Good'. And he was full of the plans he had to do up that little house you'd been offered. It wasn't in that good a condition, according to what he'd heard — the Scrivens family weren't the fussiest, if you take my meaning. Not that he knew a thing about building work or carpentry, of course, but that wouldn't have stopped him. Nothing was too good for you, Maggie, nor for the family I know he hoped you'd have —"

He broke off, pinching out his cigarette and flicking the butt into a clump of Florrie's snapdragons.

A muffled sob; he turned to look at Maggie. Her hand was pressed over her mouth, her face screwed up and her eyes closed, but the tears were squeezing out again and running down her cheeks.

"Oh Maggie, I'm sorry . . . Now I've upset you again," he groaned, wondering how he could have been so stupid as to talk about the future that Jack and Maggie had been looking forward to sharing.

"I've got to go." Maggie got up, half running across the patch of lawn.

"Maggie . . ." He caught up with her as she reached the corner of the block of outbuildings. He had no clear idea of what he intended to say or do, just that he didn't want to let her go like this. "Look, you're in an awful state . . ."

She stopped, turning back.

"It's all right. I'm all right, honestly."

But any fool could see that she wasn't. Her voice was thick with tears.

He caught her hand. "Look, why don't you stay here for a bit? At least until Ewart comes back. He'll look after you."

Maggie hesitated, like a gazelle poised for flight. Then, without a word, she suddenly turned her face into his shoulder, her free hand clutching his arm as if it were a lifeline.

For a moment, Josh stood stiff and awkward. Taken by surprise and embarrassed, he was unsure what he should do. Like most men, he hated to see a woman cry, and to have Maggie weeping into his shirt front threw him into a panic. Tentatively, he put his arm around her, patting her shoulder gently — somehow it seemed the right thing to do.

"It's all right, Maggie. You cry," he heard himself say.

And cry she did, her grief, bottled up for so long, bursting from her in a flood. For long minutes she wept, her whole body shaking, and he held her, no longer embarrassed, but only concerned for her. At last the racking sobs softened to hiccups, and she pulled away, looking up at him with eyes that were swollen and red but no longer oozing tears.

"I'm sorry."

"What for?"

She didn't answer, just gave a little shake of her head, and he pulled a handkerchief out of his pocket.

"Here — dry your eyes."

She took it, blowing her nose and then balling the square of spotted cotton into her hand.

"Look — you know where I am if you need me," he said.

"Yes. Thank you."

She looked up at him again, smiling a faint watery smile that did not reach her eyes, and then she was gone, disappearing round the corner of the outbuildings and lost to his sight.

But the scent of her hair was still in his nostrils, the sleeve of his shirt wet with her tears, and he could still feel the softness of her body pressed against his.

Josh rasped his hand over the stubble that shadowed his jaw, his breath coming out on a long sigh, his thoughts whirling. He could make no sense of the emotion that was churning in his stomach; he only knew it was like nothing he had ever experienced before. Oh, he'd wanted Maggie for a very long time, but he'd told himself it was just a passing fancy. This, though . . . this was different. A fierce, burning desire to protect her, cherish her, make her happy even.

The trouble was, it was all wrong. Maggie was Jack's sweetheart; it was his brother she was grieving for. She'd turned to him because he was the closest thing to the man she'd lost, and if he'd been of some comfort to her he was glad of it. But the way he'd felt when she was in his arms, the way he was feeling now . . . yes, it was just plain wrong.

Josh foraged for his cigarettes and lit another, blowing smoke into the clear evening air, but it didn't seem to help. Might as well admit it, he'd wanted to do more than comfort her. But the admission only made him ashamed and angry.

He'd make damn sure it didn't happen again.

CHAPTER
EIGHT

Tom Bishop grunted bad-temperedly and pushed his plate away from him.

"I don't know what you'd call that, my girl, but I call it a load of rubbish. There's more gristle than meat on that steak, and you've burned the potatoes again."

"Oh, what the hell's the matter with you?" Peggy exploded. "You've been in a filthy mood ever since you got in from work. Nothing's right for you, is it? Your bathwater wasn't hot enough, your beer not cold enough, though I've had it on the marble slab in the larder all day, and now you're moaning about your dinner. You're a miserable bugger, Tom Bishop."

"And don't you think I've got reason enough? You think I can bloody well forget that you were making a bloody fool of me with that Josh Withers?"

"It was just the once," Peggy lied.

"You expect me to believe that? Well, like I said before, you'd better not try it again, or you'll be sorry, both of you. And your lover will end up the same as his brother — six feet under."

A nerve jumped suddenly in Peggy's throat. He'd said it again — more or less the same words he'd used on the evening of the tragedy, when he'd thought it was

Josh who had been killed and she'd put him right. It had been niggling away at her ever since Sarah's visit this afternoon. What if Tom was the one who was responsible? Oh, surely he would never do such a terrible thing. But someone had. Someone who had wanted one of the men on the hudge dead. And Tom had got Josh mixed up with Jack, thought it was Josh that had been killed, and had been upset when she'd put him right.

Besides this, she knew Tom — nobody could bear a grudge quite like him, and his ruthless streak was one of the things that had attracted her to him in the beginning, that thrilling feeling that if pushed to his limits, he could actually be quite dangerous.

But this . . . this was unthinkable. Twelve men and boys were dead. Surely — surely — not even Tom would be capable of such a terrible thing? Why, he couldn't even have known for certain that the object of his cold fury would be one of those on the hudge when it went crashing down.

It was young vandals, I expect, she'd told herself. They get up to all sorts these days.

But still the suspicion had lingered like a bad taste that wouldn't go away, and now he'd said more or less the same thing again. And could it be that he was in a bad mood because he'd got rid of the wrong brother?

Peggy glanced anxiously at her husband over her shoulder as she fetched him a slice of fruit cake and a cup of tea. Should she just ask him, straight out, and set her mind at rest? But he wouldn't take kindly to that, whether he was guilty or innocent — it was sure to

138

set off the most terrible row. And in any case, she was apprehensive about what she might learn. What in the world would she do if he admitted it? Her none-too-sharp mind boggled. She'd have to tell somebody, wouldn't she? But oh, the shame of it! A husband who was a murderer a dozen times over!

He wouldn't admit it, of course, even if he was guilty. He'd deny everything, and she'd be none the wiser, still wondering whether or not he'd told her the truth. And if he thought she suspected him, and might turn him in, then perhaps he would do away with her too! A man who could cold-bloodedly send twelve men to their deaths wouldn't think twice about putting his hands around her throat if he thought she was going to send him to the gallows. No, she couldn't ask him outright. But perhaps it wouldn't hurt to mention what Sarah had told her? He couldn't read anything into that, and she'd try to judge his reaction.

"Our Sarah came to see me today," she said as she put the plate and cup on the table in front of him.

"Oh yes? Wondering why you hadn't turned up on her doorstep with all your worldly goods, I suppose?" Tom said unpleasantly.

Peggy ignored the jibe.

"She told me something awful," she went on. "She reckoned they're saying somebody cut the rope on the hudge on purpose."

Tom spluttered.

"What a load of rubbish! Folk will say anything," he said dismissively.

"No, I think it's right." Peggy was trembling inwardly, but she steeled herself to carry on. "The police are asking a lot of questions, Sarah said. They wouldn't be wasting their time if there wasn't something in it."

She slipped into the chair at right angles to him, hoping to be able to catch his expression as she spoke, but his head was bent over his plate as he poked critically at the slice of fruit cake.

"It's awful, isn't it?" she prompted him.

"What, this cake? Too right, it's bloody awful. I don't know why you can't make a decent bit of cake. This is as hard as bullets."

"No, not the cake, you ungrateful beggar. Somebody cutting the rope."

"Oh, for crying out loud, Peg, I'm fed up with hearing about that bloody hudge!" Tom exploded. "Can't you shut up about it and let me have my tea, such as it is, in peace?"

"Please yourself." Peggy got up and headed for the scullery.

Well, she'd done her best and she was still none the wiser. Just because Tom didn't want to talk about it didn't mean a thing. If he'd condemned the sabotage, she'd have felt a whole lot better, but what did she expect? His horrible, callous attitude didn't make him a murderer. He was just a nasty-tempered man who said things to make himself feel important. A nasty-tempered man she'd give anything to get away from. But she honestly couldn't see how. All very well to have planned it, and pretended she could carry it through in the heat of the moment a few days ago. Now she'd had time to think about it, she'd realised it wasn't that easy.

To begin with, she didn't have any money to call her own, nor anywhere to go to, not really. Sarah had made it pretty clear that she didn't want Peggy there — not surprising considering she had such a houseful already — and truth to tell, Peggy wasn't even sure she'd want to put up with all those children for long. There wouldn't be a minute's peace. She wouldn't have a room of her own; she'd have to fit in where she could. And she and Sarah would probably fall out before long — two women in one kitchen was a recipe for disaster. At least here she had this house to herself all day while Tom was at work, and besides . . .

A tiny frisson of excitement prickled in Peggy's stomach, an excitement she hadn't experienced in a long while.

If Tom had done this terrible thing, it must mean he thought ever such a lot of her.

But of course, he hadn't. More than likely it was a gang of young hooligans, so drunk that they'd thought it would be funny. Or a disgruntled miner who wanted the pit closed. And none of them thinking for a moment that anyone would be killed as a result of their actions.

That had to be it. Didn't it?

As she emerged from behind the outhouses opposite the Withers home, Maggie saw a figure she recognised walking in the opposite direction.

Ewart. Her heart sank. She didn't feel ready to speak to anyone yet. Although she wasn't actually crying now, she still felt weak and shaky, and she knew her eyes must be red and swollen. Really, she didn't want anyone to see her like that, even her own brother; her pride simply wouldn't allow it. Already she was horrified that she'd made such an exhibition of herself in front of Josh.

It would never have happened, she thought, if he hadn't mentioned Jack and how happy she'd made him, and it had been the last straw when he'd talked about the little house that was to be their home, and the plans Jack had been making to make it nice for her and the family they would one day have. Until then, she'd managed to remain so strong. Funny how one little thing could open the floodgates to emotion you'd thought you had under control. It didn't stop her from feeling thoroughly ashamed of herself, but at the time it had been a relief to let go, and certainly Josh had been very kind. She'd never realised before what a gentle side he had hidden beneath that Jack the lad exterior. But what must he think of her? It would have shocked and embarrassed him too when she suddenly fell apart and collapsed in his arms like that.

Now Maggie was desperately afraid that Ewart might say something to set her off again. She wished she could have at least a few minutes to compose herself, but if she turned back, she would most likely run into Josh again, and in any case, Ewart had seen her. It looked as if he had been on the point of going into their house, but now he'd stopped and was waiting for her.

142

Maggie coughed the last of the tears out of her throat, scrubbed hastily at her cheeks with Josh's handkerchief, which she was still clutching in a damp ball in her fist, and ran a hand over her hair, strands of which were escaping from the pins that were supposed to hold it in place. Nothing out of the ordinary there — her unruly hair was always falling down — but after being mussed against Josh's shoulder, it must be even untidier than usual.

"Did you manage to see Annie Day?" she asked when she and Ewart met outside the door of number six.

Ewart nodded. "I've talked to her and her brother. They're both in agreement with Josh — it's going to be best to let Sir Montague handle things." He broke off, looking more closely at Maggie. "Are you all right?"

"I'm fine," she said impatiently. "You'd better go and see Josh. He's expecting you."

"I'll go in a minute," Ewart said. "I want to talk to Mam first, try to get her to see it's for the best. The sooner this is settled, the better."

"Oh, perhaps you're right." Maggie was glad that it was Ewart and not her who would have to be the one to explain to Rose that really there was no other option.

In the wee small hours, Maggie woke with a start.

It had taken her a very long time to get to sleep; everything had been going round and round in her head, and her mother's distress at Ewart's insistence that they must go along with the mass burial had upset her all over again. But when she finally did drop off, she'd slept deeply, and she couldn't understand why she was now suddenly wide awake again.

She lay for a moment listening; the house was quiet except for the occasional creak of a settling rafter. Maggie turned over, plumping the pillow beneath her head and pulling the sheet up under her chin, but she couldn't shake the feeling that something was wrong. She wouldn't be able to go back to sleep until she'd satisfied herself that everything was all right.

She pushed back the covers and got up, padding over the rag rug beside her bed on bare feet. Her bedroom door was ajar; it never would close properly, not that Maggie minded that now, though she certainly had in the days when she had been much younger and her brothers were still at home. Across the narrow landing she could hear Ewart snoring gently — whatever had woken her hadn't disturbed him. Oh, she was probably just imagining things. She half turned to go back to bed, but the feeling of misgiving was still there, nagging at her.

And then she heard it. A muffled groan that sounded as if it was coming from downstairs.

Maggie's heart came into her mouth. She hurried along the landing and down the steep stairs that led directly into the living room. The door at the foot was closed, so the staircase was in almost complete darkness, but Maggie knew it so well she didn't need to be able to see where she was going. When she tried the door, though, it wouldn't budge. From the other side came another groan.

"Mam? Mam — is that you?" Alarmed, Maggie pushed at the door again, and managed to get it open just far enough to slide her hand through the gap. She dropped to her knees, feeling along the floor; sure enough, her fingers encountered what felt like the thin cotton of Rose's nightgown.

"Mam!" she called urgently. "Mam, can you hear me?"

"Maggie?" Rose's voice was weak, tremulous, but just hearing it was a huge relief.

"Yes, Mam, it's me. But I can't get in to you. Can you move at all?"

Rose grunted, then grunted again, but she'd managed to inch herself away from the door a little.

"Keep going, Mam," Maggie urged, but now Rose was groaning again, a low animal sound that filled Maggie's heart with dread.

"Is it the baby, Mam?" she asked urgently.

For long minutes that seemed like a lifetime to Maggie, there was nothing but the sound of Rose's laboured breathing, building to a crescendo until it died away in a whimper.

"Don't worry, Mam," Maggie said, forcing herself to sound calm. "I'll get our Ewart. Just lie still now."

She scrambled to her feet, but Ewart was already at the top of the stairs. All the commotion must have woken him at last.

"What's going on?" he asked, his voice bleary with sleep.

"It's Mam! She's fallen down — she's on the floor in the way of the door. I can't get in to her."

"Fallen down?" Ewart repeated, stumbling down the stairs. "But what . . .?"

"Just come and help me!" Maggie lowered her voice and added: "I think she's losing the baby."

She slid her arm through the gap between door and jamb again; it was definitely wider now.

"Roll over, Mam," she instructed. "Can you do that?"

More grunts and breathy groans, then a soft thud, and between them Maggie and Ewart were able to open the door a little further.

"I think I might be able to manage now . . ." Maggie turned sideways on to the gap — thank goodness she wasn't very big! — and by pulling in her stomach and twisting her shoulders was just about able to squeeze through, even as Rose began gasping again as another pain gripped her.

She took a step inside the room, which was dimly lit by the first grey light of dawn creeping in at the window. As she put her foot down, it skidded on the tiled floor. She clutched at the door to regain her balance, and, glancing down, saw that the floor was dark with blood.

Her heart lurched. Oh dear God, she'd been right! Mam was losing the baby.

Rose was lying on her side now, more blood pooling around her prone frame. Maggie dropped to her knees, feeling the hot stickiness on her own skin as it soaked through the thin cotton of her nightgown, and paying it no heed.

146

"Mam, let's move you a little bit more so our Ewart can get in . . ."

She waited until Rose's spasm of pain passed, then got behind her, slotting her arms beneath Rose's and heaving her further to one side.

Ewart pushed the door fully open and came into the room, and the look of horror on his face as he took in the grisly scene told Maggie that he was going to be of little help. This was a job for a woman — men were useless when it came to anything to do with childbirth; they always kept a safe distance. But Maggie wasn't at all confident she could deal with it either. What did she know? And a miscarriage wasn't even a normal birth.

But surely Mam shouldn't be losing this much blood, even if she was losing the baby?

"Ewart — get our Billy to go for Dr Blackmore," she instructed.

But how long would it take for Billy to run the couple of miles to Dr Blackmore's house? Probably a good twenty minutes. Then he'd still have to knock the doctor up, and Dr Blackmore would have to get dressed, harness up his pony and trap, and drive all the way over to the Ten Houses. Maggie wasn't sure Mam could wait that long before getting the medical attention she so clearly needed.

"We'd better fetch Dolly Oglethorpe too," she said. Dolly acted as a midwife amongst other things. Please God she would know what to do.

Ewart dashed up the stairs, but a moment later came clattering down again.

"The little bugger's not there!"

"I could have told you that," Rose managed between pains. "It was because of him I fell down the stairs."

Maggie didn't know what she meant. It made no sense — if Rose had fallen down the stairs, how come she had ended up on the other side of the door, jamming it closed? And where was Billy? But she couldn't waste time wondering about any of it just now. She had other, more pressing matters to attend to.

"Well, if Billy's not here, you'll have to go then, Ewart," she said decisively. "Get Dolly to come quick, and then fetch Dr Blackmore."

"Not the doctor," Rose mumbled weakly. "We can't afford . . ."

"Go on, Ewart," Maggie said, ignoring her. "And for goodness' sake make haste."

With a last horrified glance at his mother lying there in a pool of her own blood, Ewart squeezed past and hurried out. As the door closed after him, Maggie thought she had never felt more alone in her life. But somehow, once again, she had to be strong.

"Don't worry, Mam. Everything is going to be all right," she said consolingly.

And wished she could believe that it would be.

It was full daylight, a pearly summer morning, before Billy came home.

He trudged along the lane, Bullseye at his heels, head lowered, kicking at small stones in his path. He'd been walking across the fields for hours, but he hadn't been able to escape the blackness in his head, or the ache in

148

his stomach that had been there ever since the terrible tragedy of the hudge.

His dad, and all the others, dead. It was too much to take in. But his body seemed to understand what his mind could not, and wouldn't stop trembling. He couldn't sleep, either. Well, he could fall asleep from sheer exhaustion, but a couple of hours later he'd be wide awake again, with everything going round and round in his head and whirling him with it, a merry-go-round he couldn't get off.

He didn't want to go home, and he didn't want to face Mam. She must have heard him get up, though Ewart, snoring beside him, had not, and had called out of her bedroom window to him as he emerged from the back door. He'd ignored her, and he knew she wouldn't be best pleased about that. But he couldn't stay out for ever. He was hungry — he'd hardly touched his tea last night — and though he wasn't sure he'd be able to eat much now, he had to try. And maybe Mam wouldn't go on at him too much. She had Ewart home now, and Ewart had always been her favourite.

He turned into the track at the back of the rank and was dismayed to see Charlie Oglethorpe sitting on the bench outside number three. He lowered his head, hoping to get past without some sort of confrontation, but as he drew level, Charlie called out to him.

"Where have you been then, Billy the rag man?"

"Nowhere," Billy muttered.

"Well, wherever it was, you've missed all the fun. Don't you know your mam's been taken bad?"

Billy, who had been trying to sidle past, drew up short.

"What are you talking about?"

"Your mam. Your Ewart came knocking on our door in the middle of the night, and our mam's been up with her ever since. And we've had the doctor here an' all, though he's gone now. But it's something pretty bad if you ask me."

Every bit of colour drained from Billy's face and for a moment he stared at Charlie in shock. Then, without another word, he turned and began to run homewards along the track.

The back door of the house was ajar; he pushed it open and ran in. There was no one in the scullery, but he could hear voices coming from the living room. He froze, fear rushing through his skinny body in a cold wave, then he crept nervously across the kitchen and put his head round the living room door.

Maggie and Ewart were there, talking in low voices. Of Mam there was no sign.

"What's going on?" he asked timorously.

Ewart looked up and saw him. He rose from the chair, his face like thunder. "Where the devil have you been, you little blighter?"

"What's happening?" Billy asked again, ignoring the question. "Where's Mam?"

"What do you care?" Ewart raged. "This is all your fault, our Billy. What were you thinking, running out like that in the middle of the night?"

"Hush, Ewart. You're only making things worse." Maggie got up too, crossing to Billy and putting an arm round his trembling shoulders. "Come and sit down, Billy. I'll make you a nice cup of tea."

"I'll give him a cup of tea!" Ewart muttered. "And a bloody sight more besides!"

Maggie shot him a warning look.

"Come on, Billy. Ewart doesn't mean it. You're not to blame."

"What for?" Billy wailed. "What have I done?"

Maggie eased him into a chair, and while she fetched him a cup of tea from the pot that was seldom off the hob, she and Ewart told him.

Rose, it seemed, had heard Billy going downstairs and out of the back door at some unearthly hour. She'd opened her bedroom window and called to him, but he'd taken no notice and she'd tried to go after him. In her haste, she'd lost her footing on the stairs and fallen from top to bottom. Somehow she'd picked herself up and staggered into the living room, where she must have fainted, or collapsed, against the door. From the angry swelling on her head, Dr Blackmore had come to the conclusion that she'd cracked it on the tiled floor as she fell, and lost consciousness for a little while. Presumably it had been the racket as she tumbled down the stairs and the banging of the living room door as she fell against it that had woken Maggie.

And thank goodness it had, because of course that had been only the start of it. The bleeding had begun as she lay unconscious, and the labour pains — far too early — had quickly followed.

Ewart had run for Dolly Oglethorpe and Dr Blackmore. Dolly was quickly on the scene, but there was little she could do, and by the time Dr Blackmore arrived, it was all over. Rose had lost her baby, along with a great deal of blood, though thankfully the bleeding seemed to have stopped now.

"She's in a bad way, though," Maggie said. "We've got her up to bed, and Dolly is with her."

Billy's eyes were huge and haunted.

"She will be all right, won't she?" he asked, almost pleading.

"It's touch and go," Maggie said gently.

She reached out and took her brother's hand. In spite of the warmth in the kitchen, it felt stone cold.

"You mustn't blame yourself, Billy," she said. "I know you've taken Dad's death really hard, and you just want to be by yourself sometimes. I feel the same myself. But you weren't to know Mam would come running after you. A fall like that — it could have happened any time. It was just bad luck."

Billy said nothing.

All very well for Maggie to tell him it wasn't his fault — he knew it was. And if his mother died too, he'd never forgive himself.

CHAPTER
NINE

For the next few days, Rose hovered between life and death. Maggie stayed at home to look after her — although Ewart would be here at least until after the funeral and Billy, ashamed and frightened, was hanging around the house like a wraith instead of wandering off for hours on end, a woman was needed to nurse the desperately ill Rose. She wasn't to put a foot to the ground, Dr Blackmore had said; if she did, he wouldn't be responsible for the consequences, and Maggie made sure his instructions were carried out to the letter.

Her days were filled with emptying chamber pots and washing bedlinen, with making nourishing meals — soups and broths, pies and custards — and running up and downstairs to check on her mother, taking her cups of milk and mugs of locally brewed ale for good measure; Dr Blackmore had said the beer would help her regain her strength and replenish some of the blood she had lost. Maggie was glad of the activity. Exhausted though she was, at least keeping so busy left her little time for thinking, and lent a purpose to her life, filling the awful chasm left by the loss of Jack.

And Rose's incapacity meant that Maggie and Ewart were able to make the decision that Paddy would be buried along with the others in the mass funeral Sir Montague Fairley was arranging. Rose was in no fit state to argue; in fact she seemed to have resigned herself to the fact that that was the way it was going to be.

Clement Firkins, Sir Montague's agent, wearing a black bowler hat, a black tie and a lugubrious expression, had come to discuss the arrangements, but Ewart had taken care of that. Maggie didn't think she could have brought herself to be civil to him. If the hudge had been replaced by a proper cage, none of this would have happened. It was all down to Sir Montague's penny-pinching, and as his agent, Firkins was tarred with the same brush as far as she was concerned.

He had, though, delivered some welcome news. The families of the dead men would be allowed to stay in their cottages, for the time being at least.

"Sir Montague doesn't want to see anyone put out on the street when they are so recently bereaved," he said, as if that somehow made up for what had happened.

Neighbours called to ask after Rose, and Maggie fielded their enquiries, though she was surprised by the sudden show of kindness. The Donovans had been ostracised and looked down on for so long; now it was as if, with Paddy gone, they were accepted into the community. Whilst she was grateful for the concern, and for the little gifts — a tureen of chicken soup, a basket of loganberries, half a dozen fresh eggs — Maggie, who knew nothing of the beatings Paddy had

154

once inflicted on Rose, was hurt to think that their neighbours had had such a low opinion of her father. He hadn't been a bad man, just a profligate one — already she was forgetting Paddy's numerous faults and remembering only his good points. Not only didn't you speak ill of the dead, you didn't think it either, in Maggie's book, and to her, at least, he hadn't been a bad father.

Once, through the window of her mother's room, Maggie caught sight of Josh passing the house on the track below, and drew back hastily. The memory of how she'd broken down and wept into his shoulder could still make her blush, a heat that suffused not just her cheeks but her whole body too. Seeing him reminded her that she still had his handkerchief — it was under her pillow. She'd taken it to bed with her the night he'd given it to her. It smelled of him and his tobacco, and she found it enormously comforting. She really must wash it soon and return it to him, but she kept putting it off.

Apart from that one glimpse of him, Maggie hadn't seen Josh at all since that night, and she was surprised he hadn't called in on Ewart. The two had been such close friends; they'd always been in and out of one another's houses in the old days. But she supposed that with Rose so ill, he might feel he was intruding.

He and Ewart had gone to the inquest together, though. It had been held in the town hall the day after Rose's miscarriage, and both men were anxious to hear what the coroner had to say. They hadn't been able to get inside; the hall was so packed with townsfolk, there was no room for them and they'd had to make do with standing on the steps outside and learning what was going on at second hand as reports were passed back through the crowd.

By all accounts they hadn't missed a great deal. Wilfred James, the colliery manager, and Hubie Britten, who had been in charge of the hudge, had both taken the stand and stated that the rope had been in good condition — "What would you expect them to say?" Ewart snorted derisively — and a detective inspector who had been sent out from Bath to head the investigation testified that it had been severed "by a sharp instrument". No evidence had been discovered at the scene as to what that instrument was, no suspect had yet been detained, and enquiries were continuing.

"And much luck they'll have with that," Josh said disgustedly when word was passed back to them through the crowd. "We ought to make a few enquiries of our own, if you ask me. Somebody must know something."

"I wouldn't like to be in the shoes of whoever did it if we do find out," Ewart said darkly.

"Too true. He'd never live to get before a court of law," Josh agreed, and some of the crowd around them muttered their agreement. Every last man of them would have liked to have half an hour in a dark alley with the perpetrator of the terrible crime.

Next day Walter turned up as unexpectedly as Ewart had done, and the little house that had seemed so empty when they had both left was suddenly full again, though the mood was sombre, with none of the raucous

156

horseplay Maggie remembered. But having both her boys home seemed to do Rose the world of good — she kept Walter so long at her bedside, wanting to hear all about his wife and children, that Maggie was afraid she'd overtire herself and take a turn for the worse.

On the evening before the funeral was due to take place, Walter was once more sitting with Rose, and Maggie was taking the opportunity to run a mop and duster over the other bedrooms when she heard voices downstairs — Ewart, and a woman's voice, though she couldn't quite make out who it was.

Tucking her cleaning cloth into the pocket of her apron, she went down to investigate.

The door at the foot of the stairs was closed; she pushed it open and had the surprise of her life.

"Cathy!" she exclaimed. "What are you doing here?"

Cathy was dressed in the black skirt and high-necked white blouse that Mrs Freeman insisted on, but also a stylish little bonnet that Maggie recognised as one of the new stock she'd unpacked the day after the tragedy. The girl must have taken a fancy to it and bought it for herself, Maggie supposed, and she could well understand why she'd been tempted. The bonnet sat well on Cathy's dark curls and framed her pretty face, which was slightly flushed — from the exertion of the walk out to the Ten Houses, presumably.

"Miss Donovan! Oh, Miss Donovan." Even away from the shop, Cathy couldn't quite bring herself to use Maggie's Christian name. "Mrs Freeman let me leave early. She wanted either me or Beat to come and see how you are, and I volunteered."

"And you've walked all this way?" Cathy lived on the other side of town — it would take her a good hour to get home from here.

"Oh, it's nothing," Cathy said. "Mrs Freeman's worried about you. We all are. And we miss you too." She delved into the bag that dangled from her wrist, pulled out a small white box tied with a blue ribbon, and held it out to Maggie. "These are for you."

"Oh my goodness!" Maggie recognised the box — it was one of those that Mr Rawlings, the confectioner, used for his finest sweets and chocolates, the ones that were displayed beneath the glass-topped counter. She'd often looked at them longingly when she'd gone into the shop for a quarter of peppermint candy or Everton toffee, but even if she could have afforded it, she'd never have bought them. Expensive bonbons were the sort of luxury reserved for rich folk, or perhaps a special gift for a sweetheart on Valentine's Day. "Oh Cathy, you shouldn't have!"

"They're from all of us," Cathy said. "We thought they might cheer you up a bit ..." She broke off, blushing. "Oh, that's a silly thing to say. Nothing is going to cheer you up. But we thought ... oh, you know what I mean."

"That is so kind!" Maggie said, overwhelmed.

She untied the blue ribbon and opened the box to reveal the hand-decorated chocolates nestling inside — truffle balls rolled in vermicelli, rose and violet creams topped with scented sugar, fragile fluted chocolate cases filled with something pale and creamy.

"Would you like to try one, Cathy?" she asked.

158

"Oh no!" Cathy exclaimed, horrified. "They're for you."

"I hope I'm allowed one," Ewart said, his hand hovering over the box.

Maggie slapped it away.

"Certainly not! You heard Cathy — they're for me."

She put the box down on the table. Of course she'd share the chocolates with Ewart and Walter later, and Rose too if she fancied one, but she wasn't going to let her brother guzzle them now, in front of Cathy. In fact, truth to tell, they were so pretty it would be a crime to guzzle them at all!

"You'll have a cup of tea while you're here, won't you, Cathy?" she offered. "I'll make some fresh. I expect what's in the pot is all stewed."

She went off to the scullery, leaving Cathy and Ewart alone, and as she spooned tea into the pot, she could hear them chatting. Cathy even giggled once — at something Ewart had said, presumably. Maggie shook her head, actually smiling herself for the first time in days.

They made a good pair, those two. Ewart was a ladies' man, and Cathy was an incorrigible flirt. She'd do well not to leave the two of them alone for too long.

She put biscuits on a plate, and got out the best china tea set that only ever saw the light of day on special occasions — she didn't want Cathy to think they lived like paupers — then tipped sugar into a bowl and poured milk into the little rose-sprigged jug that matched the cups and saucers. When she carried it all into the living room, Ewart raised his eyebrows and winked at Cathy.

"My, you are honoured!"

"Ewart!" Maggie chastised him.

"I can't drink my tea out of those fiddly little things!" he protested. "Can't I have my mug like I always do?"

"No, you cannot!" Maggie poured the tea, noticing as she did so that Cathy was looking at Ewart from beneath demurely lowered lids, the exact same way she tempted Horace Freeman when Augusta wasn't looking. Whether it was deliberate where Horace was concerned or whether she did it from habit, Maggie was never quite sure, but she was in no doubt it was deliberate now. And from experience, she knew that the ploy worked without fail; Cathy could twist any man round her little finger, and Maggie didn't suppose Ewart would be any exception.

"I hope you're not getting ideas about my apprentice," she said when Cathy finally left. "I should warn you, she's very flighty and she looks at all the men like that."

"Spoilsport!" Ewart retorted. "Anyway, surely you know I can look after myself where girls are concerned."

"Look after the girls, more like!"

"And why not?" Ewart grinned wickedly. "She's a cracker, I must say. You've kept her well hidden."

"I've done no such thing! You haven't been here, have you? And she's my apprentice, remember. So just behave yourself where she's concerned," Maggie said sternly.

"I'm making no promises." Ewart's hand was straying towards the box of chocolates. "Can I have one of these now she's gone?"

Maggie sighed theatrically.

"Oh, go on then."

It was, she thought, the closest things had been to normality since her world had turned upside down. But the darkness was lurking, never far away.

Tomorrow she'd have to stand in the churchyard and watch as Jack and her father were laid to rest.

She didn't know how she would bear it.

CHAPTER
TEN

It was a blur, nothing but a blur of people whose faces she couldn't see. Maggie was aware only of the gravelled path that cut across an expanse of lush grass dotted with centuries-old tombs and gravestones, some ivy-covered and leaning at perilous angles, and a mound of freshly dug earth at the far side of the churchyard marking the spot that had been chosen for the mass grave. She walked as if in a dream, Ewart on one side, Walter and Billy on the other, intent only on holding her head high and her tears at bay. Her pride was, after all, all she had left, and she was grimly determined to hold on to it.

As they reached the graveside, Ewart touched her elbow, urging her to step forward. Rose had not been well enough to attend, and the family had decided that Maggie would take her place as principal mourner.

"It should be you, Ewart," she had protested. "You're the oldest."

But Ewart would have none of it.

"You were his favourite, Maggie. He worshipped the ground you walked on."

Eventually Maggie had concurred, though she was less than happy to be taking her mother's place. The responsibility of it was daunting, and besides, she would have liked to be in a position to comfort Billy, who hadn't wanted to come at all. But Ewart and Walter had given him a stern talking-to, telling him he must, that not to attend his own father's funeral would be not only disrespectful but downright scandalous.

"If we can come all the way down from Yorkshire, you can walk just down the road, and we'm going to make damn sure you do," Walter had told him.

So Billy was here, and so, almost, was Bullseye. When they'd set out, the dog had tried to follow and they'd had to tie him with a length of rope to a hook on the wall outside one of the outhouses. Maggie hoped he wouldn't get free; he was something of an escape artist, and the thought of the mayhem he would cause if he came running into the churchyard was just another thread in the nightmare that was clouding her brain and pervading her senses.

The service began — the entire ceremony was to take place at the graveside, since the church, though sizeable, would never have been able to hold so many coffins, so many mourners — and to Maggie that too was a blur. She scarcely heard the time-honoured words and phrases; they seemed to be coming from a very long way off, and the cawing of the rooks in the trees seemed more real than the voices of the vicar, the Methodist minister and the parish priest, who were officiating jointly. But she was glad Father O'Brien was here; at least she would be able to reassure Rose that Paddy had been afforded the ministrations of a Catholic priest.

Sir Montague Fairley said a few words too, though for the life of her Maggie couldn't recall afterwards what they had been. His tribute to the men who had died in his service flowed over her like a fast-moving stream over the stones in its path.

Then, one by one, the coffins were lowered into the gaping hole that had been dug in the green sward. Maggie pressed her hand to her mouth and closed her eyes. *Oh, Dad . . . Oh, Jack . . .* They had spent all their working lives in the dark passages and caverns below the Somerset countryside, but this time there would be no return. This time they wouldn't be coming home for their bath and their tea. This time the darkness would close in on them for ever . . .

A muffled sob, followed by a small commotion behind her, wrenched Maggie out of her reverie. She glanced over her shoulder and saw Billy pushing his way through the mourners gathered three deep around the grave. Walter was making a grab for him, but it was too late. To go after him would have caused even more of a commotion; in the end, Walter had no choice but to simply let him go.

Maggie, usually protective of Billy to a fault, felt a flash of irritation with her younger brother. She knew that in spite of their differences, Billy had taken the loss of his father very hard, but it wasn't easy for any of them. Billy might be only just thirteen years old, but that was no excuse. Sometime he was going to have to begin to grow up; stop behaving like a child and become a man. If only Ewart or Walter could stay to help the transition along! But in a few more days they'd

164

be gone, back to Yorkshire. It would fall to her, Maggie, to steer Billy towards manhood.

"Ashes to ashes, dust to dust . . ."

Maggie forgot all about Billy and forced herself to watch as handfuls of crumbling soil pattered down on a dozen identical coffins.

"Let's move before the mourners start leaving." Peggy's sister Sarah lifted up her toddler and sat him on the end of the perambulator in which her youngest was fast asleep so that his chubby legs dangled over the side and he could hold on to the handlebars.

The two women, along with a knot of others, had watched the funeral from the path that sloped down into the churchyard from the road above; the service was over now, people were beginning to disperse, and many of them would be heading up this path.

Peggy didn't move. She was craning her neck, trying to catch a glimpse of Josh. She hadn't seen him since the day she'd waylaid him on his way home from work; not surprising, really, given that he'd just lost his brother in the most terrible way. But even if it hadn't been for that, she wouldn't have dared go looking for him; she was too afraid of Tom and what he might do if he found out she'd so much as spoken to Josh. Things had been a little easier at home, and the last thing she wanted was to upset the apple cart again. But if Josh left the churchyard by way of the path where she and Sarah were standing, she could at least offer her condolences — surely no one, not even Tom, should he get to hear of it, could read anything into that.

"Can you give me a hand turning this pram, our Peg? It's awful heavy." Sarah was struggling, the wheels sticking on the rough ground.

Sighing, Peggy added her strength to Sarah's, and between them they managed to manoeuvre the heavy baby carriage so that it was facing the other way.

Much as she wanted to speak to Josh, it was going to have to wait for another day.

A Wednesday had been chosen for the funeral because all the shops closed at lunchtime, and from a high point in the churchyard where he could easily see and be seen, Reuben Hillman was also watching the burial. He'd chosen the spot for that very reason. It was important to him that the town should know he'd come to pay his respects to those who had died, but he also wanted to be able to see Maggie, and perhaps intercept her when the service was over to let her know that he was thinking of her, and would be only too ready to do anything he could to help.

She hadn't been at work the last few days and her absence had left him bereft. Though of course they weren't in the same shop, just knowing she was on the other side of the dividing wall was a constant excitement to him, and thinking of ways he could get to see her filled his days with a sense of purpose. When he found an excuse to go into the shop next door, her smile was like the sun coming out from behind a dark cloud, lifting his spirits, and even if she glared at him disparagingly, it was better than not seeing her at all. At least it meant she'd noticed him; at least it was communication of a sort. He wished desperately that she would come to realise how happy he could make her if only she would give him the chance. But all that would change now, he felt sure. With Jack Withers gone, the last stumbling block between them would have gone too. As he watched the undertaker's men lower Jack's coffin into the ground, Reuben felt a surge of satisfaction. He felt genuinely sorry for all those other men and boys who had died, but Jack Withers was another matter entirely. No, he couldn't regret Jack's death for an instant. Surely now Maggie would turn to him and the comfort he could offer her?

He looked at her now, standing tall and straight, not shedding so much as a tear. Surely if she'd really loved Jack she'd be weeping now? But she wasn't. It was a very good sign. She'd probably only pretended to care for Jack in order to make Reuben jealous, just as she treated him coolly for the same reason. Girls were known to have some very funny ways, or so he'd heard — he had no real personal experience of them. Yes, that was very likely it.

Suddenly there was something of a commotion at the graveside — young Billy Donovan was darting between the assembled mourners and making a run for the churchyard gate. For a moment Reuben thought Maggie or one of her brothers would go after him, but they didn't, and the boy disappeared behind the old stone wall that bordered the road beyond. But a man he didn't know did follow as far as the gateway before turning and rejoining another stranger in the shadow of the church porch.

Reuben stiffened, looking at them for the first time. The one who had made to follow Billy was quite tall and lanky. He wore a trilby hat and was clean-shaven, whilst the other, shorter and stout, had a full set of mutton-chop whiskers and sideburns.

Police. Reuben knew it instinctively. He'd heard they had arrived from Bath to investigate, an inspector and a sergeant apparently; several customers who had been into the shop in recent days had said so, and he'd been half expecting them to call in asking questions, though as yet they had not.

"I see the detectives are here," he said conversationally to two women who were standing nearby.

"Looks like it." The older of the two women, whom he recognised as the stationmaster's wife, nodded sagely. "They've come to see who shows up at the funeral, I wouldn't be surprised. They've been round the pits, I hear, asking a whole lot of questions. Even talked to Sir Montague himself!" she added in a reverential tone, as if scarcely able to credit that a mere policeman, even a detective inspector, would dare to question his lordship.

The younger woman — her daughter, Reuben rather thought — was less respectful.

"Well they would, wouldn't they? Seeing as how it's his pit where it happened."

"Oh, I know, but still . . . They can't think Sir Montague had anything to do with it, can they?"

"You never know. It was common knowledge he wanted the pit closed."

"No, I reckon it was somebody with a grudge against one of them poor souls . . ."

The two women were talking to each other now, ignoring Reuben.

"Let's just hope they catch the devil who did it," he said, trying to inveigle his way back into the conversation and make it clear where his sympathies lay. But the women turned their backs, shutting him out.

Reuben moved away a little, pretending not to mind that they didn't want anything to do with him. He should be used to being ostracised; he *was* used to it, but that didn't mean it didn't still hurt. Because it did. It did!

Except that when Maggie was his, he thought, it really wouldn't matter at all.

In many ways, Reuben Hillman was as much of an outcast as Billy Donovan, though the two could scarcely have been more different.

Where Billy was small and skinny, Reuben was plump and podgy; where Billy was red-headed, Reuben's dark hair flopped over a face that never, ever caught the sun and burned scarlet as Billy's did. But the differences ran far deeper than just the physical.

Whilst Billy had often felt the sting of his father's belt or the thwack across his buttocks of the stick used for stirring the washing in the copper, Reuben had been pampered and spoiled. The only child of elderly parents, he was the apple of their eye. He had only to express a desire for something and it was his, whether it be a toy, a sweet treat, or a trip on the train to the seaside. When he was small, his mother always ensured he was dressed in the finest silks and linens in all the latest styles — a large photograph of him, aged about two or three, hung above the mantelpiece in the sitting room of the family home, Fosse Villa. In it he was wearing a corduroy suit and a shirt with a ruffled Vandyke collar and sitting in a vast cane chair in the photographer's studio so that his plump little legs dangled over the edge of the seat. He was staring defiantly at the camera — or at any rate, at the black tent beneath which the photographer had disappeared — and his lips were pursed into a petulant pout. Anyone looking at the picture now could have been forgiven for thinking that Reuben had changed very little in the twenty or so years since.

When he was four years old, Reuben had begun attending his grandmother's dame school, and here too he was singled out for special treatment. Though his grandmother ruled with a rod of iron, and good behaviour was expected of Reuben every bit as much as of the other pupils, it was only natural that she favoured him. When there was talking in class, it was always the boy who sat next to him on the little bench seat behind the double desks who was blamed, even if Reuben had started it. He was chosen more often than anyone else to be ink monitor, and when visitors came to the school he was primed to answer the questions they might ask so that his hand would be the first to shoot up. Had he not been primed, the answers he gave might well have been the wrong ones, and sometimes still were in spite of it, for Reuben was not the cleverest of boys.

All this did nothing for his popularity, but even without it, the other children disliked him instinctively. Spoiled as he was, he was given to temper tantrums when things didn't go his way, turning red in the face and even sometimes throwing himself to the floor, squirming and kicking and punching anything or anyone within reach.

He also had a cruel streak. He liked nothing better than giving one of the other children a sly pinch and making them cry, though if they told on him, he denied it, looking so much the picture of innocence that he was always believed. He kept a beetle in a jar, delighting in its futile efforts to escape, until he tired of it, when he pulled its wings and legs off, one by one, and left the remains in the desk of one of the little girls, sending her into a fit of hysteria when she opened her exercise book and found the black fragments inside. He stole birds' eggs and smashed them, and even tormented a baby sparrow that had fallen out of its nest.

He was no more popular at big school when he started there at the age of nine, though he had grown even more sly and was better able to escape blame for the meanest of his tricks. And when he left to begin an apprenticeship at Horace Freeman's gents' outfitters, Stanley Stone, the assistant assigned to train him, made it abundantly clear that he didn't like Reuben either. Girls spurned his advances, and he squirmed inwardly as he saw them sniggering behind his back. But he told himself they didn't matter. One day he'd have Maggie, and she was the only one who mattered. When Maggie was on his arm, they'd all realise just what they were missing.

He looked at her now, the blind adoration that consumed him welling up in a hot tide. More than anything, he wanted to go over and speak to her, but there were too many people crowded around the grave and he thought perhaps this was not the right moment.

Reuben straightened his jacket, nodded to the two women who were standing beside him, and slipped away. He'd waited long enough; he could wait a little longer. Now that Jack Withers was gone, he had all the time in the world.

As Maggie turned away from the grave, one face materialised, clear and strong through the blur of her tears.

Josh. He had been standing just a few feet away from her all the time and she had not noticed him, but then Queen Victoria herself could have been there and she wouldn't have noticed. Now her heart leapt into her throat, and with it an overwhelming need that she couldn't explain and didn't try to. Behind her, Ewart was touching her shoulder, urging her to go with him, but she ignored him, taking a step or two towards Josh, as if drawn by a magnet. He didn't seem any more aware of her presence than she had been of his — he was talking to the Rogers family — but as the heel of her boot dug into the soft graveyard turf and she pitched forward, almost cannoning into him, his arm shot out to save her.

Maggie gasped, clutching for a moment at Josh's forearm, rock-hard muscle beneath the sleeve of his dark jacket. All she wanted was to bury her face in his shoulder as she had the night she had broken down in the garden, as if he could somehow miraculously take away all the raw pain that was twisting inside her and the black despair that surrounded her like an impenetrable fog. But of course she couldn't. She mustn't. With an enormous effort she regained control of herself, pulling the heel of her boot out from the turf and straightening up.

"I'm sorry . . . how stupid . . ."

"Are you all right, Maggie?" His hand was still beneath her elbow, steadying her, and his voice was low but urgent.

"Yes. It was just . . . my heel . . ."

For a long moment he looked at her, his eyes dark and narrowed with concern. Then, abruptly, his face hardened and he released her arm.

"Ewart!" he called. "Can you come and look after your sister?"

Then, without another word, he turned and walked away.

As Billy came flying round the corner of the rank, Bullseye leapt up, barking excitedly and straining at the length of rope tying him to the outhouse wall. For once, Billy ignored him, running past on legs that were shaking with exertion, so that he thought they would give way beneath him. The dog's barks turned to bewildered and disappointed yelps as Billy ran indoors, and he dropped down on to his belly, his ugly head between his paws on the dirt track, and lay there whining miserably.

Billy ran through the kitchen. His breath was coming in huge painful gasps that racked his thin chest, his lungs burned, and his face felt as if it were on fire. He had run the whole of the way home, eyes blinded by tears but unable to escape the terrible pictures that still danced before his eyes. He thought that he would see the vast open grave and the simple coffins being lowered into it for the rest of his days.

His boots clattered noisily on the stairs, alerting Rose, who had been lying in her darkened room, tormented by the fact that she hadn't been able to attend her own husband's funeral.

"Who's that?" she called sharply.

Billy had been making for the sanctuary of his own room; now he hesitated, pushed open the door of his mother's room and stood there hanging on to the handle for support.

"Billy?" Rose said anxiously. "What is it?"

Billy didn't answer. He had no breath left, and in any case there was nothing to say.

"Oh, our Billy, come here!"

Rose raised herself on the pillows, holding out her hand to him. With a sob, Billy stumbled across the room and threw himself on to the bed beside her. Her arms went round him, and he buried his head in her breast, knees drawn up, boots depositing bits of churchyard mud and blades of grass on the coverlet. As he sobbed wordlessly, Rose lowered her face to his ginger mop and wept with him.

They would still be there, clinging together, when the others came home.

On the pavement outside the churchyard, a knot of angry men was growing steadily to a rabble. They'd just witnessed an event more shocking than they could ever have imagined, and they wanted someone to blame.

"I vote we get Fairley!" one man yelled, his voice carrying over the general hubbub, and others took up the cry.

"He's to blame, the bugger!"

"Let's set fire to his bloody house!"

"Lynch the bastard!"

The commotion grew, the angry shouts shattering what had been, minutes before, a respectful silence.

Maggie, heading along the path towards the church gateway, felt a prickle of alarm, sharp and uncomfortable, as she approached the swelling band of men. The tide of fury hung menacingly in the air. Never in her life had she seen anything quite like it, and for a moment she hesitated, looking around for Ewart and Walter, but they were nowhere to be seen. Father O'Brien had buttonholed her when the service was over, and they'd gone on ahead, a little ashamed, both of them, that they no longer attended Mass and hadn't made a confession in years.

Maggie didn't often go to Mass either, but Father O'Brien always stopped for a few words if she saw him in the town, and sometimes she wished she was a better

Catholic. There was something comforting about the priest, a fatherly demeanour that loved and forgave, and she liked the perfume of incense that clung to his soutane. It stirred memories of childhood, of the little church that had once been a tithe barn, and that had felt to her like a magical place, all glowing candles and ornate statuettes, a warm, welcoming sanctuary where she whispered prayers of her own as well as the ones whose words, though familiar, she didn't understand.

Today she'd wanted to rail at him; to demand to know how his God could let something so dreadful happen. She hadn't, of course — speaking to a priest in that way was something she'd never dare do — and locked in her daze of grief, she'd barely heard what he was saying to her either. But as he squeezed her hand, his grip firm and cool, she'd been surprised to feel a moment's peace amidst the turmoil that was raging inside her, and seemed to see a chink of light in the nightmarish fog that suffocated her.

"I hope we'll see you in church soon, Maggie," he'd said, and she'd nodded.

"I will come, Father, I promise."

"I hope so, Maggie. Your faith will sustain you. We'll pray together for the souls of the departed."

And the doubts and the anger were back. What good would that do? God should have been there for Paddy, and for Jack, and for all the others when the hudge went down. If He was the loving father He was supposed to be, He'd never have let it happen.

Now, though, Maggie forgot the conversation in her anxiety about what was going on in the road outside the churchyard. A mob. It was the only word to describe the angry gathering. She couldn't hear what was being said, but she didn't need to to know that it was serious.

As she reached the gate, she saw to her horror that Ewart and Walter were amongst the ever-growing crowd. Ewart was punching the air with his fist, his lips curled in an uncharacteristic snarl, and Walter's head was thrown back as he added his voice to the swelling chorus.

Idiots! Something very nasty was brewing, and her brothers were part of it.

Maggie's anxiety flared to something close to panic.

"Ewart!" she called urgently. "Walter!"

They didn't hear her above the furore, but when she began waving frantically, she managed to catch Walter's eye, and he shouldered his way back through the crowd to reach her.

"You go on home, Maggie. We've got business to attend to here."

"And what business is that?" she demanded.

Walter's jaw was set, his usually mild expression now dark and determined.

"Never you mind. This is man's work."

His words were almost drowned out by another roar from the mob.

"Are we going to get the bugger, then?" the ringleader shouted.

"We are . . . we are . . ."

"We'll tear him limb from limb . . . bloody Fairley . . ."

"Serve 'un right!"

"Walter!" cried Maggie, horrified, as it dawned on her where this was leading. "They're not going after Sir Montague, surely?"

"He's got to be taught a lesson he won't forget in a hurry," Walter grated.

"Oh don't be so stupid! This is asking for trouble!" Maggie had begun to tremble. "Where's it going to end? You can't get mixed up with this, Walter!"

"We are mixed up, though, aren't we? That bugger killed our dad! And he's going to pay for it."

"For goodness' sake!" Maggie caught at his sleeve. "Just stop and think! Do you want to end up in prison — or worse? What about Connie and the children? What would they do then?"

The crowd was growing ever more restless and Maggie's anxiety gave way to sheer blind panic. Men she'd known all her life, peaceable men, had changed beyond recognition so that they were more like a herd of wild animals, and her brothers were amongst them. And Josh, too! Where were the police? Surely it was up to them to put a stop to this? But the only uniform in sight belonged to Will Love, the local sergeant, and he was skulking on the pavement on the opposite side of the road, unwilling, she supposed, to take on thirty or more opponents who were all fighting mad. And who could blame him? He wouldn't stand a chance on his own. If he tried to stop them, mad as they were, they'd most likely turn on him. They'd see him as the enemy, part of the same conspiracy as Sir Montague himself.

178

The only person who could persuade them was one of their own, someone who'd shared their loss . . .

It came to her in a flash. She'd lost her father and her sweetheart, the two most important men in her life. Would they listen to her? She wasn't at all sure they would; they appeared to be beyond reason, and the thought of trying to make them see sense terrified her. But someone had to stop them from doing something most of them would later bitterly regret, and which could only end badly. She must at least try.

Maggie turned and ran back into the churchyard, up a grassy bank to a spot directly above the mob on the pavement below.

"Listen to me!" she cried. "Listen, will you?"

At first she didn't hold out much hope of being heard, but when the men saw her there on the wall above them, arms outstretched like an avenging angel, they fell silent one by one, gawping at her in amazement.

"What do you think you're doing?" she cried, taking advantage of the moment's stunned silence. "You've gone crazy, all of you!"

"We'm going to give Fairley what he deserves!" a voice yelled back from the crowd. "He's killed twelve men and boys, and he's going to pay."

"He didn't kill them!" Maggie shouted back. "He wasn't the one that cut the rope. And even if he had, this isn't the way to get justice. If you do this, you're no better than him."

"No, but we'll feel better!" someone called, and another voice, one that Maggie recognised, shouted:

"He killed your pa, Maggie. Just remember that! And he killed our Frank too. I'll swing for him, so help me."

It was Harry Rogers, usually one of the gentlest of men, mad now with grief and rage.

"You want your wife to lose you as well as Frank?" Maggie cried. "She will if they hang you. What good would that do anybody? You can't take the law into your own hands. You've got to leave it to the police to catch whoever did this terrible thing."

"They'm as useless as a chocolate fire dog!" one wag yelled. "If we wait for them, we'll be waiting till kingdom come."

"But at least they won't lynch the wrong man!" Maggie was shaking from head to foot, her hands balled to fists in the folds of her skirt, but somehow she managed to keep her voice steady. "I want to see someone punished as much as you do, Mr Rogers, but this isn't the way. Your Frank wouldn't want it any more than my dad or Jack would. And neither will you when you've calmed down. Look, we've only just laid them to rest. Let's show them some respect, at least for today."

She paused for breath, not sure whether she was doing any good or not. To her, the men looked as angry and dangerous as ever, all snarling faces and bunched fists. A ripple was passing through the mob as they looked from her to one another and back again, and their muttering made a low growl, like the tide filling a cliff cavern.

Then one voice rose above the rest. "She's right, lads."

It was Josh who spoke, Josh who was elbowing his way out of the crush, running through the church gateway and up the bank beside her. The men fell silent as he leaned forward, one foot on the stone wall.

"She's right. It's no good going after Fairley. He's a bastard, yes, I know that, but he's not the one who did this. We should be trying to find out who did, not ending up in a prison cell for arson or murder. That'll do no one any good. Let's all calm down and talk about this another time, when we're thinking straight."

The muttering was quieter now, and some of the men were nodding, their faces still transfigured with emotion, but no longer the crazed fury of a few moments before. A few dropped their chins to their chests, beginning to feel a little ashamed, perhaps, that they had been carried along on the wave of madness.

"Prince of Wales tonight, lads," someone shouted.

"Tomorrow," Josh called back. "We should be with our families tonight."

To Maggie's enormous relief, the worst seemed to be over. Already the crowd was thinning out, and at long last Sergeant Love came strutting across the road, standing there ramrod straight with his hands behind his back as the men broke away in twos and threes and dispersed.

"Oh Josh, thank you!" she whispered. Her knees felt weak now, as if they would no longer support her, and the tremble she'd managed to keep out of her voice when she had been addressing the mob refused to be controlled any longer. "They'd never have listened to me."

"They *were* listening to you. You were marvellous, Maggie," he said.

She shook her head, still unable to believe she had dared address a mob of men baying for blood. "I had to do something! If you and Ewart and Walter had ended up in prison, or worse . . . Oh, it doesn't bear thinking about."

"It's time to get you home now," Josh said gently.

"Maggie, my dear . . ." Father O'Brien was approaching; presumably he'd seen what was happening from the far side of the churchyard and was now coming to offer his support. "That was a very brave thing you did. Your father would have been proud of you."

"Oh, I don't know about that . . ."

"He *was* proud of you," Father O'Brien insisted. "Very proud. Do you know what he said to me once? 'I've done a lot of wrong things in my life, Father, but there's one thing I hope will help to balance the books, and that's our Maggie. I can't be all bad, can I, if I can get a daughter like Maggie.'"

Maggie felt her eyes filling with tears.

"Thank you, Father."

She turned away. Ewart and Walter were standing awkwardly on the path, waiting for her.

But of Josh there was no sign.

Josh was heading for home as if the hounds of hell were on his heels. He overtook little groups walking on the pavement by keeping to the road, and spoke to no one. His head was bent against a stiff breeze that had blown up with a smattering of rain in it; his hands were balled to fists in the pockets of the dark coat, a size too small for him, that he'd borrowed so as to be suitably dressed for his brother's funeral. Anger and confusion were boiling inside him, fermenting into a potent mix that was driving him crazy — anger at the senseless deaths of a dozen men and boys, his own brother among them, that had made him join the mob baying for Fairley's blood, and confusion that was all down to Maggie.

What in the devil's name was she doing to him? He hadn't been able to get her out of his head since the night she'd wept in his arms, and when he'd seen her standing up there on the churchyard wall, daring to defy the furious gathering, the impulse to protect her had been overwhelming.

He could see her now through the red mist that clouded his eyes, her pretty face frightened but determined, her hands bunched in the folds of her skirt, that wayward curl escaping from its pins. Dear God, he wanted her, wanted her so badly it was a physical pain deep in his gut. But at the same time he felt heavy with guilt that he should feel this way about his dead brother's sweetheart when he'd just watched his remains laid to rest. Josh strode out along the road that would take him back to the Ten Houses in an attempt to exorcise the demons that tormented him. But the images of Maggie and of Jack were still there, and the turmoil inside him refused to be stilled.

CHAPTER
ELEVEN

As the summer wore on, a certain degree of normality slowly returned to High Compton, or at least to those not directly affected by the tragedy. The Whitsun Fair, held each year in the Glebe Field, had been cancelled as a mark of respect, but the horticultural show, with a marquee provided by Farmer Barton and a new so-called "Fur and Feathers" exhibition, went ahead — too much effort had gone into organising it to allow it to be cancelled. In July, a circus came to the town, and the same people who had watched the mass burial from a distance lined the High Street as the parade of horses, camels, jugglers and tumblers, led by a gilded coach, passed by. The annual competition for the best allotment went ahead, hotly contested as usual, and marred only by a spate of mysterious blight that ruined the cabbages and runner beans being grown by several of the favourites among the contenders. Suspicions ran high as to the identity of the culprit — weasly Sam Higgins, who was pipped at the post each year for the winner's trophy — but nothing could be proved, though there were many dark grumblings when Sam was awarded the cup for the first time ever.

184

There had been no more success in finding out who was responsible for severing the hudge rope either. At one time there had been rumours that Scotland Yard was being called in, but it hadn't happened, and the detectives from Bath were seen less and less often going about their enquiries in the town and surrounding districts.

"What d'you expect? 'Twere only miners killed," George Parfitt said bitterly when the regulars discussed it in the Prince of Wales. "'Twould have been a different story if 'twere one of the Fairleys in their grave," and the others huffed their agreement into their ale. But there was no more talk of taking matters into their own hands. Even the hotheads amongst them had come to realise that mob action against the pit owner would do no good, and would only bring down more trouble on the stricken community.

Some of the younger generation, though, were less restrained — Frank Rogers and the other lads had been their pals — and there were one or two nasty incidents. Toady Griffin, the village idiot, was set upon one night as he walked his pet goat through the town, and there was a fracas when a gang of youths attacked a family of tinkers who had set up camp in a farmer's field. But no arrests were made, the perpetrators were given a dressing-down by Sergeant Love — who, truth be told, had every sympathy with them — the tinkers moved on, and Toady went home to nurse his bruises.

For a while at the end of July and the beginning of August, talk turned to the general election that was being held, but it wasn't of any great interest, as everyone knew the Tory candidate would get in again. Though the miners detested the Tories to a man, they held little hope of ousting him in favour of the Liberal candidate — their constituency, Somerset Northern, was a rural one, and everyone knew that the landowners would make sure their man was returned. And soon there was another topic of conversation to excite their interest — the FA Cup had been stolen from a shop window where it was being displayed by a victorious Aston Villa team. Who could have taken it, and whether it would ever be found, became the burning question of the moment — it seemed the Birmingham police were having no more luck in recovering it than the Somerset force were in discovering the identity of the murderer of twelve men and boys.

Slowly life was returning to normal, and it was only the families of those who had died who were still trapped by the consequences of that terrible day back in early summer.

Ewart and Walter had, of course, returned to Yorkshire after the funeral, but they came back, both of them, over the August bank holiday. Rose, Maggie and Billy had been too much on their minds for them to be able to even contemplate not making the long journey home when they had a precious day off, and Connie was very understanding; she'd lost her own father to the miners' lung disease, pneumoconiosis, a few years earlier, and remembered only too well how much emotional support her mother had needed — and her father's health had been failing for a very long time. Rose would have had no chance to prepare herself for her loss, and on top of that she'd suffered a miscarriage and was, according to Maggie's letters, still suffering from the after-effects.

"Of course you must go to Somerset," she said to Walter. "We'll be fine. There's an outing to Scarborough on the Monday. I can still go on that and take the children — there'll be plenty of folk I know going."

"If you're sure . . ." Walter was torn; Connie was near her own time, with the new baby expected in just a few short weeks.

"I'm sure." Connie was a capable Yorkshire lass, and her sunny, stoical nature meant that very little fazed her. "Look, if your mam's still poorly, why don't you bring her back with you for a bit? The change might be just what she needs. Especially spending time with Jimmy and Edie. And another woman in the house . . . well, she'd be able to help out when the little one comes, if she's fit, wouldn't she? I wouldn't say no to that."

Walter was surprised. Big-boned and wide-hipped, Connie sailed through pregnancy and childbirth, and generally declined all offers of help, even from her own mother. But he was pleased, too; he felt he'd neglected Rose since he'd uprooted to Yorkshire, and the offer was typical of Connie's generous heart.

When he found Rose as frail and poorly as Maggie's letters had suggested, he put the idea to her, and to everyone's surprise, she didn't take much persuading.

"It would be nice to see the children, and the new baby," she said. "But what about Billy? I've got to be sure he'll be all right."

"Don't worry about Billy, Mam," Maggie said swiftly. "I can look after him. And he'll have a proper job soon anyway, I hope. That should be the making of him."

She had managed to find Billy some casual labouring, helping Farmer Barton with the harvest, and she had high hopes of him being taken on permanently; she'd played the sympathy card for all she was worth when she'd gone to talk to the farmer, and he hadn't rejected the suggestion out of hand.

So it was decided. Rose would go to Yorkshire for a bit of a break, a couple of weeks, she said, but no date had been decided upon for her return.

Ewart, Maggie rather thought, had had a dual motive in coming home for the August bank holiday. She had the feeling that he was rather sweet on Cathy, her apprentice, and was in no doubt at all that Cathy was sweet on him. She often asked after him, and when she heard he was coming to visit, there was no mistaking the way her eyes lit up.

"Really?" she breathed excitedly.

Maggie bit back a smile. "I suppose you'd like me to invite you for a cup of tea while he's here," she said wryly.

A pink flush rose in Cathy's cheeks.

"Oh . . . I didn't mean . . ."

"Get away with you!" Maggie retorted. "You know very well you did. I should warn you, though, our

Ewart is a bit of a one with the girls, but he enjoys his freedom too much to take any of them seriously."

"Well, I don't want to get serious about anybody either," Cathy said quickly. "I'm enjoying myself just as I am, thank you very much."

That was certainly true, Maggie thought. Cathy's list of conquests was a long one, and she enjoyed keeping as many of them as possible on a string. But she seemed to be taking more interest in Ewart than in any of the others.

"So, are you going to come and see me over the holiday or not?" Maggie asked, and again saw that telltale sparkle in Cathy's eyes.

"I might. You never know." Her enigmatically pursed lips curved into a broad smile. "Thanks, Maggie."

And of course, she did come, on the Sunday afternoon. Ewart was sitting on the bench outside the door, smoking, and the first Maggie knew of Cathy's arrival was when she heard voices. She'd been in the scullery, washing up the dinner things, and when she poked her head out, she could see that the two of them seemed to have picked up where they'd left off last time, flirting outrageously. She told Cathy she'd be with her in a minute, when she'd finished scouring the pans, and left them to it.

"Who's that our Ewart is talking to?" Rose had been upstairs packing some of the things she'd need for her visit to Yorkshire, and had heard the giggles floating in through the open door.

"It's Cathy, my apprentice. She's supposed to have come to see me, but . . ." Maggie lowered her voice, "that's just an excuse. It's Ewart she's come to see really."

"Oh, our Ewart!" Rose shook her head. "He'll never change. Whatever are we going to do with him?"

There really was no answer to that. By the time Maggie ventured out to greet Cathy properly, it seemed arrangements had been made, and she and Ewart were going to meet that evening. There would only be the one occasion, though — Ewart and Walter had to head back to Yorkshire the next day so as to be ready for work on Tuesday morning. But they made the most of it, Maggie guessed — it was very late that night before Ewart came home, and when she arrived at the shop after the bank holiday, Cathy looked pleased with herself.

"I take it you enjoyed yourself with our Ewart," Maggie said.

"Mind your own business!" Cathy returned pertly, and, turning away with a smile, Maggie did.

The house was quiet and empty again now with not only the two boys gone, but also Rose, but Maggie didn't mind that. She'd been so concerned about her mother, it was a relief to have only Billy to worry about, and he seemed to be much happier. Not that Billy was ever *happy* exactly, but at least he was behaving more normally, and seemed to be enjoying working on the farm.

At least the terrible tragedy had saved him from having to go underground as a carting boy, Maggie thought one day as she watched him go off along the rank with Bullseye at his heels, and was instantly horrified that she could have thought such a thing. But perhaps it was the only way to look at the blows life dealt you. To try and find a silver lining made the unbearable just that little bit more bearable, just as she believed you should always look for the good in folk, however bad they seemed to be.

It was Maggie's way. It was what helped her to survive.

The hot and often thundery purple days of August turned to the sapphire blue of September and the first yellows and ochres of October, and still Rose remained in Yorkshire. It was unlike her, Maggie thought, to stay away from home for so long — in all her life she couldn't remember a time when her mother had been absent for more than a day; perhaps to Weston-super-Mare or Weymouth. But she guessed that Rose, still weak and sickly, was dreading returning to the oppressive atmosphere of tragedy and loss, and was, hopefully, enjoying her grandchildren. Connie had given birth, as easily as always, to a little girl they'd named Eva, and when she was well enough, Rose was able to help out with her and with the other two little ones. The new life must be a bright spot in the darkness for her, even though she had lost her own baby — which, sad as it was, could only be for the best in the long run, Maggie thought. Carrying a baby to full term, delivering it and then having to nurse and raise it would have been more than Rose's worn out body could have coped with.

Billy continued to seem much happier. Farmer Barton had taken him on now as a permanent hand, and much to Maggie's surprise, she hadn't had to rouse him one single morning so far to get out of bed and off to work; he was often out of the house before she woke herself, and didn't get home until darkness fell. She didn't even have to make him snap — the farmer's wife, who perhaps felt sorry for him, gave him a hunk of bread and cheese each day for his dinner, often accompanied by a spoonful of her spicy home-made pickle.

Maggie's days fell into an ordered routine. Sometimes the grief caught up with her, a thick, suffocating cloud, and she would burst into tears for no apparent reason, crying simply because she wanted — needed — to cry. But for the most part she struggled on as she always had done, strong and stoical.

The anxiety that Sir Montague might at any time tell her she had to vacate the house was a constant niggle at the back of her mind, but with the closure of Shepton Fields, quite a few miners had left the district to find work further away, and consequently there were a number of houses empty or about to be vacated. Maggie paid the rent out of her meagre wages and hoped it would keep Sir Montague satisfied for the time being at least.

As for Josh, she had the feeling he was avoiding her, but that was all right by her. She was still embarrassed at having broken down on his shoulder that evening back in the early summer, and guilty at the treacherous feeling he had evoked in her. It was so disloyal to Jack, she thought. But that didn't stop the pang of longing when she caught a glimpse of him, a longing that quirked in her stomach and tingled in her veins before she was able to stamp on it with fierce determination — and shame. And she still hadn't returned his handkerchief either. The fact that it remained under her pillow was her guilty secret, the one little comfort she couldn't bring herself to give up.

She wasn't thinking of any of these things, though, when she left the shop one Saturday evening towards the beginning of October. Saturday was always the busiest day of the week; it was market day in nearby Hillsbridge, and people who had spent the day there often called into Augusta Freeman's drapery shop to make some small purchase on their way home. It wasn't unusual for it to be late before Maggie could escape, especially since everything had to be tidied away before she and the other assistants could leave.

The nights had begun to draw in, and it was already dark when Maggie, Cathy and Beat parted company in the centre of town. Light was spilling out from the doorway of the alehouse further up the street, but otherwise the windows were in darkness and had been for some time. Even the gents' outfitters had been closed for an hour or so — Horace Freeman was less dedicated than Augusta, and in any case not many men wanted to buy a shirt or a pair of socks on a Saturday evening — and Maggie was glad of it.

When the two shops closed at more or less the same time, Reuben had taken to waylaying her, walking with her, even, though he lived in quite the opposite direction. She had the uncomfortable feeling that he thought he stood a chance with her now Jack was gone, and she'd done her best to discourage him, but it wasn't easy without being outright rude, and outright rudeness didn't come easily to Maggie, especially since Reuben was, to all intents and purposes, being nothing but kind and solicitous. "I'm just keeping an eye out for you, Maggie," he would say when she told him she was perfectly safe walking home alone.

In any case, she actually felt a little sorry for him — he seemed to have no friends — and guilty, too, that he was so besotted with her, as if it was her fault.

As she walked up the street, the familiar noises of the alehouse floated out into the sharp chill of the evening air — the tinkling of the barroom piano belting out music hall favourites, and a cacophony of voices, some singing along to the piano, some trying to make themselves heard above the general hubbub within. To Maggie's dismay, a few people had spilled outside, and some kind of argument seemed to be going on. She hastened her step, anxious to get past as quickly as she could — the alehouse customers were known to be a rowdy crowd, who could become quarrelsome as well as merry, and neither would she put it past them to make a nuisance of themselves when they saw her, a girl out alone, at this time of night. Head held high, not so much as glancing in their direction, she marched past, and to her relief the men seemed too engrossed in their argument to notice her. But her heart was beating a little faster than usual, all the same, and when, just around the corner, an all-too-familiar figure emerged from one of the darkened doorways and planted himself directly in her path, Maggie's relief turned to annoyance.

Reuben Hillman. He should have been long gone. But no, here he was, waylaying her again.

"For goodness' sake, Reuben!" she snapped, her patience with his antics finally exhausted. "What are you doing still here?"

Reuben smirked.

"Waiting for you, of course! I thought Mrs Freeman was never going to let you go." He held out a little box, similar to the one Cathy had brought as a gift when Maggie had been off work nursing Rose, though smaller. "I got these for you."

"Chocolates." Maggie's heart had sunk even further. "Reuben, you shouldn't have. I don't want you buying me presents."

"But I wanted to!" he protested. "Cathy said you really like chocolates, and I thought they'd cheer you up. Take them, please!"

Maggie continued walking, refusing to so much as touch the box he was holding out to her.

"Thank you, but I can't accept them. This has got to stop, Reuben. It's getting beyond a joke. You must realise I'm just not interested in you, and a box of chocolates isn't going to change that."

"But Maggie —"

"No!" She stopped, turning to face him. "I'm sorry, but I don't want your chocolates, and I don't want you. Now, will you kindly stop bothering me?"

"But I just want to look after you, Maggie," he said, sounding hurt. "We're meant for each other, you and me. Don't you see? You're all alone now that Jack's gone, and so am I . . ."

"Haven't I made myself clear, Reuben?" Maggie exploded in exasperation. "Just go away and leave me alone!"

For a moment he recoiled and froze, almost as if she had physically hit him. Then his hand shot out, grabbing her by the arm. His face had changed, the silly smile gone now, fleshy lips curled back from bared teeth in an expression that was almost feral.

"You can't treat me like this, Maggie," he hissed. "All I want is to make you happy. It's all I've ever wanted. You must know that."

"I really don't care what you want, Reuben," Maggie said staunchly, though she was beginning to be very frightened.

"Don't be like this!" Reuben's fingers bit into her arm. "I can give you the sort of life you could only dream about before. Far more than that Jack Withers ever could. He's dead now, and good riddance. Don't you see, there's nothing now to stop us from being together."

Maggie's fear began to turn into outright panic. She was seeing a side of Reuben she'd never seen before — in just a few short moments he had changed from a pathetic, grovelling creature into a monster who was capable of anything in the pursuit of his twisted desires.

Could it have been him who had cut the rope? To free her, as he seemed to see it, from her commitment to Jack? In that moment Maggie wouldn't have put anything past him.

"Let me go, Reuben!" She tried to snatch her arm away, but Reuben was holding her too tightly. He did drop the box of chocolates, though — it fell open as it landed on the pavement, and expensive bonbons rolled out into the gutter, but neither of them noticed.

"I love you, Maggie!" He was holding her fast now by both arms, pulling her towards him and at the same time pushing her back against the rough stone wall of the shuttered shop. She smelled sweat and carbolic soap and tried to twist away again, but his hands slid up so that they circled her throat and his moist, fleshy lips came down hard on hers, silencing her cry of protest. In vain she tried to push him away.

"I want you, Maggie! I've wanted you for so long!" he groaned, breathing hard. "And now there's nothing to stop us being together. Nothing!"

His hand was on her breast now; this time she knew she was not imagining it. And he was trying to bunch up her skirts!

A burst of raucous laughter and raised voices carrying on the still night air reminded Maggie that they were only yards away from the alehouse and the men who'd been standing on the steps outside. She had been nervous about passing them; now anything, anyone, was less threatening than this horrible monster who was assaulting her. Gathering what little breath she had left, Maggie screamed, but if the men did hear her over the racket of the Saturday-night revelry, no one came to her aid.

Reuben was pressing himself against her now, and the horror of it galvanised Maggie. As he drove her back against the wall, his face close to hers, she lashed out with her teeth, catching his ear lobe and biting as hard as she could. Reuben sprang back, squealing in pain, and with a little more freedom of movement Maggie was able to deliver a hard kick to his shin before bringing her knee up to catch him between his legs — when a girl had three brothers, she knew exactly where it would hurt most.

Reuben doubled up, groaning and clutching at himself, and Maggie shoved at him with both hands. He toppled over in a heap on the pavement, and she squeezed past him and began to run.

Along the road she fled, terrified that he might recover himself and come after her, out into the quiet dark countryside, running, running until her breath gave out and her legs were quivering with exhaustion. She slowed, gasping, looked over her shoulder, and then, although the road was deserted, forced herself to begin to run again. She was sobbing now, tears of fright and shame blurring her eyes, and a stitch throbbed in her side, but still she kept going, more slowly but just as frantically.

Oh Jack, Jack! Where are you? Jack, please, I need you . . .

He'd been there once before when Reuben had been bothering her, but he wasn't here now, and he never would be again.

Just when she thought she would never reach it, the lane that led to the Ten Houses was there on the left-hand side of the road. Staggering now, Maggie turned into it, and then on to the track between the rank and the outbuildings. The door of number six was closed but not locked. Maggie thrust it open and ran into the scullery, where she collapsed, weeping, against the stone sink.

"Maggie?" Billy appeared in the doorway, looking puzzled and concerned. "Whatever is the matter, our Maggie?"

Maggie didn't answer. She sank slowly to the floor, knees drawn up, arms wrapped around them. The tears had begun to flow in earnest now. She buried her face in her skirts, and great shuddering sobs shook her body as she wept as she could never remember weeping before.

Billy stood staring helplessly down at his sister. He'd never seen her in such a state before. She was always so strong. The one who looked out for him. To see her like this frightened the life out of him — he felt as if the ground was shifting under his feet, everything solid in the world around him dissolving.

"Maggie! What's wrong with you?" he asked desperately.

Maggie didn't even seem to hear him, and her awful sobs filled the tiny scullery, making Billy want to cry too. He could feel his chest tightening with panic.

If only Mam were here! Or Ewart, or Walter. But they weren't. They were miles away, in Yorkshire, and he was on his own.

"Stop it, Maggie!" he begged tearfully.

Still Maggie took no notice, and Billy's panic rose until it was choking him. She wouldn't want anyone outside the family seeing her in such a state, he knew, but he couldn't leave her like this. He had to get help, or he didn't know where it would end.

Beside himself, Billy ran out on to the track behind the houses, looking wildly first one way then the other. Should he call Dolly Oglethorpe? But he hated going to the Oglethorpes', in case Charlie was there. He still avoided Charlie whenever he could.

It came to him in a flash. Josh Withers. Josh was the next best thing to Ewart and Walter. Josh would know what to do.

His breath coming in shallow little sobs, Billy ran up the track towards the Withers home.

CHAPTER
TWELVE

It was unusual for Josh to be at home on a Saturday evening; Saturday evenings were for a walk out with a young lady or a drink with your mates. These last months he'd done both, and enjoyed neither. Truth to tell, he was sick to death of the aimless small talk the men engaged in over a pint of ale, and sick to death of trying to pretend interest in a young lady. He'd romanced several — Edie Vranch, who worked in the glove factory; George Parfitt's niece, Polly, and a girl he'd met in Bath when he and some of the other lads had ventured further afield for a night out. But he couldn't work up any enthusiasm for any of them. He went through the motions, even enjoyed himself as far as it went, but afterwards there was nothing but emptiness and dissatisfaction and a restlessness that made him feel as if he'd sat down on an anthill. To make matters worse, it wasn't easy to get rid of them. Josh couldn't understand why it was he seemed to attract women like a jam jar attracts wasps — he didn't think he was that good-looking, and he certainly never went out of his way to charm the girls as some blokes did. And yet there always seemed to be one or another throwing herself at him and trying to cling on.

At least Peggy Bishop seemed to have realised he'd meant it when he said their fling was over, and he was very glad of that, but the others . . . he only had to walk out with them once or twice, maybe steal a kiss, and they acted as if the next step was a ring on their finger.

Josh felt bad about it. He didn't want to hurt or upset anyone and he certainly didn't want to lead them on. The fact of the matter was he just wasn't interested. He did wonder if the fact that he was still mourning Jack had something to do with it, but deep down he knew it was more than that. Josh had never been one of life's deep thinkers, but you didn't have to be to work out the reason.

Maggie.

He tried to avoid her whenever he could, but living in the same terrace of houses it was impossible not to catch sight of her from time to time, and every time he did, Josh felt the same kick in his stomach, the same stirring of his blood, the same quickening of his pulse. And afterwards . . . afterwards she was there in his head and in his heart and nothing he could do would banish her. Useless to tell himself to forget her, she wasn't for him. Not even the guilt that made him hate himself for envying the brother he was grieving for, and the unshakeable feeling that he was somehow betraying him, could stop the way he felt about Maggie. Love wasn't a word that figured in Josh's vocabulary, but he didn't have to put a name to it to know how he felt.

Nobody could hold a candle to Maggie, and he couldn't imagine they ever would. Perhaps eventually he'd meet a girl he liked well enough, settle down and raise a family, but she wouldn't be Maggie. Never Maggie. And for the moment, the very idea made his stomach clench and his hackles rise. One day, perhaps, he'd feel differently, but that day was a long way off.

That Saturday evening in October, Josh hadn't even thought of going out. Instead, he'd got down to a few odd jobs that needed doing — a strut in the back of one of the kitchen chairs had come loose and needed repairing, and while he had his tools out, he'd fixed the larder door that had dropped so it dragged across the flagstone floor. Then he'd settled down to spend some time working on the candlesticks he was carving out of a nice piece of oak he'd picked up.

A carpenter by trade, Josh loved wood: the smell of it, the feel of it beneath his hands, the way he could whittle it and plane it and even polish or stain it if he wanted when he'd finished fashioning it. He'd made a small table with two shallow sliding drawers that he was secretly very proud of, and a little bookcase, but as the Withers family didn't own many books beyond the family Bible, the shelves were more or less empty. At least there would always be a use for candlesticks, and if nothing else, they could sit on the top shelf of the bookcase and fill the empty space.

Engrossed in what he was doing, Josh wasn't best pleased to be disturbed by the hammering on the back door. Gilby was out for a Saturday-night pint as usual, and Florrie had gone to bed with a sick headache, so there was nothing for it but for Josh to answer the door himself. He laid the candlestick and his tools carefully on the sheet of newspaper that was protecting the

203

kitchen table and pushed back his chair, but before he got even as far as the scullery, the hammering began again.

"All right, all right! I'm coming!"

He opened the door, and was surprised to see Billy Donovan on the doorstep, his hand already raised to knock again.

"Billy! For goodness' sake! You'll bang the door down in a minute!"

"Oh Josh, can you come along to ours?" Billy appeared to be on the verge of tears.

"Why — what's happened?" Josh asked, alarmed.

"It's our Maggie. I don't know what's the matter with her, but she won't stop crying. Oh, please come, Josh, please!"

Just the mention of Maggie in trouble of some kind was enough for Josh. Without stopping for anything, he was out of the back door, leaving it open behind him, and heading down the track, Billy trailing behind him.

As he burst in through the door of number six, he almost fell over Maggie, still curled up against the scullery wall, still sobbing, though more softly now, in little trembling bursts.

"Maggie! Whatever is the matter?" He hunkered down beside her.

Maggie's shoulders convulsed, another sob catching in her throat.

"Maggie?" he said again, gently, reaching out to smooth a lock of hair back from her cheek where it had fallen. "Come on, love, tell me what's wrong."

Maggie raised her head for a moment, staring at Josh with eyes that were red and swollen from weeping, but also curiously blank and expressionless. She opened her mouth as if to say something, then abruptly closed it again, and her head sank to her knees once more.

For all that Billy had thought Josh would know what to do, truth to tell he felt as helpless as Billy had done, and he was seriously alarmed. But he had to do something.

"You can't stay down there, my love," he said reasonably. "Let's get you in the kitchen."

He put an arm round her, and to his relief she raised her head again, wiping her nose with the back of her hand and looking at him with those anguished eyes.

"Oh, I'm sorry . . . I'm sorry . . ."

"Don't be silly! Sorry for what?"

"This! I'm sorry . . . I just . . ."

Her grief had caught up with her again, he thought. He'd seen it with his mother, how she could suddenly burst into tears for the loss of Jack, set off by the smallest thing, or sometimes nothing at all, even though she'd seemed perfectly composed moments before. He'd felt it himself, too, that sudden weight of sadness and disbelief that his brother was never coming back, coming out of nowhere like a thunderclap on a clear summer afternoon.

"Come on, let's get you up from there and we'll have a cup of tea," he said encouragingly. "Put the kettle on, Billy."

Billy, who had been hanging back in the doorway, looking at his sister nervously, squeezed past them, and

Josh helped Maggie to her feet and led her into the kitchen, where he sat her down in Rose's favourite armchair.

"I'm so sorry, Josh," she apologised yet again. "I'll be all right. Billy shouldn't have come bothering you."

"No bother," he said awkwardly. "And do stop saying you're sorry. It's only natural you're upset, losing Jack like that."

Maggie gulped, and her eyes filled, and for a moment he thought she was going to start crying again.

"It was just so horrible," she managed between gasping breaths.

"You miss him. We all do."

"I just couldn't . . . I've always dealt with him before, put him in his place, but tonight . . . it was all too much . . . I wanted Jack so badly . . . I really needed him . . ."

Josh frowned.

"What are you talking about, Maggie?"

"Reuben Hillman. He frightened the life out of me. He's done it before, but tonight . . ." She pressed her hands over her mouth, closing her eyes as if she could shut out the memory.

"Reuben Hillman?" Josh repeated, puzzled. "What's he got to do with it?"

"He won't leave me alone. It's always been the same, but now that Jack's gone . . . oh Josh, he really frightened me tonight. There was nobody about, and he wouldn't let me go . . ."

Josh's face darkened.

"What did he do?"

Haltingly, she told him the whole story, and the anger grew and swelled in Josh's gut as he listened.

The little bugger! How dare he do that to Maggie? How dare he get her in a state like this! He needed to be taught a lesson, and he would be. Josh would make sure of that.

Billy, hunkered down beside the fireplace waiting for the kettle to boil, also listened in shocked silence to what Maggie was saying.

Josh got up. His hands were balling to fists, already itching to get to work on the miserable coward who had reduced Maggie to this state.

"Look after your sister, Billy," he instructed harshly.

"Why? Aren't you . . .? Where are you going, Josh?"

Josh's lips set in a hard line.

"Never you mind, Billy. Let's just say I've got business with that bloody Reuben Hillman."

"Oh Josh — no!" Maggie protested. "You mustn't!"

He ignored her, heading for the door.

"I'll look in and make sure you're all right when I get back," was all he said.

Fury was boiling white hot in Josh's blood as he marched along the lane in the direction of High Compton. He didn't suppose Reuben would still be in the town — he wasn't one for frequenting the pubs and bars — but Josh knew the Hillmans' house, a villa within easy walking distance of the town centre, and he reckoned that was where he would find the little bugger, run home with his tail between his legs.

Well, his tail would certainly be between his legs by the time Josh had finished with him!

He carried on past the alehouse, which was getting rowdy now, down the street where Freeman's drapers occupied the corner premises, and up the hill beyond. A glow of light crept through the drawn curtains of the front room of the Hillman house; Josh harrumphed with satisfaction, opened the wicket gate, strode up the path and hammered on the front door. When nothing happened immediately, he knocked again, even more furiously than before, and called loudly: "Come on out, you bastard! I know you're in there!"

He heard footsteps within, and the creak of a bolt being drawn, and bunched his fist in readiness. But when the door opened a crack, it was Clarence Hillman, Reuben's father, whose outraged face appeared in the gap.

"Who is this? How dare you —"

"I want to see your son," Josh said between gritted teeth. "I've got something to say to him."

"Well, it will have to wait for another time, I'm afraid," Clarence said coldly.

He went to close the door; Josh rammed it open with the toe of his boot.

"You'd better get him out here, or I'm coming in." He gave the door a violent shove, and Clarence staggered backwards. Josh pushed past him. "Where is he? I know he's here. Reuben, you bugger . . ."

The door to the left of the tiled hallway was ajar; Reuben himself appeared, looking alarmed.

"What . . . ? Who . . . ?"

When he saw Josh right there in the hallway, he shrank back, his podgy features melting into blubber, small eyes bright with fear.

In one stride Josh had him by the collar, bunching it up under his flabby chins so that he was lifted almost off his feet.

"I want a word with you, you miserable little rat!" he ground out. "You lay a finger on Maggie Donovan again and you'll be bloody sorry."

Reuben's eyes boggled.

"What are you talking about?" he burbled.

"Don't pretend you don't bloody know! She doesn't want anything to do with you. Understand that?"

"Let my boy go!" Clarence grabbed Josh's shoulder; he was quite a small man, and Josh shrugged him off easily.

"Understand?" he grated again into Reuben's quivering face.

Reuben's head nodded like a clockwork doll, and Josh glared into his eyes for a few more moments before releasing him.

"You'd better, or I swear I'll swing for you."

He turned, pushing Clarence aside, and had almost reached the doorway when Reuben quivered defiantly: "She's just a common tart anyway. You're welcome to her."

Afterwards, Reuben didn't know what bravado had got into him to say such a dreadful thing about his beloved Maggie, and to a man of Josh Withers's size to boot. And at the time, he certainly didn't have the opportunity to wonder. Before he knew what was happening, Josh had swung round, the black rage that was bubbling inside him reaching boiling point. His fist shot out, connecting squarely with Reuben's jaw. Reuben staggered back, collided with an occasional table and went down like a felled tree. Josh aimed a furious kick, catching him between his plump legs.

Reuben squealed in pain, Clarence froze, momentarily too shocked to do anything, and from the doorway Alexandra, Reuben's mother, gasped in horror and ran to her son.

"Get out! Get out!" Clarence yelled, recovering himself. "I'll have the police on you, you thug!"

"Do what you bloody well like." Josh stood threateningly over the stricken Reuben. "But you . . . you leave Maggie alone, all right? Or you'll get more of the same, and that's a promise."

With that, he turned and banged out of the house. He was still shaking with rage, but at least he'd done what he'd come for, and he was glad of it.

Nobody — nobody — was going to treat Maggie the way Reuben had, or call her filthy names, and get away with it. If it was the last thing he did, he'd make sure of that.

"Are you all right, Maggie?"

By the time he got back to number six, she certainly seemed to have recovered herself; she was in the scullery, washing up teacups.

"Yes . . . yes, I'm fine . . . Oh Josh, where have you been? What have you done?"

"Taught that little bugger Hillman a lesson he won't forget. I don't think he'll be bothering you again in a hurry."

"Oh, you shouldn't have! Really you shouldn't!"

"He asked for everything he got," Josh said flatly. "If you have any more trouble from him, just let me know, all right?"

Maggie wiped her soapy hands on her apron.

"Josh, promise me — you haven't hurt him, have you? I don't want you doing anything silly on my account."

"He had to be shown he can't behave like that," Josh said grimly. "The state you were in . . ."

"I expect I made more of it than I should," Maggie said. "But he's got it into his head that now Jack's gone, he stands a chance with me, and he's . . . oh, I don't think he's all there. The things he was saying! It really frightened me, it was so peculiar. He was like a man possessed. You don't think, do you . . .?" She drew a long, trembling breath. "You don't think . . . no, no, of course not . . ."

"What?" Josh asked.

Maggie shook her head, unable to put into words the awful thought that had come into her head. That perhaps it was Reuben who had severed the rope on the hudge. He was so crazy for her, so persistent, and tonight she'd caught a glimpse of a man teetering on the edge of madness — not all there, as she'd put it. Supposing he had really believed that with Jack out of the way, she'd turn to him? Supposing he really thought that he could offer her things Jack never could, and in his twisted mind had excused the wicked act by pretending he was doing it for her, for her good?

But it made no sense. He couldn't have known for sure that Jack would be on the hudge when the rope gave way. And surely not even he could be responsible for something so terrible? She couldn't believe it. She didn't.

"Nothing," she said. "I'm just being silly."

"Well . . ." Josh looked awkward suddenly. "If you're all right now, I suppose I'd better be getting home. Mam and Dad will wonder where I am."

"I'm fine, honestly. You go."

He looked at her, at the rich chestnut hair curling about a face that was still paler than usual. Her eyes were still a bit swollen, too, and her mouth quivered a little before she caught her lower lip between her teeth, biting down hard on it. But in all the time he had known her, she had never looked more kissable, and it was all he could do not to give in to the urge to do just that.

"You know where I am if you need me." He backed out of the door. "Anything at all, don't hesitate."

"Thanks, Josh." She smiled tremulously. "I just hope you don't get in any trouble over this."

"It wouldn't be the first time, by a long chalk."

"The first time on my account. And . . . oh, I don't know what you must think of me, forever bursting into tears on you. What a stupid woman I am!"

"Believe me, Maggie, that's the last thing you are," he said with feeling.

And then, before the urge to take her in his arms could get the better of him, Josh left hurriedly.

Josh had been home about an hour when there was a knock at the door. His mother and father were both in bed, but Josh was far too wound up for sleep, and was sitting in the kitchen with a tot of whisky, thinking about Maggie, and the way he felt about her.

Was it so wrong to want her? Would it be so terrible for him to see if there was a chance she felt the same way? She didn't, of course. She was still mourning Jack. But she was a young woman, she couldn't go the whole of her life alone, could she? There were women who did just that, he knew, but he couldn't see Maggie as a bitter old maid. Surely one day she'd take up with someone else, and he knew that he wanted that someone to be him. However long it took, he'd wait for her. And in the meantime, he'd be there for her. She needed someone to protect her from the Reubens of this world.

Josh swallowed a glug of whisky and refilled his glass. Yes, that was what he'd do. He'd look out for her, if nothing else. Surely that would be what Jack would have wanted?

When the knock came, Josh's heart leaped. His first thought was that it was Maggie, needing something, or Billy to say she'd become upset again. He hurried to answer it, but when he yanked it open it wasn't Maggie or Billy on the doorstep.

"Josh Withers, what have you been up to this time?"

It was a very irate Sergeant Love, red in the face from cycling over from High Compton and furious at being called out so late on a Saturday night.

Josh's heart sank. He'd had plenty of run-ins with the sergeant over the years, and though none of them were recent, he knew they wouldn't have been forgotten. Talk about giving a dog a bad name.

"Are you going to let me come in, or do I have to take you down to the station?" Sergeant Love snapped.

Josh sighed and stepped aside, and the policeman strode into the house, removing his helmet as he did so.

"I don't know, lad," he said sorrowfully, as if he were talking to a young boy rather than a grown man. "I thought you'd mended your ways. But you've really done it this time, haven't you? I've had a serious accusation made against you by a highly respected member of the community."

Josh snorted.

"Respected, my eye! He asked for it, Sergeant. And while we're at it, I've got some accusations of my own. He attacked Maggie Donovan — I don't suppose he told you that. Frightened the life out of her, and other things besides."

"Clarence Hillman attacked Maggie Donovan?" The sergeant's voice was scathing with disbelief. "I can't see that happening in a month of Sundays."

"Not Clarence. That useless lump of a son of his." Josh ran a hand through his hair, leaving it standing on end. "He waylaid her on her way home from work and . . . well, he did and said things no man should. He asked for all he got."

"Still the hothead, I see." Sergeant Love put his helmet down on the kitchen table and fished in his breast pocket for his notebook. "You ought to keep that temper of yours under control, my son. You can't go barging into decent folk's houses, taking a swing at them and knocking them out cold."

"He wasn't out cold," Josh objected. "He fell over, that's all."

"That's not the way the Hillmans tell it. I'm going to have to arrest you, you know that, don't you? A complaint has been made, and all I can say is you're lucky not to be looking at very serious charges here."

"I wish I bloody well was!" Josh flared. "It would be no more than the little bugger deserved, and I might as well be hung for a sheep as a lamb."

"You've been drinking, haven't you?" the policeman said disgustedly. "Don't deny it — I can smell it on you. And you'd been drinking when you went terrorising the Hillman family as well, if I'm not mistaken. That's half the trouble with you, getting the drink in you."

"You'd have had a drink too if you'd seen the state Maggie was in," Josh retorted. "And just for the record, when I lammed that little sod I was stone-cold sober. But charge me if you want to — I don't give a bugger. It was worth it just to see him go down like a ninepin. And I'd do it all over again. Come on then, are you taking me down the station or not?"

Sergeant Love sighed heavily. If he arrested Josh Withers and took him back to spend the night in the cells, they were going to have to walk the whole way, and the prospect, especially at this time of night, was far from appealing. The sergeant wanted his bed, and he wanted it soon, not in a couple of hours' time. Withers was home now, and no danger to anyone that he could see, and he wasn't likely to be going anywhere any time soon. In fact, the policeman was wishing he'd left the whole thing until the morning; he would have done, most likely, if the complainant had been anyone other than Clarence Hillman, the solicitor's clerk.

"If I leave you here tonight, I want you down at the station first thing in the morning," he said.

"You can bet on it," Jack said grimly. "But you can tell that bloody Hillman that if he wants to press charges against me, he'll have a few of his own to answer. Assault on a lady! That's against the law too, isn't it? And a damn sight more shameful than giving a man the smack he deserves. Tell him that and see how he likes it before you run me in."

Sergeant Love shook his head. This was getting worse by the minute.

"I still want to see you down that station tomorrow," he said belligerently. "You'll be there if you know what's good for you."

Josh raised his hands in submission.

"All right, all right. But you'd best have another word with Hillman first. Tell him what I said."

"Oh, I'll get to the bottom of it, never you fear." Sergeant Love was trying desperately to reassert his authority. He picked up his helmet and headed for the door. With his hand on the latch, he turned. "And you, my lad, had better learn to watch your temper, or you'll

216

end up behind bars. I've got your card marked. I won't stand for any more goings-on like this on my patch. Understood?"

"Yes, Sergeant," Josh said, mock-meekly.

But when the door closed after the policeman and he was alone again, he poured himself another slug of whisky.

Tonight had proved it to him — he was still too ready to use his fists, just as he always had been. When his temper was up, there was no telling what he was capable of. He might yet end up behind bars, just as Sergeant Love had predicted and as his long-suffering parents had feared when they'd sent him off to Wales to his aunt and uncle.

But whatever the consequences, he couldn't regret landing that punch on Reuben Hillman's fat, ugly nose. And if Hillman kept on bothering Maggie, he would do the same all over again.

He did report to the police station next morning as instructed, though not first thing — by the time he'd finally got to bed the previous night, he'd polished off the last of the whisky and slept like a log. Besides, he was counting on Sergeant Love speaking to Clarence Hillman before he got there, and telling him about Josh's counter-allegations. Josh couldn't see Maggie pressing charges, even if it would get him off the hook — she'd be mortified if the whole thing became public, and Josh wouldn't want to put her through that. But with any luck Reuben wouldn't want it made public either, and would have the grace to be thoroughly ashamed of what he'd done.

And it seemed that was the case.

After giving Josh another stern warning, Sergeant Love sent him on his way, and Josh found himself whistling all the way home.

It hadn't turned out so badly in the end. He had the satisfaction of having exacted revenge on Maggie's behalf and got away with it. He didn't think Reuben would bother her again. And he'd come to a decision.

He wasn't going to avoid Maggie any more. He was going to look out for her, and hope that one day he'd be more to her than just Jack's brother.

"You stupid, stupid boy!" Clarence Hillman said. "Why in the world would you want anything to do with one of those Donovans? Have you been chasing after her? Is it true?"

Reuben, nursing a black eye and swollen cheek, avoided his father's eyes and said nothing.

"From your silence, I assume you were," Clarence fumed. "How could you place me in a position like this? It's intolerable! All I can hope for is that I can be assured that is the end of this foolishness. Well?"

"Yes, sir," Reuben said sullenly.

But inwardly he was seething. His desire for Maggie was as strong as ever; he'd never let her go — never! But stronger even than his desire was the burning anger and his hatred for Josh Withers. Oh, he wouldn't forget this. The humiliation. The pain when Josh had landed his punch and kick. And worst of all, the suspicion that

218

something was going on between him and Maggie, and that Josh was closer to her than he, Reuben, had ever managed to be.

Just you wait, Josh Withers! he thought bitterly. Just you wait!

Revenge was a dish best served cold, so the saying went. However long it took, Reuben was determined on one thing. When he got his revenge on Josh, it would be something he'd never forget. And Reuben would relish every moment of it.

CHAPTER
THIRTEEN

"I'm a bit worried about Mam," Maggie said.

She'd eaten her evening meal and was sitting at the kitchen table with a cup of tea when Josh called in, as he'd taken to doing most evenings since the night she'd been assaulted by Reuben Hillman — to make sure she was all right, he pretended to both of them, though in reality he knew it was much more than that.

If Billy was there he didn't stay too long, but tonight the lad wasn't yet home from work.

The moment he'd walked in he'd thought Maggie looked preoccupied, and she didn't get up to make him a cup of tea as she usually did. Now he pulled out a chair and sat down, and Maggie picked up an envelope lying on the table in front of her, pulled out a couple of sheets of writing paper and unfolded them.

"I got this letter from Walter today. He says Mam's not been at all well."

"Oh, that's a shame." Josh was typically nonchalant.

"He says she's off her food — well, she's been sick too a couple of times — and she's complaining of pains in her stomach." Maggie ran her finger down the page, tracing Walter's neat, slanting handwriting. "And the day he wrote this, she stayed in bed most of the morning. That's not like Mam. She likes to be up and doing."

"I expect she ate something that upset her," Josh said reasonably.

"Connie's a lovely cook," Maggie argued. "She wouldn't give Mam anything that was going off."

"She's picked something up, then. You know how these things go round."

Maggie sighed.

"I hope you're right. I just hope it isn't anything to do with . . ." She hesitated, fighting shy of mentioning Rose's miscarriage in so many words. "What happened back in the summer," she said instead.

Josh shifted in his chair, as uncomfortable with discussing women's problems as Maggie was.

"She's never been right since," Maggie said. "I reckon they ought to get the doctor to her, but whether they will . . . Walter's got a family to keep, and doctors cost money."

"He'll find it if he thinks it's needed, or your Ewart will," Josh said. "But I wouldn't mind betting she's fine by now."

Maggie chewed her lip, still staring down at Walter's letter as if she could change what it said by sheer willpower.

"She could be, I suppose. I certainly hope so. But I've got this really bad feeling . . ." She broke off as the dark dread filled her again, dragging her down to a place she really did not want to be. It had been hovering about her all day, even before she'd opened the letter, and it frightened her. Useless to tell herself she was simply still raw from the terrible things that had happened in the last months; she recognised that feeling of sick apprehension, and until she'd got home and read the letter there had been no reason whatever for her to be feeling that way. It was as if, deep inside, she knew something was terribly wrong, even when she hadn't the first idea what it was. But now here it was in black and white: Mam was poorly again, and Maggie was horribly afraid that what she was feeling wasn't just ordinary anxiety but an instinctive knowledge that was somehow compellingly different.

"I don't know what I'd do if anything happened to Mam," she said, folding both hands tightly over the letter and lowering her eyes. "I just couldn't bear it on top of everything else."

"Nothing is going to happen to your mam, Maggie, trust me." Josh reached across the table, covering her hands with his own.

Such a gentle touch, the smallest comforting squeeze, but it made Maggie quiver inwardly, and warmth ran through her veins in a glowing tide from the place where his fingers lay, making her almost forget the awful foreboding that had been suffocating her.

"Try not to worry," he said comfortingly. "Your mam is a strong woman. She'll be fine, you'll see."

Maggie nodded. She didn't trust herself to speak.

"You're just looking on the black side," he went on. "It's not surprising, with all that's happened, but it's not like you. You're the one who generally keeps everybody else's spirits up."

She smiled faintly. "Am I?"

"You certainly are. And I've got to take my hat off to you, the way you've held things together since . . . you know . . . There's plenty who'd have gone under, with all you've had to deal with."

"I just do what I have to do," she said simply. It was no more than the truth.

"Well . . ." his fingers tightened on hers, "you're not on your own, Maggie. You know that, don't you? Whatever you need, I'm here for you."

Her skin was even more sensitised now, the little tingles that ran from his hands into hers sharper and more compelling, and she experienced a moment's panic and almost snatched her hand away. But somehow she didn't. For one thing, she didn't want to. She wanted him to go on holding her hand for ever. It felt so good and so safe, as well as exciting in that darkly dangerous way. And what would he think if she did? He didn't mean anything by it; he was just trying to comfort her, the most natural thing in the world. He was Jack's brother, after all, and she'd known him all her life. If she pulled away suddenly, it would give away her own treacherous thoughts and feelings, and make things horribly awkward.

Oh, what in the world was the matter with her? How was it he could make her feel like this? It was something she'd never experienced in her life before, and the longings it aroused in her shocked her and filled her with shame. She'd relived those longings often, lying in bed at night with Josh's handkerchief pressed to her face so she could smell the familiar scent of soap and tobacco, and wondered what on earth was happening to her. Jack had never made her feel this way, and she had been going to marry him. The thought of going beyond kisses had been repellent to her. Now . . . Maggie was aghast to realise she actually wanted — craved — the very things the thought of which had made her cringe where Jack had been concerned. What sort of a woman did that make her? One who was no better than she should be, that was for sure!

Besides that — even worse, perhaps — was the way she couldn't stop thinking about Josh. He was there, somehow, in everything she did. As she cooked a meal for herself and Billy, she imagined she was cooking it for Josh too. As she sorted boxes of haber-dashery, she thought how nice it would be to sew buttons on his shirt and darn his socks. As she walked home along the lane in the falling dusk and heard a nightingale sing or an owl hoot, she wanted him there, sharing the moment with her. It was madness, utter madness, and though it made her feel horribly guilty that she should harbour such thoughts about Jack's brother when Jack was scarcely cold in his grave, she couldn't help feeling her heart soar and her imagination take flight.

This was the man who'd taken up cudgels on her behalf, gone after Reuben Hillman and punched him on the nose in his own front room; the man who'd climbed on the churchyard wall beside her when she'd been trying to dissuade the mob of angry miners from marching on Sir Montague's house after the funeral. It lent him an aura of romance, as if he were a knight in a fairy tale, and the dangerous edge of his wild youth, still there, though well hidden these days, added a little thrill of excitement that made the chemistry that existed between them even more potent.

It was there now, tingling in the place where his fingers touched, spreading warmth through her veins, twisting in her gut. And with it the familiar feelings of guilt and confusion.

"You wouldn't hesitate to come to me, would you, if there's anything you need, anything at all?" Josh went on.

"Thank you," she said quietly. "But I'm all right, really I am. It's just that sometimes I get this awful feeling that something else dreadful is going to happen. I expect I'm just being silly, though."

"Like I said, hardly surprising."

"I suppose."

She raised her head, looking at him, trying to smile, and as their eyes met, something quite extraordinary happened.

The potent attraction was there again, sparking like an electric storm, but this time it felt to Maggie that it wasn't only she who was experiencing it. In that moment it seemed to her that her own tumultuous emotions were reflected in Josh's narrowed dark eyes. The breath caught in her throat as they gazed at one another, and for a long hiatus in time they remained perfectly motionless, frozen in a white-hot bubble of ice. Then Josh's hands closed more tightly over hers and he leaned towards her across the table, at the same time drawing her towards him. She offered no resistance. It was, she thought afterwards, as if she were nothing but an iron filing being sucked up by a magnet. His features were no longer in focus and she couldn't see him clearly, but the scent of him was sharp in her nostrils: soap and tobacco smoke, and something else, something so unmistakably male it took her breath away.

His breath kissed the soft skin of her cheek and she could almost taste his mouth on hers. She parted her lips, closing her eyes, floating in a universe that had become unreal as a dream.

And the dream shattered.

Neither of them had heard the back door open, but there was no missing the bang as it shut. Maggie jumped, startled out of her trance, panic rushing through her in a flood tide. She snatched her hands away from Josh's, half rising from her chair just as her brother came into the kitchen.

"Billy! You're home, then! Farmer kept you late tonight . . ." She was gabbling, she knew, but she couldn't help it. "You must be tired out. Sit down . . . I'll get you something to eat."

Billy slumped down in the easy chair.

"I'm all right. Farmer's wife cooked us bacon and egg."

"Well, I'll get you a cup of tea anyway. You're bound to be thirsty."

She couldn't look at Josh, couldn't meet his eyes.

He stood up too.

"I'd better be going. Try not to worry about your mam. She'll be fine, I'm sure of it."

"What's wrong with our mam?" Billy asked sharply.

"Oh, it's something and nothing, I expect," Maggie said. "She hasn't been too well, but our Walter will look after her."

"Oh . . . well . . ." was all Billy said, but there was still a pinched, anxious look on his pale little face. Billy missed his mother a lot, Maggie knew; apart from herself, Rose was the only one who was always there for him, and she hoped desperately for his sake as well as her own that it really was something and nothing, and that Rose would soon recover from whatever it was that was ailing her.

In the doorway, Josh paused and turned.

"Just remember — you know where I am if you want me."

Hot colour flooded Maggie's cheeks. *If you want me . . .* He didn't mean it like that, of course, but all the same, the words were a bit too close to home for comfort.

She nodded, but for the life of her couldn't bring herself to say anything.

And then he was gone, and Maggie was left alone with Billy, and with the confusion that now raged in her more fiercely than ever.

As he walked back up the track to his own home, Josh burned with pent-up frustration. Why the hell had Billy chosen that very moment to come bursting in?

But for all that, he was elated. There was no mistaking what had so nearly happened between him and Maggie.

He'd been taking a hell of a chance there, of course, making a move like that this soon. If she didn't feel anything for him, it could well have been the end of his hopes. But she hadn't drawn back. She hadn't given him a slap, which would probably have been no more than he deserved. She'd been ready to let him kiss her. More than ready, he reckoned . . .

He could see her face now, close to his, lips parted, eyes closed, and the fire in his belly flared like a burning hay barn. But he could wait. If he thought he stood a chance with her, he could wait a bit longer. And just at this moment, he thought he definitely stood a chance.

Josh kicked at a small stone in his path, sending it scudding merrily ahead of him, and whistled a music hall tune as he headed for home and a much-needed tot of whisky.

That same evening, Peggy Bishop was visiting her sister Sarah. She'd given up calling on her in the day; there was never a chance to talk properly when all the children were running around — a noisier, more demanding brood Peggy couldn't imagine, and she was only glad she'd never had any of her own. What sort of a life was that? Washing filthy nappies, wiping runny noses, bathing scraped knees, making piles of jam or dripping sandwiches, cleaning muddy floors, and all to the endless whines and cries and unintelligible chatter. Oh, she could do without all that, thank you very much!

They were sitting now in Sarah's cramped little kitchen, Sarah busy darning the toes and heels of much-worn socks that had been passed down from one growing child to the next, Peggy nursing the last dregs of a cup of sugary tea. So far, to Peggy's annoyance, they'd talked about nothing but the children — or at least, Sarah had talked and Peggy had been forced to listen to tedious accounts of teething problems and growing pains, bilious attacks and temper tantrums until she found herself wondering why she'd bothered to visit at all. The warmth of the fire was making her drowsy and she was, in fact, half asleep when Sarah unexpectedly changed the subject.

"Do you ever see anything of Josh Withers these days?"

Peggy roused herself.

"Not for ages," she said. "Why? What made you think of him?"

"Oh, nothing really, but I heard he was in trouble with the police again a couple of weeks ago."

Peggy pricked up her ears.

"Whatever for?"

"Fighting. Well, worse really. He went to Clarence Hillman's house, forced his way in, and let into his son. Knocked him out cold, I heard. He's lucky not to be up before the court by the sounds of it. I don't know — there's some as will never learn."

"Why ever would he go picking on Reuben Hillman?" Peggy wondered. "I wouldn't have thought he even knew him."

"Well, according to Tilly Yates, young Cathy Small, what works at Freeman's along with him and Maggie Donovan, reckoned he'd been making unwelcome advances to Maggie. I wouldn't like to say for sure, of course, but it sounds about right. When blokes start knocking twelve bells out of one another there's usually a girl involved, and I don't suppose Josh Withers is any different."

Peggy snorted in disgust. The thought of Josh picking a fight with Reuben Hillman on behalf of Maggie Donovan was very hurtful to her, especially since he'd given her such an uncompromising brush-off. But she wasn't going to let Sarah know she cared a hoot.

"Silly sod," she said contemptuously.

Sarah snipped through her wool and jammed the darning needle between her lips while she paired the sock she had been working on and dropped the roll into a basket at her side.

"To think that not so long ago you were thinking of running off with him!" she said. "You've changed your tune."

"Maybe I have and maybe I haven't," Peggy said evasively.

Sarah gave her a sharp look as she cut another length of grey darning wool.

"You and Tom getting on better, then?"

"We're all right at the moment," Peggy said, wishing Sarah would go back to talking about her children, boring as it was. She had no desire to tell her sister about the strange change in her relationship with her husband, and the peculiar shift in her own feelings towards him. Truth to tell, she couldn't quite understand it herself, and it certainly wasn't something to be shared, not even with Sarah, who'd known most of her secrets since they were girls. For over the past weeks, her awful suspicion that Tom might have been the one who severed the rope and caused the terrible disaster at Shepton Fields had given rise to something that was close to excitement. It wasn't something she was proud of — she barely wanted to admit it, even to herself — but it crackled and buzzed inside her all the same.

If she was right, if Tom had done something so unspeakably awful in order to punish the man who had been her lover, then he must care far more about her than he ever let on. That in itself was gratifying, but it was more than that. A dangerous man was also an attractive one, and the very idea of it titillated her. Oh, she'd always known Tom could be dangerous, of course, but in a mean, sly way that belittled him rather than enhancing his image in her eyes. This, though . . .

Somehow it had failed to occur to Peggy that cutting through a rope under cover of darkness was just as sly and cowardly as anything Tom had ever done — she saw only a man who could commit murder, and although on one level it shocked her, she was too exhilarated by the spice it added to their relationship to care.

Tom seemed to be behaving differently too, perhaps because of the change in her attitude towards him. Oh, he could still be surly and unpleasant and controlling but he sometimes surprised her with little generosities, and certainly he was very appreciative of her warm response in bed. And when he did say nasty things, she didn't feel as resentful as she used to; she just saw it as further evidence of the hard man he was, and even found satisfaction in allowing herself to be dominated, whereas before she had rebelled. It was almost as if she was falling in love with him all over again, but with the real Tom and not some idol she'd placed on a pedestal only to knock down in the cold, hard light of day. Others might regard him as a monster if they knew what she thought she knew, but the secret she was hugging to herself was strangely erotic.

Yes, at the moment she was more than satisfied with Tom, and with the surprising fillip all this had given to their love life.

"We're all right now," she reiterated, and thought that she might just decide to leave Sarah and her tedious chit-chat and go home in the hope of an early night with her husband.

"There's nothing for it, Firkins. We shall have to raise the rent on all the tied cottages."

Sir Montague Fairley stood, swaying slightly on his bow legs, a brandy glass in one hand, decanter in the other, in the centre of the Persian rug that covered his drawing room floor.

He'd already had a bad day. Alfred Nicholls, the police superintendent from Bath, had called to see him this morning and informed him that the enquiry into the pit accident was being scaled down. Every avenue had been explored, no progress was being made, and the manpower they had expended could no longer be sustained.

Sir Montague had been incensed; he was aware that there was talk in the town that he was to blame, and he wanted a culprit brought to book. But the superintendent refused to be moved with regard to the number of officers assigned to ask questions around the town, though he did attempt to appease the coal owner by promising that the case would remain open and that he personally, along with one of his best detectives, would continue the investigation.

Sir Montague was having none of it.

"You should have called in Scotland Yard at the outset," he growled.

"They couldn't have done any more than we have done," Nicholls asserted. "Less, in fact. They don't know the locals as we do. I'm sorry, Sir Montague, that we have had no success so far, but I can assure you I still regard the case with the utmost seriousness, and it's my sincere hope that there will be a satisfactory outcome."

"There had better be, or I shall see about calling in Scotland Yard myself," Sir Montague threatened.

"I'm not sure that's within your power." The superintendent sounded confident enough, but he was fiddling nervously with his collar stud as he said it.

"We'll see about that," Sir Montague barked, his blood pressure rising dangerously. "I want this matter laid to rest and I shall ensure that it is, whatever it takes. Now, are you willing to reconsider this so-called scaling-down?"

But the superintendent remained adamant.

"I'm sorry, I can't do that. We'll speak again when, and if, I have anything further to report."

The unsatisfactory interview had made Sir Montague's hearty lunch lie heavily in his stomach, while his gout was playing him up too. So when Clement Firkins, his agent, had arrived with the news that two more families were leaving the area for work elsewhere and their houses would be falling vacant, his temper had reached boiling point.

"Good God, at this rate I'll be bankrupted!" he exploded. "Rents will have to rise to compensate. With immediate effect."

Clement Firkins stirred uneasily, and his highly polished boots squeaked on the varnished boards that surrounded the Persian rug.

"I'm not sure they'll be able to afford to pay, Sir Montague. Especially those who lost their breadwinner in the accident."

Sir Montague juggled the brandy decanter and glass.

"They'll find it somehow. They will have to, if they want to keep a roof over their heads. I've been more than generous so far, but I'm afraid all good things must come to an end. They can remain in their homes until I have need of them, but they'll have to pay for the privilege. Do I make myself clear?"

"Perfectly, Sir Montague." The agent knew better than to argue if he wanted to keep his job.

"Very well, see to it." Sir Montague poured himself the refill he was craving. "Close the door on your way out, Firkins. It's the maid's evening off, blast her."

234

"I'll do that, Sir Montague," Clement Firkins replied, with all the dignity he could muster.

"Bloody business!" muttered Sir Montague as the door closed after the agent.

And took a healthy gulp of the fine cognac, which he needed, he'd convinced himself, for medicinal purposes.

CHAPTER
FOURTEEN

"Are you going out tonight, our Billy?" Maggie asked.

It was Sunday evening; Billy knew without questioning her why she was asking. Maggie liked to have a bath on a Sunday evening, ready for the week ahead, and in any case, he could hear the water simmering in the copper.

"It's all right," he said. "I think I'm just going to go to bed. I'm as knackered as Barney's bull."

It was no more than the truth; as Rose had warned him long ago, farm work was no easy ride. As always, he had been up before dawn, toiled away all day in the pouring rain, and only got home when darkness had fallen. No days off for him. He didn't mind, though — he liked it on the farm, and since he had no real friends to go out with, he was happy enough just to catch up on some sleep before it was time to begin all over again.

"Do you want me to fetch the bath in for you?" he asked.

"No, you get off to bed if you're that tired."

The rain was still falling heavily. Maggie scooted across the track to fetch the tin bath from the outhouse, and by the time she returned, little rivers of water running down her face, there was no sign of Billy.

Bullseye was still there, though, sitting on the rug in front of the fire, the exact place where she wanted to put the bath. She ought to push him outside where he belonged, but she didn't have the heart. Instead she made him go and sit in the corner, then, using the metal dipper, ladled scalding water from the copper into the bath. She fetched soap and a towel and got undressed, folding her clothes neatly and piling them up on a chair.

She winced as she stepped into the hot water, wiggling about from foot to foot, then eased herself down to a sitting position and relaxed, enjoying the luxury as she always did. There was something so cosy about a bath in front of the fire at this time of year, with the glow of the embers the only light in the room and the warmth flushing her face as well as her body.

Maggie slid down so that the water covered her head and washed her hair with soap shavings. Then she scrubbed herself all over and settled back again to make the most of her weekly treat before the water cooled.

She was feeling much happier than she had done recently; she'd had a letter from Walter yesterday in which he said Rose seemed to be picking up, and that was a weight off her mind. But she did have another concern: Clement Firkins, Sir Montague's agent, had been to see all the families in the Ten Houses and informed them that their rents were to be raised.

It wouldn't be easy to find the extra; money was already tight. Whereas before Paddy had died she'd been able to keep a bit back for herself when she handed Mam her wage packet at the end of the week, now it was all eaten up on paying for the essentials. But she'd just have to cut her coat according to the cloth, Maggie thought. And she should be due a small rise in her wage at the end of the month — another whole year she'd been at the draper's. She'd manage somehow; really, she had no choice.

The warmth was making her drowsy, but a tin bath was no place to go to sleep, even if she rested her head on her knees. Maggie levered herself up and got out, shivering a little now as she towelled herself dry. Then she slipped into Rose's old dressing gown, which she'd laid out ready — Rose hadn't taken it with her, arguing that it would take up too much room in her suitcase, and Walter had promised to buy her a new one; not before time, he'd said.

Maggie put milk for a cup of cocoa to warm in a pan on the trivet and was just towelling her hair dry when there was a knock at the door, followed almost immediately by the creak of someone trying to turn the handle.

"Oh my goodness!" Maggie flew into the scullery. "Who is it? Who's there?"

"It's me, Josh. Can I come in?"

"No! No, you can't . . . I'm . . ."

"I'm getting soaked to the skin out here!"

"No, you can't! I'm not decent."

"Have a heart! It's pouring down."

"Oh . . . wait a minute, then." Relenting, Maggie undid the dressing gown sash and retied it tightly, then, with one hand holding the edges closely together around her throat, she unlocked the door.

"I wasn't expecting anyone at this time of night," she said defensively as Josh came into the scullery, shaking himself like a rat. "I've just had a bath."

"I could do with a nice bath myself," he said jokingly. "Is the water still hot?"

"No, it's not! You go back to your own home if you want a bath, Josh Withers, 'cos you're not getting one here!" Maggie retorted, flustered but not wanting to show it.

He pulled a wry face. "You're a hard woman, Maggie. If you aren't going to be nice to me, I might just change my mind about what I've come to say."

He was struggling to keep his voice light, struggling not to gaze at her. Her hair still damp and mussed up, falling in an untidy curtain to her shoulders. Her face flushed and rosy from the bath. The clean, soapy smell of her, sweet in his nostrils, lighting a fire in his blood. He'd never wanted her more; it was almost too much for a man to stand. Especially with her so close here in the cramped scullery, where there was scarcely room to swing a cat.

"So, what did you come to say?" she asked, her tone still short with embarrassment.

"Let's go in the kitchen and I'll tell you. You'll catch your death out here."

It was no more than the truth — away from the warmth of the fire, the cold air of the October evening had invaded the scullery, and in spite of the dressing gown, Maggie could feel chilly shivers running over her skin.

"Oh, come on then, if you must."

She led the way into the kitchen and he followed. The milk on the trivet was beginning to skim over and bubble up; she bent to pull it to one side.

"I'm just making a cup of cocoa. Do you want one?"

"I wouldn't say no."

"I'll get some more milk, then."

She eased past him back into the scullery, where the jug of milk lived on a cold slab, and his eyes followed her. God, she was beautiful! It was all he could do not to grab hold of her, untie that stupid sash, and —

"How's your mam?" he asked to distract himself.

"A bit better, thank goodness. I got another letter from Walter yesterday."

She was bustling back and forth, pouring more milk into the saucepan and returning it to the trivet, setting out cups and spooning sugar and cocoa into them.

"There you are, what did I tell you? Didn't I say she'd be fine?"

"I don't know that she's *fine* exactly."

"But she will be. She's tough, your mam."

"Like me, you mean." There was a hint of teasing in her voice now.

"I didn't say you were tough, Maggie. I said you were hard," he responded, taking up the teasing.

"That's even worse! You make me sound like a walnut!"

"Could be! Hard shell, but sweet inside. Well worth cracking . . ."

"Josh Withers, stop it this instant!"

She was flirting, she realised! She could hardly believe it.

"So tell me why you're here, interrupting my bathtime."

"And enjoying myself, too. But if you insist . . ."

"I do! I want to get to bed before I catch my death, as you so nicely put it."

"To bed, eh?"

Colour flamed in her already rosy cheeks.

"Josh Withers! I've never heard the like!"

"Then perhaps it's time you did . . ."

She drew herself up.

"Stop it! You're as bad as Reuben Hillman!"

"Oh, him! That's a nice compliment to pay me, I must say."

"I swear you are. And if you don't stop this right now and tell me why you've come bothering me . . ."

"Yes, what?" he challenged.

"Well . . ." Her eyes were wide with pretended indignation, her lips pursed. "You'll just have to punch yourself on the nose, won't you?" she said, a giggle escaping even before she finished the sentence, and both of them dissolved into laughter.

"Come on, then." With an effort, Maggie recovered herself. "What did you come to say? Something nice?"

"Well, I hope you'll think so . . . Hey, watch that milk, it's going to boil over."

Maggie swooped on it, poured scalding milk into the cups and then returned the lot to the saucepan.

"All right, I won't keep you in suspense any longer," Josh said as she stirred the pan vigorously. "I found out today that they're having a dance at the Miners' Welfare next Saturday. There's a band coming out from Bath,

241

and it sounds as if it might be a bit of fun. I wondered if you fancied going."

"Oh Josh, I don't know . . ." Maggie stopped stirring and glanced over her shoulder, serious again suddenly. "Don't you think . . .? Well, isn't it a bit soon?"

"How do you mean?" he asked, though he knew.

"Well . . ." She bit her lip. "Dad . . . and Jack . . ."

"You've had a tough time, Maggie. We all have. I reckon we deserve a bit of fun. We can't shut ourselves away for ever. That's what the organising committee thought, I expect. That's why they're putting it on, so we can enjoy ourselves for a change. Hey, come on . . . I know I'd like to go. But not on my own."

"You'd have plenty of partners, Josh Withers. Half the girls in the district would be lined up and waiting for you."

Josh took a deep breath.

"Maybe. But not the one I want."

For a moment he thought he'd gone too far. Maggie stood stock still; he could almost hear the beating of her heart. Then she moved abruptly, pouring the steaming cocoa into the cups and pushing one across the table towards him.

"Well, if it's an act of charity, I suppose I'd better say yes," she said drily. "Now, drink your cocoa and go on home. We've had quite enough of this nonsense for one night."

Tired as he was, Billy couldn't get to sleep. It was too often like this nowadays; whereas once it was waking up that had been the problem, since the tragedy at

242

Shepton Fields there hadn't been a single night when he'd been able to drop off and sleep right through to dawn. Every time he closed his eyes, it seemed, the horror of what had happened was there, chasing around and around inside his head until he thought it would drive him crazy. And when he did manage to sleep, there were the nightmares, not always about the accident, often making no sense at all, but dark and suffocating, awful, nebulous scenarios from which he couldn't escape when he woke, sweating and trembling. He was afraid then to go back to sleep in case the horror was still there waiting for him.

Tonight he'd lain with the sheet pulled up to his chin, staring into the darkness and listening to the rain gusting against the window but hearing only screams and cries inside his head. When he could stand it no longer, he pushed aside the covers and got up. He'd fetch Bullseye. Maggie would be cross with him for having the dog on the bed — it wasn't hygienic, she said, and it wasn't him who had to wash the sheets and pillow-cases either — but there was comfort in feeling the dog's weight on his feet, or pressed alongside him, and hearing the little snorts and snuffles the dog made when he was asleep. Sometimes he even barked softly and his feet made little scrabbling movements — dreaming that he was chasing rabbits, Mam said; no nightmares for him. And if Billy was feeling really scared, he could reach out and stroke the wiry hair, tweak one of the dog's misshapen ears, and Bullseye might stir enough to lick his hand, or even his face. That always made Billy feel better.

At the top of the stairs, though, he hesitated. He could hear voices in the kitchen below — Maggie's, and a man. It sounded like Josh Withers. Billy frowned. Maggie had been going to have a bath — in fact, he'd heard her bring the tub in, and the scent of her soap had filtered under the gap around the door and up the stairs.

So what was Josh Withers doing here? Billy's mind boggled. She wouldn't have let him in, surely, if she wasn't decent? Unless . . .

Suddenly it was another unpleasant memory that was uppermost in Billy's mind — the sounds he'd heard sometimes coming from his mam and dad's room. Oh, surely Maggie wouldn't . . . would she? He knew from talk he'd overheard amongst the men and boys that it wasn't only married folk that did *that thing* — like the cows humping in the farm fields. But Maggie . . . Maggie would never think of doing anything like that, would she? Why, he'd never even seen her not properly dressed; she'd shout at him to stay out of the room even when she was wearing her camisole and bloomers.

A kind of shocked curiosity overcame Billy. Hardly daring to breathe, he crept down the stairs, keeping as close to the side of the treads as he could to stop them from creaking. The occasional one still did, though, and each time he froze, waiting. But the door didn't fly open, with Maggie yelling at him and demanding to know what he thought he was doing, and when he reached it, he could still hear the rise and fall of voices coming from the other side.

244

Ah — there was Josh, perched against the kitchen table. And Maggie . . . as he peeped round the door and saw her bending over the trivet and doing something with a saucepan, his first reaction was one of relief. She wasn't naked. She wasn't even in her underwear. She was all wrapped up in Mam's old dressing gown.

But hot on the heels of the relief came a wash of something that was almost disappointment.

He hadn't wanted to catch Maggie and Josh doing *that thing* — he hadn't! But the very thought of it fascinated him, teased at him, in a way he couldn't really understand.

As he watched, Maggie straightened up, turning, and Billy withdrew hastily, pulling the door closed and holding his breath. A moment later a scratch at it made him almost jump out of his skin. But it was only Bullseye. He'd seen his young master, even if Maggie and Josh hadn't. Billy opened the door again, keeping well back to allow Bullseye through unnoticed. Then, the dog at his heels, he crept back up the stairs and into his room.

He slipped into bed and Bullseye jumped up and settled down beside him. Well, at least now he had his pal for company. But Billy thought it would still be a long while before he would be able to get to sleep.

Except that this time it wasn't the terrible tragedy on his mind, but something quite different.

The rain was still coming down in sheets. Josh pulled up his coat collar and tucked his chin into it as he jogged back up the track. With his head bent, he didn't notice Hester Dallimore emerging from the privy in the block on the opposite side to the houses. He cannoned into her, and one of the spokes of the umbrella she was holding over herself struck his cheek a sharp, painful blow.

"Hey, look out!" Hester exclaimed shrilly. "You trying to knock a body over?"

"Sorry, Mrs Dallimore."

"You want to watch where you're going. You could have done me an injury, and broke my umbrella into the bargain."

"Sorry," he said again.

He was in no mood to argue, or give her cheek as he might sometimes have done. He was elated. He'd done it! He'd bloody done it! He'd invited Maggie to the dance, and she'd accepted! Why, he felt like dancing right now! What would Hester Dallimore say if he caught hold of her and whirled her round, out here in the middle of the track in the pouring rain?

The very idea made him chuckle. Hester, hearing, called after him in annoyance.

"It's no laughing matter, Josh Withers! You're nothing but a young hooligan."

"You're right there, Mrs Dallimore," he called back over his shoulder. "But let's look on the bright side. At least you didn't manage to put my eye out with that brolly of yours."

He didn't catch her reply, just the angry slam of her door, and he laughed again from sheer exhilaration. He wasn't going to let a miserable old biddy like her upset him. Not even his stinging cheek bothered him, though he thought there might be blood trickling down his face along with the rain.

He was going to take Maggie to the dance. There was a long way to go yet, but it was a start. And Josh couldn't have been happier.

Maggie was really looking forward to going to the dance on Saturday. Josh was right, she could hardly remember when she'd last had any fun. The whole of the summer had been lost in a black morass of grief, worry and work. She hadn't been to a single social event, not the fetes, not the circus, and certainly not a dance.

Not that she'd ever been to many dances, and usually they had been the ones that followed one of the summer galas, when folk gathered on the recreation field or in the town square, and the Salvation Army band, more often than not, played. Jack had taken her once or twice, but since neither of them knew more than a few steps, it was more a case of jiggling about in time to the music than really dancing, and it had usually ended up as an excuse for a cuddle — well, if Jack got his way, anyway. Maggie was always too conscious of making a show in public and had tried her best to keep him at arm's length. It had been fun, though; the music always set her feet tapping and she wished she could learn to do it properly, as the gentry did.

But it wasn't just going to the dance that was exciting her. It was the prospect of a whole evening with Josh. Try as she might, Maggie couldn't forget the sparks that had crackled and fizzed between them that night when he had so very nearly kissed her, couldn't forget the heady euphoria and the longing that had rushed through her in a flood tide. Though she knew she shouldn't, she couldn't help imagining how it would be to dance with him, his arm around her, or at least his hand on her waist, and when she did, she felt dizzy with pleasurable anticipation. And the best part was that no one would think anything of it. It was what you were supposed to do when you were dancing, and there was no danger of things getting out of control when you were surrounded by other people.

Just as long as they didn't think she had no business being out enjoying herself, with her father and Jack dead only a few months . . . Just as long as they didn't think that she didn't care . . . The ever-present anxiety cast a shadow over her eager anticipation, but she tried to tell herself that surely no one could begrudge her one evening when she could forget about her troubles, and that the other revellers would know that Josh was simply escorting her because he was Jack's brother, and was looking after her for him.

But did she believe that any more? Was it just wishful thinking on her part, or had something really changed between them?

Josh had called in almost every evening over the last week, and though nothing untoward had happened, she was sure she'd felt that chemistry sizzling between them. The slightest of accidental touches set her skin shivering, the shared smiles filled her with joy, and

248

when their eyes met, there was something in his gaze that made her almost believe he felt the same way she did. You've taken leave of your senses, she told herself. But daring to think he might made her feel good, so good that she didn't want to put an end to it.

Saturday came at last. All day, butterflies fluttered in Maggie's stomach, and she could barely concentrate on her work — she gave customers the wrong change twice, and then managed to spill a paper twist of pins all over the counter.

"What's up with you today, Miss Donovan?" Cathy asked, helping her to scoop them up again. "You're like a cat on hot bricks."

Maggie, down on her knees looking to see if any of the pins had fallen on to the floor, hesitated. She was reluctant to tell Cathy, who wouldn't be able to keep it to herself for a moment, but then after tonight, everyone else who attended the event would know anyway, wouldn't they?

She rescued some stray pins and got up.

"I'm going to a dance," she confided. "Josh is taking me. But I'm still not really sure whether I should go or not. What do you think?"

Cathy's face was a picture.

"Of course you should go! Why ever not?"

"It's not that long, though, is it, since Dad and Jack . . . You don't think I should still be in mourning?"

"You *are* in mourning!" Cathy said. "But you need something to cheer you up. And I should think Josh

249

Withers is just the right person to do it. He's quite a one, isn't he?"

Maggie bit her lip. *Quite a one*. He certainly was. At the unbidden thought, colour flooded her cheeks, and Cathy's eyes widened.

"Miss Donovan!" She pursed her lips as if trying to suppress a giggle. "I do believe you fancy him!"

"Don't be silly!" Maggie snapped, but Cathy was still looking at her in that knowing way, and she relented.

"I do like him," she admitted. "That's the trouble, really. It makes me feel so guilty."

"Now you're the one that's being silly," Cathy said pertly. "You've nothing to feel guilty about. It's only a dance, isn't it? Whatever is wrong with that? Jack would want you to have some fun. He wouldn't want you turning into a dried-up old maid."

"I suppose not, but . . ."

"You just go and enjoy yourself. I wish I was going myself. Now if your Ewart was here . . ."

Maggie smiled. She'd wondered how long it would be before Cathy got around to mentioning Ewart.

"He was asking after you the last letter I had," she said. "But Yorkshire is an awful long way away, Cathy. You'd be far better off with a local lad."

"Mm." Cathy looked regretful.

The doorbell jangled; a customer was coming in.

"Just you stop worrying, Miss Donovan, and go out and have a lovely time," Cathy whispered as the two girls lined up behind the counter, ready to serve. "And let's just hope Mrs Freeman doesn't keep you too late tonight."

250

"Let's hope not," Maggie whispered back.

It was something else that had been worrying her a little; by the time she got home and changed into the fresh blouse and skirt she'd put out ready, they were bound to be late arriving at the dance. She'd warned Josh that she couldn't be sure what time she'd be able to get away, and he had said it didn't matter.

"Just as long as we get there before the beer's sold out, and in time for the refreshments," he'd joked. "We don't want to miss out on those."

"Speak for yourself, Josh Withers!" she'd retorted. "I don't know as I want dried-up sandwiches, and I certainly don't want any beer!"

But she knew Josh would be both hungry and thirsty, and she wasn't even sure whether they would make it in time for the interval refreshments if there was a stream of late customers coming into the shop.

She was watching the door anxiously when, just before seven, Augusta Freeman called her into the back room. Maggie's heart sank — she was in for a rollicking, she thought, over all the silly mistakes she'd been making today. But to her surprise, Augusta regarded her benignly.

"I'm quite happy for you to get off now, Maggie. I'm sure we can manage without you until closing time."

Maggie's jaw dropped, and Augusta smiled — a fairly rare occurrence.

"You have a social evening to attend, I understand."

"Well, yes, but . . ."

"Off you go, then. You don't want to be late."

"Thank you, Mrs Freeman." Maggie felt quite flustered, the butterflies skittering again.

"Don't thank me, my dear. Thank Cathy. She's offered to do all the jobs you generally do when we close for the weekend."

"Oh, that's really nice of her!" Maggie was quite overwhelmed.

Fancy Cathy taking it upon herself to go to Mrs Freeman and beg time off for her!

"Let's not waste any more time, then." Augusta resumed her usual stern manner, but Maggie thought she saw a twinkle in her employer's eye. "And do try to enjoy yourself, Maggie, and forget all your troubles for a little while at least."

"Thank you, Mrs Freeman," Maggie said again.

And as the nervous excitement swelled inside her, she almost ran from the shop.

Reuben Hillman, standing by the glass-panelled door of the gents' outfitters next door so as to watch out for potential customers, saw Maggie leave and burned with the rage of frustrated desire and injustice.

He'd kept away from her since the night Josh had come after him and punched him in his own front room, because he was scared of what might happen if he didn't. Like all bullies, Reuben was a coward. He didn't want Josh going for him again, and neither did he want to incur his father's wrath. Clarence had been furious with him, as if the whole sorry incident had been his fault, and the atmosphere at home had been horrible for days afterwards, with his father glowering at him over the breakfast and dinner table, and his mother looking ready to burst into tears. They were disappointed in him, he knew, and their opinion meant a great deal to him. They were the ones, after all, who made him feel good about himself when nobody else seemed to like or admire him, and he couldn't bear it when even they seemed to turn against him.

But none of this changed the way he felt about Maggie. He couldn't shed his obsession with her like a snake shedding its skin. He wanted her as badly as ever, and he was just as determined that one day he'd have her. He just had to let this blow over. At least Jack Withers was out of the picture now, and though Josh had taken up cudgels on her behalf, he couldn't believe she'd look twice at a thug like him, not his lovely Maggie. He'd find a way to make her see that they were meant for each other, and when his parents got to know her, they'd love her too and welcome her into the family.

As the days had gone by, Reuben had talked himself into believing that this was the way it would be, curbing his impatience with the promise of what was to come — soon, very soon.

And then today, when he'd gone into the draper's side of the business to get change for the outfitter's till, he'd overheard Cathy Small asking Augusta Freeman if she'd let Maggie go early that evening as Josh Withers was taking her to a dance at the Miners' Welfare.

Reuben had scarcely been able to believe his ears. What in the world was Maggie thinking of? How could she turn him down and yet agree to go out with that varmint?

In that moment he hated her almost as much as he hated Josh Withers, and as he watched her hurry away across the street long before the shop closed, it boiled up in him again.

Who do you think you are, to treat me like this? he fumed. *I put you on a pedestal, and you're as bad as him!*

Until today, he'd never had a single bad thought about Maggie. Even when she'd spurned him, he'd made excuses for her. But this . . . this was a step too far.

As she disappeared into the darkness, Reuben moved away from the door. His hands were balled to fists, his flabby mouth pursed, and tears of anger and disappointment were gathering in his throat.

"Damn you, Josh Withers!" he muttered. "And damn you too, Maggie."

For the first time he was realising what a fine dividing line lay between love and hatred. For the first time he was thinking that if he could put his hands around Maggie's throat again, he'd strangle the life out of her. She wouldn't spurn him then! She'd be begging, pleading — and he'd be the one in control. Oh, that would feel good, so good. And she would be his at last, for ever.

Reuben's anger was suddenly superseded by a strange, wild elation. Maggie might be going to meet Josh Withers tonight, but his turn would come. He'd make sure of that.

CHAPTER
FIFTEEN

Maggie flew along the track behind the Ten Houses and rapped on the door of the Withers house.

It was answered by Florrie, still wearing the big wraparound apron that womenfolk had usually taken off by this time of day. A delicious smell of baking wafted out around her.

Maggie felt a moment's nostalgia for the times when she'd come home from work to find their own kitchen full of the same appetising smell — Rose's fruit cakes were legendary, and they'd never lasted long when there was a hungry horde to demolish them, but Maggie thought those days had gone for good. Even if Rose was ever fit enough to make a cake again, she likely wouldn't bother, with only Maggie and Billy to eat it before it went stale.

But she was too excited tonight to dwell on times past.

"Oh, Mrs Withers, can you tell Josh I'm home? Mrs Freeman let me go early. I've just got to get changed now, that's all. If he gives me ten minutes, I'll be ready."

"All right, Maggie, I'll tell him." There was a certain reserve in Florrie's tone. She wasn't sure what she thought of Josh taking Maggie to a dance so soon after

Jack . . . But she wasn't going to say so to either of them. Maggie had had a hard time lately, what with one thing and the other. She could do with something to take her out of herself. And if Josh had ideas about taking his brother's place, well, Maggie was a lovely girl whom anyone would be glad to have as a daughter-in-law. She just wished the thought of it didn't stick in her throat, but there it was. Maggie was bound to take up with another lad sometime, and what would be would be.

Maggie rushed home. Billy was in the kitchen, tucking into a plate of cold meat and bread, Bullseye sitting expectantly at his side.

"Oh good, you've got yourself something to eat, then," she said. "I got it ready before I went to work this morning because I knew I'd be in a rush when I got home. I'm going out."

"Yes, so you said."

"I'm sorry, Billy, but I can't stop to talk now. Josh will be here for me in a minute. You'll be all right, won't you?"

"I 'spect so," Billy said, chewing on a mouthful of ham.

"I might be late home."

"I'll be fine, our Maggie. I'm not a baby any more."

"No, of course you're not."

She hurried upstairs, slipped out of her working clothes and into her best blouse and skirt. The blouse had leg-of-mutton sleeves, and fastened at the cuff with a row of tiny pearl buttons; Maggie's fingers were shaking so much it seemed to take forever to do them up. Then she pinned a small silk rose on to the high collar band at the base of her throat — she'd experimented with it yesterday, and decided this was the best place for a touch of colour. And she'd been right. Now it seemed to reflect the pink glow of her cheeks that came partly from hurrying home and partly from excitement.

As she tidied her hair at the mirror on top of the chest of drawers, and slid a pretty comb into the knot at the nape of her neck, she heard voices downstairs. Josh was here! No time for anything else but to pinch some colour into her lips and check her image one last time before grabbing her shawl and running downstairs.

"Ready! How's that for a quick turnaround?"

His eyes were running over her appreciatively. The colour flamed in her cheeks again, and something sweet and sharp twisted inside her.

"You look lovely, Maggie," he said. "But are you going to be warm enough? Didn't you ought to wear a coat?"

"Oh, I don't want a coat!" It was the literal truth; she didn't want to spoil the effect of her best blouse and skirt by covering them with her old everyday coat, the only one she possessed. And she wasn't going to wear a hat either and risk dislodging the comb, which had cost her quite a lot of money in the days when she had had some of her wages to spare. "It's a lovely night out now the rain has stopped, and I expect I shall be more than warm after all the dancing I'm going to be doing."

"You reckon you're going to be dancing, then?" Josh said with a wicked twinkle.

"I certainly hope so! I thought that was the whole idea."

"Like I told you, it's the supper and the beer I'm interested in."

"Oh — men!" Maggie raised her eyes heavenward, knowing she was flirting again, and really not caring. When she lowered them, she encountered Josh's gaze, and there was another of those moments when their eyes held and time seemed to stand still. Then Josh crooked his arm, tucking her hand into it.

"Come on then."

Maggie giggled.

At the door, she stopped, looking back over her shoulder.

"You will be all right, Billy, won't you?"

"Oh, for goodness' sake, Maggie!"

"We'll see you later, then."

"I expect I'll be in bed by the time you get home."

There was an expression on his face that she couldn't read. But then that was Billy all over. When did you ever really know what he was thinking? She remembered Mam once saying that Billy was different, and it was true, he was. Sometimes it felt as if he didn't belong on this planet, never mind in this family.

She wasn't going to worry about that now, though.

Josh opened the door and they stepped out into the cold, clear night.

By the time they arrived at the Miners' Welfare hall, the dance was already in full swing, the music floating out of the half-opened windows. It wasn't quite what

258

Maggie had been expecting — a couple of fiddles and a squeeze box, by the sound of it — but it sounded jolly, and when they climbed the flight of steps and went into the hall, they were greeted by the sight of dozens of people lined up in the centre of the floor, clapping as they executed something that looked like a grown-up version of "Oranges and Lemons". The couple at the end had their arms raised to form an arch, and another couple, holding hands, were scooting down the space between the lines, ducking beneath the arch and taking up their new position.

"Whatever are they doing?" Maggie asked.

"Looks like a country dance," Josh said.

"What's that? I've never seen anything like it!"

"Then you haven't lived." He laughed. "Come on, get rid of that shawl and we'll join in."

"No!" Maggie was horrified. "I wouldn't know what to do!"

"You don't need to. That bloke's calling out the moves. All you have to do is what he tells you."

A short, fat, bewhiskered man was indeed shouting instructions, his voice just about audible over the wheeze of the accordion. But even so . . .

"Let's watch for a minute," Maggie begged. "We can't just barge in anyway."

"Fair enough." Josh grinned at her. "But don't think you can get away with it for ever. Next dance — we're in. Now, let's see if we can get a drink before the thirsty crowds hit the bar. What would you like?"

"Oh, I don't know . . ." Maggie wasn't a drinker. In her book, drinking was for the menfolk. There were women, she knew, who liked a drop of gin, but she didn't think it was very seemly. She associated it with those who were no better than they should be, like Aggie Weeks, who lived in a hovel in the courtyard behind the Prince of Wales, and was known to entertain gentlemen visitors in exchange for money to pay for her habit. Not that they were gentlemen, of course, far from it, but at least the expression described what was going on there without sounding vulgar.

"Leave it to me." Josh escorted her to a vacant seat on the edge of the dance floor and made for the bar.

As Maggie sat watching the dancers, she began to feel a little less intimidated. At least there was a pattern emerging — they seemed to be doing the same routine over and over again.

Josh still hadn't returned when the dance ended; there was quite a crush in the bar, Maggie supposed, with a lot of people waiting to be served.

"Hey! That's my seat you're sitting in!"

A buxom woman was standing right in front of Maggie, glaring at her belligerently. It was Peggy Bishop.

"Oh, I'm sorry . . ." Maggie rose quickly, feeling flustered again.

"Didn't know these chairs were booked out, Peg."

Maggie hadn't seen Josh returning amongst the crowd of dancers who were now leaving the floor. But here he was, a glass in each hand.

"Josh!" Peggy looked startled. "I didn't expect to see you here."

"Well there you are, life's full of surprises," he said easily.

260

Peggy backed off a little.

"It was our seats, though."

"We weren't to know that, were we?"

"Come on, Peg. There's room over there." Tom Bishop appeared at Peggy's shoulder, looking rather uncomfortable.

That wasn't like Tom Bishop, Maggie thought. He had a reputation for being nasty-tempered. But she was relieved, all the same, as he gave Peggy a little prod and led her off. She'd have willingly vacated the seat rather than cause trouble, but she had a feeling Josh intended to stand his ground. In spite of his affable tone, there had been a determined set to his face. He wasn't going to see her pushed around, and knowing it more than made up for the awkward moment.

"Here we are, then. I got you a sweet cider." Josh handed her a mug brimming with amber liquid and sat down beside her. "See what you think of that."

Maggie took a tentative sip, then another.

"It's quite nice."

"Haven't you ever had cider before?"

She shook her head.

"Take it steady, then. I don't want to have to carry you home." he warned her.

Maggie thought secretly that she would quite enjoy that. But of course she didn't say so.

From the opposite side of the room, where they'd found fresh seats, Peggy Bishop was glaring surreptitiously at Maggie.

What was she doing here with Josh? What was Josh doing here at all, come to that? She'd never have expected to see him at the dance — but then she was quite surprised to find herself and Tom here. When she'd heard about it, and mentioned that she quite fancied going, she'd expected him to pooh-pooh the idea. He hadn't taken her to a dance since their courting days. But to her surprise he'd come around. "Well, we could go if you like, I suppose," he'd said. She'd still expected him to change his mind at the last minute, but tonight, after they'd had their tea, he'd spruced himself up and here they were. He was even dancing instead of propping up the bar as she'd expected. He was acting differently lately, not a doubt of it. Ever since the accident at the pit, really.

The twist of strange dark excitement stirred in Peggy, the same excitement she felt every time she wondered if Tom might have had something to do with it. Strange as it seemed, things were better between them than they had been for years, as if fires that had all but gone out had been rekindled.

The band was getting ready to start up again, the caller inviting couples to take to the floor. Peggy saw Josh put his beer beneath his seat and get up, taking Maggie's hand.

In spite of her revived feelings for Tom, a little bolt of jealousy she couldn't contain shot through her, making her eyes narrow and her mouth tighten. She still fancied Josh, always had, always would. But perhaps it was all to the good that he was here tonight with Maggie Donovan and Tom had seen them together.

He'd know that if Josh was courting Maggie, he wouldn't be sneaking off to meet Peggy. She thought again about what Tom had said after the terrible tragedy of the hudge. *He'd better leave you alone if he doesn't want to end up like his brother.* Yes, much as it stuck in her craw to see Josh with Maggie, perhaps it was for the best. She didn't want any more deaths on her conscience.

Though the windows had all been left partly open to the cold autumn air, it was hot and muggy in the hall from the sheer number of folk and their exertions, and Maggie's skin felt quite sticky under her blouse.

They'd been dancing almost non-stop, and she was really enjoying herself. Josh had been right, it wasn't difficult to follow the instructions of the caller, just as long as you could hear him over the band, and if you did make a mistake it didn't really matter; everyone was getting things wrong, and just laughing about it as the set descended into chaos.

The great "grand chain" was fun, going hand-over-hand round a circle of dancers and never knowing who you would end up with as your partner, though Maggie was always glad to get back to Josh. She watched as he came nearer and nearer, her heart beating expectantly, and groaned inwardly if they had to pass and go on again. But best of all she loved the dances where he was required to whirl her round and round, his hands on her waist to steady her — and she certainly needed steadying! She'd had two glasses of cider now, drinking the last one down almost as if it were water in spite of

Josh's warnings, and the spins were making her quite giddy. Then there were the exhilarating moments when she, Josh and another couple had to form a tight knot, arms around each other, and circle so fast that she and the other girl were lifted clean off their feet. Maggie screamed as her boots left the floor and her legs swung out behind her. But she was perfectly safe, supported by two strong men and hanging on to them herself for dear life, and when she was lowered again she collapsed against Josh, laughing and resting her head on his chest as the room spun around her.

"I think I need some fresh air," she admitted.

"Get your shawl, then. It'll be cold outside."

"That's exactly what I need!" Maggie said recklessly. "I don't want to bother with a shawl — I just want to cool off! Come on!"

She pulled Josh towards the door and down the steps. The night air was cold on her hot cheeks and she breathed it in, crisp and clean after the heat and the tobacco fug inside the hall.

"Oh, this is such fun!"

"Glad you're enjoying it."

"I am! Oh, I am!"

He caught her hand, pulling her in close with his arm around her, and she didn't resist. Her head nestled against his shoulder, and it felt so good, and at the same time just a little unreal, as if she were in a dream. They walked along the pavement to where an alleyway ran along the side of the hall. Josh turned into it, and before she knew it, Maggie was in his arms.

It was dark here; only the faintest glow from the gas lamp on the main street reached the alcove in which they were standing, so she couldn't see his face. But the scent of him was in her nostrils, intoxicating her — that familiar masculine scent of tobacco and beer and just the slightest hint of fresh sweat — and the nearness of him was making her skin prickle and her pulses race. She raised her head from the solid wall of his chest, and as his mouth came down on hers, something sharp and sweet twisted deep inside her.

His kiss was gentle at first, then, as her lips moved and parted beneath his, it became deeper, more urgent, and Maggie felt her own excitement rising with his. She'd never experienced anything like it in her life before; she'd quite enjoyed Jack's kisses, just as long as he didn't try to go any further, but this . . . this was something quite different. She felt as if she were floating outside her own body, and yet she was more aware of every nerve ending, every inch of skin, every bit of the deepest parts of her than she could ever have imagined possible. Except that she wasn't imagining, or even thinking. There was no room for thought. Only feeling. Ecstasy. Desire. A pressing need to be closer, closer still . . .

Suddenly Josh held her away.

"I think it's time we were going." His voice was rough. "You wait here and I'll get your shawl."

Without waiting for a reply, he walked away from her, back towards the entrance of the hall, leaving her there in a state of shock. She felt bereft, suddenly, disappointed and frustrated. One minute he had been kissing her as if he wanted it every bit as much as she did; the next . . . Why had he walked off like that? Had she done something wrong? She was hopelessly inexperienced in such matters, she knew. Josh was probably used to kissing girls who knew what to do much better than she did. And yet every fibre of her body ached with longing, and more than anything she wanted to experience that exhilarating madness again.

After just a few minutes he was back with her shawl. As he went to put it round her shoulders, she shivered.

"You're cold," he said. His voice still sounded rough. "I told you you would be."

"I'm all right."

"No you're not."

It was true. The perspiration soaking her blouse had cooled, and the fabric now felt unpleasantly cold and damp against her skin.

"Here, have my coat, at least until you warm up." He shrugged out of the jacket he'd retrieved from the hall along with her shawl, and draped it around her shoulders. She shivered again at his touch.

"Josh?" she said in a small voice. "Don't you want to kiss me again?"

He snorted.

"You know damn well I do!"

She turned to him, shamelessly placing her hands on his chest, raising her face to his.

"Why don't you, then?"

"Because if I do, I can't guarantee what will happen, Maggie. Don't you know you're driving me crazy?"

"Oh!" The warmth was seeping back into her veins, even if it hadn't yet reached her chilled skin, and recklessness overcame her. "I just really, really want you to kiss me again . . ."

"And I want a lot more. So I think we ought to get going before I do something I'll regret."

"What if I want it too?" She couldn't believe she'd said that, but the madness was spiralling out of control and she could think of nothing but how much she wanted him, needed him. Really, nothing else in the whole world mattered.

"Maggie, you don't know what you're saying," he said, sounding agonised.

"I do, Josh! I really, really want you."

"Come on," he said shortly. "I'm going to take you home."

His good intentions didn't last long, with Maggie snuggling beneath his arm, her head resting on his shoulder, stumbling a little as she walked. Her hair smelled sweet and soapy; he lowered his chin to drink it in, and when she turned her face up to his, he couldn't resist kissing her again.

The attraction between them was a force field, showering them with sparks even as it magnetised and drew them together; they were lost in it. The walk home took much longer than usual because clinging together slowed their steps and they stopped frequently to kiss again, kisses that only ratcheted up the intensity of the desire that was consuming them. They scarcely spoke; there was no need for words.

The terrace was in darkness, but for a lamp burning in an upstairs window of number four. Annie Day, unable to sleep again, no doubt. She was still in a terrible way at the loss of Fred.

When they reached Maggie's door, they kissed again. It was beginning to feel right now, comfortable as well as exciting.

"You want me to come in?" Josh asked softly.

"I don't want you to go."

She opened the door and Josh followed her into the deserted kitchen. Good as his word, Billy must have gone to bed and taken Bullseye with him; there was neither sight nor sound of either of them.

Almost before the door had closed behind them, they were in each other's arms again, kissing, clinging, touching. And this time, neither of them had the will to stop.

CHAPTER
SIXTEEN

Once during the night Maggie woke. She had no idea what time it might be, and she cared less. Cocooned in the darkness, she lay quite still for a few moments, drowsily basking in the rosy glow of contentment that suffused her. Her whole body felt replete and languorous, but she gradually became aware of little aches niggling in the pit of her stomach, and the place between her legs burned a bit too.

She slid her hands beneath her nightgown, wriggling it up over her thighs, and ran them over her stomach. The skin felt moist and slightly sticky, and as her fingers explored, a little echo of the sensations that had overwhelmed her earlier stirred deep within her.

As she relished it, the memory of all that had happened floated through her mind, precious, exciting, and yet hazy, as if it had all been a dream.

Josh's hands caressing every inch of her body, his mouth on her lips, her throat, her breasts. The sharp but somehow wonderful shock as his teeth closed over her nipple. The desperate ache of longing deep inside her as she raised her hips to his. The moment's fierce, searing pain as his body entered hers. The glory of feeling him moving inside her. His shout of triumph.

And then, when it was over, the wonderful contentment that came from lying in his arms, his heart beating next to hers, their legs entwined, breathing synchronised.

And yet still she had wanted him, still the need yawned deep within her, still every inch of her flesh tingled, sensitised, drawn to his as if by an invisible magnet. It wasn't over yet; she was still yearning for him with every nerve ending, every tiny muscle, every breath.

And he seemed to know it. He took her again, there on the rug in front of the last faintly glowing embers of the fire, slowly this time, slowly and gently until the frantic need was screaming within her. His tongue was where his fingers and body had been and she'd writhed in delight, shameless with desire.

Oh Josh, oh Josh!

Nothing mattered, nothing, but to have him inside her again.

And he was. Moving rhythmically, deeper and deeper. Withdrawing so that she arched her back to find him, then thrusting deep within her once more. She'd thought she was going to die with the intensity of the sensations she was experiencing. Her nails raked his bare back as they grew more and more powerful, and she was swept up to a plateau of ecstasy that seemed to last for ever.

She gasped, then screamed, and Josh's hand covered her mouth, quietening her. Afterwards, lying once more in his arms, she was terrified that she might have woken Billy, but the house was quiet, the only sounds her own uneven breathing and Josh's voice, soft in her ear.

"All right, my love?"

"Yes . . . oh yes . . . oh Josh . . ."

She didn't want him to go, she wanted him to stay here for ever, holding her in his arms until the end of time. But he couldn't, of course. She watched as he got dressed, the faint glow of the firelight making planes and shadows of the long, hard muscles and the hollows that lay between them. She slipped into her blouse and stepped into her skirt with a reluctance she knew he shared, because as she did up her blouse, he took her in his arms again, kissing the valley between her breasts before fastening the tiny pearl buttons himself. He kissed her again, then kissed his fingers and pressed them to her lips, and on his fingers she could taste and smell her own self.

She followed him to the door, wanting to watch him walk up the track, to drink in every last moment of him, but he shook his head.

"Go back inside, Maggie. I want to know you're safe. I'd put you to bed myself, but . . ."

But with Billy asleep in the room across the landing, that wasn't an option.

Maggie tossed her head, regaining a little of the pertness that seemed to come naturally with Josh these days.

"I'm perfectly capable of putting myself to bed, thank you very much!"

"Mind you do. No falling asleep in the chair or you'll catch your death. Night night, my love."

"Night night."

And he was gone.

Now, half asleep, Maggie had very little recollection of getting ready for bed. She must have undressed again and put on her nightdress, since she was wearing it now, and she must have pulled the curtains and climbed into bed. But it was all something of a blur.

I do believe that cider made me tipsy! she thought, and giggled softly. For the moment, nothing mattered but that she and Josh had shared something utterly wonderful, and for the first time in her life she felt complete.

It was still dark when Maggie woke again, but she knew it must be almost morning because she could hear Billy up and about, getting ready for work, and guessed it must have been him who'd disturbed her.

The niggles were still there in her stomach, but now they felt more uncomfortable than pleasurable; her head was thick and muzzy, her mouth horribly dry and her throat parched, and a dull ache throbbed beneath one eyebrow. And it wasn't just the aches and pains that were bothering her now, either. Conscience had begun to prick her too, and the first barbs of shame.

What in the world had she done? The memory of it was no longer warm and exciting, but horrifying.

Oh! Maggie thought, beginning to tremble. How could I have let something like that happen? How could I have behaved so shamelessly?

She knew, of course. It must have been the cider, two whole glasses when she wasn't used to so much as a single sip. She had a sudden vision of her father tumbling up the stairs after he'd had too much beer and maybe a whisky chaser or two, and a memory of one long-ago night when a young Ewart had been found asleep in the grassy bank at the turning to the rank after a wild night out with some of his friends. But she couldn't understand how she could have been so stupid. Drunk! No better than her father. No better than the gangs of youths fighting and roistering outside the alehouses. No better than Aggie Weeks, tippling away at her gin and then going with men to get the money to buy more.

Oh, the shame of it!

And worse, far worse, allowing Josh liberties such as she'd never imagined in her wildest dreams, and enjoying every moment of it! Josh, of all people! Jack's own brother! How could she ever face him again? How could she face anyone, knowing what she'd done?

Maggie pressed her hands over her mouth, closing her eyes as if she could somehow erase the memory of it, make it all go away.

Oh Jack, Jack, I am so sorry! Oh, what have I done? How could I? How could I?

Shame, regret, disgust with herself, anger with Josh for taking advantage of her when she'd been in that awful, inebriated state, all welled up inside her, and, shaking, Maggie buried her throbbing head in the pillow and wished she could die.

The morning was half gone before Maggie felt well enough to get up and go downstairs. She didn't know when she'd last stayed so late in bed, but each time she'd tried to get up she'd become nauseous and dizzy

273

and her head felt as if Walter Browning, the blacksmith, was hammering on his anvil inside it. There was a certain safety to be had in the blankets bunched around her. She could, if she wanted, pull them right over her head and shut out the world.

The very thought of having to face a single living soul was a sickening one. They'd know, they must do, what a terrible thing she'd done, what a terrible woman she was. To behave like a common floozy, and not only that, to betray Jack's memory so flagrantly with his own brother! As if she hadn't been betraying it for weeks with her feelings for Josh. That had been bad enough — but this . . .

Every time she thought of it, Maggie cringed and her cheeks flamed scarlet. But eventually there was nothing for it but to struggle downstairs and make herself a cup of strong tea.

When a knock came at the door at about midday, she didn't want to answer it. She hung back, hoping that whoever it was would think there was no one home and go away. But the door clicked open, and a moment later the last voice on earth she wanted to hear was calling her name.

"Maggie? It's me!"

Josh. Panic filled her.

"What do you want?" she demanded as he came into the scullery.

"That's a nice welcome, I must say!" He brushed drops of moisture from his shoulders; it must be raining again. She hadn't noticed, she'd not so much as glanced out since coming downstairs.

274

"Are you all right?" he asked, giving her a concerned look.

"I've got a terrible headache, and I don't feel very well."

"Ah." He pulled a sympathetic face. "A hangover. Bit of a bugger, aren't they? That's what it will be."

"If you say so. I wouldn't know. I've never had one before."

He grinned. "No, I don't suppose you have. But you were certainly letting into that cider last night."

The confusion she was feeling was making her angry; anger was far preferable to the awful combination of embarrassment and shame.

"You shouldn't have bought it for me. You know I don't drink."

He raised an eyebrow.

"Maggie, you're a grown woman. You didn't have to drink it. Anyway, I thought it was doing you good. It was nice to see you enjoying yourself for once. Forgetting all the bad stuff for a bit."

The bad stuff. The accident. Mam's miscarriage. Dad. Jack. Most of all, Jack.

"That's what was behind it, I suppose — you getting me drunk. It was *myself* you wanted me to forget. And I did. Oh, I'm so ashamed! I'll never forgive myself, never!"

"Hey, wait a minute, Maggie, I did not get you drunk, at least not on purpose. Oh, come here, you silly girl . . ." He took a step towards her, and she backed off as if facing a rabid dog.

"Stay away from me, Josh!"

He raised both hands in submission, frowning now.

"All right, all right! What in the world has got into you? Last night —"

"Don't mention last night!" She was trembling now, and the colour was hot in her cheeks. "Don't ever mention it! I don't know what got into me! Well, I do . . . the drink . . . but to do what I did . . . Oh!" She broke off, covering her mouth with her hands. "What must you think of me?" she whispered from behind her splayed fingers. "And Jack. What would Jack think if he knew? Letting myself down like that? Letting you . . . What if he does know? What if he was watching us?"

"Oh Maggie, love . . ."

"No, what if he was?"

"Maggie, Jack is dead," he said gently.

"But his spirit's still alive. He could be here, right now, looking down . . . What would he *think?* He'd be so hurt, Josh. So hurt!"

The tears were coming now; her throat was thick with them.

"Oh Maggie, don't torture yourself like this," Josh groaned.

"Why not? Isn't it what I deserve? And you? Don't you feel the least bit guilty? Betraying him like that? Taking advantage of me?"

Something of what she said struck a nerve.

"Dammit, you wanted it as much as I did," Josh growled, thrown suddenly on the defensive.

"Don't try to put the blame on me!" Maggie flashed. The tears were flowing now, running down her cheeks and trickling between her fingers, tears of guilt and grief and shame.

"Oh Maggie, don't cry!" Josh said helplessly. "All right . . . it was my fault. I should have realised you didn't know what you were doing. But you can only push a man so far, and the way I feel about you . . . you're more than flesh and blood can stand, Maggie. These last few weeks — well, I thought you felt the same way. Seems I was mistaken, and if it wasn't what you wanted, then I'm sorry."

For a long moment she stood motionless as his words sank in, then slowly she raised her eyes, still sparkling with tears, looking at him over the tips of her fingers.

"Oh Josh . . ."

She didn't need to say any more; it was there, written all over her face. Josh experienced a jolt of elation. He hadn't been mistaken. She did feel as he did. Then she started sobbing again.

"But it's wrong! So wrong! How can I want you so much when Jack's scarcely cold in his grave? How can I feel like that? We were going to be married. Married! And yet I never . . ." She broke off, unable to say those final words of betrayal: that for all their closeness, she had never wanted Jack as she had wanted Josh last night — as, in spite of everything, she still wanted him. Even now, mortified as she was at what had happened, her treacherous heart was aching for Josh, her body crying out for the comfort of his touch.

"I am a wicked, wicked woman," she whispered, and the tears began again.

"Maggie, don't, please!" He came towards her again, and this time she didn't back away. He put his arms around her and she laid her head against his chest, sobbing softly, not really knowing any more why she was crying except that the weight within her was too great to bear.

At last her sobs quietened to hiccups and the tears slowed and stopped. As she lifted her face, he scrabbled in his pocket for his handkerchief.

"Here . . ."

She dried her eyes, blew her nose, thrust the handkerchief back at him.

"You'd better take it this time, or you won't have any left."

He gave her a puzzled look, and she sniffed a wry half-laugh.

"The one you lent me before. I've still got it. Under my pillow. How stupid is that? I just . . . like it being there."

He smiled. "You can have every handkerchief I own if that's what you want."

"Oh — just one's enough."

He brushed that stray lock that never would behave away from her cheek, let his fingers caress the lobe of her ear, slide down to stroke her neck.

"Better now?"

She nodded. "Mm. My head's still pounding a bit, though."

"I'm not surprised. It will go soon, I promise. Come and sit down, sweetheart."

278

He sat down himself in Rose's armchair and pulled her on to his lap.

"So — what are we going to do?"

"What do you mean?" Maggie asked, puzzled.

"About us. I want you, Maggie, and I think you want me."

At his words it all came rushing back: the guilt, the shame — and the despair.

"There's nothing we can do, is there? Not with things the way they are. It would be an insult to Jack's memory if we . . ." Her voice tailed off miserably.

Josh was silent, not knowing how to counter her argument. He wanted to say that Jack wouldn't want Maggie to mourn him for ever. That he'd want her to find happiness — the happiness that Josh believed they could share. But he couldn't find the words. It would simply sound as if he was chasing his own selfish ends.

"What would people say?" Maggie went on distractedly. "Oh, I don't care about myself. I've learned not to take much notice, although it isn't always easy. But I do care that they don't think Jack can be forgotten so easily. Because he can't. He never will be."

"Of course he won't be forgotten. But —"

"But it would look to other people as if he had been. As if we didn't care. You must see that, surely? I can't just take up with someone else, not now, not yet. And especially not his own brother. It makes a mockery of what we had. Besides . . ." Maggie hesitated, biting her lip, "to be honest, I'm not sure I'm ready. It's too soon. This morning I felt so guilty, not just about what we did, but about the way I feel. I just hated myself. I can't live like that, Josh. Do you understand?"

He shrugged helplessly. This was all getting too complicated for him. Josh was a simple man who didn't go into things too deeply.

"All I know is that I want you, Maggie, and I think you want me. That's what really matters."

"But it wouldn't be right. And I don't just mean what other people would think. If I feel this guilty now, how much worse would it be if we were openly courting? What if every time we . . . well, you know . . . did what we did last night, all I can think about is that I'm betraying Jack? You'll get angry with me, and I'll hate myself, and it would spoil everything. You must see — I just can't do it, Josh. Not yet, not for a long while yet."

Josh felt deflated, but he could see that pressurising Maggie just now would do no good.

"All right, we'll take it slowly," he said.

"No." Maggie wriggled out of his arms and stood up, crossing the kitchen, then turning to face him. Her lips were a tight, determined line. "That won't work either. We've got to stop seeing each other. It's the only way."

"For goodness' sake, Maggie, this is ridiculous!" he exploded.

"Look, to begin with, however discreet we might be, people will find out. They will! They're not stupid. They saw us at the dance together last night. They'll see you coming here; they'll put two and two together. Your mam and dad especially, and that would be bound to upset them. And being secretive about it somehow makes it all the worse. It just goes to prove we have something to be ashamed of. We'd be the talk of the town before long, just as much as if we were open about it."

"Oh Maggie . . ."

"And then there's the other thing." Hot colour flooded her cheeks. "What we did last night. That can't happen again. It mustn't."

"What if I promise to make sure it doesn't?"

Even as he said it, Josh was wondering if he'd be able to find the strength to control himself when they were alone, and Maggie, clearly, was thinking the same thing.

"That's easier said than done." She wiped her damp palms on her skirt. "If we're here, on our own — what was it you said just now? 'More than flesh and blood can stand'? No, the only way is to stop seeing one another altogether until . . . well, at least until there's a decent interval and I don't feel I'm being unfaithful to Jack just being with you, let alone anything else."

Josh's dismay came out on a snort.

"And will you ever feel that?"

Maggie bowed her head.

"I honestly don't know. I'm sorry. All I can tell you is how I feel right now."

"Well if that's how you feel, I suppose there's nothing more to be said." His tone was aggressive; he wasn't going to let her see how much her rejection was hurting him.

He strode to the door, looked back just once, perhaps hoping that she might relent even now. But her mouth was set in a firm line though he could see tears glistening again on her lashes.

"I'm sorry, Josh," was all she said.

There had to be a way. Dammit, there had to be!

Josh had thought of nothing else for days, and it was driving him crazy. He'd drunk too much and slept too little, he was in the foulest of tempers, and each time he caught sight of Maggie, his gut wrenched and the blood raced in his veins.

All very well to have salvaged his dignity by walking away from her as if he'd accepted her decision and didn't care too much about it. The truth was, he couldn't stand being so close to her and yet so distant. If she was going to refuse to see him, he had to get away. But where? Not that it really mattered, just as long as he wasn't confronted daily with a tantalising glimpse of the woman who'd stolen his heart, his senses, his every waking thought.

He'd leave High Compton. He'd worry about her constantly, he knew, but it was the only way he could hold on to his pride and his sanity. He had a trade — surely he'd be able to find work as a carpenter pretty well anywhere? Wales, perhaps? He knew folk there, and could stay with his aunt and uncle until he found permanent lodgings. But their farm was in a remote spot, and besides, he could imagine his aunt asking too many questions that he didn't want to answer. Explaining to his mother and father why he was going away would be bad enough; there was no way he was going to admit to the truth.

282

Josh turned the possibilities over endlessly, and eventually came to a decision. He'd go to Bristol; Bristol was a busy port and he was confident he'd be able to find work there. It also had the advantage of being only fifteen or sixteen miles from High Compton, far enough to be well out of Maggie's way, but not so far that he couldn't get back if there was a family crisis — or if she needed him. And who knew? Maybe when he'd got a job and sorted out somewhere to live, she'd join him. She might feel less guilty about marrying him if they weren't under the noses of the people who knew she'd been engaged to Jack.

Marry him! Josh smiled to himself. He'd never so much as considered marriage before; now the thought of it came as easily to him as breathing. He wanted to marry her — nothing less would do. And the best way to achieve that was a fresh start for both of them, far from the scene of the tragedy and the people who mourned, out of sight of the black batches that were a constant reminder of the sacrifices of those who toiled far beneath the green fields.

Perhaps he'd ask her before he left. He couldn't see her accepting here and now, but at least she'd be left in no doubt about his feelings for her, and time might change her mind where he could not.

On the Sunday morning exactly two weeks after their last encounter, he decided to take the bull by the horns. Sunday was the one day he could be sure of finding her at home and Billy at work, the one day he could talk to her without fear of interruption. If she'd talk to him at all. She might well slam the door in his face . . .

Tension was a tight knot in his chest as he walked down the track. Josh, who took most things in his stride, admitted to himself that he had never felt more nervous in his life.

Maggie was making a stew. Cold and murky weather had set in and comfort food was called for. A good big pot of scrag end beef and vegetables would last for days, ready to be warmed up when she got home, chilled to the marrow and perhaps wet through, after a hard day's work, and ready for Billy too if Farmer Barton's wife hadn't already fed him.

She'd found planning meals a chore these last two weeks; she seemed to have no energy or enthusiasm for anything, really. A shroud of depression had settled around her, thick and persistent as the fog that descended each evening — so dense it was difficult to see even the outhouses on the other side of the track, never mind the end of the rank — and sometimes lingered, grey and moist, most of the day. Maggie, usually sunny-natured and optimistic, felt trapped and miserable. After all the terrible things that had happened, she'd glimpsed joy and fulfilment beyond her wildest dreams, but that was all it could be, a glimpse, and even that had been spoiled by the feelings of guilt she couldn't ignore. What hope was there for her, torn between that guilt and her longing for Josh? None whatever, really. She was trapped between her conscience and her heart; she could see no way out, and it was a bad place to be.

It had been all she could do to summon the energy to begin making the stew, but now the beef was beginning to come to a simmer on the trivet over the fire, the carrots were peeled and cut up ready to pop in, and she was skinning the onions, which were already beginning to make her eyes sting. She blinked hard in an effort to keep them from running, but she knew she was fighting a losing battle. Before long, tears would be streaming down her cheeks and she'd barely be able to see what she was doing.

She tutted when she heard the knock at the door; she just wanted to get the job in hand over and done with. She put down her knife, and with the onion still in her hand went to see who was there and what they wanted.

As she opened the door and saw Josh standing on the step, her heart lurched, and her hand tightened over the half-peeled onion.

"Oh!" For the moment, no other words would come.

"Maggie, I have to talk to you," Josh said. "Can I come in?"

"No! No, you can't!" Conflicting joy and dismay made her begin to tremble; really these days her nerves were so dreadfully on edge. "You know . . . we agreed."

"I didn't agree to anything," Josh stated baldly.

"You shouldn't be here." Maggie tried to close the door, but his foot was in the way. "Josh, please . . ."

"Would you rather I said what I've come to say out here, where all the world can get an earful?"

"Oh — you are impossible!"

Beaten, Maggie opened the door. She didn't want anyone seeing him coming into the house when she was alone, but neither did she want to have an argument with him on the door-step. In a close-knit terrace like this one, there was little privacy, and though not everyone was as nosy as Hester Dallimore, they didn't miss much.

Josh came into the scullery and closed the door behind him. Suddenly she was aware of him with every fibre of her being. It was exactly what she was afraid of, that the nearness of him would make her weaken; lure her, before she could save herself, into doing something she'd very quickly come to regret.

She put the onion down on the cupboard top, wiping her hands on her long wraparound apron.

"Let's go in the kitchen."

There was more room in the kitchen; she wouldn't be forced into such close proximity to him as in the cramped scullery. But it was also the very place where they'd —

Maggie cut off the memory. It horrified her, and yet it could still make her glow with remembered warmth. She and Josh on the rug in front of the fire, limbs entwined, bodies united. The glory of it. The contentment. And the shame.

"Just say what you've come to say and go," she said shortly.

"Oh, for goodness' sake, Maggie!" Josh exploded. "I'm not about to ravish you again, much as I might want to."

The hot colour rushed to her cheeks. *I want it too! Oh, you have no idea how much!*

"That's all right then," she heard herself say instead. "Just as long as —"

"What do you take me for?" he demanded. Though he'd intended to keep his cool whatever her response, his defences were coming up and making him sound aggressive again. "The only reason I'm here is because I've decided to go away. I thought I ought to tell you, and make sure you're all right before I leave."

It was something else that had been preying on his mind; he didn't think it was likely Maggie would have fallen pregnant as a result of that one night of passion, but you never could be sure. His meaning was lost on Maggie, though; she'd heard only one thing, and her heart seemed to have stopped beating.

"You're going away? Where?"

"Bristol, I thought. I'm sure I can get a job there, better paid, too. I just thought you ought to know."

"But why, Josh?" Maggie felt as if her world was falling apart around her.

"I can't stay here with things as they are. It's driving me crazy."

"But I don't want you to go!" she said before she could stop herself.

He shook his head ruefully.

"You can't have it both ways, Maggie. You've made it pretty clear that there's no hope for us for the foreseeable future, and it seems to me it would be a darned sight easier for both of us if I was out of the way."

"But . . . *Bristol!*" To Maggie, it felt as if he was proposing to fly to the moon.

Distractedly she rubbed her eyes, and instantly the onion juice on her fingers was stinging, making her wince and squeeze them tight. "Oh, blooming onions!"

Josh didn't know whether to be grateful for the distraction. He was confused by the mixed messages Maggie was sending him. In one breath she was telling him she didn't want to so much as speak to him; in the next she was seemingly horrified by the idea of him moving away.

It was now or never, he decided.

"You could always come with me," he said, quite flippantly.

Her squinting eyes appeared over the top of the back of her wrist.

"What are you talking about?"

"Come to Bristol with me. Nobody there knows us. It would be a fresh start. Oh, for goodness' sake, don't look so shocked, Maggie. I'm not trying to turn you into a scarlet woman. I'm asking you to marry me." There. He'd said it.

All the breath seemed to leave Maggie's body in a rush and her mouth dropped open.

"Marry you!"

"Is it such a daft idea?"

Maggie's pulses were racing. She could not imagine anything more wonderful. But she was totally stunned by Josh's proposal. It wasn't as if they'd been courting properly; he'd taken her out only the once. In any case, Josh had never seemed to her to be the marrying type — quite the opposite. What could have brought it on?

288

Was he feeling guilty because of what had happened between them?

"A daft idea? Well, yes, it is really," she said, more curtly than she meant to. "Given the way things are."

His ready defences were up.

"In that case, I'm sorry I asked." His tone, too, was short, belying what this meant to him. "But seeing as I'm going away, I thought . . ." He turned for the door.

"You thought what? That you'd better offer to make an honest woman of me?" she shot after him. "That's very commendable of you, but it's really not necessary."

"That's all right then." He was in the scullery now, his hand on the door latch. "I won't bother you again, don't worry."

Maggie's heart was pounding in her throat. This was all happening too fast.

"Josh, please don't go, please . . . not like this."

He turned back, and beneath the hard lines of his face she could see the hurt, clearly written. This wasn't just a proposal to save her honour; he'd asked her to marry him because it was what he wanted. He wasn't a man for flowery sentiments. They came no more easily to him than they had to Jack; perhaps even less so. But that didn't mean they didn't come from the heart.

"There's nothing I'd like better than to marry you, Josh," she said. "But I can't, don't you see? Not now. Not like this. We've been through it all before. You know how I feel. It's all very well to say that no one in Bristol would know about me and Jack, but people here would find out, they'd be bound to. Your mam and dad for a start. You can't keep something like that quiet.

Besides, I'd know, and I can't do it yet, I just can't. It feels all wrong, and it's no way to start a life together."

He grimaced.

"Fair enough. I more or less knew what you'd say, but I thought it was worth a try. I know it's still Jack with you."

"You're wrong. You couldn't be more wrong!" *I love you!* she wanted to say, but she couldn't bring herself to.

"Well that's how it seems from here," he said ruefully. "We look alike pretty much, so I'm the closest you could get to having him back."

"No!" But how could she explain that she had never felt this way about Jack without doing the very thing she was trying so hard not to do — denigrate his memory? "It's not that at all!"

"Then come with me. Marry me." It was one last desperate throw of the dice.

"Oh Josh . . ." Maggie felt as if she was being torn in two. "I've tried to explain that I can't, not yet, and if you don't understand, I don't know what else I can say. In any case, I couldn't just up sticks and leave. There's Billy to think of. I can't abandon him — you know what he's like."

"Your mam will be coming home soon, surely?"

"I don't know . . . it hasn't been mentioned yet. But even if she did, she's still not a well woman. She'd need a lot of looking after herself."

"Seems to me," he said, "you're looking for excuses."

"They're not excuses — they're reasons!"

"Well, call it what you like. It comes to the same thing in the end. You don't want to come to Bristol with me."

Maggie was tired of arguing, of saying the same thing over and over again.

"I can't, Josh," she said simply.

He nodded.

"That's that, then." He opened the door, turned back. "When I've sorted out somewhere to stay, I'll write and let you have an address so you know where to find me if you want to."

And he was gone. Maggie felt that her heart was breaking, but what choice did she have? She covered her face with her hands, and this time it was not just the onion juice on her fingers that brought the ready tears.

CHAPTER
SEVENTEEN

Later, much later, when there was no escaping the reality of what was happening, Maggie couldn't understand how she had managed to avoid it for so long. Hadn't Josh hinted at the possibility that last Sunday morning when he'd come to tell her he was going to Bristol? But she'd been so confused that day, desperate to tell him how much she wanted him, how much she'd love to marry him, but unable to find the words; torn apart by her longing for him and her loyalty to Jack. She'd been overwhelmed by her emotions and by the responsibility she felt to her own family, and the possible consequences of their night of passion had passed her by.

She had been a little anxious a few weeks later when she realised she hadn't had a period for a while, although she wasn't sure just when it was due — she had too many other things on her mind to remember exact dates, and certainly no time to make a note of them. She had niggly little pains in her stomach, which she hoped meant her period was about to start, and she felt a bit queasy, but she put that down to getting herself in a bit of a stew, as her mother would have described her state of constant anxiety. And then she had a little bleed, lighter and for a shorter time than normal, but undoubtedly fresh blood, and, relieved, she'd thought that everything was going to be all right.

She had made a note of the date this time, but there were few spare minutes to think about it. With Christmas fast approaching, Freeman's was very busy, and it was often late in the evening before she could leave. Besides this, Ewart had written to say that he was bringing Rose home for Christmas. She still really wasn't well, but she was insistent that it was what she wanted. They would travel down the day before Christmas Eve and he'd stay over for the festivities.

Though she was looking forward to seeing her mother again, Maggie couldn't help worrying as to how she'd manage if Rose needed a lot of looking after. She was concerned too that Rose might think she'd let things slide in her absence, and when she got home from work each evening, dog tired, she set herself the task of giving every room in the house a thorough clean. She made the beds up with clean sheets, and even bought dried fruit to make two Christmas puddings and set them to boil in the copper.

No wonder she was feeling under the weather, she thought when she got up one morning vaguely nauseous and a little faint. And still it didn't occur to her, until she was having a good strip wash at the scullery sink — much easier than carrying hot water upstairs to the jug and basin in her bedroom when Billy was at work and she had the house to herself — and realised her breasts felt tender. Strange! She didn't ever remember them being tender before. She glanced down and was shocked to see the nipples standing out like soldiers at attention and the areolas around them dark against her pale skin.

It must be the poor light here in the scullery, she thought; on these dark December mornings, very little filtered in through the small window. But when she went upstairs to dress, she looked again, carrying the free-standing mirror from her chest of drawers to the window, and this time there was no mistaking it. They *were* different, the usual rosy pink darkened to a dark reddish brown.

The first flutters of alarm stirred in Maggie. No! It couldn't be, surely? She'd had the curse last month, hadn't she? But it had been very light, only a couple of soiled towels rather than the outpouring she usually experienced . . .

Panicked, she searched for the old envelope she'd used to note down the date, failed to find it, and instead tried to remember something that would peg the date the bleed had begun. She'd still been anxiously awaiting it on Bonfire Night — she remembered the smoke hanging heavy in the foggy air as she crossed the track to the privy hoping to find that she'd started. But she'd thought everything was all right by her birthday, which she always celebrated on 12 November, though no one was exactly sure whether that was the correct day or not, and of course, with only Billy for company, there had been no celebration at all this year.

So — Maggie consulted her mother's Old Moore's Almanac — that meant she was late again.

294

Her stomach seemed to fall away, and though she tried to persuade herself otherwise, Maggie knew the truth with a conviction that refused to be denied. The evidence was all there; she could ignore it no longer.

Pregnant. A hot tide of horror suffused her. This couldn't be happening! But it was. In all her life, she didn't think she'd ever felt more frightened or alone.

It was a nightmare she couldn't wake up from, the last thing she thought of at night and the first thing in the morning, and it hung over her in a dark cloud every minute of the day.

Though she still clung desperately to the hope that the curse would come as it had last month, in her heart she knew it would not. That little bleed had just been some sort of hiccup in the scheme of things, perhaps the start of a miscarriage that hadn't, in the end, happened. Maggie took a bath, as hot as she could stand it, in the hope of setting things off again; she drank gin and swallowed syrup of figs, but the gin only made her violently sick and the syrup of figs kept her running to the privy all the next day, and still there was no sign of a bleed.

In a strange sort of way she was almost glad. The baby growing inside her was Josh's baby, and the thought of losing it through her own actions was something that made her shrink inwardly. As for seeking out someone who could use more certain methods to get rid of it, she never considered such a thing for a moment. It was against all the tenets of the Catholic church, which were ingrained in her though it was a long time since she'd attended Mass regularly, and besides, she'd heard it could be very dangerous.

But what was she going to do? Oh, if only Josh were still here! If only she'd agreed to go with him as he'd asked, at least she wouldn't have to flaunt the evidence of her betrayal of Jack in front of all the folk who'd known him. But now . . . was it too late? Did Josh still want her? Or had he moved on, building a new life that didn't include her? Maggie had the most awful feeling that that might be the case.

She'd received just one letter from him since he had left, giving the address of the house in Bristol where he'd found lodgings, and since then nothing. Unsurprising, really, since she'd decided not to reply, but she'd kept the letter, folded neatly beneath a stack of handkerchiefs in the top drawer of her tallboy. She got it out now, though she knew it almost by heart, spread it out on the kitchen table and fetched writing paper and pen.

For a long while she pondered what she should say, and even then it took three attempts before she was satisfied.

Dear Josh.

I hope this finds you well. Something awful has happened and I really need to talk to you. Are you coming home for Christmas? Do you think you could, even if you weren't planning to? It's really important.

Please write soon.

I remain, your ever-loving Maggie.

She posted the letter and waited impatiently for Josh's reply.

None came.

Rose and Ewart arrived as planned on the day before Christmas Eve. Maggie was unable to meet them, as the drapery shop was open until late, but she arranged for Fred Carson to be there with his pony and trap — Rose would be far too tired after the long journey to walk all the way from the station to the Ten Houses, she knew. But Billy, finishing work earlier now that it was dark by four o'clock, was able to make it, and rode home sitting beside Fred, with Rose and Ewart and their luggage piled in behind.

Maggie had left a plate of cold cuts and a pan of potatoes peeled and ready to be boiled, and by the time she got home, the others had eaten. But Rose had a plate of mash and cabbage keeping warm for her over a saucepan of simmering water on the trivet, and the table was laid with pickles and chutney, just as it would have been when she was late home from work in the old days.

"Mam!" Maggie hugged her mother, realising with a shock just how thin Rose had become. Why, she was little more than skin and bone! "Oh Mam, I've missed you so much! It's so lovely to have you home! But you haven't been eating properly, have you? What have you done with her, Ewart? She's as skinny as a rake!"

"Oh, I've no appetite these days," Rose said. "It's not Ewart's fault, or Walter's. They've been looking after me very well. Though I must say it's nice to be back in my own kitchen."

She held Maggie away, regarding her critically.

"You don't look so good yourself, my girl. Have you been overdoing things?"

Maggie's stomach contracted. She was dreading having to admit the truth to Rose, and this was not the moment.

"I'm fine, Mam," she said. "I've just been really busy, that's all."

"Well, you've kept everything nice, I must say. Now, come and have your tea before it spoils."

Bullseye was standing beside the table, nose raised and twitching expectantly.

"You've still got that darned dog, I see," she added tartly, lifting the lid from the plate and setting it down in the place that was laid ready for Maggie.

"And you're still as stubborn as ever when it comes to taking things easy," Maggie returned.

"Yes, well. Eat up now."

The trouble was, Maggie had no appetite whatsoever; hadn't had since she'd realised the awful truth about her condition. But she made a heroic effort anyway. She didn't want Mam or Ewart to suspect anything was wrong — not yet, anyway.

"Is Cathy still working at the shop with you?" Ewart asked as Maggie cut ham into small, manageable pieces and forked up mashed potato.

Maggie managed a smile.

"Oh yes, and she's very excited that you're home. I suppose you'll be seeing her while you're here?"

"I certainly hope so. She's a little cracker, your apprentice." Ewart, who had been sprawled in the chair in front of the fire, got up. "Well, now that you're home, our Maggie, I think I'll go up and catch up with Josh."

Maggie's heart lurched.

"I don't think you'll find him at home, Ewart. He's gone to Bristol to live."

"Gone to Bristol?" Ewart repeated, staggered. "What do you mean?"

The potato was going round and round in Maggie's mouth; she simply couldn't swallow it.

"He left — oh, it must be a couple of months ago. He wanted a change, I suppose."

"You *have* taken me by surprise!" Ewart scratched his head. "Well, I think I'll go up anyway, see if he's coming home for Christmas. If not, they're sure to have an address for him. I wouldn't want to lose touch."

Maggie lowered her eyes and said nothing. She didn't want to admit that she had an address — Ewart would wonder how she came by it, and why. Besides, Josh's family might have more up-to-date news, and she too was anxious to know whether he was coming home for Christmas. It could be that he was, and that was the reason he hadn't replied to her letter. She couldn't imagine he was much of a letter-writer, and if he'd thought he'd see her in person, he might well have put it off.

But she knew she was clutching at straws. Really it didn't bode well that he hadn't put pen to paper, and Maggie couldn't avoid the horrible feeling that he'd guessed exactly what it was she wanted to talk to him about and had decided he'd rather not know.

Ewart was back almost before she'd finished her tea, and she steeled herself not to appear too eager to find out what he'd learned, leaving it to Rose to ask.

"Well, he's not coming for Christmas as far as they know," Ewart told her. "But at least I've got an address for him — in Totterdown, wherever that is."

"Totterdown! That doesn't sound like much of a place," Rose commented, but Maggie found a small crumb in the fact that the address she had was in Totterdown too. At least Josh hadn't moved on and failed to let her know. But the news that he wasn't expected home for Christmas made her heart sink. She so desperately needed to talk to him; she didn't know how she could cope with the situation on her own.

She felt the now-familiar stirrings of panic, and tried to ignore them. She'd just have to get through the festive season, and then decide what to do. But it wasn't going to be easy. Oh, it wasn't going to be easy at all.

In houses all over High Compton, families were preparing for Christmas. Kitchens and parlours were decorated with freshly cut holly — "The blooming birds have had most of the berries this year!" Peggy Bishop complained as she stuck the best sprigs she'd been able to find behind the pictures that hung on her kitchen walls — and bunches of mistletoe were suspended in doorways. The Hillmans had a Christmas tree in their parlour that reached almost to the ceiling,

300

and a goose in the larder on the cold slab. Maggie unwrapped the cloth that she'd tied over one of her puddings so that her mother could poke it with a skewer and make sure it was done in the middle — Rose didn't totally trust her to have boiled it for long enough — but the skewer came out clean except for a few soggy raisins. And Rose sniffed the pudding and pronounced it a job well done.

"I know it won't be like yours, Mam," Maggie said apologetically as she tied a fresh piece of string around the cloth her mother was holding in place over the top of the basin. "It wasn't made early enough, for one thing."

"We had other things to think about when we should have been making puddings," Rose said. "We'll have one for Christmas Day and put the other one in the larder for next year. It'll be all the better for keeping."

Then her eyes misted as she looked at the chair Paddy had used to occupy, empty now.

"Who'd have thought it?" she said sadly. "Who'd have ever thought last Christmas that it was going to be your father's last? And all those others too . . . However must they all be feeling? I can't understand how Josh Withers could have gone off and left his mam and dad like that when he's the only one they've got now, and not so much as come home to see them on the day. And what about all those little children without a father this year? It doesn't bear thinking about."

Maggie said nothing. She'd seen little Lucy Day staring forlornly out of the window of number four when she'd passed on her way home from work, and could only guess at what a miserable Christmas she would have with her father gone and her mother barely holding herself together. There wouldn't be any spare money for little presents or good things to eat either, with the breadwinner gone and Sir Montague pressing for increased rent on the house. Maggie had managed to find the extra, though it had meant she'd had to buy a boiling fowl for Christmas dinner instead of the cockerel she'd planned on, and the fruit and nuts they usually treated themselves to had had to stay in the shop. But at least she was in work — for the moment, anyway, though what would happen when she started to show, she didn't dare think about.

"Well, we'll just have to make the best of it," Rose went on, pulling herself together. "At least our Ewart's here, and that'll be nice, and I've got you and our Billy too. And that blooming dog!" she added.

Bullseye was lurking beneath the kitchen table, and Maggie knew the reason why. She'd taken to feeding him covertly, bits from her plate that she just couldn't stomach but didn't want to leave to invite comment from her mother. Even now Rose was studying her closely and frowning.

"Are you all right, Maggie? You look a bit peaky to me."

"I'm just tired, I expect," Maggie said. "You know what it's like in the shop at this time of year."

"And you've had everything to do here too," Rose said. "Well, I'm home now, and you'll be able to take it a bit easier."

"Mam, you're not well yourself, remember."

"There's nothing wrong with me," Rose said shortly, and Maggie thought ruefully that they were both good liars.

Christmas Day passed in a haze of unreality. Ewart had brought presents for them all: a brooch for Maggie, slippers for Rose — "to go with that new dressing gown," he said — and a bright spotted neckerchief for Billy.

"Oh Ewart, you shouldn't have!" Maggie said, unwrapping the delicate porcelain oval set in a make-believe gold surround. "I haven't got anything for you. I just haven't had time to go to the shops."

But to her surprise, Billy went upstairs to his room and returned with small packages that he handed round — tobacco for Ewart, who had taken to smoking a pipe, and sweets for Maggie and Rose, all bought from his meagre wages. He also had a marrowbone for Bullseye, who fell on it eagerly and had to be pushed outside where he could gnaw on it to his heart's content without leaving grease and bone splinters all over the kitchen floor.

There was an extra parcel in Ewart's bag, Maggie noticed, which he'd made no attempt to give to any of them.

"Who's that for then, Ewart?" she asked, though she had a pretty fair idea.

Ewart flushed a little and folded the bag over the little parcel.

"Never you mind, Miss Nosy-Poke."

"I can guess. You can't fool me. You'll be going out later to see a certain young lady, if I'm not much mistaken."

"I might be," Ewart admitted, and grinned. "Don't suppose she'll want to come out tonight, but there's always tomorrow." He sighed. "And then I suppose I shall have to be heading home."

Home. It still jarred with Maggie that he referred to Yorkshire now as home instead of Somerset.

"Why don't you move back here?" she suggested.

It was a vain hope, she knew, but she couldn't help the irrational feeling that somehow, if Ewart was here instead of miles away, things wouldn't seem quite so bad.

That hope was quickly dashed.

"Back to Somerset and the conditions here?" Ewart said scathingly. "I wouldn't want to do that. No, I'm far better off in Yorkshire. Our Walter would tell you the same. Oh, Cathy's a nice girl. I like her a lot. But not so much that I'd come back to this hellhole."

"And I wouldn't want you to," Rose said. "Look what happened to your father and all the others."

"Accidents can happen anywhere." Maggie was clutching at straws, and she knew it.

"That's true enough," Ewart conceded, "but there's nothing here but faulted seams, and buggers like Fairley. Look at Josh: he's gone off further afield, and he wasn't even down the bloody pit."

Maggie lowered her eyes. Without blurting out the truth, there was no way she could tell Ewart that Josh's leaving had nothing whatever to do with the work to be found in High Compton, and she was nowhere near ready to do that.

Ewart left the day after Boxing Day.

"Are you sure you're not coming with me, Mam?" he asked, and Rose assured him she was perfectly sure.

"I couldn't be doing with a long journey like that again so soon," she said, and it was true, she did look very tired.

To Maggie's knowledge, Ewart had seen Cathy twice, and had been very late coming home the previous evening. Under normal circumstances she would have been looking forward to seeing her assistant when she returned to work the following day to find out her side of the story, but as things were, she had far too much on her mind to give it a second thought.

She absolutely had to decide what she was going to do. Though she thought her waist looked a little thicker and her breasts a little fuller when she checked her reflection in the mirror, that might be just her imagination; certainly the casual observer wouldn't notice any difference. But it wouldn't be long, certainly not more than another couple of months, before she would no longer be able to hide it, however tightly she laced her corset.

Her mind ran in frantic circles, but always it came back to the same thing.

Josh. She had to talk things over with Josh. Had to know whether he would be prepared to stand by her. She could write again and be more explicit this time, she supposed, but she couldn't abide the thought of more weeks of waiting for a letter that didn't come.

In desperation, she came to a momentous decision that both scared and excited her.

She would go to Bristol in person, find the address he'd sent her, which must be correct seeing as he'd given his parents exactly the same one, and speak to him face to face.

Daunting though the prospect was for a girl who had scarcely set foot outside of High Compton, for the first time in weeks Maggie felt that at least she was taking control of her dire situation.

CHAPTER
EIGHTEEN

The house was tall and narrow, one of a terrace, but totally unlike the terrace that was the Ten Houses.

Maggie paused to catch her breath. After the steep climb up the hill from the railway station, it had taken her forever to find the right place, asking passers-by and even a rag-and-bone man for directions. But this was it. Now all she had to do was walk along the street and look at the numbers on the doors.

Her heart pounded, and not just from her exertions. Would Josh be at home? She'd chosen a Sunday as the most likely day to find him in, but there was no guarantee. And if he was, how would he react to seeing her on the doorstep, and to what she had to tell him? *How* was she going to tell him, even? On the train journey to Bristol, she'd run over and over it in her head, but still she wasn't sure it would come out right. And however she put it, the news was bound to come as a dreadful shock to him. Maggie shrank from the dismay she could imagine seeing on his face, and worse . . . Supposing he turned her away without even discussing it? What would she do then? She'd have to go home, admit to Mam that the excuse she'd made about spending the day with Cathy was a lie, and tell her the truth that she wasn't going to be able to conceal for much longer.

Pull yourself together, she told herself. *You've come this far, you can't give up now.*

But her heart was still pounding, and the nerves fluttering in her stomach were making her feel far more sick than the nausea she sometimes experienced in the mornings.

She started along the street, checking house numbers as she went. It was far from deserted: a lad bowling a hoop almost cannoned into her, and on the pavement, children, well wrapped up against the cold winds of early January, played hopscotch in squares they had marked out with a chalky stone. Outside one house an old man squatted collier-style smoking a pipe; from an upstairs window a woman called to one of the children that dinner was ready.

Maggie found the house she was looking for, swallowed hard at the nervous lump that had formed in her throat, and knocked at the door.

It was less well kept than its neighbours, she noticed, green paint peeling away to reveal a muddy brown beneath; the knocker and doorknob didn't look as if they'd been polished in a while, and the curtains at the window were greyish and grubby rather than the white lace they had once been.

Maggie waited a moment, then knocked again, desperately hoping she hadn't come all this way only to find no one at home, and anxiously listening for some sound of life within.

"He's probably down the boozer, love." She turned quickly to see a short, rotund woman in the doorway of the house next door. "He's always down the boozer of a Sunday dinner time. That's if it's Albie you want. Or if it's Cissie, you're out of luck there too."

So — the neighbours here could be just as nosy as they were in High Compton.

"No, I was looking for —" Maggie got no further, for she heard a bolt being drawn on the inside of the door she'd been knocking at.

"It's all right, there is someone home," she said quickly, and the rotund woman retreated a little, though Maggie was sure she'd keep her own door ajar so as to listen and satisfy her curiosity.

The door scraped open and Maggie found herself face to face with a giant of a man, so tall and broad he filled the narrow doorway. A head of unkempt hair and a full beard obscured much of his face; a calico shirt was open to the waist revealing a none-too-clean undershirt, which was, mercifully, buttoned to the neck. Braces dangled from their fastenings, allowing his trousers to hang low beneath an ample belly.

Albie, she assumed. Not the sort of man you'd want to meet in an alleyway on a dark night!

"Mr . . . um . . ." she began nervously, though she had no idea of what his second name might be.

"Who wants him?" The tone was belligerent, and he was squinting at her as if the pale January sun was hurting his eyes.

"Actually, I'm looking for Josh Withers," Maggie said, taking her courage in both hands. "He lodges here, I think."

The man grunted and swore — a word Maggie had never heard before, but which she knew instinctively was incredibly vulgar.

She bit her lip, striving to maintain her dignity.

"I have got the right house, have I?"

"Ah, you've got the right house, but you won't find 'im here no more," the man said shortly. "He's gone — and my missus too — and good riddance to the pair of them."

Maggie's mouth fell open.

"What do you mean?"

"What d'you bloody well think I mean? They run off together, didn't they? And don't ask me where, 'cos I don't know and don't care. So you might as well get on back to where you come from. All right?"

These statements were all peppered with expletives, and before she'd had time to take in what he was saying, let alone ask more, the door slammed shut in Maggie's face.

She stood staring at it stupidly, too shocked to move.

"Oh, he's a bad tempered bugger, that one."

Maggie had been right: the woman next door had been listening to every word. Now her door was fully open again and she was leaning against the frame, arms folded across her ample bosom.

"What he said's right, though," she went on. "If you're looking for that young chap that was lodging with them, you won't find him here. He's been gone now . . . oh, a couple of weeks before Christmas it must have been."

"And . . . that man's *wife*?" Maggie could barely string two words together.

"Seems that way. I couldn't tell you the ins and outs of it," the woman said regretfully. "All I know is Albie was working away — he's a ganger on the railway — and when he came home, he found them both gone. He's in a bit of a way about it, but I can't say as I blame Cissie. She's far too good for the likes of him, and that Josh is a handsome fellow."

She paused to take a wheezing breath, and then went on: "He'll have his work cut out with her, though. She's a bit of a one, is Cissie. He isn't the first lodger she's carried on with. There was another one a year or so back. Albie came home and caught them red-handed. Well — the to-do! You could hear it right through these walls. I thought they was going to end up killing one another. So I was real surprised, I can tell you, when he let one as young and good-looking as that Josh into the house. He should have known it was asking for trouble." She squinted at Maggie, mean little eyes bright in her doughy face like currants in a steamed suet duff. "You a friend of his, are you?"

Maggie didn't reply. She was still reeling in shock; all she wanted to do was get away from this dirty-looking house — how could Josh have lived here? — away from the belligerent cuckolded husband, and most of all, away from this horrible woman who was glorying in every detail of the scandal.

311

Grasping her bag tightly between both hands to keep them from trembling, she turned away and started back down the street. The view of the city from here was breathtaking, the river cutting a broad swathe through the valley, wooded hills rising beyond and the majestic sweep of the suspension bridge spanning it. But Maggie scarcely noticed.

Josh had run off with another man's wife. Though he'd never made any promises to her, it still hurt dreadfully. She could scarcely believe it, and yet it must be true. These people had no reason to lie to her.

In some ways, though, it wasn't so unbelievable. Josh had always been a rascal, in scrapes of one kind or another, and he'd always been irresistible to women. She'd dared to think that he had feelings for her, and perhaps he had, for a little while. But when she'd turned him down, it hadn't taken him long to look for pastures new. She'd had her chance and she'd thrown it away, and Josh had wasted no time in finding someone to take her place.

Hot tears stung Maggie's eyes as she made her way back down the steep hill to the railway station. What would she do now? She hadn't the faintest idea. But even so, frightened as she was at facing her problems alone, it was the thought of Josh with another woman that hurt the most.

Oh Josh, Josh!

The loss of his love — if love it had ever been — was a pain in her chest so sharp that she thought her heart was breaking.

312

"Is there something wrong, Maggie?" Augusta Freeman asked. "Something you'd like to share with me, perhaps?"

It was late February, cold, dark and wet, and business was slow, as it always was at this time of year. There'd been plenty of quiet moments for Augusta to observe Maggie, and she'd seen the change in her. Whereas usually Maggie was industrious, efficient and sociable, these last weeks she'd seemed preoccupied and withdrawn. And with her sharp eyes, used to assessing measurements as accurately as any tape, Augusta had noticed that Maggie's wasp waist had thickened, so that the waistband of her skirt strained around it, puckering into tiny pleats.

Augusta found it hard to believe that Maggie was the sort of girl to let herself down, but of course these things sometimes happened, and to the ones you'd least expect it of, whilst the tramps and trollops often got away with it. What really shocked her was that it was a good nine months since Jack had been killed, and if Maggie had behaved foolishly with him, the evidence would be far more obvious than this by now. That she should have gone with someone else was almost unthinkable — to Augusta's knowledge, she'd been mourning the loss of her fiancé and not so much as looked at another man. But as the days passed, her suspicions grew, and today she had decided it was time to say something about it.

Now, one look at the girl's face was enough to confirm her worst fears. Guilt and panic were written all over it, and her hands flew to that too-tight waistband.

"Oh Maggie!" Augusta said heavily. "We'd better go somewhere quiet and have that talk."

Maggie's shoulders slumped and her chin quivered, and Augusta sighed. This wasn't something she wanted to do; quite the opposite. But first and foremost she was a businesswoman, and fond as she was of Maggie, she couldn't let that make any difference.

As she led the way through the back of the shop into the living room of the house beyond, her mind was already made up. If Maggie confirmed what Augusta was certain she already knew, she would be left with no choice.

"You leave me no choice, Maggie," she said. "I have to give you notice, with immediate effect. I'll pay your wages up to the end of the week, but I'd prefer it if you didn't come in again.

"But I'm not showing yet." Maggie was close to tears. "I won't be for ages."

"I noticed, didn't I?" Augusta said tartly.

"If I was to tighten my corset . . ."

"And have you fainting in the shop? I don't think so, Maggie. And besides, there is the moral aspect to consider. How do you think Cathy's mother, or even Beat's, would feel about me allowing her to work with you?"

"They wouldn't catch it from me like the measles," Maggie blurted with a flash of her old spirit.

314

Augusta's lips tightened. "Cathy, especially, is a young and impressionable girl. Whilst you, I am afraid . . ." She closed her eyes and gave a sharp shake of the head, indicating her reluctance to put a name to the kind of woman Maggie had shown herself to be. "I have to think of the customers too," she went on. "And the good name of this establishment. I can't — won't — be seen to be condoning immoral behaviour. I'm sorry, Maggie, but I have to let you go."

It was, of course, no more than Maggie had expected. She'd only hoped she could delay the inevitable for as long as possible. How on earth they were going to manage for money without her wage, she had no idea — the pittance Billy earned would be nowhere near enough to provide what they needed to live on. He could barely afford to keep himself, let alone Rose, and herself and a baby, especially now that Sir Montague was demanding more rent.

"But you'll be short-staffed," she said in one last desperate attempt to achieve a reprieve.

The faint hope was quickly dashed.

"We're very quiet at this time of year, Maggie. Beattie is quite capable of taking over as chief assistant, Cathy is coming along nicely, and I shall take on a new apprentice."

She's got it all thought out, Maggie thought wretchedly.

"How in the world did it come to this, Maggie?" Augusta was shaking her head sadly. "I would have thought you were the last girl to get herself into this sort of trouble, and so soon after the death of your fiancé, too. Will the father stand by you?"

Maggie couldn't bring herself to reply.

"Who is he?" Augusta asked. "Perhaps if Horace was to speak to him, remind him of his responsibilities . . ."

Still Maggie was silent.

"Well, if you won't tell me who it is, there's nothing I can do to help you," Augusta said shortly. "This really is a most regrettable business. I've been more than satisfied with your work, and I had great hopes of you. To see you come to this . . . Wait here and I'll go and make up your wages. Then I would like you to go home without further ado."

"Can't I even go and say goodbye to the girls?" Maggie asked miserably.

"I think it would be best all round if you just leave quietly," Augusta said firmly. "Anything else would only cause a great deal of distress and embarrassment. I'll explain the situation to them in my own good time."

She disappeared back into the shop, closing the door after her.

In all the time Maggie had worked at the drapery, she'd only ever been into this room once before, and then she'd marvelled at the beautiful furniture — a green velvet-covered chaise longue, a highly polished table, a glass-fronted display cabinet filled with ruby cut glass and highly decorated bone china, and the carved case clock, gleaming brass candlesticks and figurines of a shepherd and shepherdess on the mantel above the fireplace. Now she stared at it all and saw nothing but a swirl of darkness so thick she felt as if she were falling into it.

A few minutes later Augusta was back with a brown envelope in her hand and Maggie's coat over her arm.

"I've put in a little extra," she said, handing Maggie the envelope. "Now, I'd like you to leave by the back door. We don't want to cause an upset in the shop."

"Thank you, Mrs Freeman," Maggie managed.

She slipped on her coat and pushed the envelope containing her wages deep into the pocket. Then Augusta led her through to the private side entrance and opened the door.

"I hope you are able to find some way of resolving this, Maggie," she said, sounding genuinely regretful. But her ramrod back and the tight lines of her face were as unyielding as before.

Augusta could not, would not, allow the slightest smear of scandal to threaten the business she had built up through hard work and acumen, even though it meant turning her most valued employee out on the street to manage as best she could. And if she felt the slightest sympathy for Maggie's plight, it was far outweighed by her disappointment and disgust.

A biting wind whipped at Maggie's thin coat as the door closed behind her, funnelled by the corner of the building, but she noticed it no more than she had noticed Augusta's fine furniture and ornaments. She felt dazed now, unable to gather her thoughts, lost in the dreadful fog of fear and anxiety that seemed not only to weigh her down but to have crept right inside her.

She crossed the road and began walking in the direction of home, dreading having to explain herself to Rose when she got there. But she could see no way of avoiding it. And very soon it wouldn't be just Rose who knew the truth, but the whole of High Compton.

What had she done? How could she have been so stupid as to get herself into this terrible predicament?

She knew, of course. The drink was to blame — that and her crazy passion for Josh. A wave of longing for him engulfed her. Even now, she still wanted him with every fibre of her being, wanted to see him, to speak to him, to have him put his arms around her and tell her that everything was going to be all right. But that wasn't going to happen. Josh had left her and run off with another woman. She was alone in this dreadful nightmare.

Just out of the centre of town, a break in the footpath made way for a narrow road leading off to the right. As she reached it, Maggie's steps slowed to a halt. At the end of the road was St Christopher's, the Catholic church. She hadn't set foot inside it for years, Easter and Christmas excepted, and this year she hadn't even gone at Christmas. But now, for some reason she couldn't explain, she felt drawn towards it. A reluctance to go home — or something more? Maggie didn't know, and didn't even pause to wonder. Without making any conscious decision, she turned up the rough track.

The church had once been a tithe barn. It sat in an oasis of lawn and garden, bare now, but vibrant with roses and fuchsia in the summer. Maggie approached the heavy oak door, grasped the iron ring that served as a handle and turned it. The door opened with a loud creak, and as she stepped inside, the scent of incense enveloped her, heady and oddly comforting.

She stood for a moment breathing it in as her eyes roamed around the once familiar interior. The vast beams supporting the low ceiling — when she was a child she'd been afraid one might come crashing down, and the roof with it, but Paddy had said God would never allow such a thing to happen. The rustic pews into which she and her brothers had crowded — Ewart would never sit still, he'd fidget and pull faces to try and make her laugh, and once a marble he'd got out of his pocket to play with had rolled away, right down the aisle to where Father O'Brien was consecrating the bread and wine for Mass, all in Latin, of course, of which Maggie didn't understand a word, and which seemed to drone on for ever. The brightly painted statues set in alcoves along the north and south wall — the Holy Mother in azure and white, St Martin, rich brown, St Theresa with her pink roses, St Agnes draped in a green shawl with a lamb in her arms. Often candles burned in the little votives set up before each shrine, but today there were only the blackened stubs — there had been no service this morning, and it was not a day when folk would leave the warmth of their homes unless they had good reason to. Even the candles on the altar were unlit, and the grey light filtering in through the small windows barely reached the magnificent tabernacle, yet still there was that aura of welcoming mystery.

Maggie dipped her fingers into the little bowl of holy water beside the door and dabbed it on her forehead, bobbed a genuflection towards the altar, and walked slowly down the aisle, her boots clicking on the paved stone. She paused there for a moment, then turned towards the narrow side aisle and the effigies in their little alcoves. She hesitated at that of the Holy Mother, then passed by, averting her eyes. How could she pray to the Blessed Virgin in her state of sinfulness? But when she reached St Theresa she stopped, took a little candle from the basket at the saint's feet, and fell to her knees on the wooden step that served as a prie-dieu. Of all the saints, it was St Theresa to whom she had always been drawn, though other children usually chose St Agnes, because of the lamb.

She had no way of lighting the candle, but she clutched it between her hands anyway, holding it close to her heart as she gazed up into the beautiful face of the saint. If she left it in the votive, someone would light it later, and whilst it burned it would waft her prayer towards heaven.

"Please help me, dearest St Theresa," she whispered, and then no more words would come, though her heart was full of them.

"Help me, please," she whispered again, crossing herself, before placing the candle in the votive and getting up to stand for a few more moments, unwilling to leave the delicately fashioned figure.

320

A thud, loud in the silence of the church, startled her and she swung round to see the black soutane-clad figure of Father O'Brien, who had emerged from the sacristy — the thud must have been made by the door closing after him.

Maggie's heart lurched and she felt as guilty as if she'd been caught stealing from the offertory box. Father O'Brien was bound to wonder what she was doing here in the middle of a working day. But he was coming towards her, and Maggie could see no way of avoiding him.

"Maggie, my dear." He smiled at her warmly. "It's not often we see you here these days."

"I know, Father. I just . . ." She gestured towards the votive.

"Would you light my candle for me, please, when you have time?"

"Of course. It's a comfort to you, I hope, praying for their souls. And I am sure our heavenly Father will hear your prayer."

Guilt suffused Maggie; she hadn't said a single word for the redemption of her father and Jack, who could well be languishing in purgatory waiting for enough Hail Marys to be said to speed them on to heaven.

"I know, my child, I know," he went on comfortingly, mistaking her guilt for grief. "It's hard, and beyond our understanding. But be sure they are in a better place."

"Oh Father . . ." Quite suddenly it was all too much for Maggie. His sympathy was only making her feel worse — she didn't deserve it! The weight of the secrets she was keeping felt too heavy for her shoulders; she couldn't bear it a moment longer. "Father . . . will you hear my confession?"

The priest's expression grew concerned, but he responded in the same gentle tone.

"Of course, my child."

He indicated that she should make her way to the confessional, but when they reached it, Maggie hesitated. She'd always hated the tiny enclosed space, hated the musty smell and the darkness, the way the priest's voice filtered, disembodied, through the grille in the wooden wall that separated them, hated the feeling of being trapped in what had always seemed to her to resemble a coffin. Now, more than ever, the similarity frightened her.

"Couldn't we do it out here?" she asked. "There's nobody but us."

"If that's what you want . . ." Father O'Brien sounded reluctant, but Maggie was insistent.

"It is."

"Very well. Shall we sit down, then?"

He led her to the front pew, right beside the figurine of the Holy Virgin, Maggie noticed uncomfortably.

"You're going to think I'm terrible," she said in a small voice.

"My dear, we are all sinners. That's why Jesus died for us. So that, through him, we might be saved."

"I think I'm beyond that," Maggie said wretchedly.

"No one who repents is beyond the mercy of our heavenly Father." The priest folded his hands together in his lap and waited.

Maggie swallowed hard, uncertain where to begin.

322

"I've done something so wrong. I've betrayed Jack, I've let myself down, and oh — I know I deserve what's happening, but Mam doesn't, and . . . oh, Father, it's awful, really awful, and I don't know what to do . . ."

The priest was starting to guess what it was that was troubling Maggie, but he said nothing, waiting for her to tell him in her own words. After a further brief hesitation, Maggie began.

"What am I going to do, Father?" she asked miserably.

The formal part of the confession was over, Father O'Brien had spoken the words of the absolution, and given Maggie a penance of five decades of the rosary to be said for five consecutive days. Now he looked at her sadly, seeing only a young woman who had fallen from grace as so many before her had done and would go on doing for as long as men and women lived and loved. A decent girl, even if her attendance at Mass was not what it should be, a girl who had slipped only the once if her confession was to be believed, and been caught out where so many, far more promiscuous than she, escaped retribution. And she had been through so much these last months! Small wonder she had sought comfort where she could find it.

She would be forgiven, of that he had no doubt, but that wouldn't solve the terrible problems she faced, and the disgrace was the least of these. Her lapse would have been forgotten eventually if the father of her baby had been prepared to marry her, but that, it seemed, was not an option. Maggie would have to raise her child alone, with no means of support, and Rose, and Billy too, would suffer, since they were dependent on her. Already she'd been dismissed from her position at the drapery shop, and it was hard to see who would offer employment to a fallen woman. She'd be ostracised, penniless, homeless too, in all likelihood. She needed more than absolution — she needed practical help, and Father O'Brien felt not only obligated to do what he could, but found himself desperately wanting to.

As always when he felt helpless, the priest reached for the crucifix that dangled from his girdle, holding it between his palms and pressing his fingertips together in an attitude of prayer. And quite suddenly, as if his prayer had been answered, inspiration struck.

"Maggie." He raised his eyes, looking at her over the tips of his fingers. "I can make no promises, but there's just a possibility I may be able to help. Come back and see me in a day or so, and I'll be able to tell you if I've been successful."

Hope and bewilderment in equal measure flickered in her eyes.

"What do you mean? How can you help?"

"No." Father O'Brien shook his head. He didn't want to raise her hopes only to have them dashed. "There's someone I need to speak to before I say more. But I shall be praying that God has provided an answer to our supplications."

"Oh!" Tears sprang to Maggie's eyes. "Oh, I'll pray too, Father! You don't know how hard I'll pray!"

"Just remember to say those rosaries, my child."

As she left the church, the wind seemed to have dropped and the cold was less biting. And to Maggie it felt miraculously as if a weight had been lifted from her shoulders and she was filled with a sense of peace as well as hope.

It seemed almost foolhardy to dare to think that Father O'Brien could really do anything to help her situation. Yet in that moment, anything seemed possible.

CHAPTER
NINETEEN

The house stood in the centre of a triangle of land, bordered on all three sides by roads — a main and two lanes — about six miles west of High Compton. Maggie, who had walked the whole way in driving rain, made her way around the perimeter until she found a gate in the high laurel hedge.

Oh, why couldn't it have been a fine day? She tucked a straggling end of wet hair back under the shawl she'd tied over her head and brushed moisture from her cheeks. She wasn't looking her best — in fact she felt like a drowned rat — and it was so important she should make a good impression. All very well for Father O'Brien to have recommended her to Lawrence Jacobs, the man she had come all this way to see; if she looked slovenly and unkempt, it wasn't likely he'd want to take her on as his housekeeper.

Housekeeper! It sounded very impressive, but Maggie had little idea of what such a position entailed, though Father O'Brien had assured her it would be well within her capabilities.

"Lawrence lives a simple life," he'd told her when she'd gone back to see him and he was elaborating on the idea he'd mentioned the day he'd taken her confession. "All he needs is someone to keep his house clean, his clothes laundered, and food on his table. He rarely entertains, and mostly he's immersed in his work."

"What does he do?" Maggie asked, though to be honest, it scarcely mattered if it meant an income to help support herself, her unborn child, Rose and Billy.

"He works in stained glass," Father O'Brien told her. "He's made windows for some of our finest churches. That's how I came to meet him — he restored a window for the abbey. I found the process fascinating, he allowed me to visit his workshop, and we've been friends ever since."

"Goodness!" Maggie was impressed. She loved looking at stained-glass windows, the vivid colours glowing when the light shone through them, but she'd never really stopped to wonder about the process involved or the artist who had recreated saints and martyrs from a mosaic of glass shards. "Like the window over the altar, you mean?"

"Exactly." Father O'Brien smiled. "Our own window is but a poor example, I'm afraid. Lawrence's work is far superior, and I understand he is very much in demand. The trouble is that when he is busy with a commission, he forgets to eat and sleep, let alone keep his home clean and tidy, and the woman who looked after him for many years has fallen into poor health and can no longer carry out her duties. I knew Lawrence needed someone to replace her, and it occurred to me you might suit him very well. I've spoken to him, and he seems to think so too. He would like to meet you. So, what do you say?"

The prospect of a lifeline was so overwhelming, Maggie was almost speechless.

"Oh, thank you so much!"

He patted her arm.

"Don't thank me yet, Maggie. I've secured an interview for you, nothing more. It will be Lawrence's decision as to whether you are the right person for him."

"Does he know about . . ." Maggie felt the hot colour of shame rush to her cheeks.

Father O'Brien nodded. "Of course. I wouldn't have recommended you under false pretences.

"And he doesn't mind?"

"Lawrence judges no one. He leaves that to God. As do I."

Now, soaking wet, and with her heart hammering with nervousness as she unlatched the wicket gate, Maggie reminded herself of the priest's words, and hoped desperately that he was right and this opportunity would prove to be the answer to her prayers.

The house — a rambling cottage half covered in creeper — was all in darkness, no glimmer of the light of an oil lamp showing at the windows, though given the oppression of the lowering skies it must have been very dim inside, and when Maggie tugged on the bell rope outside the porch door, all was silence. She tugged again, harder, hoping against hope that she hadn't come all this way on a fool's errand. She had the right day and time, she was sure, but if Lawrence was as vague about practical matters as Father O'Brien had suggested, perhaps he had forgotten. Then a voice from behind her made her turn.

A man was emerging from an outbuilding set amongst shrubs and hawthorn trees to the left of the path, calling to her as he approached.

"It's all right, my dear, I'm coming!"

He hurried towards her, holding an old piece of sacking over his head to keep off the rain. He was, Maggie judged, well into his fifties, of medium height and wiry build, and his gait was uneven, as if one leg was considerably shorter than the other.

"Mr Jacobs?" she said tentatively.

"And you must be Maggie. I'm sorry, my dear, I was in my workshop." He opened the front door and stood aside. "Do go in. You're soaked to the skin."

The door led directly into a living room, long, low and narrow. A fire burned in an open grate on the far wall, stairs led upwards from a corner. The room was comfortably furnished, but dreadfully untidy — open newspapers, a pile of books, used crockery and a bowler hat and cane left not an inch of space on the dining table; more books were stacked beside the chintz-covered sofa, and on the settle that stood in front of the little lead-paned window. Mud and leaves, trodden in from the garden, littered the stained board floor and a threadbare carpet. Lawrence Jacobs, however, seemed blissfully unaware of the chaos, even when his toe connected with yet another pile of books and sent it toppling.

"Let me take your coat. I'll put it by the fire, though I doubt it will dry much before you need it again. Can I offer you a cup of tea, or perhaps a nice hot chocolate?"

Maggie wasn't at all sure she fancied either. Judging by the state of the room, she could well imagine the cup and saucer would need a good wash in hot soapy water before it would be fit to drink out of — if, indeed, there was any unused crockery left in the house.

"Don't bother on my account, please," she said.

"No bother at all! It will warm you up."

"No — really — I'm fine."

"As you wish. Do please sit down, Maggie. May I call you Maggie?"

"Yes, of course."

Maggie perched in a space on the sofa, knees tightly drawn together, hands in lap, trying to appear demure. Somehow she had to override any preconception this man might have of her.

Lawrence took a seat himself opposite her, moving a pair of fire irons from an easy chair and stacking them untidily in the fireplace before he did so.

"So, Maggie, how is your mother?"

Maggie was quite taken aback — of all the questions she had expected him to ask, this was not one of them. Of course, Father O'Brien would have told him that Paddy had met his death in the terrible accident last spring, and perhaps Lawrence was simply trying to put her at her ease. But even so . . .

"She's bearing up," Maggie said. "She really isn't well, but she spent some time in Yorkshire with my brothers Walter and Ewart, and I think that helped."

Lawrence shook his head sadly.

"A terrible business. Terrible. I'm sure it hit you all very hard."

"Yes," Maggie said. "It did." For a moment there was silence, and Maggie shifted awkwardly in her seat. "Father O'Brien says you're looking for someone to . . ."

"Look after me. Yes." Lawrence smiled slightly, the narrow face between the mutton-chop whiskers taking on an expression of faint embarrassment — the first time he'd acknowledged the chaos that reigned in his home. "As you can see, I'm not particularly good at doing it myself."

Maggie tactfully refrained from agreeing.

"I've never worked as a housekeeper, Mr Jacobs, but I do know all about keeping house. Well — I can cook a little, and light a fire, and iron a sheet . . ."

"I'm sure you can." He smiled again. It was a kind smile, Maggie thought; it reached his eyes and softened the lines etched deeply into his face. "I'm sure you've been well schooled, and my needs are simple. As long as the house is kept tidy and I have clean clothes to put on and good, plain food on the table, I shall be more than satisfied. And I may need you to remind me to eat sometimes." He chuckled. "When I'm hard at work, I do tend to forget."

"That's not good for you," Maggie said.

"Indeed it is not. The sooner we can come to an arrangement, the better, don't you think?"

Maggie was surprised. Lawrence Jacobs was talking as if he had already decided to take her on, and he hadn't asked her a single pertinent question.

"Don't you want to know something about me?" she blurted.

Lawrence waved a hand airily. His fingers were long and fine, Maggie noticed, though they sprang from surprisingly broad palms.

"I think I know all I need to, my dear."

Again, Maggie was surprised. Father O'Brien must have given a very thorough report on her — and a glowing reference. She really must begin going to church regularly so that he'd know how grateful she was.

"You're going to take me on as your housekeeper, then?" she asked before she could stop herself.

Lawrence hesitated, his long, thin fingers tracing invisible lines from his knees to mid thigh and back again.

"That is not quite what I had in mind. I'm afraid there would be all kinds of problems with such an arrangement." He half rose from his chair. "Are you sure you won't take a cup of tea?"

"I really don't want one, thank you." Maggie was beginning to feel anxious as well as puzzled. "I just want —"

"I know my dear. I'm prevaricating, I expect. I often do, when really it would be much better to get to the point. The thing is, I don't think it would be seemly to take you on as a housekeeper, for a number of reasons."

"Oh," Maggie said dully, wondering why had he brought her all this way if he had no intention of offering her the job. And why had he talked as if he was about to do just that?

"Let me explain," Lawrence said as if he had read her mind. "You live some distance on the far side of High Compton, don't you? It would be impractical for you to get here each day to carry out your duties and then have to go all the way home again."

"I don't mind," Maggie said swiftly. "I walked it today and —"

"And got soaked through. Besides, before long I can't imagine such a long trek would be advisable, or even feasible."

Maggie flushed; it was the first time any mention had been made of her condition, and having a gentleman allude to it, even obliquely, made her dreadfully uncomfortable. He was right, of course. How much longer would she be able to walk the six or so miles here and home again? By the time she was seven or eight months gone, it would exhaust her, especially as the weather might well have turned hot in those last weeks. And afterwards . . . what then? She'd assumed that once she'd finished nursing, she could leave the baby at home with Rose while she was at work, but by then it would be winter. Suppose it was a hard one? How could she plough all that way through deep snow?

Maggie bit her lip. How could she have been so stupid as to not think of it herself? She'd been so

333

carried away with euphoria at the prospect of having her problems solved that she hadn't considered it sensibly, she supposed.

"It really would not be practical, would it, my dear?" Lawrence went on. "A housekeeper has to live in if she's to carry out her duties. But in your case, I don't think that is the answer either. Can you imagine what people would have to say? A young lady, single, living alone under the same roof as an old bachelor?"

Maggie didn't know whether to laugh or cry. He was talking as if she was perfectly respectable, and had a reputation to maintain.

"I'm afraid they're going to be talking about me anyway," she said with a small ironic laugh.

"Perhaps. But what I'm going to suggest might help to alleviate that — in time, anyway — and restore your good name. My offer is for you to come here not as my housekeeper, but as my wife."

For a moment Maggie was too startled to speak, or even to think. This couldn't be right! She must have caught a chill and be hallucinating. This man, this stranger, asking her to marry him? It was beyond belief.

"I've shocked you," Lawrence said. "I don't expect you to give me an answer right away, of course. You'll need time to think it over. But let me state my case. I would ask nothing of you beyond the duties we've already discussed. I have been celibate for most of my life, and I'm content to remain in that state. What I'm offering is a completely platonic relationship, but one that would benefit both you and your child. You would gain the respectability that comes from being a married

334

woman, and your child would escape the stigma of being known as what our cruel world calls a bastard. Tongues may wag for a little while, but it would soon be forgotten, and in any case you would be far enough away from High Compton for it not to bother you unduly.

"Then there's the financial aspect. You'd have no need to worry any more with regards to supporting yourself and your baby. Or, indeed, your immediate family. I'm not a wealthy man, perhaps I should make myself clear about that, but I'm comfortably off, enough to ensure you'd want for nothing. And when I die, everything I have would be yours. There should be enough to keep you free of worry in that regard for as long as you are in need, and perhaps a little longer — as long as the man you choose to marry after I'm gone isn't a gambler or a spendthrift."

When I die . . . Dazed as she was, his choice of words leapt out at Maggie, and again he seemed to read her mind.

"It's unlikely I have more than a few years left," he said, without the slightest hint of regret or self-pity. "I was very sick as a child — infantile paralysis, they called it — and besides a withered leg, I was also left with a weak heart and chest. This winter I've been fortunate, and I have managed to avoid the chills and fevers, but that won't always be the case. If next winter is harsh and I succumb, there's no telling what might happen. I wouldn't like you to find yourself in the position of being without means of support again so quickly, and with a young baby to care for into the bargain."

Maggie's thoughts were reeling.

"I don't understand," she said faintly. "Why would you . . . ?"

Lawrence smiled, and Maggie saw a twinkle in those kindly eyes.

"You're wondering what benefit there is in this for me? Well, it's obvious, surely? I gain a young and comely wife, which will considerably raise my standing in the eyes of all those who think of me as a dry old stick! No . . ." He became serious again. "It's true that I'd much prefer to see a pretty face when I come in from my workshop. Mrs Hoskins was a wonderful cook, and a good soul, but beauty was never one of her attributes, even in her younger days. And of recent times, having her here puffing and wheezing over even the least onerous of tasks has, I confess, been something of a trial as well as a cause for anxiety. She's been good to me, and I shouldn't speak ill of her, I suppose, but there it is. If I became sick, she certainly couldn't have cared for me — she could barely care for herself."

His eyes levelled with Maggie's.

"Perhaps I should lay a little more emphasis on my tendency to periods of ill health," he said. "It may well be that I am in need of a nurse as well as a housekeeper. So there you have it. If you agree to my suggestion, I shall be assured of someone I can depend on in time of need, and you will gain financial security and a degree of respectability. It's not such a bad bargain, is it?"

336

"No . . . no, but . . ." Maggie was still in a state of disbelief that something as life-changing as a proposal of marriage should have come out of the blue like this. "You don't know me at all. I could be the sort of woman who —"

"Would rob me of all my money and run off and leave me in my hour of need?" he interrupted her, his eyes twinkling again. Serious as he might appear, at least Lawrence had a sense of humour, she thought later. "Well, I don't know you, of course. But I have a mind to trust you, Maggie."

"On Father O'Brien's word?"

"Not entirely." His eyes narrowed, and he appeared to be staring intently yet unseeing at some point beyond Maggie's shoulder.

"Well, that's my offer to you," he said, coming back abruptly from wherever he'd been wandering. "It won't have been what you were expecting, I know, and I'm sure you will want some time to think it over. But I very much hope you'll come to see it as not entirely disagreeable to you."

"No," Maggie said, making up her mind.

She couldn't let an opportunity like this slip through her fingers, and it wasn't such a bad deal. Though she'd only just met him, Lawrence seemed kind, and she felt sure Father O'Brien would never have sent her to him if he knew different. She would, of course, be tying herself to a man she didn't love, for whom, in fact, she had no feelings whatsoever, but so long as he expected nothing from her but the same duties she'd been prepared to take on as his housekeeper, then she could hardly complain.

In any case, what was love? She'd thought she'd found it with Josh, and what had that got her? A disastrous situation and a broken heart. What Lawrence was offering her was far more than she could have dared hope for. Security. Respectability. A home for herself and her baby. Support for Rose and Billy.

"No," she said, and Lawrence looked at her questioningly, thinking perhaps that she was turning down his proposal. She hastened to assure him otherwise.

"I don't need time to think," she said swiftly. "I'm not even sure I have it, before tongues start wagging. I'd like to accept your kind offer."

"Only if you are sure, Maggie," he said. His eyes levelled with hers.

"I'm sure," she said with all the confidence she could muster.

And thought: in the last resort, what choice did she have?

The rain had eased a little by the time Maggie left, though with her thoughts whirling, she barely noticed. What in the world was Rose going to have to say about all this?

She'd been in a dreadful way, of course, when Maggie had confessed that she was pregnant and had been dismissed from her job because of it.

"Oh Maggie, you silly, silly girl!" she'd said, wringing her thin hands. "What were you thinking of?"

338

"I wasn't thinking," Maggie replied miserably.

But she'd refused to answer Rose's next question as to the identity of the father, just as she'd refused to tell Augusta. And she hadn't told her about the interview Father O'Brien had arranged for her either — she didn't want to raise her mother's hopes only to have them dashed. She'd made some excuse about going to Hillsbridge to look for work.

"On a day like this?" Rose had said. "Why don't you leave it until the rain's stopped?"

"I can't just sit at home doing nothing," Maggie had replied. "A drop of rain won't hurt me."

Now there could be no more prevaricating. As she walked, Maggie ran over all the options.

"Mam, I'm going to be married to a man I met this morning."

"Mam, there's no need for you to worry any more about how I'm going to manage."

"Mam, I expect you'll think I've gone funny in the head, but . . ."

She shrank inwardly as she imagined Rose's shocked reaction. Would she be relieved? Would she be horrified? Maggie had no idea. Both, probably.

In the event, the one reaction she didn't expect, hadn't considered for even a moment, was the one that actually happened.

Rose fainted clean away.

As Maggie told her haltingly about Lawrence Jacobs, she saw the colour drain from her mother's face, saw her clutch at the neck of her blouse and sway.

"Mam?" she said urgently. "Are you all right?"

Rose didn't reply. Her knees were buckling, and though her eyes were still fixed on Maggie, they'd gone unfocused. She went down slowly, almost gracefully, though her head made a horrible thud as it connected with the tiled floor.

"Oh Mam!" Maggie wailed.

She rushed to fetch the smelling salts, wafting them under Rose's nose, and after what seemed like an eternity, Rose's eyes opened and her head rolled from side to side.

"Have a sip of this, Mam," Maggie held a cup of water to her mother's lips.

"I don't know what happened to me," Rose said faintly. "Oh dear, I feel ever so sick . . ."

Maggie hurried to the kitchen to fetch a bowl. Mercifully, Rose wasn't sick, but she was still paper white.

"What an old fool I am!" she groaned.

"No, you're not. I gave you an awful shock." Maggie felt dreadfully guilty as well as anxious. "Oh Mam, I am so sorry . . . about everything."

Rose was recovering herself little by little.

"What's done's done. No use being sorry."

"But . . . you think I'm wrong to agree to marry a man I don't really know at all?"

"Well, of course I wish things were different. But he's a good man and he'll take care of you."

"How can you know that?" Maggie asked.

For a moment, Rose's mouth worked, though no words came. Then:

"Father O'Brien wouldn't have sent you to him if he wasn't. No, it's for the best, I expect."

"I honestly don't think I have any choice," Maggie said.

In the grey light of early morning, Billy was driving the herd of cows along the lane for milking. His head was bent, chin resting on chest, and rain dripped in a steady plop-plop from his hat on to the waterproof cape he wore over his coat, sometimes even finding its way inside his collar and trickling down his neck. He scarcely noticed. He could think of nothing but that Maggie was going to be married to a man he didn't even know, his mother was going to move to Yorkshire to live with Walter and Connie, and his own future was horribly uncertain.

It had been suggested he should go to Yorkshire too, and he had wondered if it might be a good idea to leave High Compton with all its terrible memories and start afresh. But he liked his job on the farm — Billy was always more comfortable around animals than people — and if he moved to Yorkshire, he might be expected to go down the pit like his brothers. The thought of it made his stomach clench with fear. The very idea of the descent into the bowels of the earth terrified him just as it always had. Besides, there was Bullseye to think of. Connie might not want a dog in the house, and leaving Bullseye behind to fend for himself was unthinkable.

But where would he live? He couldn't stay on in the family home; he couldn't have afforded the rent even before Sir Montague increased it, and he didn't suppose he'd be allowed to anyway. He'd have to find lodgings somewhere, but again Bullseye came into the equation. He'd sleep rough on the streets rather than be parted from his beloved dog.

Maggie had suggested he should ask Farmer Barton if he could have a room at the farm, or even a cottage, and that, he thought, was the best option. But he was pretty sure there were no cottages vacant, and Farmer might not want him in the farmhouse. There was nothing for it, of course, but to take the bull by the horns and ask, but Billy was still struggling to get up the courage. It wasn't so much that he was afraid to; rather that if Farmer refused, he didn't know what he'd do next.

One of the cows had stopped to feast on the lush grass that grew along the side of the road and the others were bunching up behind her. Billy swished his stick to move them on, then gave the culprit a smack on the rump and yelled at her to get going. He could hear the clip-clop of a horse's hooves coming along the lane behind him — it sounded like a pony and trap, Fred Carson maybe. Well, he'd just have to be patient; Billy couldn't make the cows go any faster and they didn't have much further to go now.

As he plodded stoically on, he found himself wondering yet again why Maggie was marrying this Lawrence Jacobs. No reason had been given for it, but he'd heard Mam and Maggie talking together in low whispers, and as far as he was aware, there was really only one reason for a rushed job like this. If it had been Josh, or Jack before he was killed, Billy would have been able to understand it. But why this Lawrence Jacobs? Surely Maggie hadn't been putting herself about with strangers to make ends meet? He huffed disgustedly at the thought and tried to block it out, just as he tried to block out all the other things that were too disturbing to think about. Sometimes he succeeded, and sometimes he didn't, but right now he had to concentrate on working out what he was going to say to Farmer about his future living arrangements. One thing at a time.

Billy shrugged deeper into his waterproofs and trudged the last few yards to the gate that led to the milking parlour.

Three weeks later, Maggie and Lawrence were married quietly by Father O'Brien at St Margaret's, the Catholic church in Hillsbridge. St Margaret's was the sister church to St Christopher's in High Compton, and Father O'Brien shared the ministry with a monk from the nearby abbey. The witnesses were Billy and Ewart, who had travelled down from Yorkshire and would be taking Rose back with him.

Rose did not attend the ceremony. She'd been very quiet ever since Maggie had told her the news, but though she looked pale and drawn, it hadn't occurred to Maggie that she was so ill she wouldn't be able to come to the church to see her daughter married. On the morning of the wedding, though, she told Maggie that she felt very poorly, and was afraid she was going to have to miss it.

"How can I get married without you there?" Maggie asked, distressed.

"You wouldn't want me fainting again in the church, would you?" Rose said. "Think of the upset it would cause! No, it's best I stay at home." She smiled weakly. "And you know you have my blessing. That's all that matters."

"If you're feeling that bad, perhaps you shouldn't be travelling all the way to Yorkshire," Maggie said anxiously. "Perhaps you should wait a few days until you feel a bit better."

"I'll be all right," Rose assured her. "I'll have to be. Our Ewart can't lose more time off work.

"Oh Mam . . ." Maggie put her arms round her mother's thin frame, hugging her. "I should be here for you. It's all so wrong."

Rose was silent for a moment, but the stiffness of her shoulders and the shallowness of her breathing told Maggie that she was struggling to keep from crying. Just one soft gulp escaped her, then she held Maggie away, trying to smile.

"It'll all work out for the best, Maggie, you'll see. The Lord alone knows I wish it could have been different, but like I said before, you've got a good man there, even if he's not the one you'd have picked, given the chance. And you'll come and visit me, won't you, after the baby is born? I'd like to see it — and I shall be dying to see you."

"Of course I will, Mam," Maggie said, tears pricking her own eyes.

Rose wiped her nose with the back of her hand.

"Get off with you now. You don't want to be late for your own wedding."

Ewart was waiting for her, all spruced up in a white shirt with a wing collar.

"Don't worry about Mam," he reassured Maggie. "I'll take good care of her."

"I know you will, Ewart," Maggie said.

The pony and trap Lawrence had hired to take them to Hillsbridge would be waiting at the end of the lane — Maggie hadn't wanted the neighbours to see them go — but if it was there for much longer, someone was certain to walk past and start wondering about it.

Maggie hugged Rose one last time and walked out of the house that was the only home she had ever known. She knew it was unlikely she would ever return.

When the brief ceremony was over, another hired pony and trap took Maggie and Lawrence back to his house on the outskirts of town. There they celebrated with a small glass of sherry and a fruit cake Maggie had baked under her mother's instruction, and sat for a while talking.

"I don't suppose this is how you imagined your wedding day would be," Lawrence said thoughtfully.

"Not really." Maggie sighed wistfully. "But then things don't very often work out the way you expect, do they? Dreams . . ." She bit her lip. "Dreams are just that. For children."

The minute she'd said it, she regretted it, afraid he would think her ungrateful.

"I mean, when I was little, all I wanted to do was draw pictures, or make clothes for my doll," she went on hastily. "I thought that when I grew up and didn't have to go to school, I could do that all the time. Sell my pictures, or design dresses for fine ladies." She laughed shortly. "Imagine it! That someone like me could do something like that! The closest I ever got was dressing the window at the shop, or putting ribbons and flowers together to trim a plain bonnet. Now I don't even have the chance to do that."

"But life may yet have some pleasant surprises in store for you," Lawrence said gently. "You're far too young to give up on your dreams. One day, perhaps, some of them will come true in ways you could never imagine."

"Perhaps," Maggie said, anxious not to make the mistake again of saying anything that might give him the idea that she was ungrateful; not wanting to hurt his feelings, she realised. Rose had been right: he was a good man.

"I'll make some tea," she said.

Lawrence nodded. "That would be nice, my dear."

Later, when the fire was burning low and the lamp flickering, Maggie went upstairs to the cosy room under the eaves that was to be hers, leaving Lawrence downstairs. As she was undressing, she heard the side door beneath her window open and close. She looked out; his shadowy figure was making its way along the path to his workshop, a storm lantern held aloft. Relieved that he was keeping to his side of the bargain,

Maggie finished her toilet and slipped beneath the patchwork quilt.

The narrow bed was comfortable enough, and the sheets were freshly laundered — she knew, because she'd made up the bed herself. But homesickness was already beginning to gnaw at her, and a feeling of being trapped.

This was not, she thought, how she had imagined her wedding day would be. But Lawrence Jacobs had offered her a lifeline, and she must be grateful for it.

CHAPTER
TWENTY

Gossip and speculation was rife in High Compton, but not a single person, apart from Father O'Brien, knew the whole truth. All that was certain was that Maggie was no longer employed in the drapery, and number six Fairley Terrace was all shut up, with no one at home. Ewart had been there for a couple of days, the neighbours said, and they thought he'd taken Rose back to Yorkshire with him, but that didn't explain Maggie and Billy's absence, and no one had seen Bullseye either. He wasn't hanging about outside the locked-up house waiting for someone to come home; one or other of the Donovans must have taken him with them. But where had they gone without a word to anyone — and why?

Theories abounded. That the family owed money they couldn't repay and had done a moonlight flit was one of the favourites. Billy was in trouble with the police was another, but this had to be discounted when it was discovered that he was still working at the farm, and now living in, Bullseye with him. And of course, the one that was closest to the truth — that Maggie had got herself in a pickle and she too had gone to Yorkshire, where no one knew her, to hide her shame.

The bolder and more curious, Hester Dallimore among them, found excuses to go into Freeman's shop in the hope of learning something of interest, but got nowhere. The girls who worked there became nervous and uncomfortable at the mention of Maggie's name — unsurprising, really, since it elicited a warning glare from Augusta, who was known to be a strict disciplinarian, and who would come down hard on any employee who engaged in gossip about another. In fact, the girls knew little more than anyone else.

"Mrs Freeman wouldn't say why she gave Maggie the sack," Cathy told her mother when she asked. "And we never got the chance to ask Maggie herself. Mrs Freeman let her out the back way, and we haven't set eyes on her since."

Cathy, of course, was unhappy that she'd lost her contact with Ewart, besides being concerned about Maggie.

Then a surprise snippet of information added spice to the mix. Hester Dallimore was discussing the mystery with a cousin who lived in Hillsbridge when she struck gold.

"Maggie Donovan, did you say?" the cousin asked. "I'm sure someone of that name had their banns called in our church a few weeks back."

Instantly Hester was all ears.

"Your church?"

"St Margaret's. Yes."

"And Maggie Donovan had banns read there?" Hester probed eagerly.

"I couldn't say for sure, but I think that was the name. We were all saying to one another — 'Who's that when she's at home?' And we didn't know the chap's name either. It was all double Dutch to us."

"I thought you had to live in a parish to have your banns called," Hester said.

"Well, strictly speaking, you do. But if you leave a suitcase with your clothes in for a couple of weeks, and the priest's on your side, you can get round it, or so I understand. It doesn't often happen, but it's not unheard of."

"Well!" Hester was agog. "So you reckon Maggie Donovan's got married on the OT!"

"I wouldn't know about that." The cousin, knowing Hester's reputation as a gossip, was beginning to wish she'd kept quiet.

"And you don't know who it was she was marrying?"

"That's what I said."

"It wasn't Josh Withers, was it?"

"I can't remember, our Hester. And that's the truth."

"I'll bet that's who it was!" Hester was triumphant. "He's gone off somewhere too. Well, well. Maggie and Josh Withers! And she was engaged to his brother, the one that got killed at Shepton Fields. No wonder they wanted to hush it up!"

It didn't take long, of course, for Hester to begin sharing her juicy news. When it reached the ears of Josh's mother she was quick to deny it, but Hester was not to be deterred.

"Florrie reckons he's away working, but that's her story," she said smugly as she spread the gossip ever further. "You should have seen her face! Scarlet, she was. Scarlet!"

"Well I never! There's a thing!"

"No wonder poor Rose's took bad and gone off out of the way . . ."

"Maggie Donovan and Josh Withers! You reckon they had to do it in a hurry?"

Oh, it was a juicy story right enough, and it spread like wildfire, gaining embellishments along the way.

For a few weeks it provided much-needed entertainment in a town that was still in mourning for its lost sons.

Just two weeks after Maggie O'Donovan married Lawrence Jacobs, an envelope had dropped through the letter box of the Withers home.

When she saw it lying on the tiled floor, Florrie swooped on it eagerly. It was a good while now since Josh had written — he wasn't much of a letter-writer, she knew, and she couldn't expect weekly missives like the ones she got from her sister, who was married to a policeman and lived in Torquay, but she did like just a line or two so that she knew he was all right. Though he was a grown man, she still worried about him, especially since the awful thing that had happened to Jack.

She carried the envelope into the kitchen and sat down at the table, reaching for the magnifying glass. Her sight wasn't as good as it used to be, but there was no way she could afford to see an oculist and be fitted for spectacles. The writing on the envelope was certainly Josh's, but to her surprise Florrie saw that the postmark was Belfast, Ireland. Puzzled, she tore open the envelope and took out the two sheets of lined writing paper covered with Josh's hurried scrawl.

Dear Mam and Dad, *she read*. I hope this finds you well.

I expect you will be surprised to hear that I am in Ireland now, working at the Harland and Wolff shipyard. I couldn't get anything in Bristol, only casual labouring at the docks. It wasn't paying enough to keep body and soul together really, but then somebody told me they were looking for carpenters in the shipyard here in Belfast and I thought I'd try my luck. I came over to have a look at the place and see what was going, and they offered me a job.

There was a bit of a to-do when I got back to Bristol to pick up my belongings. Cissie, my landlady, had left her husband and run away, and he thought we'd gone off together. Fat chance of that! He was all ready to pick a fight over her, but I soon put him right. She was seeing a chap who used to lodge with them before me, I know. He came to the house once or twice when Albie was away working, and Cissie told me he was a Londoner who bummed around with a travelling funfair when he couldn't find work in the docks. I told Albie his missus was sitting in a caravan somewhere gazing in a crystal ball and getting her palm crossed with silver (she used to tell fortunes reading the tea leaves if anybody asked her to) and he said he'd give her crystal ball if she came back! Well, it was on those lines, but I don't want to shock you, Mam, with telling you what he really said.

Anyway, I packed up my stuff and left him to it, and now here I am in Ireland.

It's a great place, and I'm earning good money. I wanted to settle myself somewhere before I let you know as I thought you'd only worry, but now I've found nice lodgings with a couple of pals. So I'm writing to tell you I'm doing fine, and if you want to write back, you will find me at this address.

I will write again soon.

Your loving son

Josh

PS Do you see anything of Maggie? Is she all right?

"Well, well, well!" Florrie said wonderingly, and she read the letter again before going out into the garden, where Gilby was digging parsnips for dinner, to tell him the news.

She wished with all her heart that Josh hadn't gone away at all, especially not as far as Ireland. But at least it sounded as if he was doing well for himself, and perhaps one day he'd get tired of foreign places and come home. It was the best she could hope for.

On the same day, the postman pushed an envelope containing an almost identical letter through the letter box of number six. It was addressed to Miss Maggie Donovan. The postman wondered idly who would be writing to both Maggie and the Withers family all the way from Ireland, but then he was forever asking himself questions about the mail he delivered to which he'd never get the answers. As long as the letters went to the right address, his job was done. It wasn't his concern that there was no one at home to receive them.

"I suppose you've heard — your boyfriend's got married." Tom Bishop pushed back his empty dinner plate and belched loudly.

Peggy turned away, pretending to be clearing the table.

"Oh, is that right?" she said non-committally, though in fact she already knew — Sarah had told her yesterday when she'd visited with half her brood in tow. Peggy had pretended with her too — that it couldn't matter less — but in fact she'd been dismayed. Though it had been all over between them for a long time now, she still carried a torch for Josh that had been burning more brightly lately. Tom was slipping back into his bad old ways — surly, discontented — and the novelty of imagining he might have ruthlessly murdered a dozen men and boys for the love of her was wearing a little thin.

If Josh had finally settled down, it put an end to any hopes Peggy might have had of rekindling their affair, and she was surprised at how much that could still upset her.

"Done all right for himself, too," Tom was going on. "That Maggie Donovan's a little cracker. Though from what I hear of it, there'll be a nipper along soon to spoil their fun and games. Dipped his wick once too often if you ask me."

"Don't talk so disgusting," Peggy snapped.

Tom guffawed sarcastically.

"Don't like to think of him putting it about with anybody but you, is that it? Well let me tell you this, Peg, he wouldn't look twice at you now. Even if I hadn't scared the blighter off, he's got better fish to fry. And just as well he has, 'cos he knows if he came sniffing round after you again he'd get what was coming to him."

He belched again, and something snapped in Peggy. She wheeled round, humiliation and disgust with Tom, his nasty tongue and his filthy habits, making her throw caution to the winds.

"It was you, wasn't it, you bugger!" she accused.

"What you talking about, woman?"

"The rope on the hudge. It was you cut it. You mixed Josh up with Jack, and you cut that bloody rope to get your own back on him."

The light in the kitchen was too dim for her to be able to see his face clearly, but she heard his quick intake of breath.

"Have you took leave of your senses?" he snarled.

Peggy straightened up, hands on ample hips.

"You can't fool me, Tom Bishop. I know you, and I know your nasty temper. But you needn't worry. I

355

haven't said anything to anybody else, and I won't. I don't want folk knowing I'm married to a murderer."

"You bloody stupid woman," Tom grunted.

Peggy half smiled. "In any case, I quite like it that you care that much about me. So come on, you might as well own up. It was you, wasn't it? Tell the truth and shame the devil."

Tom leaned back in his chair, his chest swelling, and patted his full belly.

"You'd like to know, wouldn't you? You fancy having something over me. Well, you can just go on wondering, m'dear. Now, I think I'm going out for a pint — unless there's something better on offer here."

"And what would that be?" Peggy demanded, a little saucily. Talking about what had happened was having that erotic effect on her again, making Tom seem more attractive, making her forget Josh and that stupid Donovan girl. Josh might be a bit of a stud, but he'd given her the brush-off long before he'd taken up with Maggie Donovan, and in any case, she couldn't imagine he'd ever have done what Tom had done, even if he'd been mad for her.

Tom caught hold of her arm, yanking her roughly towards him.

"Come here, Peg, and I'll show you."

He pulled her down on to his lap, and Peggy smiled to herself as he rucked up her skirts.

Oh, Tom might be uncouth, he might be ill-tempered, but first and foremost he was what she thought of as a real man.

Peggy Bishop was not the only one dismayed to learn that Maggie Donovan was married.

Reuben was in the living room, sorting the latest acquisitions for his stamp collection and being hassled by his mother to pack it away so that she could lay for tea when his father came home from the office.

It was unusual for Reuben to be at home before Clarence, except, of course, on a Wednesday, which was early-closing day in High Compton, but he was suffering from a severe head cold and Horace had sent him home the previous day saying it was unhygienic for him to be sneezing all over the customers.

"We're not busy, nor likely to be," he had said firmly. "Have a hot toddy or two and come back when you're no danger to the rest of us."

Reuben hadn't been sorry. He didn't feel at all well, and since Maggie had disappeared from the drapery shop, there was no incentive for him to struggle in to work. He couldn't understand what had happened to her; he didn't like to ask, and in any case he had a strong feeling that he would get no answer. When Stanley Stone, his fellow assistant, had asked if she was on holiday, Horace had simply replied that she was no longer an employee, and his expression had forbidden further discussion of the matter.

Reuben was puzzled — and wretched. Even though she had rejected his advances, even if she could barely bring herself to look at him, let alone speak to him these days, it was as if a light had gone out in his world. He'd even walked out to the lane leading to the Ten

357

Houses one evening in the hope of seeing her, though he'd had no idea what he would say to her if he did. He'd stood on the road in the freezing cold, stamping his feet and blowing on his hands for a good half-hour before he'd given up and gone home.

In an effort to forget Maggie, he'd decided to ask Cathy if she would go out with him. He'd waited for her outside the shop one night, but Cathy had been rude and scornful.

"I wouldn't go out with you, Reuben Hillman, if you were the last man in England!" she'd said, with a toss of her hair. "And you'd better not start mithering me the way you mithered Maggie, or my brothers will be after you. They won't just give you a punch on the nose like Josh did, either. They'll put you in the hospital!"

"Don't worry, I didn't really want to go out with you anyway," Reuben had retorted before slinking away with his tail between his legs. But his pride was badly dented, not least for being reminded of the ignominy of being felled by a single blow from Josh Withers.

Now he was about to be reminded of it again.

"It would seem," Clarence said, when he'd taken his coat off and draped it over the back of one of the dining chairs, "that that hobbledehoy Withers, who came here and violated our home, has left the district. And he has taken the Donovan girl with him. In fact, if the story I heard today is to be believed, he has married her. So I think it unlikely that we will be troubled by either of them again."

Reuben's stomach fell away and his already congested airways seemed to close completely so that he could hardly breathe.

Maggie — married! No! He couldn't believe it. Couldn't bear it!

"I'm very glad to hear it," Alexandra said. "Perhaps you'll forget about her now, Reuben, and find yourself a nice young lady."

"He's forgotten her already, haven't you, son?" Clarence smoothed his hair, shiny and sleek with macassar oil. "He was taken in by a pretty face, as young men often are. But common sense has prevailed, I'm glad to say. A girl like that was never good enough for him, and he knows that now. Isn't that right, Reuben?"

Reuben mumbled something unintelligible, found his handkerchief and blew his blocked-up nose.

"That's all right then," Alexandra said, approaching the table with the cutlery box. "Now, if you could just pack up what you're doing, Reuben, I can get this table laid."

Reuben stuffed his handkerchief back into his pocket, somehow managing to brush his carefully sorted stamps so that they were all over the place again. Some had even fluttered to the floor. Normally he would have been annoyed, but right now he was past caring.

Nothing seemed of the slightest importance by comparison with the fact that Maggie was now out of his reach for ever. Misery overwhelmed him, and with it a wave of hatred for Josh Withers. The man who had humiliated him in front of his father. The man who had stolen the love of his life.

I'll get back at him if it's the last thing I do! Reuben vowed silently as he scrabbled around under the table for the last stray stamp.

Revenge. Planning it really was the only consolation left to him.

In the isolation of her new home, Maggie was blissfully unaware of all the furore her marriage had caused in High Compton, though, truth be told, even if she had known about it, she would have spared it little thought. There were far too many other things on her mind.

Rose for one. Her failing health was a constant worry, and the long journey to Yorkshire wouldn't have done her any good. Walter, Connie and Ewart would take good care of her, Maggie knew, but they weren't miracle-workers, and the way Rose had fainted the day Maggie had told her she was getting married, and the fact that she had felt too unwell to attend the wedding ceremony, didn't bode well. Ever since she'd suffered the miscarriage, it had seemed to be one thing after the other. Until then, although she'd always looked as if a puff of wind would blow her away, she'd had an iron constitution, but now it seemed to Maggie that her mother was slipping away, little by little, and there was nothing she could do to stop the relentless deterioration.

It could be it had started even earlier, with the accident and Paddy's death, of course, and Maggie had been too distraught herself to notice. But whatever, the decline could no longer be denied, and it was a constant weight on Maggie's mind.

Then there was Billy. Farmer Barton had agreed to let him have a room over the stables, and Billy had seemed happy enough with that — at least it meant an extra half-hour in bed for him in the mornings. Farmer's wife was feeding him, too, and Maggie had no doubt that it would be good, wholesome food. But she wasn't so sure about the accommodation, which would be cold and damp at this time of year, she felt sure. And good as Farmer's wife might be, she wasn't family. Billy was such a loner, so difficult to communicate with, and though he'd always been one to go off on his own when something upset him, he'd always had her and Mam to come home to, comforting him simply with their presence even if there was nothing they could say to help.

Well, at least he had Bullseye with him, Maggie comforted herself. And he seemed to think more of that dog than he did of any human.

Last but not least, Maggie worried about being a good wife to Lawrence. As he'd told her the very first time she met him, his needs were simple enough, but Maggie felt duty-bound to go above and beyond the bare essentials. Lawrence had given her so much — a home, respectability, financial security — and soon there would be a baby in the house, which was bound to disrupt his way of life, however bound up he was in his work and however much Maggie tried not to let it. She cooked the meals she thought he'd enjoy — roast meats and hearty soups, bread and butter puddings, fresh custards, and Victoria buns, a recipe from a cookbook by Mrs Beeton that she discovered in a cupboard in the living room, and which was proving a godsend.

She washed and scrubbed, dusted and ironed, spreading a thick blanket over the kitchen table and heating the flatirons over the fire. She opened the windows to air the upstairs rooms when the weather was good enough, and tidied Lawrence's numerous books on to shelves that had previously been filled with clutter. She polished the brass and swept last year's dead leaves away from the doorstep; she went to market in Hillsbridge once a week to buy butter, cheese and fresh vegetables, thankful that no one in the town knew her and that she did not know them. And still she felt it was not enough.

What company was she for him? They had no shared experiences or interests, no friends in common apart, she supposed, from Father O'Brien. Confined to the house most of the day, she had nothing of interest to relate. And Lawrence was not, by nature, a talkative man. Too many years of his own company had made him quietly introspective, and Maggie felt obliged to fill the silence over the meal table, or when they sat down in the evenings in the chintz-covered chairs one each side of the open fire, even though she worried that her chatter was either boring or annoying him, and perhaps both.

He did sometimes ask her questions about her family and her past, it was true, but then he would retreat into himself so that she wasn't sure whether or not he was listening, and, uncomfortable, she would force herself to bite her tongue.

But what had she expected? Lawrence was fifty-six — more than ten years older than her father had been. He was an educated man; the books she tidied away bore witness to that — volumes of poetry and plays, works of philosophy and history. Some of them weren't even in English but Latin, which she recognised though she didn't understand it, and other languages she didn't recognise at all. There was evidence amidst the clutter that he'd travelled, too. Programmes from the opera in Paris, musical recitals in Berlin and Rome, a well-thumbed map of London. Small artefacts that looked as if they'd been picked up along the way — a piece of crystal, a phial containing what looked like red sand, a wallet whose cover depicted a scene of warriors in a mosaic of multicoloured leather. And the inevitable religious icons too, rosaries and medallions and tiny statuettes, none of which looked English.

They stirred something in Maggie, a thirst for experiences beyond her mundane existence that had always lurked at the edges of her consciousness but which she had put to one side as silly and fanciful. But they also emphasised the huge gulf of experience that yawned between her and Lawrence.

How could she ever hope to connect with such a man? Maggie wondered, without any real hope of finding an answer.

As for his work, which occupied almost every moment of his day, she knew next to nothing. He rarely talked about it, and she'd never so much as set foot in his workshop — he'd told her it was the one place she didn't need to keep clean and tidy and she'd thought that he was afraid she might damage something or interfere with a delicate stage of the process, whatever that might entail. All she knew was that he was engaged on an important project that he'd been working on for a year or more, and which would continue to occupy him for some months to come.

"But what is it?" she'd asked, and he'd told her that he had been commissioned to make a triptych window for a cathedral in New York.

Maggie's eyes had widened in amazement and awe. New York! Why, that was half a world away!

"How did you come to get a job like that?" she'd asked.

"Through a friend I made when I was training in London, many years ago," he said, looking a little embarrassed at her open admiration. "Jacob was an American, and a master craftsman, over here to carry out some highly specialised restoration work. He taught me all I know. But he's too old now to do the things he used to, his sight is failing and his hands are too stiff, and when he was approached he suggested I should be commissioned in his place. There have been times, I confess, when I've wondered whether my health would allow such a thing, but I've carried on with the making of the windows just hoping I would be able to oversee their installation for myself, and I think that hope has proved to be justified." He smiled at her. "Since I've had you to take care of me, my dear, I've never felt better."

"I do my best," Maggie teased. "But how will you get the windows all the way to America when they're finished?"

"They will be crated up and sent by sea," Lawrence told her. "Then, God willing, they will be mounted in the lady chapel they are intended for. But that's a good way off yet, and will continue to be unless I get to work. I'll leave you to whatever you need to do, my dear."

He had gone out to his workshop and Maggie had been left with a thousand unanswered questions and a tickle of excitement bubbling deep inside that felt in some strange way as if she were almost within reach of her childhood dreams, something precious and secret.

There were numcrous examples of Lawrence's craftsmanship scattered about the house — a lampshade that glowed, jewel-like, when the candle it covered was alight, a circular plate hung by a length of wire over one of the window panes, and many more, and she had often marvelled at them as she dusted and cleaned, wondering how the facets had been shaped and fitted together into the lead strips that held them in place, but she had not asked. It seemed to her that Lawrence's art went beyond the skilful; there was a mystique about it that bordered on the sacred, and to question him about it would somehow be irreverent.

After a while, however, her curiosity began to overcome her reluctance to pry into his private world, the world that existed within the tumbledown walls of the workshop, and one day when she'd finished her chores and he was still missing, she wondered if she dared pay a visit to his mysterious domain. There could be no harm in showing an interest, surely? She was, after all, his wife! But still her heart was beating a nervous tattoo at the very thought of it.

Rain was falling, thick and steady, as it had seemed to do incessantly these last weeks. Maggie pulled a shawl over her head and ran down the unevenly paved path to the workshop, tucked between shrubs that were beginning to sprout new growth for a spring that still seemed a long way off. As she tapped at the door, rainwater dripped from the overhanging branches of the sycamore tree, splashing on to her face and hands, and she turned the iron handle and opened the door a crack.

Lawrence was at a vast bench, his back towards her.

"I just wondered if you'd like a cup of tea," she said hesitantly.

"Oh, my dear, come inside, do!" Lawrence said without turning round.

"Are you sure?" Maggie felt once again that she was trespassing in a holy of holies.

"Well of course!" He glanced over his shoulder and smiled at her before bending to his work once more.

Maggie stepped inside. It was surprisingly warm in the workshop, the heat emanating from a kiln, inside which a heap of coke glowed fiery red. Various tools and brushes lay on side tables or were affixed to wall racks, and long, thin strips of what she assumed was lead hung over a bracket. But it was the panel spread

366

out on the workbench that drew, and held, her attention. Some five feet in length, and half as wide, it took up almost all of the bench, and Maggie could see it was nearing completion.

"Oh, that's beautiful!" she gasped before she could stop herself — and so it was.

The panel depicted a woman, almost life-size. Her flowing robes were sapphire blue, and a halo, white and gold, shimmered around her head. Her hands were clasped in prayer, her feet bare against emerald grass, and above her, in an azure sky, a tiny cherub emerged from a fluffy cloud, blowing on a silver trumpet.

"The Holy Mother," Maggie whispered reverently.

"Indeed." Lawrence nodded. "She is one of the three windows that make up the triptych — her place will be to left of the central, which will be of our Lord Jesus Christ on the cross. I haven't begun work on that yet, but the right-hand panel, depicting St Joseph, is already complete."

"May I see it?" Maggie asked eagerly.

"You may, but not just yet. I have it stored for safe keeping, and for you to fully appreciate it would mean unwrapping it and bringing it into the light."

"Oh, I don't want to cause you any trouble," Maggie said hastily. "This . . ." she nodded towards the Blessed Virgin, "is more than enough for me. But however do you do it? Those little pieces — how do you get them to be the right shape; how do you know where each of them goes, and stick them together? I can't begin to understand!"

"It's a long process, my dear," Lawrence told her. "There are many stages, and it takes years to learn them all. Most craftsmen concentrate on one or the other — the design, the cutting and painting, the lead work, the firing. I couldn't be satisfied with that — I was fortunate to be able to learn them all. The only thing I don't do myself is the painting of the cartoon. I make a rough drawing of the design required and call on the help of a friend who is a much more talented artist than I. When the picture is finished, and has my approval and that of whoever has commissioned the work, I make a tracing to work from and continue from there."

Already Maggie was quite lost in the explanation. Drawing — tracing — cutting — painting — leadwork — she didn't understand any of it. Seeing the bewilderment on her face, Lawrence smiled.

"I know. It must seem unfathomable to you. Let me finish the Blessed Virgin, and when I begin working on the crucifixion, you can follow me through each stage. As you learn, you can perhaps make a small panel of your own, if you'd like to."

"Oh, I'd love that!" Maggie said, delighted. "But what about my usual duties? I can't neglect them."

Lawrence shrugged.

"As long as we have a meal on the table and clean clothes to put on . . . there are better things in life, Maggie, than a continuous round of domestic tasks. I'd like to think I'd introduced you to some of them. Now, why don't you make us that cup of tea and you can watch me working . . . until, of course, you become bored."

"Oh, I won't be bored for a moment!" Maggie protested.

She could imagine nothing more fascinating than watching as this beautiful window was made ready to go to the home for which it was destined. A home goodness only knew how many miles away, on the other side of an ocean. On the other side of the world!

CHAPTER
TWENTY-ONE

Winter softened into spring, spring blossomed into summer. The window portraying the Blessed Virgin was finished now and stored beneath its protective covering as the one of St Joseph had been. Now Lawrence had begun work on the central window, depicting the terrible beauty of the crucifixion, and Maggie had fallen into the habit of hurrying through her daily chores so that she could join him in his workshop and watch as he worked, talking her through each stage of the process with a patience that was typical of him. She now knew the names of the tools, each of which had its proper place, and something of the different types of glass, though remembering them all was still beyond her. She had helped Lawrence carefully unroll the drawing of Christ on the cross, and he had allowed her to trace some of the outlines, and even make some of the bolder cuts, though he had executed the more intricate pieces himself, running the diamond over the glass, then holding the sheet between finger and thumb as he teased out the required shape. She'd seen him make the square-cornered framework, and stretch lengths of lead, with one end firmly under his foot whilst he pulled with all his strength on the other.

370

She'd even tried her hand at painting, using first the camel-hair matting brush, then the badger, laying down a wash with vertical strokes as he showed her. She had learned how to fire the kiln with coke and charcoal, and she had drawn a simple design of her own, a pit wheel in the centre, a Davy lamp, a helmet, a slag heap and a pickaxe arranged in sections around it, and traced it as she had seen Lawrence do on to a small piece of glass.

"You have a talent for drawing," Lawrence had said. "I can see that I'll be able to dispense with the services of my artist friend before long."

Maggie had flushed with pleasure and pride.

"I've always loved to draw," she said shyly. "When I was a little girl, I was forever doing pictures with coloured pencils on every bit of scrap paper I could get my hands on. But I haven't done anything like that for years now. I've never had the time."

"Well, you have the time now," he said kindly. "Practice is what you need, and lots of it, and then I think we might make an artist of you."

"Oh, I'm not so sure of that!" Maggie knew that whatever talent she possessed was raw and undeveloped, and it would be a long time before she could hope to produce anything good enough to form the basis of one of Lawrence's beautiful windows.

She was, though, happier than she had ever believed possible. There was a purpose now to her days that she'd never experienced before; the moment she woke in the mornings, she was filled with a sense of anticipation and eagerness that bubbled inside her like a fine wine — though Maggie, who had never so much as tasted a fine wine, was unable to make the comparison. All the pressures of her previous life seemed to have melted away; it was as if she inhabited a different world. Lawrence made no demands on her, the news from Yorkshire was encouraging — the warmer weather was suiting Rose, it seemed — and even Billy worried her less. He seemed to have settled in well to the life of a farmhand, and though when he first came to visit he was awkward and sullen, Lawrence treated him with enormous kindness and patience, and slowly Billy began to respond.

"I'm sorry — our Billy can be very difficult," she'd said after that first time, when he'd lowered his eyes and shuffled his feet whenever Lawrence spoke to him. But Lawrence had only smiled, that kind, gentle smile that seemed to belong more to one of the saints in his stained-glass creations than to a flesh-and-blood man.

"He's young and shy," he said. "I was much the same myself once."

Maggie found it hard to believe that Lawrence had ever been as awkward as Billy, but she was grateful to him for his understanding. She didn't argue that Ewart and Walter had never behaved the way Billy did; that seemed unwarranted and cruel. He was just different, as Mam had always said, and that far she did go one day when Billy had been particularly rude to Lawrence. "Different, yes." Lawrence nodded. "But one day he'll find his metier, just as we all do."

Maggie didn't recognise the word, or really know what it meant, but she got the gist of it. She was learning all the time, she thought, simply from being in

Lawrence's company: new words, new manners, new customs, and of course, most of all, new skills.

And she was learning, too, that love came in many forms, not simply the blind passion she had felt for Josh, or the fierce loyalty of blood ties. She was coming to love Lawrence, she realised — his kindness, his gentleness, his modesty, his enduring faith in a God to whom he had dedicated his life in his own way. This love was a seed planted in gratitude, and it grew and deepened with each passing day, fed and watered by the interest they now shared, he as the teacher, she as his student. Josh seemed now more like a distant dream, an ache in her heart with which she had learned to live, and though she still woke sometimes in the night with tears on her cheeks and the longing for him strong as ever, she had trained herself to put it away.

Josh had left her. He was with someone else. He had never loved her as she loved him. But a part of him was with her still. As her stomach swelled to a baby-shaped mound, as she felt the child move within her, as she traced her fingers over small protruding lumps that she knew were either a fist or a tiny foot, she experienced something close to a sense of triumph.

This child was Josh's child, and that fact alone made it very special, the last thing she had, would ever have, of the man she had loved with all her heart. Yet it was also her child and hers alone, and no one and nothing but God or a cruel fate could take it away from her. Thanks to Lawrence, the baby had a future that was secure, holding far more than he could otherwise have hoped for. He wouldn't be branded a bastard; he wouldn't have to fight bigger boys who called him names; he wouldn't have to wear hand-me-down clothes that were shabby, threadbare or too big for him. He wouldn't have to give up his education and toil in the darkness far beneath the green fields. And if he turned out to be a she, she wouldn't have to go into the drudgery of service — though Maggie felt quite certain that the unborn baby was a boy.

Caressing her swollen stomach, she reflected on all this, and vowed that she would never do anything to jeopardise her baby's assured future. Even if that meant devoting herself to Lawrence and forgetting that Josh ever existed.

This was her life now; she would be content with it.

And she was, she was.

The telegram was delivered one morning in early July.

Maggie had been up since dawn. She'd had a restless night, and the old feeling of foreboding she'd learned to dread had been nagging at her, indeterminate but too strong to ignore. Besides this, the niggling ache low in her back that had kept her from settling was growing more intense. She'd been trying to ignore it and get through her daily chores so that she could join Lawrence in his workshop; today she was due to begin the delicate task of cutting the tiny fragments of glass that would make up the sections of sky that peeped between the spokes of the pit wheel in the plate she was making, and she was eager to begin. The concentration required would soon make her forget this stupid ache, she told herself.

When the doorbell jangled she was upstairs, debating whether or not to change the bedlinen. It was a fine, warm day; if she washed the sheets and pillowcases they'd dry quickly on the line that ran the length of the garden outside the kitchen window. But the thought of carrying buckets of hot water from the copper, heaving the wet fabric up and down in the sink, rinsing, and then, worst of all, running the lot through the mangle was not an appealing one, so the sound of the bell was a welcome distraction. She was puzzled as to who could be calling, though; visitors were a rarity, and it was too early for the baker, who came twice weekly. Sometimes a gypsy would come to the door with a basket of clothes pegs to sell, or a bunch of lucky white heather — if they had set up camp in the nearby countryside, their route into Hillsbridge took them past Lawrence's home. Perhaps it was a gypsy; well, she'd just have to send them on their way. She didn't need clothes pegs and she wasn't sure Lawrence would approve of the lucky heather, being a devout Catholic and scathing with regard to superstition. Then again, he might give them a few pennies or a silver threepenny bit out of sympathy. But it wasn't her place to raid his purse, and she had no intention of interrupting him to find out if he was feeling charitable today.

She glanced out of the window and saw a bicycle propped up against the gate. Not gypsies, then. Maggie descended the stairs slowly, her bulk making her feel a little unsafe, and the doorbell jangled again.

"All right, I'm coming!" she muttered, crossing the living room and rubbing her aching back as she did so.

As she unlatched the door and saw the uniformed boy on the doorstep, holding out a small buff envelope, her heart missed a beat. A telegram! Though she'd never received one in her life, she knew what it was, all right. And she knew too that telegrams rarely brought good news.

"Mrs Jacobs?" The boy thrust the envelope towards her. "For you."

"For my husband," she corrected him automatically.

"No, missus, for you." The boy had a cheeky little face, red from the exertion of pedalling out from Hillsbridge as fast as his legs would take him, and a voice to match, a reedy voice that had not yet broken.

Maggie took the envelope, and her heart thudded again as she saw that it was indeed her name emblazoned on the front of it.

"Thank you," she said faintly.

The boy made no effort to leave.

"Do you need paying?" she asked. She had no idea of the protocol involved.

"Sixpence wouldn't come amiss," the boy replied. "It's a long way out here, you know."

"Very well. Wait a minute."

Maggie went back into the house; Lawrence's purse was, she knew, in a dresser drawer. She opened it and found a sixpence. Though she wouldn't have done it for the gypsies, this was different. This was official.

She returned to the door, gave the sixpence to the boy, and he went whistling down the path. Only when he had retrieved his bicycle and pedalled away did she go back into the house and tear open the envelope.

376

The ache in her back was forgotten now, but she felt sick with dread, and as she unfolded the sheet of paper and read the message it contained, her worst fears were realised.

It was brutally brief and to the point — not a single word beyond what was necessary — as telegrams, she supposed, always were.

Mam passed in the night. Will write. Walter.

Her stomach fell away and the ground seemed to be dissolving beneath her feet.

It shouldn't have been a shock, though recently Mam had apparently been better; wasn't this exactly what Maggie had been fearing for the last year and more? And yet it was.

Mam, dead? No! Oh, please, no!

Mam dead, so far from home, and Maggie hadn't been with her. She would never see her again; Mam would never see her new grandchild. The thought was almost more than she could bear.

For long moments she stood, swaying on her feet, her mind racing in wild circles. What should she do? What *could* she do? Should she go to Yorkshire? She so wanted to be there, with Ewart and Walter — oh, how she wanted that. But with the baby due at any time, it didn't seem possible. And Billy — how was she going to tell Billy? He was going to be so upset. The thought of his distress only added to her own.

Lawrence. She must tell Lawrence. He would know what to do. But her feet seemed welded to the floor and she shrank from the thought of making all this real by putting it into words.

"Maggie?" Lawrence's voice from the doorway. "Maggie, my dear, whatever is wrong?"

He must have heard the clang of the bell and come to see who was calling.

"Oh . . ." Maggie whispered, and still the words would not come. "Oh . . ."

Lawrence took the telegram from her, reading it with one quick glance.

"My dear . . . I'm so sorry . . ." His distress was genuine. "She was a good woman . . . such a good woman . . ."

Maggie was briefly puzzled by his words. As far as she knew, Lawrence had never met her mother. But as he reached for her hands, squeezing them tight between his own, the shock and grief came rushing in, and she could think of nothing else. Tears gathered in her eyes and ran down her cheeks unchecked.

And not only her cheeks. Moisture was running down her legs in a hot rush. For a horrified moment Maggie thought her bladder had released, but it wasn't that.

"Oh dear God!" she gasped. "I think . . ."

But she was unable to articulate that either. How could she find the words to tell a man — even her husband — what was happening?

Her waters had broken, Maggie knew. Her baby was coming.

One in, one out. The old adage popped into Maggie's head more than once in the hours that followed, in between the spasms that were now gripping her. At first they weren't much worse than the ache that had been troubling her since the middle of the night, but gradually they increased in strength so that when they came she could no longer think of anything at all beyond riding out each excruciating wave and waiting for the next. Only the despair remained, an overwhelming wretchedness that needed no coherent thought but lent an aura of nightmare to the contractions that racked her.

Lawrence had arranged for a midwife and a doctor from Hillsbridge to attend her, a luxury Maggie would never have been afforded in her former life. As soon as it became evident that she had begun her labour, the midwife was sent for, a big-boned, capable-looking woman named Mrs Harvey. She came bustling in, divesting herself of her cape and looking around critically at the small, cluttered living room.

"Let's get you upstairs then, missy, and I can have a good look at you."

Maggie, who had been walking the length of the room and back again, over and over, went, obedient as a child, leaving an anxious Lawrence downstairs.

In the bedroom — which warranted more critical looks — Mrs Harvey tied a voluminous apron around her ample frame and examined first the bed — "Are these clean sheets? Best put some old ones on if you don't want them all mucked up" — and then Maggie. Maggie hated that; it was both humiliating and painful. Mrs Harvey seemed unnecessarily rough, and Maggie had to grit her teeth against the prodding fingers.

"You'll be a good while yet," the midwife pronounced.

"Oh, I was hoping it wouldn't be too long," Maggie said, before catching her breath as another pain racked her, and Mrs Harvey snorted derisively.

"You'll have a lot more than that to put up with before this is over," she said, and it seemed to Maggie that she was taking pleasure in the prospect.

Oh Mam, she thought, tears pricking her eyes. *Where are you? I need you! Where have you gone?*

But Rose wasn't here, and never would be again, no matter how much Maggie wanted her. There was only Mrs Harvey, bossy and unsympathetic, and Maggie could only hope she was as good at her job as her reputation suggested. It was she the Hillsbridge doctor had recommended when Lawrence had taken her to see him, and she had been booked on the strength of his advice.

The doctor, at least, had seemed nice, though much younger than Dr Blackmore in High Compton. But he was a Scot, with a strong Highland accent, and Maggie had had trouble understanding a word he said. Everything and everyone was alien to what she was used to, and although she was only a few miles from home, she felt lost and frightened, cut off from the comfortable and familiar.

It would be some time, anyway, before the doctor arrived. He had better things to do than sit by the bedside of a woman in labour, and would only be sent for when the redoubtable Mrs Harvey deemed it necessary.

380

As the day wore on, it seemed that moment would never come. The room was stiflingly hot, the windows all closed and the fire in the grate burning fiercely as Mrs Harvey kept it well stoked up from the coal bucket that stood beside it. Maggie tossed and turned, wriggled and writhed, tugging on the old pillowcase that the midwife had tied around the bedhead for her to hang on to when the pain became unbearable. Sweat poured down her face, gathered in the hollow between her breasts and soaked her nightgown. She wanted to get up and try to walk about — anything, she thought, would be better than lying on the bed with sheets that were rumpled and untidy no matter how often Mrs Harvey smoothed them out, and damp with Maggie's perspiration — but the midwife wouldn't hear of it. She wiped Maggie's forehead occasionally with a cool wet flannel and allowed her sips of water, but neither seemed to help.

The pain was almost continuous now, one long agony from which Maggie could not escape, and still Mrs Harvey, after more painful prodding and poking, maintained she wasn't anywhere near ready to deliver her baby. Eventually, though, Lawrence took matters into his own hands.

Dimly Maggie was aware of his uneven gait on the stairs and a tap at the door. Mrs Harvey harrumphed impatiently — husbands were most definitely not welcome in what had become her domain — but she opened it a crack and there was a whispered conversation.

"Mr Jacobs wants to get the doctor," she said, disapproval evident in her tone. "I've told him it'll be hours yet, but he thinks he knows best."

Maggie was past caring and certainly past arguing, but she felt a wave of relief all the same. Surely the doctor would do something? This couldn't go on for much longer. She couldn't stand it! She stuffed her fist into her mouth to keep herself from crying out as another pain built to a crescendo — even now her pride wouldn't allow her to let herself down, as she thought of it, in front of this hatchet-faced woman whom she was coming to dislike more with every passing hour. But she couldn't help herself from whispering, "Oh God, dear God, please help me!" only to evoke the sharp retort: "He is helping you, my girl."

The light outside the window was fading, and Mrs Harvey had fetched an oil lamp and placed it on the chest of drawers beside the bed by the time the doctor arrived. He came into the room, dumped his medical bag on the chair Mrs Harvey had been sitting in between her ministrations and crossed to Maggie. His tall, lanky form seemed to tower over her, and she still couldn't understand a word he said, but his thin, angular face was kindly, and when he examined her, he was far gentler than Mrs Harvey had been.

"Och aye, you're doing fine."

Miracle of miracles, she understood that! And miracle of miracles, now that he was here, nothing seemed quite so bad.

"Oh Doctor, is it going to be much longer?" she whispered.

And was quite suddenly overcome with a powerful need to push. Though it was what she had been waiting for all day, she was still startled by the strength of the compulsion.

"Ah, that's the way, hinny." The lilting accent was soothing, and for all that the pain had reached new dimensions, Maggie felt safe with him. Even in those panic-stricken moments when she thought her body was being torn in two, that lilting voice and kind eyes had the power to calm her.

More lamps were brought, fetched from every corner of the house at Dr Mackay's request, even the candle lamp with the stained-glass shade, and it was on that that Maggie focused as she strained and pushed with each contraction. Darkness fell and the candle flame glowed, an oasis of light in the darkness that seemed to surround her.

And at last — at last! — Maggie felt a soft rush as her baby slipped from her into Mrs Harvey's waiting hands and uttered his first mewling cry.

"A little boy! You've got a beautiful little boy!" the midwife told her, triumphant as if she herself was solely responsible for the new life.

Maggie fell back against the rumpled pillows, too exhausted to even try to peek at her baby. But a little while later, when the midwife placed the small, tightly swaddled bundle in her arms, she gazed in awe at the little red face, puckered into creases around a perfect pursed mouth, as if he was angry at having been kept waiting so long to be delivered; at the mass of fine dark hair covering a pointed head, and at shell-like ears that lay flat against his skull, and a wave of love stronger than any she had experienced before in her life swept through her.

But oh! Her heart twisted. He was so like Josh!

Not possible. Surely it was far too early for him to look like anyone. Yet that first impression was too strong to be denied, and Maggie didn't know whether to be angry or glad.

"What is the bairn to be called?" asked Dr Mackay, washing his hands in the china bowl on the washstand. How was it she could now understand him, though his accent was as thick as ever? The shared experience, perhaps?

Maggie looked at Lawrence, who had at last been allowed into the bedroom and was standing beside the bed gazing at the baby with much the same awe as Maggie was feeling.

They hadn't talked about a name. Though Maggie had run over a few, testing them on her tongue to see how they sounded, she'd never asked Lawrence's opinion and he hadn't offered it. But now the baby was here, flesh and blood, a real, living human being, not just a swelling beneath her petticoats. He deserved a name, and Lawrence, who had given her refuge and the baby a future, deserved to be consulted.

"Lawrence?" she said softly.

"You're calling him after your husband?" Dr Mackay asked, misunderstanding, and then, after just a moment's hesitation, Maggie said:

"We could, yes."

"Oh, I think not!" Lawrence shook his head, smiling. "That would be far too confusing. And besides, a baby doesn't want to be named for an old duffer like me."

"You are not an old duffer," Maggie said stoutly. "And we could always call him Laurie to make the distinction. Laurie . . . I like that . . ." She paused for a moment. "And perhaps Patrick besides, after my father."

"Patrick Lawrence, then," Lawrence said. "We'll decide later." But Maggie thought he looked pleased and as proud as if he was the baby's real father.

"Patrick," she whispered, and smoothed one peachy cheek with her thumb. "Patrick Lawrence . . ."

But her eyes were drooping. With her baby nestled against her breast, Maggie fell asleep.

CHAPTER
TWENTY-TWO

September 1897

The little house on the outskirts of Hillsbridge was a flurry of activity. The three tall stained-glass windows were finished at last, crated securely and ready to be shipped across the Atlantic, and Lawrence was to go to New York to see them safely fitted in the lady chapel of the cathedral. His passage was booked — he was to sail from Liverpool on the steam ship *Campania* in just a few days' time, and Maggie was helping him to pack a trunk with all he would need and a suitcase with sufficient to see him through the voyage.

As she folded shirts and undergarments, Patrick waddled around behind her on plump little legs, which sometimes collapsed beneath him so that he landed in a heap on his bottom, lost patience with the business of walking and scrambled after her at a rapid crawl.

He was growing fast, no longer a baby but a little boy. His hair, thick and dark even when he was born, was now a mass of curls and ringlets falling around cheeks rosy with health. His nose had grown straight, and his eyes turned from that first clear blue to hazel, the exact same colour as his father's, and Maggie could not look at him without thinking how like Josh he was.

She found it hard to believe, in fact, that no one else could see it, but of course no one in Hillsbridge knew Josh, and when Ewart had come to visit, in early summer, if he'd seen the likeness he didn't comment on it, and for that she was grateful. No one beyond her immediate family knew the truth; as far as the outside world was concerned, Lawrence was Patrick's father, and if they questioned it in private, she never knew it.

In the first months after Patrick was born, she'd walked into Hillsbridge often, pushing him in his perambulator, and the people she met in the shops and the market would coo over him. Maggie was glad they thought he was Lawrence's, even if perhaps they wondered in private how an old man like him could have fathered such a beautiful child. It wasn't just that she wanted to keep her secret; it seemed to her to be a little tribute to the man who had given her a whole new life.

And what a life! Scarcely a day passed but Maggie counted her blessings. She never had to worry for a moment as to where the next penny was coming from; Lawrence gave her a generous allowance for housekeeping and paid without questioning for everything she needed for herself and Lawrence. She had a nice home, she had the most beautiful son, and a husband who demanded nothing of her that she was unprepared to give. Though Lawrence had insisted the laundry be sent once a week to a washerwoman, and brought in a girl to help with the spring cleaning after the chimney sweep had been, her days were full, and they were for the most part happy.

There had been dark ones, of course, in the months following Rose's death, days when she had been ready to burst into tears, and times when she had railed at the heavens that Rose had been taken without seeing her grandchild. There were times when she worried about Billy, as much the loner as ever, perhaps even more so, for his beloved Bullseye had died, too, in the long, hard winter — he'd gone missing for a few days before Billy had found him lying in a corner of the barn, curled up and half hidden behind the threshing machine. And there were times when she still ached for Josh, longed for him with a fervour that was, she told herself, far more than he deserved. But she had little time for such thoughts. When she wasn't engaged in domestic duties, her every waking moment was occupied with helping Lawrence work on the precious stained-glass window.

She had a talent for it, Lawrence had said, and that filled her with pride, though she was all too aware of her limitations. The plate she'd made to her own design looked clumsy and amateurish compared to Lawrence's fine work, so intricate and precise, but it would come with practice, he assured her, and she could almost believe him, for she was beginning to be able to see exactly what needed to be done, even if her fingers were not yet nimble enough to always follow suit.

"Try your hand at a new piece of your own whilst I'm away," Lawrence encouraged her, and she promised she would, though she wasn't sure how she'd manage it now that Patrick was walking. She wouldn't be able to take him into the workshop with her with only one pair of eyes to watch what he was up to; there were far too many dangers there, from the kiln to the cutting tools and the collection of sheets of glass. Even if she took some of his toys with him, he'd most likely find the unfamiliar attractions far more interesting, and she couldn't risk him cutting or burning himself. But perhaps she would be able to snatch a little time while he was asleep. The evening hours would be long and lonely while Lawrence was away.

She was going to miss him, Maggie realised. The man who had once been no more than a kind stranger had become her closest friend, and where she had once felt shy and awkward with him, now she told him everything. Though he was as quiet as ever, Maggie more than made up for it, filling what could have been long silences with her chatter, relating every detail of her day and reporting on Patrick's latest development.

It was because of Patrick that the bond between them had grown and strengthened, she thought — Lawrence doted on the little boy. But he was also unfailingly kind and caring towards her, and surprisingly fond of Billy, whom he encouraged to come to the house whenever he had a day off. He'd been especially good when Bullseye had died, spending time with Billy and seemingly comforting him, not so much with words as simply by being there. Perhaps it was because neither of them were outgoing that they were able to communicate with few words spoken, Maggie thought. They understood one another. And now that he was about to leave for America, Lawrence had asked if Billy could come and see him off.

Maggie hadn't been sure if it would be possible, or even if Billy would want to. But when the day came, and the pony and trap deposited her, Patrick and Lawrence at the Hillsbridge railway station, Billy was there, leaning against the fence beside the entrance, the bicycle that he'd borrowed from Farmer propped up beside him.

They all trooped on to the platform, the elderly porter, who had appeared as if by magic, wheeling Lawrence's trunk on a set of trucks. The stationmaster himself emerged from his office to speak to Lawrence, and Maggie realised yet again how well regarded he was in the town. It wasn't long before a signal clanked and the level-crossing gates closed across the main road, then the train was pulling into the station. Patrick squealed excitedly, his little face animated as he pointed with chubby fingers at the clouds of steam coming from the engine. Lawrence's trunk was manhandled into the guard's van and the porter held a door open for Lawrence to climb into the carriage.

He turned, chucking Patrick under the chin, and squeezed Billy's shoulder.

"Look after your sister while I'm gone."

Billy nodded. "I will, sir," and Maggie thought how odd that was — she'd always been the one to look after him.

Last but not least, Lawrence embraced Maggie, and then there was nothing for it but to get into the carriage, though he wound down the window and stood looking out as the porter slammed doors up and down the train. The guard blew his whistle and raised a green flag, then with another hiss of steam the train pulled away, Lawrence still at the open window.

Maggie waved her handkerchief until the train rounded a bend in the line and was lost to sight. She felt utterly bereft.

"I suppose I'd better get home," she said to Billy.

"I've got to go too," Billy said. "Farmer will dock my wages if I'm gone too long."

"Will you come over and see me when you get some time off?" she asked.

"If you like."

The pony and trap were waiting for her. The driver lifted Patrick up, then handed her in. As the pony trotted off, she looked back over her shoulder; Billy was still standing beside his bicycle watching her go and looking as small and lost as ever.

"It's going to be funny without your daddy, isn't it, my love?" she said to Patrick, but his eyelids were drooping, long lashes fanning out across his soft, plump cheeks. Maggie cradled him to her, burying her chin in his curls, and long before they left the town behind, he was fast asleep.

She'd been right — she did miss him. There was suddenly a Lawrence-shaped space in the little house, and even with Patrick tumbling about, it felt strangely empty and silent. Patrick's attempts at speaking were mostly unintelligible garbles, with the occasional "Ma-ma" or "birdie" thrown in, and when she talked to him it tended to be about the mundane and the infantile.

Loneliness crept up on her unawares; she wished she could venture into High Compton to meet up with Beat and Cathy, and one day she pushed Patrick in his perambulator almost to the outskirts of the town. But there she stopped, before turning around to go back the way she'd come. It was too far, she told herself; by the time she made it all the way home again, it would be well past Patrick's tea time. And it was too hot — one of those scorching days of Indian summer; her back and armpits were moist with a sheen of perspiration beneath the leg-of-mutton sleeves of her blouse, and her feet felt swollen inside her laced boots. But in reality she knew she'd turned back for quite another reason — how could she simply walk into the drapery shop and face Augusta and the girls after all this time? She had nothing to be ashamed of now — she was a respectable married woman, after all — but Mrs Freeman knew the truth even if the girls did not, and she simply couldn't bring herself to do it.

"Let's go and listen to the echo, Patrick," she said — there was a spot in the woods only a little off the beaten track where a shouted "Hello!" would reverberate off the railway arches across the valley, and she thought it would amuse him.

But when she began calling out, a terrible feeling of sadness overcame her. For Mam, for Jack, for Paddy . . . all dead and gone. And then for Josh, the father Patrick would never know, and also for Lawrence, who was by now half a world away.

"Be safe, Lawrence," she whispered, tears misting her eyes.

"Ma-ma?" Patrick was staring up at her, his clear hazel eyes puzzled, as if he'd picked up on her change of mood and he too might begin to cry.

"It's all right, my love," Maggie said, swallowing her tears and managing to call out again to the echo, making him smile.

Then she bumped the perambulator over the rough ground until they were back on the road, and walked briskly off in the direction of the place she now called home.

Lawrence had been gone for more than two weeks when Maggie took Patrick to market in Hillsbridge one Saturday morning.

The market was a huge affair, as much a social event as a commercial enterprise. There was a vast purpose-built hall with entrances on three sides, which was always filled with stalls, and even then there wasn't space for them all. They spilled out on to the cobbled square outside, which also formed the forecourt of the George Hotel: fruiterers, butchers, fishmongers, grocers, a stall selling butter, cream and cheese, though this one was of course inside in the shade. Smasher the chinaware man was there, tossing plates and cups into the air and letting them crash into a thousand pieces on the cobbles to attract attention to his wares; a pair of Indian doctors were selling pills and potions they claimed would cure all ills, and there was even a wagon where a swarthy man with what looked like an enormous pair of pliers would pull aching teeth in full view of the watching crowd.

The market would continue well into the evening, and sometimes the Salvation Army band would play and people would dance while a tiny woman went around with a hat, collecting money to go to good causes. Maggie had never been there in the evening, of course — before she was married, she'd always been at work herself for late-night opening, and now she had Patrick to think of. Besides which, she had heard, things could turn rowdy later on. The miners would have divided up their week's wages earlier on in the bar of the Miners' Arms, just across the street from the George, and some of them would have whiled away the day spending too much of it on a few drinks.

When Maggie arrived soon after ten in the morning, however, all was respectable hustle and bustle. She bought butter, bacon, and a small wedge of cheese from the dairy stall, apples and vegetables from the greengrocer, and half a pound of biscuits from the grocer, loading it all into the well of the perambulator. On the way back down the aisle between the stalls she made a detour to one that sold novelties, and treated Patrick to a little paper windmill on a stick. Outside, she was showing him how it turned by blowing on it, for there was not enough wind to do it for him, when she heard someone call her name.

"Maggie!"

She looked round, startled — who in Hillsbridge would call her by her given name instead of Mrs Jacobs?

Then her stomach fell away and her heart seemed to stop beating.

Pushing his way towards her through the crowd was the tall figure of the man she'd tried so hard to forget.

It was Josh Withers.

She couldn't move, couldn't speak. If she hadn't been holding on to the handle of the perambulator, she thought her legs might have given way beneath her.

"Maggie! Thank goodness!"

From somewhere she found her voice.

"What are you doing here?"

"Looking for you, of course! Hester Dallimore said she thought she'd seen you at the market last week, so I came on the off chance you'd be here again."

"You came specially looking for me?" There was no containing that spurt of fierce joy.

"I've been trying to find you ever since I got home and found you gone. Nobody at home seemed to know what had become of you, not even Mam and Dad. You certainly know how to give a man the runaround!"

"Really!" Quite suddenly that joy was soured with anger. "I've given you the runaround! Well, that's rich coming from you, I must say! And it's a bit late to be looking for me, isn't it?"

"Oh Maggie!" Josh's eyes went to Patrick, who was staring up, round-eyed, from the perambulator, his new windmill forgotten. "It was right, then, what people are saying. Why didn't you tell me?"

She raised her chin, remembering all too clearly the despair she'd felt that day she'd made the trip into Bristol looking for Josh. Oh, he had a nerve, all right!

395

"And how was I supposed to do that when you disappeared from the only address you gave anybody and ran off with somebody else, I'd like to know?"

"Maggie, I didn't! And I wrote, soon as I was settled . . ."

"Oh, don't lie to me, Josh!" she snapped. "You didn't give a fig about me. Well, I'm all right now, so just leave me alone."

She turned away, manoeuvring the perambulator through a gap in the shoppers. Josh followed.

"Maggie! Wait! We need to talk . . ."

"I've got nothing to say to you, Josh." A red mist flaring in front of her eyes, she forged a path towards the road, thinking of nothing but escaping from her churning emotions and the man who was responsible for them. The railway delivery wagon was approaching, the horse at a fast trot, but she didn't even notice it until Josh grabbed the handle of the perambulator, stopping her abruptly.

"For goodness' sake, Maggie! Are you trying to get yourself and the baby killed?"

She was trembling violently now, realisation that she had very nearly pushed Patrick into the path of the oncoming wagon piling in on the shock of meeting Josh so unexpectedly.

"Please, just go away!" she begged.

"I'm not going anywhere until we've had the chance to talk."

He had never sounded more determined, his voice a low growl, and quite suddenly the fight drained out of her.

She was all too aware of the nearness of him, his hand brushing hers on the handle of the perambulator; all too aware of the maelstrom of emotion churning inside her. No matter that he'd let her down, no matter what he'd done or not done, she loved him still.

"Oh Josh," she whispered, and all the despair, all the longing was there in her voice. He was here, right beside her, but he might as well have been a million miles away. "It's too late."

"I can see that." His eyes went to her hand, and her wedding ring. "I'd still like to sort things out."

"Not here. I don't want the whole town knowing my business. We'd better find somewhere quiet. We could go in the churchyard, there's a bench there . . ."

"Churchyard, eh?"

"It's on my way home. I can't be too long, Patrick has his dinner at midday."

It wasn't what he'd hoped for when he'd come to Hillsbridge this morning in search of her, but he reckoned it was more than he had a right to expect. He was cursing himself, as he had cursed himself every day since he had come home and found Maggie gone, that he hadn't made more of an effort to check with her that she wasn't pregnant before he went off to Ireland. But she'd made it crystal clear that she couldn't allow them to be together, for a long while at least. He'd written to her from Bristol and she hadn't even replied, and when he planned to go to Belfast in search of work in the Harland and Wolff shipyard, he'd written again, to both her and his parents. He'd asked Cissie to post the letters for him, and assumed she had, but now he knew she'd had other things on her mind — namely running off with her fairground lover. By the time he wrote again, with the address of his new lodgings in Belfast, it was, of course, too late. Number six was all shut up and the Donovans were gone, his mother had told him.

How much had she known? he wondered now. She'd been very evasive, and wouldn't speculate beyond the rumours that had been circulating, one of which was that Maggie had got herself into trouble.

"If that's what's behind it, I hope it wasn't anything to do with you, my lad," she'd said, giving him a dark look. "I hope that isn't why you went off to Ireland, to get out of doing the right thing by her."

"What do you think I am?" Josh had growled, and Florrie had merely said: "Well, that's all right then," and let the subject drop. But Josh couldn't forget it, any more than he could forget Maggie.

There was a job going for a colliery carpenter at Northway pit; Josh had gone to see the manager, secured it, and returned to Belfast only to pick up his belongings. Back in High Compton, he'd tried every which way to find out what had become of Maggie, and got nowhere. Not even Beat or Cathy could tell him anything, though Cathy had promised to write to Ewart and ask for information — a good excuse to get in touch with him, Josh suspected; her face had turned very pink when she mentioned his name. But both girls seemed seemed genuinely concerned to know what had become of their friend.

And then, as he'd told Maggie, the gossip of the rank, Hester Dallimore, had spotted her at the market one Saturday.

"And she was pushing a pram with a nipper in it, about a year old, I'd say!" she added triumphantly as she spread the news far and wide.

Josh's stomach had turned over when he heard it. If Maggie had a child about a year old, there was no doubt in his mind that it must be his. It was no more than he'd feared, but he couldn't stop castigating himself for not having been here for her when she needed him. His stupid pride was to blame, he thought — when she'd told him she wouldn't go with him to Bristol, didn't know if she'd ever be able to be with him, he'd thought it was because he was just a poor second to Jack. He'd been badly hurt and had gone on the defensive, and when she hadn't replied to his letter he'd taken it as further evidence that she didn't want him. Why the hell hadn't he been more assertive? Or more dogged? Why the hell had he assumed that if she wanted, or needed, him, she would come to him?

And where did they go from here?

Josh had never before been in the Hillsbridge churchyard. A path led around the old grey-stone building, opening up into a vast expanse of grass, dotted with headstones so old they were beginning to totter and crumble, but beyond the church door the ground sloped upwards and the graves there were clearly newer and well tended. Near the path a bench had been set under a tree — a magnolia, Josh thought, but he wasn't that good at identifying flora, and just at the moment couldn't have cared less.

Maggie parked the perambulator next to it, lifted Patrick out and set him down on the dry grass with a soft knitted toy and his new windmill.

"Play with this like a good boy," she said. "And don't poke the sails like that or you'll break it."

But still the little boy couldn't resist — sticking a chubby finger into the gap in the paper and wriggling it round.

An unfamiliar emotion twisted within Josh. He'd barely ever taken notice of a baby before, but this one, he knew, was his, and the tenderness mixed with warmth and pride he was experiencing now took him completely by surprise.

"Well," Maggie said, sitting down on the bench, "what's happened to this woman you ran off with, then?"

Josh sighed. So many misunderstandings, and yet in the end it all came back to one thing.

"I never ran off with any woman, Maggie," he said. "You've got to believe me when I say there's never been anyone for me but you."

"So where were you?" she demanded. "Where were you when I came to Bristol to find you? And why did her husband tell me you had? That's what I'd like to know!"

"If you'll just hush up for a minute I'll tell you," Josh said.

"What are we going to do, then?" Josh asked when he had finished.

"There's nothing we can do." Maggie's eyes were full of tears. She had a feeling of déjà vu. First the ghost of Jack had stood between her and Josh; now it was Lawrence, a living, breathing man who had been so kind to her, who had offered her a refuge when she had desperately needed it. He was her husband, she loved him, though in a quite different way to the way she loved Josh, and she wouldn't, couldn't, hurt or betray him.

Patrick, who had been playing quietly all the time they had been talking, was becoming restless. She'd had to get up a few times now to go after him when he toddled or crawled too far away, and now he was pulling at her skirts, his small face twisting into an expression of discontent that she knew was the precursor to tears. He was getting hungry, she guessed, as well as being bored.

"I'm going to have to go," she said.

"I want to see you again. You — and Patrick."

Oh, how she wanted to see him too! But . . . She shook her head.

"That wouldn't be a good idea."

"I let you go once . . . I'm not going to let you go again," he said fiercely.

"Oh Josh, don't make this harder for me, please!" She lifted Patrick, holding him between them.

"But if your husband is away . . . I could come and see you both . . ."

"And where would that end? You know as well as I do. No, I'm sorry, Josh, but it has to stop here. When Patrick is older, perhaps he can come and visit you — if

401

Lawrence doesn't mind, and always provided you still want to see him, of course. But you've got to forget about me. I took marriage vows to Lawrence, and I intend to keep them."

"I see. He matters more to you than I do, then."

"Oh, don't do this to me, please!" she begged.

"What am I supposed to think? If you loved me . . ."

Maggie set Patrick down in the perambulator and turned to face him.

"Oh Josh, believe me, I love you. I've always loved you, and I always will. But . . ."

The tears were pricking her eyes again, Patrick had begun to grizzle and bounce restlessly so that the perambulator rocked on the uneven ground. Holding on to the handle to steady it, Maggie leaned towards Josh and kissed him briefly on the cheek.

Then, before she could weaken, she turned the perambulator, steadied it back down the slope to the path and walked away without a backward glance.

CHAPTER
TWENTY-THREE

Lawrence arrived home two weeks later, the pony and trap that had brought him from the railway station pulling up outside the cottage just as dusk was falling on a blustery autumnal day.

Maggie ran to the door to greet him, Patrick in her arms.

"Oh Lawrence, it's so good to have you back!" she exclaimed, and it was. She'd been feeling really down since her encounter with Josh, with too much time on her hands to think about what might have been. Now, as Lawrence hugged her and Patrick, taking the little boy from her and swinging him round to make him laugh, she knew that for all her regrets, she had done the right thing. Though he'd probably hide it behind a patient smile, he would be so terribly hurt if she left him to be with Josh. And she didn't like to think of him left alone either. He was such a solitary soul, but she knew he was glad of what she and Patrick had brought into his life, and would miss them dreadfully.

"How have you been, my dear?" he asked when he'd taken off his coat and was sitting in the wing chair with Patrick on his knee.

"We've been fine, haven't we, Patrick?" Maggie still hadn't decided whether to tell him that Josh was back in the area — she'd hate him to hear about it from anyone but her — but this wasn't the moment.

"That's good." Lawrence jiggled Patrick on to his good leg so that he could reach for the cup of tea Maggie had placed on an occasional table beside him. "Because I'm afraid I'm going to have to go back again, and soon."

"Go back? But why?" Maggie was astounded.

"Unfortunately, one of the windows was damaged in the transportation," Lawrence said.

"Oh no! Which one?"

"The Blessed Virgin. How it happened, I don't know. It was so securely crated and went with clear instructions that it should be handled with care. But somehow the damage has occurred, and I have agreed to go back to New York to make the necessary repairs there rather than risk it on yet another Atlantic crossing."

"Why didn't you do it while you were there?" Maggie asked.

"Well, for one thing I wanted to ensure that the glass is the same as I used originally — the blue of the Virgin's robe is a very particular shade, and I wasn't sure I'd be able to match it. Besides which, I'd much prefer to use my own tools; foolish, I suppose — one badger brush is much like another — but there you are." Lawrence took a sip of his tea. "But the main reason is that the damage is really quite extensive and the repairs are likely to be rather a long job. I didn't feel

404

I could stay to complete them without coming home first to make sure you were all right. And I have to confess, I was rather hoping that perhaps you might come back with me."

"To New York?" Maggie was staggered.

"Why not? I think you'd enjoy it. It's a wonderful city. And with your new-found skills, you could help me with the repairs."

"Oh my goodness!" Maggie shook her head, overwhelmed by the enormity of the suggestion. "But I couldn't take a baby all that way on a steamship!"

"The voyage took only six days, and the *Campania* is a marvellous vessel. The public rooms are all panelled in oak and satinwood, with thick carpets and velvet curtains and richly upholstered furniture. There is even an open fireplace in the smoking room, and the dining salon . . . my dear, you should see it! It must be ten feet high, and in the centre a well rises up through three decks to a skylight. When I unpack, I'll show you the handbook each passenger was given. The crossing alone would be a tremendous experience for you."

"It sounds . . . amazing . . ." Maggie was lost for words.

"You'd enjoy working with me in the cathedral, too," Lawrence went on. "And I could do with your assistance. Sometimes I think my eyesight isn't what it was, and you could help me so much when the light is failing."

"You've almost persuaded me," Maggie said, laughing.

"Good. Because I have taken the liberty of booking passages for all of us on a sailing at the end of November," Lawrence said with a twinkle. "I know, I shouldn't have done it before I'd discussed it with you, but truth be told, I was missing you and this little fellow." He smiled at Patrick, who was trying to pull on his whiskers. "I don't want to miss any more of your growing up, my lad. Goodness knows, I've missed enough already! Where has that little baby gone, I'd like to know?"

A sharp pang gnawed at Maggie. Lawrence wasn't the only one missing the precious stages of Patrick's development. Josh was missing them too, not just a month or so, but all of them. But she mustn't think about Josh. Lawrence was her husband, he was a good man and she had promised to love and to cherish him until death did them part.

If it was the last thing she did, Maggie would see to it that she kept her marriage vows. And if that meant going to New York with Lawrence, then that was what she would do.

"Are you seeing that bugger again?" Tom Bishop demanded.

"No, I'm bloody not!" Peggy, poking a fork into the potatoes that were boiling on the trivet to see if they were done, wheeled round. "I haven't so much as set eyes on him since he got back."

That wasn't the whole truth; she had caught sight of Josh a couple of times in High Compton and her heart had given the same little flutter it always did. Once, they'd come face to face on the pavement outside the ironmonger's, but Josh had merely nodded at her and crossed the road — to get out of her way, she'd thought, hurt and disappointed.

"You'd bloody well better not be," Tom growled.

"Leave it be, can't you?" Peggy grabbed the handle of the saucepan and lifted it off the trivet with a vicious jerk. Boiling water splashed on to her wrist and she squealed, almost dropping the pan. "Oh — now I've burned myself! You and your stupid fancies!"

"You should be more careful, you clumsy mare."

Although it was the first time Josh's name had been mentioned since Tom had come home from work one day and told her that he was back, spats like this one happened pretty well every day now. Tom had reverted to his old surly ways and things had gone back to being as bad as they'd ever been, perhaps worse. These past weeks, since he'd turned up at work one day and spotted Josh walking across the colliery yard, he'd been in a foul mood most of the time.

"Was that Josh Withers I just saw out there?" he'd asked as the men collected their helmets and lamps from the lamp room.

A couple of the men shrugged, but Hughie Saunders, who knew everything, confirmed it.

"Oh ah, he be working in the carpenter's shop. Started last week. They've been one short since Skiffy Small took bad, and Gaffer took 'im on. He's a bloody good carpenter, so they do say."

"Bloody good for nothing!" Tom retorted, jamming his lamp into place.

"He been working in Ireland, I do hear," Hughie went on, keen to share his superior knowledge. "Now he's come home, living with his mam and dad again. They be glad to have him back, I shouldn't wonder. His brother was one of them got killed over at Shepton Fields when they had that terrible do."

"We all know that, Hughie," Tom snapped, and strode out of the lamp room seething.

Of all the pits in High Compton and Hillsbridge, why in the world had Josh Withers had to get a job here, at Northway? Right under his nose? It was the bloody limit!

Every time Tom caught a glimpse of Josh striding across the yard or squatting collier-style under the wall outside the carpenters' shop, his blood boiled. Arrogant sod! The picture of Peggy rolling around in the grass with him that long-ago night was burned into his brain. He'd never forgotten it, never would. And he'd never trust Peggy again either. She'd been acting funny lately, miserable as sin and telling him to leave her alone when all he wanted was his husband's rights. Well, she'd better not be messing about with Josh again or he'd teach the pair of them a lesson they wouldn't forget in a hurry.

Tom simmered with a fury that was just waiting to boil over. Josh Withers had made a fool of him once; he would make sure it didn't happen again.

"Did 'ee know they'm asking questions again about the accident over at Shepton Fields?" one of the Northway miners asked.

The men had finished their shift and, in a group, Tom amongst them, were smoking and sharing a chinwag before going their separate ways.

Instantly he had everyone's attention. Though time had passed, feelings about the terrible tragedy still ran high, and always would. Something like that would never be forgotten, even by those who had been fortunate enough not to lose a friend or family member.

"Oh ah, they were down the club last night," Hughie Saunders supplied, nodding his head sagely. He always had to be in the know, though several of the others had been there too. "Fairley's stirred things up, from what I hear."

This last, at least, was something of a revelation, but it was in fact not far from the truth. Hughie had got it from his niece, who was in service at Fairley Hall, and, being as nosy as her uncle, was given to eavesdropping whenever the opportunity arose.

A new superintendent had recently taken charge of the police division; Sir Montague had been in his company at a pheasant shoot and expressed his displeasure that no one had ever been brought to book for the cutting of the rope on the hudge, and the new superintendent, keen to make his mark and show that he was far superior and more efficient than his predecessor, had reopened the case. He'd visited the Hall himself, along with a sharp young detective he was nurturing, and when Nellie, Hughie's niece, had been instructed to serve them tea, she'd managed to listen at the door long enough to overhear the gist of their conversation.

"They'm never going to find out who did it after all this time," one of the men said now, and the others muttered their agreement.

All but Tom. As they were talking, he'd seen Josh Withers leave the carpenters' shop and stride across the yard, cocky as ever, and the loathing and desire for revenge had boiled up in him, potent as ever.

"I reckon I've got a pretty good idea who did it," he said darkly. "That Josh Withers. I wouldn't put anything past him."

"Josh Withers? Never!"

"His own brother were killed."

"Why would he do a thing like that?"

"Well, he were after his brother's girl, weren't he?" Tom said. "I seen them together with me own eyes at that dance in the Miners' Welfare not long after the accident. He'd set his cap at her all right, and he wanted his brother out of the way so he could step in."

"Never!"

"But she bain't here now. He's living back home, and I don't know where she be."

"He were gone, though, weren't he, and her too. My missus reckoned there was some funny business there. 'Twouldn't surprise me if they didn't get off out of the way 'cos they had something to hide."

"An' then she found out what he done and they fell out . . ."

"You never do know."

"Josh Withers! Well, I'll be damned . . ."

The story had started, and it would grow and spread, embellished a bit here and a bit there. Josh was unaware of it, barely even noticed the suspicious looks, the whispers behind cupped hands. Until, eventually and inevitably, it reached the ears of the bright young detective who had been assigned to the case.

At twenty-nine years old, Alfred Turner was already making his mark in the force, with a promotion to inspector and a move out of uniform and into the criminal investigation department, but he was ambitious, and impatient to climb the ladder. If he could make an arrest in the Shepton Fields case, it would be a real feather in his cap that he'd succeeded where others before him had failed, but so far he'd run into just as many dead ends as the officers who had conducted the first investigation.

Now, for the first time, he had the name of a suspect, and when he made enquiries of the local officers, he was elated to learn that this Josh Withers had a record stretching back to his youth. What was more, not so long ago he'd burst into a house and assaulted a young man for no other reason than that the boy had shown an interest in Maggie Donovan — the very same young lady who'd been engaged to Withers's brother, one of the victims of the tragedy. He was clearly a violent man who had no control over his temper, and if he could punch a lad on the nose for merely looking at the girl he was besotted with, then it was certainly possible that he would go much further if he thought he was about to lose her for ever.

"Bring him in," he instructed a shocked Sergeant Love.

"Oh, I don't think Josh would do anything like that," the sergeant protested. "He's been a hothead and a rascal in his time, but —"

"That is the trouble with this case," Alfred stated pompously. "You all find it impossible to credit that someone you've known all their life could be responsible. But it was a local, I'm convinced of it. And I am determined to clear up the matter once and for all. So if you'd kindly do as I say and get the man in, we'll say no more about it."

Sergeant Love was bristling with anger at being spoken to in such a way, but he knew he had to bite his tongue and bide his time. With any luck, this cocky young upstart would fall flat on his face, but for the moment he had no choice but to bring Josh Withers in as instructed.

"Where in the world have you been?" Florrie Withers demanded when Josh eventually got home close to nine o'clock that evening. "Not in the pub, I hope! Well, your dinner's ruined. I threw it in the bin an hour ago."

Josh sank down into the chair and buried his head in his hands.

"It doesn't matter about my dinner, Mam. I couldn't have eaten it anyway. I just want a bloody drink."

"But whatever . . .?" Florrie couldn't understand it. Josh hadn't been himself since he'd come home and found Maggie Donovan married, but this was something else. "What's happened, Josh?" she asked.

412

For a moment he didn't move or speak, then he straightened, stretching his neck and massaging it with the tips of his fingers.

"I've been down the police station most of the day," he said flatly. "They've only just let me go, and they'll be hauling me in again tomorrow, I shouldn't wonder."

"What!" Florrie gasped. "But why . . .? Oh Josh, what have you been up to now? Not fighting again, I hope."

Josh snorted a hollow laugh.

"I wish that's all it was, Mam."

"Then what is it?"

Again he was silent, not knowing how to tell her.

"Josh, what have you done?" Florrie asked again.

He looked up, his face showing the strain of the terrible day he'd endured since Sergeant Love had arrived at the carpenters' shop this morning and told him he was wanted at the police station for questioning.

"It's not what I've done, Mam, it's what they think I did. They've got it into their heads that it was me cut the rope on the hudge. They reckon I wanted our Jack out of the way so I could have Maggie."

"What!" Florrie had turned white; she sank into the chair on the opposite side of the fireplace. "But that's ridiculous! I've never heard such a thing . . ."

"That's what they're saying. And how can I prove otherwise? I can't remember for sure where I was the night before the accident, and even if I could, it's no help. I could have crept out of my bed in the middle of the night and gone across the fields with no one any the wiser — that's what they're saying."

"Oh, I'm not having this!" Florrie's shock was turning to anger. "Let me get my coat and I'll go down to that police station and have a word myself — tell that Sergeant Love what I think of him!"

"It's not him, Mam — it's some jumped-up detective from Bath. Sergeant Love couldn't do anything even if he wanted to."

"But they've let you go . . ." Florrie was looking for any crumb of comfort.

"For now. But like I said, we haven't heard the last of it. This Inspector Turner's made up his mind it was me, and truth to tell, who can blame him? He's desperate to find the culprit, and I fit the bill, don't I? With my record, and what he thinks is a motive . . . Oh, they'll be having me in again all right, and I wouldn't be surprised if I didn't end up on a charge of murder."

"We've got to do something," Florrie said determinedly. "What you need is a solicitor. I reckon we ought to go and see Mr Beaven first thing in the morning. He'll be able to tell us what to do."

"Oh Mam, I don't know . . ."

"When your dad gets home from the Prince of Wales we'll talk about it again. But that's what I reckon. First thing in the morning, we'll see Mr Beaven."

Josh was too drained, too weary and too upset to argue.

"I've got the right man, I'm sure of it." Alfred Turner, looking smug, was reporting back to the superintendent before returning to High Compton the next morning. "He had motive, he had means, and he had

414

opportunity. He has no alibi — how could he have? The rope could have been cut at any time between the pit closing in the evening and the miners turning up for work next morning. And he has a history of violence. His record alone will be enough to convince a jury of his guilt."

The superintendent looked doubtful.

"You may well be right. But I'd prefer it if you could come up with something concrete before we charge him. We don't want this falling apart when it gets to court. Hard evidence is what we need, Turner. A credible witness, perhaps. Go back and do a bit more digging and we'll talk again. But well done anyway. This is more promising than anything has been so far."

"Thank you, sir," Turner said, as he knew was expected of him.

He didn't actually hold out much hope of finding either; the trail of hard evidence had had too long to go cold, and the community was too tight-knit to produce a credible witness. If no one had been prepared to speak out at the time, he couldn't imagine that they would now.

Little did he know that exactly what he wanted was about to fall into his lap.

Reuben Hillman's excitement knew no bounds. At last his chance to wreak revenge had come! His father had arrived home that evening with the news that Josh Withers had been to see Jeremiah Beaven, the solicitor for whom he worked, seeking legal advice, as he thought he was about to be charged with the murder of twelve men and boys at Shepton Fields.

Clarence Hillman should not, of course have been discussing it at all — what was said within the bounds of the solicitor's office should have remained there and been treated with strict confidentiality. But he was quite unable to keep the news to himself.

"That dreadful man who came here and assaulted you is suspected of being the one who cut the rope on the hudge," he said, failing to hide the triumph he was feeling. "As far as I can make out, an arrest is imminent. But Mr Beaven is of the opinion that what the police have against him is not enough on its own. I hope and pray it is, but we shall see, we shall see. The man should have been charged with assaulting you, Reuben. Sergeant Love should never have let him get away with it. He's a danger to the community. I can only hope they find further evidence so that he doesn't get away with this — the most dreadful crime imaginable. A witness, someone who saw him that night where he shouldn't have been, that's what's needed."

Reuben's cheeks had turned pink with excitement, and his thoughts were racing. All the police needed was for someone to say they'd seen Josh that night . . . someone who would be believed. Well, *he* would be believed, wouldn't he? He held a responsible post — why, only a month ago he'd been promoted to chief assistant to Horace Freeman. He'd never been in any sort of trouble. His father was clerk to a solicitor, his mother was forever doing good works in the town, his grandmother had run the dame school, which everyone knew was where the best families sent their children to learn their letters, their numbers, and good manners too.

It was the perfect opportunity to get back at Josh Withers.

"I saw him, Father," he said eagerly.

"You saw him? Where?" Clarence asked, astonished.

"Going across the fields that night," Reuben blurted.

"But how could you have seen him?" Alexandra asked, puzzled. "Shepton Fields is a good two miles from here."

"I'd walked out that way in the hope of seeing Maggie," Reuben said. His mother and father wouldn't be best pleased at the admission, but what did that matter compared to the satisfaction he'd get from seeing Josh Withers charged with murder? "I was standing by the gate, and I saw him."

"What time was this?" Clarence asked.

"Oh, I'm not sure, but it was beginning to get dark," Reuben said.

"But you saw him clearly enough to know it was him?"

"Oh, it was him all right," Reuben confirmed. "And he had a knife in his hand," he went on, embellishing the story enthusiastically. "I thought it was peculiar, but —"

"Why did you not say something at the time?" Clarence demanded. "Why wait until now?"

Reuben thought furiously. His father wouldn't be the only one to ask that question if he took his story to the police.

"I was afraid to," he said. It wasn't a very flattering thing to confess to, but it sounded quite plausible. "You know what he's like, Father. How nasty and violent he can be. I thought if I said anything and the police didn't believe me, he'd come after me, give me a good hiding, or worse. A man who could do something like that . . . well, he might do anything. But if the police have got him, they'll make sure he doesn't hurt me, won't they? Won't they?" he repeated pitifully.

"Oh Clarence . . ." Alexandra was looking extremely worried. "Reuben's right! What if this Josh Withers should come after him? He'd be no match . . ."

"I'm quite sure Reuben would be afforded protection," Clarence said confidently. "You must speak out, Reuben; be a man and tell the police what you know. In fact, I think we should go down to the police station right away. I don't suppose the detective will be there now, but you'll find it easier speaking to someone you know. Sergeant Love will pass it on to the appropriate quarter."

"Let him have his tea first," Alexandra begged. "The poor boy needs to keep his strength up."

Clarence's own stomach was rumbling, and the lamb that had been roasting half the afternoon smelled good.

"Very well," he said. "But when we've eaten — well, we must do what we must do."

"I will, Father," Reuben promised.

But he thought he would have difficulty swallowing so much as a single mouthful.

It was two days later when Maggie and Lawrence were startled by the bell jangling fiercely, followed by a frenzied knocking at the door. Patrick was upstairs sleeping soundly and they had been enjoying a nightcap by the fire before retiring themselves.

"What in the world . . .?" Maggie made to get up and answer it, but Lawrence raised a cautionary finger.

"Stay there, my dear. I'll see who it is."

He crossed to the door, Maggie following anxiously in spite of his admonition. She couldn't think who could be hammering so urgently at this time of night. Lawrence drew back the bolt and opened the door, and Billy tumbled into the living room, dishevelled, wild-eyed.

"Billy! Whatever is the matter?"

Billy's face crumpled, and for a moment he couldn't speak.

"Billy!" Maggie said again.

At last the words burst from him.

"It's Josh!" he gasped, still breathless. "They've arrested Josh! They think he's the one who cut the rope on the hudge!"

CHAPTER
TWENTY-FOUR

Time seemed to stand still. Maggie felt as if the ground were dissolving beneath her feet.

"Josh?" she repeated in a disbelieving whisper. "But that's ridiculous! Where did you get this from, Billy?"

"Farmer. He went to bank this afternoon. Everybody in town is talking about it. They say Josh was the one cut the rope. They say he'll hang for it." Billy's face crumpled, and tears rolled down his flushed cheeks.

"He's been arrested, you say?" Lawrence asked. "You're sure you're not mistaken?"

"No. They came for him at work. Took him off — in handcuffs!" Billy was beside himself.

"It's ridiculous!" Maggie said again. "There must be some mistake. Why would they think it was Josh cut the rope?"

"It was that Reuben, the one you used to work with." Billy's teeth were chattering so violently he could scarcely get the words out. "He says he saw Josh going across the fields to the pit that night with a knife."

"What? He's lying! He has to be! Surely no one would believe him!"

"But they do!" Billy gasped. "I told you — why won't you listen to me? They've taken Josh off to prison! Oh Maggie, what are we going to do?"

Maggie was still too shocked, too stunned, to reply. It was Lawrence who went to Billy, putting an arm around his thin, shaking shoulders.

"Come on, my lad, sit down. You look all in. Maggie will make us a nice cup of tea and then you'll feel a lot better."

He urged Billy towards the sofa and the boy's legs seemed to collapse beneath him as he sank down, but almost at once he was up again like a jack-in-the-box on the end of a spring.

"We've got to do something, Maggie!" He shook off Lawrence's soothing hand, running after his sister. "Maggie, please! Maggie . . ."

"For goodness' sake, Billy!" Maggie said impatiently, unable to understand just why Billy was so distressed. It was most peculiar. She was upset, of course she was. Josh was the love of her life, the father of her child. But Billy . . . Josh had never been anything to him beyond a neighbour and a friend of his brothers. She'd always looked after Billy, tried to comfort him when his funny moods dragged him low, but just at the moment it was more than she could cope with.

"Never mind the tea, Maggie. I think we could all do with something a bit stronger." Lawrence was at the dresser, opening the cupboard door and taking out a bottle of cognac and some glasses. He poured a little into one and folded it into Billy's shaking hands. "Here

you are, my lad. Take it steady, though. It's strong stuff."

Billy sipped it and coughed.

"He'll be sick," Maggie said. "Mam always used to give us a drop of brandy to make us sick if we had an upset stomach."

Lawrence ignored her comment, passing a second glass to her.

"This is the best cognac money can buy. Have a little drop yourself. It'll do you good."

The smell was enough to turn Maggie's stomach, but she took a sip anyway, and didn't dislike it. It was much smoother than the rough, cheap brand Mam used to dispense, and as it trickled down her throat, the warmth seemed to spread into her veins. She'd been shaking too, she realised, chilled by the shock of Billy's news.

The brandy didn't seem to be doing anything to calm Billy, though. He was still jerking like a marionette on a string, still crying, his mouth working as he tried to control the sobs. His nose was running, a trail of slime reaching his upper lip. He looked, Maggie thought, exactly as he had looked when he was ten or eleven years old and being bullied by the older boys.

"Pull yourself together, Billy, do," she said.

"But what if they hang Josh?"

"They won't hang Josh." She said it firmly, as much to convince herself as to comfort Billy. "There's been a terrible mistake. Josh didn't cut that rope."

Billy's lip trembled. "I know."

"Of course he didn't. Reuben Hillman is just making up a story to get back at Josh. I'll go and see Sergeant

422

Love in the morning, tell him how Reuben used to follow me around, how he used to frighten me until Josh put a stop to it. I'll tell them what a nasty piece of work he is, and . . ."

She broke off, realising the futility of what she was saying. Would anyone take the slightest notice of her? Somehow she doubted it. The police had wanted to arrest a culprit, Sir Montague Fairley wanted it. If they had someone to pin the blame on at last, they weren't likely to let it go so easily, and her testimony would be brushed aside, especially if it came out that Josh was the father of her child.

Even worse, if the case came to court, as it almost certainly would, and it was Reuben Hillman's word against Josh's, it was going to be Reuben a jury would believe — Reuben who, in spite of being a horrible little toad, had not a stain on his character, whilst Josh . . .

"Oh my God," she whispered, as the horror of it washed over her in an icy tide.

Billy was right. If the jury believed Reuben Hillman, Josh could be sent to the gallows for a crime he didn't commit. For he hadn't done that terrible thing, of that she was perfectly certain.

"What can we do, Lawrence?" she asked pleadingly, unconsciously echoing Billy's words of a few moments ago.

Lawrence laid a hand on her arm.

"My dear, I'm not sure there's anything we can do."

"But he's Patrick's father!" It was the first time she'd ever said it out loud. In her anguish, she'd almost forgotten Billy was there, but in any case, though she'd never told him who the father of her child was, she thought he would have guessed. He'd seen them together, after all.

"I can't see him hanged! I can't!" she wailed. "Whoever did that terrible thing, I know it wasn't Josh."

"Oh Maggie." Lawrence put his arms around her and she laid her head against his shoulder, her whole body contorting with the waves of panic that were sweeping through her.

A sudden crash made her jump, and she jerked round to see the occasional table overturned, the books that had been heaped on it scattered across the floor, and Billy darting towards the door.

Lawrence released her and made to go after the boy, but his limp slowed him down, and Maggie reached the door first, running after Billy into the garden.

"Billy!" she called. "Billy — wait!"

Down the path he ran, disappearing into the shadows. She'd never catch him, she thought, and almost abandoned the chase. But as she reached the gate, she heard the sound of sobs coming from the other side of the hedge, and when she rounded the corner, she saw the dark bulk of a figure crouched against the darker foliage.

"Billy! Whatever is it?" she asked.

For long moments he didn't answer. He was bent double, arms wrapped around himself, shoulders shaking, breath coming in long, tearing gasps between the sobs.

"Oh Billy, don't, please!" Maggie begged helplessly. "You mustn't take it so hard. None of this is your fault."

His head jerked up. By the light of the moon, which had emerged from behind a cloud, she could see his tear-stained face, his mouth working as he mumbled something unintelligible.

"What?" she asked.

"I can't . . . I can't . . ."

"Can't what, Billy?"

"Tell you . . ."

"Tell me what? For goodness' sake, Billy . . ."

Another gasp. Another sob. More garbled muttering. And then, on a heart-rending wail, the words she would never forget as long as she lived.

"It was me, Maggie. It was me!"

Maggie froze, and the world seemed to have frozen around her too.

"You mean . . .?" She couldn't bring herself to put into words the awful suspicion that was assailing her. "You mean it was you who . . ."

Billy couldn't answer; his only reply was the sound of his sobs.

"Oh Billy! Oh Billy!" Maggie, too, was lost for words. She just pulled her brother to her, wrapping him in her arms and burying her face in the spiky red hair while tears of her own rolled down her cheeks.

"Whatever possessed you to do such a thing?" Maggie asked.

They were back in the living room, Maggie sitting on the sofa beside Billy, holding both his hands in hers and gently rubbing his nails, bitten to the quick, with the tips of her fingers. His frenzied weeping had quietened now to intermittent gasps and sobs. Lawrence crouched beside him, a gentle hand laid on the boy's bony knee. Every line of his face reflected the shock and horror he'd felt when Maggie and Billy had returned to the house and Maggie told him of Billy's confession; every small pouch between sagged with anxiety.

"I never meant for anybody to be hurt," Billy said in a tearful whisper. "I didn't want to go down the pit, and I thought if the hudge was broken they wouldn't be able to make me."

"He was terrified," Maggie said to Lawrence, needing to make some excuse for the terrible thing Billy had done, wanting desperately to make Lawrence understand. "They said he had to go underground, as a carting boy, and he was terrified."

"So you sawed through the rope?" Lawrence said.

Billy nodded. "With Mam's kitchen knife."

With something of a shock Maggie suddenly found herself remembering how she had been unable to find it when she was preparing a meal in the days following the accident, and Mam saying: "Oh, blame our Billy. He went off with it when he was in a state about having to go underground. You'll have to ask him what he did with it."

She hadn't asked; she'd used another old knife, and forgotten all about the missing one. Now she wondered why it had never occurred to her that Billy might have used it to sever the rope in a desperate attempt to avoid going underground the next day. But she hadn't. Not for a moment. They'd been so fixated on trying to think who could have had a motive for deliberate murder that such an explanation had never occurred to any of them.

"I thought the hudge would just fall down when I did it," Billy whispered. "I never knew . . ." He began crying again, more softly this time.

"But it didn't," Lawrence said. "You didn't cut the rope right through."

"No, but I didn't know . . . honest, I didn't know . . ."

"It's all right, Billy," Maggie said gently.

It wasn't, of course, it would never be all right. Maggie felt she was being torn in two, witnessing his obvious distress, knowing how he must have suffered this last couple of years. No wonder he'd become ever more withdrawn. No wonder he'd turned and fled from the graveside when the victims of the disaster were being laid to rest. It had been so much more than grief that had driven him. The guilt, the regret must have been unbearable.

Now, however, it was time for Billy to face up to the consequences of what he had done. Josh had been accused of the crime and might well suffer the ultimate penalty for it. Even if it had been anyone but the love of her life whose freedom was at stake, she'd have felt the same. Billy couldn't allow someone else to pay for what he'd done; he couldn't have that on his conscience too.

As if reading her mind, Lawrence patted the boy's knee gently.

"You know what you have to do, don't you, lad?" he said quietly.

Billy nodded wordlessly.

"Would you like me to write down a confession for you? That might be the easiest way."

Billy nodded again. He could write; in spite of his withdrawn ways, he'd learned at school as easily as the others. But Lawrence was an educated man; he'd know how to put the confession together in a way that would be easily understood, he'd know how to spell the long and awkward words, and hopefully he would be able to show exactly Billy's terrified state of mind when he'd done what he'd done — the fact that he had never meant anyone to come to harm — and present the mitigating circumstances in such a way that the judge would show some mercy when the case was heard.

Lawrence rose with some difficulty from his cramped position on the floor beside Billy, fetched a pen and writing paper and drew up a chair so he was facing the boy.

"Tell me everything, Billy," he said. "In your own words. I'll write it down for you."

It was a long and laborious process. Billy spoke haltingly; Lawrence asked him questions from time to time, considering the answers carefully before incorporating them in the statement. The police would do it all again, of course, but Lawrence believed this first confession could also be introduced as evidence, and might help to sway the outcome in Billy's favour.

At one point Maggie said she thought she heard Patrick crying, and excused herself to go to him, but

Patrick was sleeping soundly and Maggie knew that she'd used him as an excuse to escape the relentless retelling of every detail of that fateful night. By the time she returned, they were almost done. Lawrence was reading the statement back to Billy, and when the boy nodded his agreement, Lawrence passed him the paper and pen and Billy signed in his round, childish hand.

"Will they hang me?" he asked fearfully, and Maggie's heart contracted painfully. Until a few hours ago, she'd willingly have assisted the hangman herself in fastening the noose around the neck of the perpetrator of the terrible crime, and triggered the trapdoor that would send him to his death. Now she looked at the pathetic little figure of her brother, guilt-ridden and tormented, and prayed only for mercy for him.

"I don't know, Billy." Lawrence answered him with honesty. "I do think at the very least you will go to prison for rather a long time."

Maggie saw the terror in his eyes again, the terror of confined spaces that had always plagued him, and wanted to cry.

"All I can promise," Lawrence said, "is that you will have the very best legal representation that money can buy. I'll see to that, have no fear. And now I think it would be best if we all try to get some rest. We have a long and trying day to get through tomorrow."

"You can have my bed, Billy," Maggie said at once. "I'll sleep down here on the sofa."

Lawrence spoke quietly in her ear.

"If you can bear it, my dear, we could always share my bed."

For all the closeness that had developed between them in the time they had been man and wife, never once had Lawrence made the suggestion, and neither had Maggie. The intimacy had always seemed a step too far. Now, however, she realised she wanted nothing more than the comfort of another body close to hers.

"We'll do that, Lawrence," she said softly.

Maggie took Billy upstairs to her room, drew the curtains and turned back the covers on the narrow bed. Then she kissed him on the forehead as she hadn't done since he was a child, whispered: "Try to get some sleep, Billy," and left him.

Lawrence was already in his nightshirt when she went into his room. He climbed into bed, and Maggie undressed as quickly and modestly as she could and slipped in beside him.

"God moves in mysterious ways, Maggie," he said softly. "Try not to worry, my dear. This has been a dreadful shock for you, I know, but I'm sure everything will work out in the end."

Maggie wished she shared his confidence. She lay for a while carefully keeping the distance between them, then slowly she crept closer, curling herself around the curve of his back. Then and only then did her eyes grow heavy, and for a little while she slept.

A sound somewhere in the house wakened her. Her eyes flew open and she lay motionless, listening, as the dreadful disclosures of the previous hours came rushing in on her like a cloud of dark-winged ravens, fluttering, suffocating. All was silent, though, and she was beginning to think she'd imagined the sound when she heard another coming from downstairs, a scraping, followed by a thud.

Maggie slid away from the sleeping Lawrence, pushed aside the covers and rolled out of bed. The boards were cold against her bare feet as she crept out of the bedroom, silvered by moonlight, and the night air chilled her warm skin. Across the landing she went, pushing open the door to her own room. Just as she had suspected, there was no human-shaped mound beneath the covers, no ginger mop on the pillow. Anxious, but still reluctant to disturb Lawrence, she crept downstairs.

The living room and kitchen were empty, not a sign of Billy. Maggie went to the front door, which was unlatched, opened it and looked out, but he was nowhere to be seen. He'd gone out, she was sure of it, but where? Back to the farm, or just for a walk to clear his head? She couldn't go after him in her nightgown and with nothing on her feet, and she wasn't sure whether she should in any case. Perhaps he needed some time alone. But she'd wait up for him — there was no way she'd be able to go back to sleep now. She'd make herself a hot drink if there was enough warmth left in the fire to heat the milk; her mouth felt dry from the after-effects of the cognac she'd drunk a few hours earlier.

The moon had disappeared again in cloud and the room was in darkness. Maggie lit a candle, found a lamp and lit that too. It was when she set it down on the table that she saw it — a single sheet of paper placed centrally. A sheet of paper covered not with Lawrence's neat, sloping script but by Billy's s round, childish hand.

Apprehensive suddenly, she picked up the paper, tilting it towards the light so she could read it, and felt her stomach fall away.

I am so sorry, Maggie. I am gone to Newby Pond. I won't bother you any more. Please tell them all I'm sorry. I never knew wot would happen. I can't stand it any more.
Your loving brother
Billy

Newby Pond! Billy had gone to Newby Pond! Men went there to fish sometimes in summer, children went to pan in the shallows for tadpoles. But Maggie knew several people who'd gone there for quite another reason — well, she didn't actually know anyone who'd done it, but she'd heard all right. "He went to Newby Pond" was a euphemism for "he killed himself". And the wording of Billy's note left her in no doubt. He hadn't gone there in the middle of the night to admire the scenery or take a dip — he couldn't even swim. Billy had gone there to end his torment in the dark, muddy waters.

Her heart racing with terror, Maggie rushed upstairs.

"Lawrence! Lawrence! Wake up! Something terrible has happened!"

"What . . .? What in the world . . .?" Lawrence sounded confused, bleary.

"It's Billy! He's gone to Newby Pond! I've got to go after him . . ." She was shedding her nightgown, all pretence of modesty forgotten now, dragging on the clothes she'd stacked neatly last night on the bedside chair.

Lawrence was shaking off sleep, barely able to comprehend what Maggie was saying.

"He's left a note. He's gone to Newby Pond!"

"Oh no!" Fully awake now, Lawrence thrust aside the bed covers. "Leave this to me, Maggie. I'll go after him. You stay here."

"I must come too!"

"And leave Patrick alone in the house?"

"I can run faster than you. I've more chance of catching him."

"And if you don't? He has a head start. Our best hope is that he has second thoughts and delays doing anything stupid. But if not . . . I don't suppose you can swim, can you?"

"No, of course I can't . . ."

"But I can." Lawrence was more or less dressed now. "Look after Patrick, and pray God I'm in time to save Billy."

Maggie followed him downstairs, and stood in the doorway watching as he went, at a surprisingly fast pace, down the path and disappeared into the darkness.

Her heart was pounding and terror was making her sob, but Lawrence was right, there was nothing she could do now.

Nothing but wait, and pray.

It was a mile or so from the cottage to Newby Pond. Lawrence hastened as fast as his gammy leg would allow along the road, then turned down an uneven track that grew ever narrower between overhanging trees and dense thicket. Sometimes the moon emerged from behind the scudding clouds, but he saw no sign of Billy ahead of him. A stitch pricked painfully in his ribs, and his leg ached horribly, sending sharp jolts into his hip, but he pressed on, driven by desperate anxiety and black dread.

"Oh, the silly boy! The silly boy!" He kept hearing his own voice, but knew it was only in his head — he had no breath left to speak aloud.

After a few hundred yards the path forked to left and to right, skirting the perimeter of the pond, a dark expanse before him. Lawrence paused, casting his eyes about in the hope of catching sight of Billy, but there was no one to be seen and no sound but for the mournful hooting of an owl and the rustle of a creature of the night in the undergrowth.

Fearful that he might be too late, Lawrence paused for a moment, scanning the murky water. He thought he saw a dark shape breaking the surface close to the bank a little further along and hurried towards it in an agony of suspense. But it was just a thick fallen branch that had snagged in the mud. Again he looked to left and to right, calling Billy's name, and heard the rustling in the thicket again and twigs snapping, louder this time. Could it be a fox or a badger? But it wasn't likely

that either would come so close to the water's edge —
the open fields would be their hunting ground.

"Billy!" he called again. "I know you're there! Come
out, there's a good lad, so we can talk."

For a moment the silence was complete, then, with a
suddenness that startled him, a flurry of disturbance,
and the thin figure of Billy emerged from the thicket
just yards from him. He stood unmoving, like a terrified
deer at bay, then, as Lawrence moved towards him, he
turned and darted away.

"Billy! Come back! Please . . ." Lawrence knew he
had no hope of catching the boy, but Billy stopped
again, looking over his shoulder.

"Don't try and stop me." His voice was reedy and
thin, shaky but determined.

"This isn't the answer, Billy," Lawrence said. "It's a
mortal sin, you know that."

"I don't know nuffin' any more," Billy wailed. "Only
I can't stand it, that's all."

"We'll sort something out. Just come home with me.
Maggie is going out of her mind with worry."

"Maggie hates me."

"That's not true, and you know it."

"'Tis. She's bound to hate me. Everybody will."

"They'll understand you didn't mean for it to
happen. You've owned up to us now, that was the
hardest part, and we don't judge you, I promise." He
took a step towards Billy, but at once the boy retreated
further.

"Don't come any closer!"

"All right, all right." Lawrence raised his hands in submission. "But stop and think. This is no answer. What would your mother say if she was here?"

"But she's not here! She never will be again!"

"It's true she's in a better place, but she is with you in spirit, watching over you. And what would it do to Maggie? Don't you think she's suffered enough?"

Billy clapped his hands over his ears, crumpling in torment.

"Let's go home to her, Billy."

Lawrence took a tentative step towards the boy, then another, holding his breath. He had almost reached him when Billy suddenly let out an agonised wail and turned and fled once more. Lawrence started after him, calling to him again, but Billy ran on. The path was higher above the water here; a muddy bank fell steeply away from the edge to the deepest part of the lake. Lawrence felt his feet losing purchase on the carpet of wet leaves that covered it and had to slow his pace, but Billy raced on.

"Be careful, Billy!" Lawrence shouted.

Too late. To his horror, he saw Billy slip and lose his balance. Over the edge of the rise he went, and there was a loud splash as he hit the water.

"Oh dear God!"

Disregarding his own safety now, Lawrence half ran towards the spot where Billy had been. As he did so, Billy surfaced, flailing wildly, coughing and screaming for help. Whatever his intentions when he had come to the lake, now that it was a reality, all his instincts for

436

self-preservation had taken over. Lawrence didn't hesitate. Stripping off his coat and boots, he jumped.

The icy-cold water closed over his head, and he fought his way back to the surface. He had hoped that he would be near enough to Billy to grab him, but he was still feet away, and the boy's struggles were taking him further out into the lake. Lawrence swam towards him, the cold of the water making him breathless, the weight of his sodden clothes slowing him down. He reached Billy and tried to get a hold of him, but Billy, totally panicked and still struggling wildly, grabbed him around the neck, dragging him down so that the water closed over the pair of them. "Don't fight me, lad!" Lawrence managed to say as they surfaced once more, gasping and spluttering, before once again Billy dragged him down.

How long the dance of death went on, Lawrence had no idea; he only knew that if Billy kept struggling, he would drown them both. He had swallowed a lot of foul-tasting water and he was weakening fast when suddenly Billy went limp and the terrifying battle ceased. Lawrence knew nothing of life-saving techniques; he simply grabbed a handful of Billy's hair and with the last of his strength made for the bank, towing the unconscious boy behind him.

He had forgotten, though, how far above the water the bank was at this point. There was no way he could even climb out himself, much less get Billy out. Driven on by willpower alone, he made for a spot where the bank was shallower, scrambled out and dragged Billy on to the rough path. Though he was of slight build,

Billy's waterlogged clothing made him heavy, but somehow Lawrence managed it. He turned the boy on to his stomach, head to one side, and began to pump as hard as he could between Billy's shoulder blades. Water came out of him in a rush and, daring to hope that he would begin breathing again, Lawrence redoubled his efforts.

To no avail. Again Lawrence lost all count of time as he worked to try and save Billy, but at last, shivering and exhausted, he realised it would do no good.

"Oh lad, lad, what have you done?" he groaned, sitting back on his heels and surveying the sodden, lifeless body. And then, as his religion had taught him, he began to pray.

After a few minutes, he got up and went to retrieve his coat. He had trouble forcing his feet into his boots, and his hands were shaking so much he was unable to tie the laces properly.

He had failed. There was nothing more he could do for Billy now but ensure he was given a proper Catholic burial. Heavy of heart, dreading telling Maggie what had happened, and shivering uncontrollably, Lawrence set out for home.

CHAPTER
TWENTY-FIVE

All of High Compton was buzzing with the news. Billy Donovan was the one who had cut the rope on the hudge. He'd confessed, and then he'd drowned himself in Newby Lake. The town had rarely known such excitement. There were some who had the story correct, that in the end Billy's death had been an accident, but not many folk believed this version — it was far more satisfying to think that, overcome by guilt, he'd taken his own life.

"Just as well, if you ask me," Sarah said to Peggy. "If he was still alive and kicking, he'd be lynched and that's a fact."

"I expect you're right," Peggy said. She didn't know whether to feel regretful or relieved to discover that it wasn't Tom who'd cut the rope after all.

"I can't understand it," Reuben Hillman blustered. He was worried that there might be repercussions with regard to the statement he'd made to the police that had led to Josh's arrest. "It was definitely Josh Withers I saw going across the fields with a knife that night."

"Nobody doubts you, my boy," his father replied. "He was setting snares to catch rabbits, I expect. But whatever he was doing, he was up to no good, of that you can be sure. You did the right thing in speaking out."

"But what if he comes after me?" Reuben snivelled. "If he knows it was me told on him, goodness knows what he'll do."

Clarence paled. He did not want a repeat of the night Josh had forced his way into the house. But he put a brave face on it.

"He won't do any such thing unless he wants to end up back in prison. Don't worry, son, I'll seek advice from Mr Beaven first thing in the morning, and speak to Sergeant Love, too, if needs be. But I think you'll find that Josh Withers has learned his lesson."

"Oh, poor Maggie!" Cathy Small said when she heard the news. "First her father and Jack, then her mother, and now Billy! It's her whole family gone, all but Ewart and Walter. Whatever will she do?"

But she was unable to suppress a spark of quite inappropriate hope that Ewart would come home for the funeral. He'd been writing to her from time to time — that was how she'd learned of Rose's death — and though she'd walked out with a few boys in the last year, none of them measured up to Ewart in her eyes.

But it was for Billy that Florrie Withers's heart was breaking once Josh was released from prison and was home again, the terrible charges against him dropped.

"That poor little boy," she said, shaking her head. "Oh, it's too awful to think about."

"That poor little boy killed twelve men and boys, including your own son, and damn nearly got the other one hanged for it," Gilby said grimly. "Don't you go wasting your tears on him, our Florrie."

"But he owned up in the end, didn't he?" Florrie argued stoutly. "When he heard our Josh was being blamed. And he never meant for it to happen, any of it. All he wanted was not to have to go underground, and he just didn't think. You know what he was like, Gilby. Scared of his own shadow. Always bullied by them as was bigger and bolder than him. The state he must have been in ever since the accident . . . well, it doesn't bear thinking about. And then to go and drown . . . dear, dear, dear. It fair breaks my heart."

"Well, perhaps we'll find out at last what became of Maggie Donovan," Hester Dallimore said to Dolly Oglethorpe. "The funeral's going to be here, or so I hear. Will she come, do you think?"

"I don't know, Hester, and to tell you the truth I don't care much," Dolly said. "I wouldn't think there'd be many that'd go to the church or the cemetery anyway. Not for the funeral of a lad who did what he did. And if you ask me, those as do go are just plain nosy!"

And that, she thought, had put Hester in her place, and about time someone did it too.

Around and around went the gossip and the comment, and perhaps the only person who remained silent on the subject was Josh.

He was relieved, of course he was, to have been cleared — he'd thought Reuben Hillman's testimony might well put a noose around his neck, and almost as bad was knowing that all the people he knew and respected would believe that he had been responsible for the terrible accident, so jealous of his brother that he'd been prepared to end the lives of twelve men and boys in the most dreadful way. But, like Cathy Small, it was Maggie of whom he was thinking. He wished with all his heart that he could go to her and comfort her, but he knew he couldn't. If she hadn't been prepared to leave her husband for him before, then she would be even more determined not to do anything to hurt him now that he had apparently made such a heroic attempt to rescue Billy from the lake.

He loved her, he knew that now; she would always be in his heart and his mind. But there was not a thing he could do about it.

As Dolly Oglethorpe had predicted, few folk attended Billy's funeral. Most stayed away to show their disgust at what Billy had done; others, though bursting with curiosity, didn't want to be seen as ghouls. But those who did come were treated to their first glimpse of the man Maggie had married, and it caused quite a stir as she walked up the aisle behind the coffin holding tightly to his arm. There were nudges and exchanged glances and whispers that were drowned out by the organ before they all remembered themselves and lowered their eyes in respectful silence. There would be plenty of time later for discussing the sensation — Maggie Donovan married to a man old enough to be her father.

Cathy was amongst the congregation — it was a Wednesday afternoon, so early closing at the shop — but she managed to stop herself from looking at Ewart, who was sitting with Walter and Maggie in the front pew. It wasn't seemly to be having romantic thoughts at such a time.

The Withers family were there too, and similarly, Josh managed to avoid looking too long at Maggie, though he had noticed how deathly pale she was beneath her black veil as she followed the coffin past the pew where he was sitting. A small group of other neighbours had filed in self-consciously and taken seats at the back of the church.

Farmer Barton and his wife arrived late, after the service had started, causing a few raised eyebrows as Farmer's boots clumped noisily on the flagged floor for all his best efforts to move stealthily. He hadn't wanted to come, but his wife had insisted, and he stood staring glumly at the hymn book as she sang lustily, glad only that it wasn't to be a full requiem Mass. If it had been, he'd have clumped out again long before it was finished, on the excuse that it would be milking time and he was a hand short.

But Maggie was almost unaware that the church was half empty and that those who were there were goggling at her and her husband. She was lost in a horrible fog, too upset — and too worried about Lawrence — to notice anything. He'd taken a chill after his heroic exploits of a few days ago, and she had tried to persuade him to stay at home. But poorly as he was, he had insisted. He was all right; nothing would persuade him to stay at home in the warm.

She glanced at him now, sitting beside her, as Father O'Brien recited the prayers. She could hear the rattle in his breathing, and try as he might, he was unable to suppress the persistent cough that had kept her awake most of last night. He was flushed, too, but shivering, so she was sure he had a temperature. And no wonder! When he'd arrived home on the night of Billy's death, he'd been exhausted, chilled to the marrow and in a state of shock. She'd got him into clean, dry clothes, relit the fire and made him a hot toddy — though she was in shock herself, she'd done what had to be done as mechanically as if she'd been one of the automatons in a glass case on the pier that went through jerky actions when you put a penny in the slot. But it didn't seem to have helped. Lawrence was going to suffer for his selfless actions, and the unfairness of it was just another cross she had to bear.

At last the service was over, and the mourners filed out behind the coffin. There wasn't a graveyard at the church; instead, a part of the town cemetery had been dedicated for Catholics, and as Maggie and the other family members set off up the road, friends and neighbours followed at a discreet distance; all but Farmer and Mrs Barton, who headed for home. The committal was as brief as the service had seemed interminable — Maggie bowed her head, fighting back tears as the clods of earth thudded down on to the dark oak coffin that Lawrence had insisted was the only kind good enough for Billy.

"Oh Maggie, you've had trials enough these last couple of years to last you a lifetime," Father O'Brien said, squeezing her hand when the official part of his business was over. "But remember, God never sends us more than we are able to bear, and you have a good man here." He smiled briefly at Lawrence.

"I'll take care of her, Father, never fear," Lawrence said, but as he began coughing again, Maggie was overcome with concern for him. It was going to be the other way around if she was not much mistaken.

"I think we should get you home and into the warm, Lawrence," she said firmly.

As they approached the cemetery gate, Maggie was startled to see Josh there, standing on the path outside. For a brief moment their eyes locked and she felt the familiar wrench in her gut. Then, with just the briefest nod of acknowledgement, he turned and was gone, and there was nothing left for her to do but help Lawrence into the trap that was waiting for them, the pony pawing the ground impatiently. She mustn't think about Josh. All that mattered was getting Lawrence home. They wouldn't have the peace that she would have liked when they got there — Connie was there with her brood, looking after Patrick while Maggie attended the funeral, and with Ewart staying too, the house would be overflowing. But tomorrow they'd be heading back to Yorkshire — the men couldn't afford to lose another day's work — though Ewart had hinted he might be back soon, looking for work back in Somerset.

Much as she loved them all, under the circumstances Maggie thought she would be glad to see the back of them. Just now, all she wanted was to be alone with her husband and son.

* * *

Lawrence had taken a turn for the worse, and Maggie was desperately worried about him. His temperature was raging, and he had fits of shivering so violent that he couldn't even hold a cup of water to his lips; he also coughed constantly, a tight, chest-racking bark that took his breath away and wouldn't loosen, despite the doses of the linctus Dr Mackay had prescribed and the tar rope she had tied around his neck, an old remedy of her mother's.

"There's nothing more to be done," the doctor had said the last time he came to see Lawrence. "All we can hope for is that the infection runs its course quickly and his heart is strong enough to withstand the strain this is putting on it."

Maggie nodded wordlessly. The black dread was hanging over her in a thick cloud. Would all this never end? Surely, surely Lawrence wouldn't be taken from her too?

Just to make matters worse, she thought she was coming down with a cold or influenza herself. Her throat and mouth were dry and tickly, her eyes itchy, and she felt drained and distant, as if she were a million miles away. She couldn't be ill, she told herself firmly. If she was, who would look after Lawrence and Patrick? She was exhausted, that was all, from running up and down the stairs and trying to keep Patrick from disturbing Lawrence. But her determination was not enough. Her nose began to stream and she started coughing herself, a chesty cough which though not tight and painful like Lawrence's still left her feeling weak and ill.

On the Sunday, to her surprise and, she had to admit, relief, Cathy arrived unannounced at the door.

"Tell me to go if I'm not welcome, but I've been worried about you," she said.

On the point of asking how Cathy had known where she lived, Maggie realised — Ewart must have told her. He'd gone out the evening following the funeral, no doubt to meet Cathy, and if she wasn't mistaken, that was what was behind his statement that he was going to look for work back here in Somerset. He must be as keen on Cathy as she was on him if he was prepared to return to the narrow, faulted seams here when he'd got used to better conditions in Yorkshire.

"You know you're always welcome, Cathy," Maggie said now. "I'd have got in touch ages ago if it hadn't meant coming into the shop and making things awkward for you with Mrs Freeman. And I have to admit I'm pleased to see you now. I've got my hands full here, and I don't feel too good myself."

"You look awful," Cathy stated bluntly. She set her basket down on the table and took out a jug covered with a clean muslin cloth. "I brought some of my mam's chicken soup and what a good thing I did. It's just what you need if I'm not much mistaken."

Maggie made a cup of tea for them both and the two girls sat chatting for a while, Cathy filling Maggie in on all the gossip from the shop, Maggie content to just listen. She really didn't feel up to talking, and she guessed Ewart would have acquainted Cathy with all the details of what had happened to Billy, for which she was very grateful. Having to go over it all again was the last thing she wanted just now.

The one subject she couldn't avoid was Patrick, who was scooting round their feet chasing a wooden horse on wheels that Lawrence had bought for him.

"What a lovely little chap he is!" Cathy said. "There's no mistaking who his father is, though. I am right, aren't I?"

Maggie swallowed hard at the lump that had risen in her throat.

"Lawrence is his father," she said stoically.

Cathy raised an eyebrow.

"If you say so."

"He is, in every way that counts." Maggie had to pause to blow her nose. "Really, Cathy, I can never repay him for everything he's done for us, and he adores Patrick, every bit as much as if he were his own. Josh . . ." She bit her lip, turning her head so that Cathy would not see the tears in her eyes. "I don't want to talk about it really."

"Look, Maggie," Cathy said after a moment. "Why don't I take Patrick out for a bit of a walk and you can have a rest?"

Maggie hesitated. She could scarcely bear to let Patrick out of her sight, and she lived in fear that he would catch the same bug that was affecting her and Lawrence.

"It's a bit of a cold wind . . ."

"But it's nice in the sun. If he's well wrapped up, the fresh air will do him good and he'll be out of your hair for a bit."

Maggie relented. "All right. If you're sure you don't mind . . ."

"I wouldn't have offered if I minded," Cathy said smartly. "You put your feet up for half an hour. You look done in, honest you do."

When they were ready, Cathy manoeuvred the perambulator down the path a little awkwardly. She paused at the gate for Patrick to wave to Maggie, and called a goodbye. Still feeling a little apprehensive, Maggie went back indoors. It was nice of Cathy to give her a little time to herself, but much as she would have liked to, she wouldn't feel comfortable sinking into a chair and perhaps dozing off when Lawrence was upstairs alone. She made another cup of tea for herself and one for him and carried them up to the bedroom.

"How are you feeling?" she asked anxiously; she'd been able to hear the angry rasp of his breathing from halfway up the stairs.

"Never mind me. What about you?" It was typical of Lawrence to be more concerned with Maggie than with himself.

"I'm all right. Cathy's come to visit and she's taken Patrick out for a walk, so there's nothing to stop me sitting with you for a bit."

She pulled the chair up to the bedside and sat down, close enough to be able to take the cup if Lawrence should get one of his shaking fits. But he didn't seem to want the tea; he set it down on the bedside table and took her hand in his.

"I've been wanting to talk to you, Maggie. You know, don't you, that if anything happens to me, you are well taken care of."

"Nothing is going to happen to you!" Maggie protested.

"I hope not, but you heard the doctor. My heart . . ."

"Don't even think such things!" But she admitted to herself that it was hard not to when just talking was making him horribly breathless.

"Listen, Maggie." Lawrence turned his head on the pillow so that he could look at her. "The stained-glass window. If I'm not able to do it, I want you to."

Maggie frowned. Her head felt thick and muzzy and Lawrence wasn't making any sense. Was he delirious? she wondered.

"What stained-glass window?" she asked.

"The Blessed Virgin. The one that was damaged. If I'm not able to, I want you to go to New York and repair it."

"Me!" she exclaimed. "I couldn't . . ."

"You could. You've learned so much and you have a talent. Everything you'd need to do the job is put together ready in my workshop. All you have to do is pack it safely."

"But . . . I couldn't go all the way to New York without you!" Maggie gasped, horrified.

A small smile lifted the corners of Lawrence's mouth.

"Oh, you underestimate yourself, my dear. You are the most independent and resourceful woman I have ever met. Going to New York would be nothing

450

compared with all you've endured. The passages are booked, as I told you. You'd need only to get yourself and Patrick to Liverpool, and on to the ship, and my old friend will take care of you when you arrive in America. You'd enjoy it, I'm sure. And experience and travel broaden the mind. You'll come back a different woman, Maggie."

"Oh, I don't know . . ."

Lawrence's fingers tightened over Maggie's hand; glancing down at them, she thought that they were nothing but skin and bone, like the talons of a bird.

"Please, Maggie. It's very important to me that I keep my promise to restore the window and see it safely installed. If I am not able to do it, I want you to do it for me. Is that so much to ask?"

"Oh Lawrence . . ." What Lawrence had done for her was, as she had told Cathy, a debt she could never repay, and this was the first thing he had ever asked of her. Of course it wasn't too much.

"Please, Maggie," he said again.

"Very well." She sighed. "If it comes to that, I'll do it. But it won't. You're going to get better and you'll be able to do the job yourself."

"I don't know that I am, Maggie," he said quietly, and indeed he looked dreadfully drained as he sank back again into the pillows. "Thank you, my dear." It was no more than a whisper, and when his breathing had quietened again he drifted off into an exhausted doze. Maggie could do nothing but sit beside him, still holding his hand in hers.

The next day the fever flared again. Out of her mind with worry, and still full of a cold herself, Maggie ran up and downstairs in between making food for Patrick and doing the necessary chores, dabbing Lawrence's forehead with a cool flannel and urging him to take tiny sips of boiled water, which she left in a carafe beside his bed. She desperately wanted to call the doctor again, but she couldn't leave Lawrence and there was no one she could get to relay a message.

As if an angel had answered her prayers, the doorbell rang at around midday, and when she answered it, there on the doorstep was Dr Mackay himself.

"I'm out on my rounds and thought I'd call in," he said in the lilting accent she still found quite difficult to understand. "How is Lawrence?"

"Awful, Doctor. I'm so glad you're here."

"Hmm. I'll have a look at him, but as I told you, there's little I can do, I'm afraid." The dreadful sound of rasping breathing could be heard now throughout the house, and Dr Mackay stood for a moment listening to it before making for the stairs.

Maggie followed, Patrick in her arms, and stood by the window as the doctor approached the bed and examined Lawrence.

Sweat was pouring from him and he seemed almost unaware that anyone was in the room. He was mumbling something, but Maggie couldn't make out the words, and the ones she did hear seemed to make no sense.

"He's delirious," Dr Mackay said by way of explanation. "I don't think the crisis can be far off."

"The crisis?" She knew what he meant, but asked automatically.

"The moment when either the fever will break or . . ." His lips set in a tight line and he gave a small shake of his head. "I have seen him like this before and he's pulled through, but I don't think he has ever been quite this bad. His lungs are dreadfully congested, and his heart . . . To be honest, I'm not sure how much more strain it will take."

Maggie nodded dumbly. The doctor was really only telling her what she already knew.

"You are a silly fellow, Lawrence," Dr Mackay said. "Jumping into an icy lake in the middle of October in your state of health. What on earth were you thinking of?"

"Billy."

Out of it as Lawrence had seemed a moment ago, that word came out loud and clear.

"Yes, yes, I know. And very commendable too. But you should never have done it. You had no hope of saving him from what I hear; he almost drowned you both, and look where it's landed you."

"Had to!" Lawrence was becoming agitated. "Had to save him! My son!"

"Not your son, old boy. But never mind . . ."

"My son!" Lawrence insisted.

The doctor moved away from the bed, shaking his head.

"He's confused. It's not unusual. The Lord alone knows where his poor troubled mind is wandering.

He's imagining, I expect, that it was Patrick he went into the water to save."

"Not Patrick! Billy!" Lawrence's agitation was increasing, and the doctor returned to his medical bag.

"I'll give him something to quieten him down. You need to save your strength," he said to Lawrence. "If you don't, I won't be answerable for the consequences."

With difficulty, since Lawrence was still protesting, he managed to get a spoonful of tincture into the sick man's mouth, and almost immediately he fell back on the pillows, his head rolling from side to side for a few minutes before his eyes closed and there was nothing but the tortured breathing.

"Is there someone I can call to help you out with your husband's care?" Dr Mackay asked as he repacked and closed his medical bag. "It really is too much for you to manage alone."

Maggie shook her head. "There's no one."

"Would you consider getting in a nurse, then? I'm sure Mrs Harvey would be willing to assist you."

Maggie's heart sank at the thought of having the horrible woman under her roof again at such a time, but Dr Mackay was right, she didn't think she could manage alone.

"Isn't there anyone else?" she asked.

"I don't know of anyone better qualified."

Maggie was thinking furiously. Dolly Oglethorpe had attended Billy's funeral; there was no longer any need for secrecy. And she'd always got on well with Dolly. Suddenly she was yearning for a familiar face.

"There's someone who used to be a neighbour of mine, a Mrs Oglethorpe," she said. "It's a long way for her to come, I know, but if I sent a pony and trap for her . . . Would you be able to ask her, at least? I don't care what it costs, and I'm sure Lawrence wouldn't mind either."

"I'll see what I can do," the doctor promised. "And I'll call by again tomorrow, though I should warn you . . ."

"I know." Maggie didn't want to hear him say the words she was dreading; that it was very possible Lawrence would not live to see tomorrow.

Dr Mackay touched her arm briefly.

"Take care of yourself, Mrs Jacobs. You're doing a fine job."

"Thank you, Doctor."

But Maggie was not at all sure that what she was doing would be enough.

Dr Mackay must have gone straight to High Compton and spoken to Dolly, for by mid afternoon, Fred Carson's pony and trap was drawing up outside the gate and Dolly came bustling in.

"Oh, thank you so much for coming!" Maggie said.

"Just doing my job, dear." She cocked her head, listening to the dreadful rasping breathing coming from upstairs. "I don't like the sound of that. Pneumonia, is it?"

"I think so. And his heart is very weak, too."

"Well, at least I'm here now and you won't be on your own." She smiled at Patrick, who was peeping from behind Maggie's skirts. "He's a bonny one, and no mistake."

"Yes, he is, isn't he?" Maggie was wondering if Dolly had noticed the likeness to Josh, but she had too much on her mind to worry about that.

"You take care of him and I'll sit with your husband," Dolly said, taking off her coat. "Just you get on with whatever you've got to do and I'll call you if there's any change."

"I am so grateful," Maggie said, and meant it with all her heart.

As day wore on and night fell, Maggie had ever more reason to be grateful to Dolly. They took turns at sitting beside Lawrence's bed, which Maggie found almost unbearably distressing. But even that was preferable to trying to do what she had to do elsewhere with that terrible breathing invading every corner of the house.

"You try to get a couple of hours' rest or you'll be good for nothing tomorrow," Dolly said as the clock chimed eleven. "I'll wake you, don't worry, if he gets any worse."

Maggie couldn't see how Lawrence could possibly be worse. He was tossing and turning, obviously delirious, but he was quite unaware of her presence, and Dolly was right: she was exhausted and needed at least a catnap in order to be fit to deal with whatever tomorrow might bring. She sponged him down one last time, then made a hot drink for herself and Dolly and went to her room. She'd thought sleep would be impossible, but almost the moment her head hit the pillow, black oblivion closed in.

The dream, when it came, was muddled but vivid. She was by the lake, except that it was a much vaster expanse of water than Newby Pond and the wind was whipping the surface into huge waves. A feeling of nightmarish dread was making her shiver, though at first she couldn't understand why. And then she saw them, Billy and Lawrence, out there in the water, splashing, struggling.

There was a small boat pulled up on the bank nearby; almost choking on panic, she managed to get it afloat and climbed in. But the oars were on the bank; she couldn't reach them. Somehow she began to paddle with her hands, but she was making no progress. She couldn't see Billy now, but Lawrence was still there, waving to her, calling for help. She paddled more desperately, but still she could not reach him. The waves were so high they kept hiding him from her view, and Maggie was desperately afraid that the next time they subsided, Lawrence would be gone like Billy. She redoubled her efforts, but the boat was rocking now, rocking so violently she was sure it would capsize —

"Maggie! Maggie, wake up!"

Maggie came abruptly through the layers of sleep and realised that the rocking boat in her dream was in fact Dolly shaking her hard. In an instant she was up, her heart beating so fast it seemed to jar the whole of her chest.

"What is it? Lawrence . . .?"

"I think you should come, Maggie." Dolly's voice was low and urgent.

Stopping only to grab Mam's dressing gown, which she had left on the bedside chair for just such an emergency, Maggie flew across the landing and into Lawrence's room.

He was gasping now, long, shuddering, painful gasps with ominous silences between them. Maggie dropped to her knees beside the bed, taking his hand in hers.

"I think he's going, Maggie," Dolly said quietly, and retreated to the doorway so as to afford them some privacy.

"Oh Lawrence, I do love you so much, and I'm going to miss you so," Maggie whispered. "But don't worry, my love, I'll be all right, and I'll do as you asked. I'll go to New York and I'll do my very best with the window. It'll be the finest in the whole cathedral, I promise."

Lawrence didn't answer; Maggie didn't know if he even realised she was there. But suddenly a faint smile lifted the corners of his mouth. One last shuddering gasp, and all was silence.

With a sob, Maggie laid her head against his chest, listening for a heartbeat, or a whisper of breath in his lungs. There was nothing.

"He's gone, Mrs Oglethorpe," she said, and her voice was surprisingly steady. She kissed Lawrence on the lips, and laid her face on his chest again. Then the tears began, hot and bitter, tears for the man who had rescued her when she had been in the depths of despair, and who had shown her a life she could never have dreamed of.

CHAPTER
TWENTY-SIX

Another death. Another funeral. Would it never end? Maggie felt as if she were living in a nightmare from which she could not escape. Even Patrick, who usually brightened her days, was subdued, picking up on the atmosphere that pervaded the little house.

She had to keep going for his sake, of course, and at least she was not alone. Ewart had dropped everything and come down from Yorkshire, and Cathy was there for her too, taking a few days off from work with Mrs Freeman's blessing.

Removed as she felt from everything around her, Maggie was pleased to see the two of them together. They were so well suited, comfortable in one another's company, and clearly in love. It gladdened her heart to think that at last Ewart seemed to have found a girl to make his life complete, and she liked the idea of having Cathy for a sister-in-law.

But nothing could ease her grief for long. It hung over her, dark and heavy, clouding her every thought and making every action an effort; grief not only for Lawrence, but for all those she had loved and lost. Maggie wondered if she would ever be happy again.

"Well that's it, then, I've got myself a job at Northway pit," Ewart said.

It was a few days after the funeral. He and Maggie had finished their evening meal and were lingering over a cup of tea.

"Oh Ewart, that's wonderful," Maggie said. "Northway is so much better than any of Fairley's pits. Josh . . ." She broke off.

"It was through Josh I got the job," Ewart admitted. "And it's also the reason I didn't mention it before. I know he's a touchy subject as far as you're concerned."

Maggie ignored that.

"I suppose you and Cathy will be getting married, then?"

Ewart flushed.

"I haven't asked her yet . . ."

"Well you'd better — and quickly!"

"I've got to find somewhere for us to live first."

"That's no problem. You can live here."

"There's not a lot of room," Ewart said doubtfully. "We wouldn't want to put you out."

"You wouldn't be. You see, there's something I haven't told you. I'm going to America in a few weeks."

She laughed at Ewart's amazed expression, the first time, it seemed, that she had laughed in a long time.

"I'd better explain."

"You certainly had!"

She told him the story from the beginning, and Ewart listened, amazed and a little awed.

460

"Well, I suppose nothing you do should surprise me, our Maggie. But this time you've got me beat!" he said when she'd finished. "How long will you be gone?"

"Judging by the time it took Lawrence in the first place, and given that I'm nowhere near the craftsman he was, I'd say a year at least," Maggie said. "So you see, there's no need for you to be in any hurry to find a place of your own. I'll be glad to know someone is looking after this house, keeping it warm and aired for when I come back. If I do come back," she added after a moment.

"What do you mean?" Ewart asked, alarmed.

"I mean I might just decide to stay in America. It's a wonderful land of opportunity, so they say. What a start in life it would give Patrick! And . . . well, there's nothing to keep me here now."

"That's not quite true, though, is it?" Ewart broke off, unwilling to admit he'd been discussing Maggie with Josh. "Think about this, Maggie, for goodness' sake, before you do anything silly. This is your home. You'd miss it, though you might not think so at the moment. *I* missed it, and I was only in Yorkshire. America — well, that's a whole different kettle of fish."

"There's nothing to think about," Maggie said flatly. "I promised Lawrence I'd do this, and I'm going to keep my word. It's the last thing he asked of me, about the only thing that made any sense in those last few days. Most of the time he was talking nonsense."

"Well there you are!" Ewart argued. "He wasn't thinking straight. He wouldn't expect you to go all the way to America on your own with a baby."

Maggie shook her head. "No, he knew what he was saying all right. He was desperate to make me understand what he wanted and get me to promise to do this one last thing for him. It was different from all the other stuff, when he was wandering goodness knows where. Why, at one time he was even trying to say that Billy was his son. Where he got that from, I don't know. He was very fond of Billy, of course, really good with him, but still . . ." She trailed off, fighting back tears.

"He said Billy was his son?" Ewart said wonderingly.

"Yes. That's the sort of nonsense he was talking."

Ewart was silent. He'd gone very thoughtful suddenly, his face creased in concentration, his eyes distant.

"What?" Maggie asked.

"Oh, it's nothing . . ."

"Come on, what are you thinking?" Maggie pressed him.

Ewart blew breath over his top lip.

"I'm being stupid, I expect, but you've just made me think," he said reluctantly. "When we were little, Mam used to go out charring a couple of days a week. I don't know where it was, but I know it was quite a long way from home. Dad used to go on at her to give it up because the long walk tired her out."

"I don't remember that," Maggie said.

"I don't suppose you would; you were only little, but I was old enough to know there was something going on. I heard rows that really frightened me."

"There were always rows."

"True enough. Like I say, I'm just being stupid. Forget it."

"No, wait a minute." The hairs on the back of Maggie's neck were prickling. She sat forward, elbows on the table. "Are you saying you think it might have been Lawrence Mam was charring for, and they . . . had an affair? That Lawrence was speaking the truth when he said he was Billy's father?"

"I don't know what I was saying, Maggie. I was talking even more rubbish than Lawrence when he was delirious." Ewart scraped back his chair. "I'm going to see Cathy, tell her the news."

"And ask her to marry you?" Maggie was trying to push aside the thoughts that were assailing her and introduce some levity.

"Maybe." Ewart grinned at her, his old self once more. "If I do, I promise you'll be the first to know."

Left alone in the house, and with Patrick tucked up and fast asleep, Maggie found her thoughts returning to what Ewart had said. It was preposterous, of course. Ewart hadn't believed it for a moment, and neither did she. But all the same . . .

Now that the seed had been planted in her mind, she couldn't forget about it. The thought of the aesthetic Lawrence having an affair with anyone, especially her mother, was almost beyond belief. Yet he had been young once — was it such a stretch of the imagination to think that perhaps he had known lust and love? Priests swore celibacy, but some had been known to stray, and Lawrence hadn't been a priest. As for Rose, she had been a pretty woman before hardship and toil had worn her down. Was it possible that she had worked for Lawrence in those days? And that the two of them . . . Was that the reason why Rose had fainted clean away when Maggie had told her she was going to marry Lawrence? And why she had excused herself from attending the wedding? She'd claimed she was ill, yet she had been fit to travel to Yorkshire the very next day. Had the real reason been that she didn't want to come face to face with Lawrence?

Try as she might to push such thoughts out of her head, Maggie couldn't. She kept returning to them, as compulsively as picking at a scab. In some ways it would explain so much — how different Billy was to the other Donovan boys, for one thing. He'd never been rough-and-tumble like them; he was shy and sensitive, a target for bullies. It would also explain why Lawrence had been so ready to help her when she had been in trouble, offering her not just a job but a home and respectability. He had been so kind to her, making sure she wanted for nothing, even teaching her the art that was his life. He had adored Patrick. And he had taken Billy under his wing, showed him endless patience and understanding, and in the end given his life for him.

And something else . . . the memory flashed unbidden into Maggie's head. "She was a good woman," Lawrence had said. Maggie had thought it strange at the time that he should speak of Rose as if he had known her, but had then forgotten all about it. Now she remembered, and remembered too how sad

464

he had seemed. She had thought his sadness was for her, that she had lost her mother. But might it have been something quite different?

And now that she came to think about it, Rose had said something similar about Lawrence. Though to Maggie's knowledge she had never met him, she had seemed convinced that he was a good man who would treat Maggie well.

Maggie sighed, shaking her head. She really didn't know, and she supposed she never would now. All those who would have known the truth were dead. The rest was nothing but a little boy's imperfect memory and a whole lot of conjecture. But strangely enough, Maggie found comfort in the idea.

Rose and Lawrence. It would be nice to think they had shared some happiness, however fleeting.

Smiling wistfully, she went upstairs to check on the sleeping Patrick.

"I have some exciting news, Reuben," Clarence Hillman said.

Reuben, who had just arrived home from work, had barely had time to take his coat off before his father approached him. His eyes narrowed in his pudgy face. The only exciting news he could imagine his father bringing home would be that the police believed they had got things all wrong and Josh Withers had been arrested after all for the severing of the rope. The debacle of his accusation still stung badly. Though his mother and father insisted he had done the right thing in reporting what he had seen, he couldn't help feeling embarrassed every time he thought of it. He wasn't ashamed, or sorry for what Josh had been put through — in Reuben's book it was no more nor less than a bounder like him deserved. But he thought that he'd been made to look a fool. It was that that really hurt.

"Josh Withers is in trouble again?" he said hopefully.

"No — well, not so far as I am aware." Clarence stroked his whiskers, a small satisfied smile playing about his face. "This has nothing to do with that unfortunate business. It's your future we are talking about, my boy."

"Oh!" Reuben was startled.

"Mr Beaven is looking to take on a junior clerk," Clarence went on. "I've taken the liberty of putting your name forward for the post, and Mr Beaven responded very favourably to the suggestion. He'd like to see you as soon as possible to discuss it, but I think we can be reasonably confident the job is yours. Now isn't that good news?"

"I suppose it is, yes," Reuben said, a little uncertainly. His first thought was that his father wanted him where he could keep an eye on him, and that rankled. They'd go to work together and come home together; there would be no minute of Reuben's day when he wasn't under supervision, no opportunity to pursue some secret fantasy of his own, no real freedom.

But on the other hand, it would certainly be a step up in the world. He was becoming a little tired of working in a gents' outfitter's. The attraction had been Maggie working just next door, and of course she was no longer there. And there was a certain prestige about being a solicitor's clerk, even if he would only be a junior to begin with.

"Well, what do you say, my boy? It's a wonderful opportunity, isn't it?"

Reuben considered. If he could tell the young ladies that he had such a job, perhaps they would be more inclined to take a second look at him. Maybe even Maggie. She was, after all, a widow now. The thought lifted his spirits and he nodded vigorously.

"Yes, Father. I'm sure you're right," he said.

The date for her departure to America was fast approaching. Maggie had sorted out all the things she would need for the restoration of the damaged window and they had already been dispatched. Now all she had to do was pack a trunk for herself and Patrick.

She was upstairs putting clothes in neat piles on the bed when there was a ring at the doorbell. She scooped Patrick up and went to answer it — if she left him up here alone, he would very likely pull all the things she was laying out into a jumbled heap on the floor, or he might attempt to come down the stairs by himself and take a tumble.

With Patrick still in her arms, she opened the door, expecting to see the baker's boy with his basket full of pound loaves and currant buns. But it wasn't the baker's boy.

"Josh!" Maggie said, taken completely by surprise.

"Maggie."

"What are you doing here?"

"What do you think? Ewart tells me you're going to America."

"Well, yes, I am."

She should have known, of course, that Ewart would at least mention her departure to Josh. But it hadn't occurred to her that he would turn up on the doorstep. She'd thought that after their last encounter he would find someone else; forget her and all the heartache she had caused him. If, of course, she had caused him heartbreak. Maggie still found it difficult to believe that Josh cared for her as deeply as she cared for him; that it wasn't just the fact that she was out of his reach that made her attractive to him.

"It's madness, Maggie!"

"No, it's something I have to do."

"Ewart says you might not come back. That you might stay in America."

"I don't know. I don't know anything at the moment. It's too early to be making decisions that affect my whole future."

"And my son's future!" Josh rammed his fist into the door frame. "Oh, I know you don't give a damn about me, Maggie. I know you'll always find some excuse why we shouldn't be together. But this is beyond the pale."

How was it that when they were not in one another's arms, they always seemed to end up yelling at one another? Maggie sighed.

"Josh, I am not deliberately doing this to hurt you."

"That's how it looks from where I'm standing."

"Well, it's not." The wind was whipping waves of fallen leaves around Josh's feet and gusting through the open door. "You'd better come in."

In the living room, she set Patrick down on the floor amongst the toys she'd scattered earlier to amuse him.

"I owe this to Lawrence. Please try to understand."

Josh's face was set and grim.

"All I know is you're running away again."

"I am not running away!"

"Last time we talked, you told me you wouldn't leave Lawrence because you didn't want to hurt him. Well, he's not here now, is he? He's dead. And still you're using him as an excuse."

"How can you be so callous?" Maggie flared.

"There's always some reason why you say we can't be together. First it was Jack, then this husband of yours, now some stupid promise you made him. It's hardly surprising that I'm fed up with it."

"I'm sorry," Maggie said wretchedly. "I suppose it must seem that way. It's not what I want, honestly it's not, but I have to do this. I owe him so much and I must do as I promised. When I come back . . ."

"*If* you come back. You said yourself that you might not. And even if you do, what makes you think I'll still be here waiting?"

Maggie bit her lip.

"That's a chance I have to take. I do love you, Josh. I'll never love anyone the way I love you, but you must see I have to do this."

He shook his head.

"You and your conscience."

"I can't change the way I am," Maggie said defiantly.

"Oh Maggie . . ." He looked so defeated suddenly, all the fight gone out of him. Maggie had always seen him as being so strong, but in that moment she caught a glimpse of the vulnerability that lay beneath the rugged exterior.

"I'm sorry," she said again, helplessly.

"I know. And I suppose I wouldn't have you any other way. I love you just the way you are."

Had she heard aright? He'd said he loved her?

"Oh Josh . . ." She had no words left. She bit hard down on her lip, overcome with conflicting emotions. If only things had been different, if only they'd somehow managed to discover one another at the right time, when they would have been free to explore a relationship. If only . . . but things were as they were. She couldn't go back on her promise to Lawrence, however much she might want to, any more than she had been able to desecrate Jack's memory. And for all the strength of their feelings, it was creating an impossible gulf between them.

"I'd better go, hadn't I?" Josh said.

She nodded. "I think you had."

If she had had her way, she would have put her arms around him, kissed him, loved him, but from bitter experience she knew where that would lead. And she couldn't find herself pregnant again now. She couldn't go to New York and do what she'd promised if she was carrying a child.

470

Josh knew it too. He pulled her toward him briefly, kissed her on the lips, then let her go while he still could. Maggie felt as if her heart were breaking.

"I almost forgot." He fished in his coat pocket and pulled out a toy railway engine. "I made this for Patrick."

Through a haze of tears, Maggie looked at it. Perfectly carved in what looked like light oak, varnished to a high sheen, the toy must have been many hours in the making. And Josh had attached a string to the front fender, so that Patrick would be able to pull it along behind him as well as pushing it on its sturdy wheels.

"Oh Josh, it's beautiful."

"It's OK. I was going to make some trucks or carriages to go behind, but . . ." He left the sentence unfinished. *If you're not going to be here, there's no point.*

"Here you are, little man. This is for you."

He crouched down beside Patrick, offering him the toy in the palm of his hand; then, as Patrick took it wonderingly and tried to stuff it into his mouth, he eased it out of the chubby fingers, set it on its wheels and pushed it back and forth in front of the little boy. Patrick gurgled in delight, reached out to do the same, then picked it up and once again tried to stuff it into his mouth.

"Patrick — no! It's not a cake." Maggie bent to retrieve the engine, and for a moment she and Josh were but inches apart, heads almost touching. Then Josh rose abruptly.

"It's all right, I didn't use anything that would harm him if he does try to eat it. But he'll soon discover he doesn't care for the taste, I expect."

He smiled, but his eyes were moist. He ruffled Patrick's hair, dropped a kiss on the top of Maggie's head and moved towards the door.

Maggie followed him with tear-filled eyes. *Please don't go!* she wanted to implore him, but she bit back the words. Her last promise to Lawrence must be kept.

As the door closed after him, she bent her chin to her chest, covered her face with her hands, and let the tears come.

Peggy Bishop could scarcely believe it. She'd come to see Dr Blackmore because she'd been feeling poorly for a while now; well, not exactly poorly, maybe, but certainly more tired than usual, and her stomach was swollen. At first it was hardly noticeable beneath the rolls of fat that came from too many helpings of rice pudding and fruit cake, and she'd made a half-hearted effort to eat less and take more exercise, but it hadn't made any difference. In fact she'd had to loosen the waistband of her skirt yet again. But it was when she started to experience niggling aches and shooting pains that she'd become seriously worried. Did she have a growth? She had gone cold at the thought. Tom, almost as worried as she was when she told him, had suggested she go to the doctor on a Saturday morning so that he could accompany her to the surgery.

He hadn't come into the consulting room, though — that wouldn't have been seemly. Instead she'd left him sitting on a hard bench in the waiting room along with the other patients awaiting their turn.

Now she gazed open-mouthed at Dr Blackmore.

"That can't be right, Doctor!"

The doctor smiled thinly.

"There's no mistake, Mrs Bishop. You are going to be a mother in about — oh, three months, I'd say. Had you no idea?"

"No . . . none . . ." It sounded stupid, she thought, but it was no more than the truth. All these years she'd been married, all the times she'd allowed favours in the past, and never so much as had a scare, so that she'd come to believe she never would. The possibility of it now simply hadn't crossed her mind.

"It is good news, I hope?" the doctor said, looking at her over the wire-framed spectacles that perched on the end of his nose.

"Well . . . I don't know, Doctor. You've given me that much of a shock . . . You are sure?"

"No doubt about it, Mrs Bishop. None at all. You'd better start getting used to the idea. I can see you're surprised, but sometimes these things happen just when you think they never will."

"You can say that again, Doctor," Peggy said.

"Don't worry, I'm confident you will carry this baby and bear it with no problems." Dr Blackmore hitched his glasses up his nose again. "You're young and strong — healthy, too. Eat well, have a glass or two of good strong ale when you fancy it, and rest if you're tired, and you'll sail through. And you know you can call me

473

when the time comes. Would you like me to make a booking for your confinement?"

"Oh not now, Doctor. I shall have to talk to Tom about that."

She left the surgery in a daze, and nodded briefly at Tom, who got up and followed her on to the street.

"What did the doctor say, Peg?" he asked anxiously.

Peggy gave a small shake of her head.

"Not here, Tom. Let's wait until we get home."

"Is it bad news, then?" For the first time in years, Tom was seriously concerned for his wife. If it was a growth . . . the thought of losing her made him feel sick to the stomach. Oh, she got on his nerves sometimes, and she hadn't been the most faithful of wives, but then maybe he hadn't been the best of husbands. He caught her arm.

"For God's sake, Peg, tell me the worst."

"I'll tell you when we get home. I can't talk about it here in the street."

She stepped out determinedly and he took her hand and tucked it through the crook of his arm, all manner of unwelcome thoughts flashing through his head. The minute the front door closed after them, he sat her down on a chair and stood facing her.

"Come on, Peg, I can't stand this any longer. You're not going to die on me, are you?"

Peggy started to laugh, covering her mouth with her hands.

"No, I'm not going to die on you. But by the time this is over, you might be wishing I had. I'm going to

474

have a baby, Tom. In about three months' time, Dr Blackmore says."

"What!" Tom was almost as flabbergasted as Peggy had been.

"It's true. I know — I couldn't believe it either. I'm going to be a mother. And you are going to be a father."

"Well, well, well!" Tom huffed breath over his top lip. "That is a turn-up for the books."

Peggy looked at him anxiously.

"You aren't cross?"

She'd half expected an explosion from Tom. They'd agreed long ago when no children had come along that they didn't really want them anyway, but now, quite suddenly, Peggy was feeling differently about it, as if just by carrying a baby, albeit unknowingly, she was developing maternal feelings and fulfilling a need she hadn't realised she had. Now she was hoping desperately that Tom wouldn't object too strenuously.

"Cross? No!" Tom huffed again. "Taken aback, more like. And all this time I've thought I was firing blanks . . ." His eyes narrowed suddenly with suspicion. "You haven't . . . have you?"

"Of course not!" Peggy snapped, ludicrously indignant given her past history. "I never did really. I only liked a bit of fun, that's all."

Tom's brow cleared, all too ready now to believe her.

"Well, well, well!" he said again, shaking his head. Then a beam split his face from ear to ear, replacing his usual surly expression. "Me a father! Who'd have thought it! There's one or two that'll be surprised at that! Wait till I tell 'em there's life in the old dog yet!"

"Oh, get on with you! You're not old!"

"Old to be a father for the first time. Well, I'll show the young 'uns they bain't the only ones with fire in their bellies!" He glanced at her solicitously. "Do you want a cup of tea? I'll make one for you if you like. You'd better start taking things a bit easy, my girl."

Consideration of this kind was the very last thing Peggy had expected. She watched Tom setting the kettle on the trivet over the fire with almost the same disbelief with which she had received the news of her pregnancy. He actually seemed pleased with the news. Could it be that some of his bad temper had come from believing he was less of a man than his mates? Had it been eating away at him secretly, making him sour and snappy?

Well, only time would tell, but for the moment he was a changed man, and Peggy was determined she would make the most of it.

CHAPTER
TWENTY-SEVEN

Liverpool docks. Maggie had never seen anything like it in her life. The sprawling warehouses and the containers piled high, the small ships darting amongst the big ones, the hustle and bustle, the dirt and the noise. And amidst it all, the splendid liner that was the *Campania*, towering majestically above the wharf, dwarfing everything around her. How in the world could such an enormous vessel stay afloat? Maggie wondered, trembling with nervousness as she approached the gangplank. Surely the sheer weight of her would take her straight to the bottom of the ocean! But she made the crossing regularly, Lawrence had said, and since he'd sailed on her twice, Maggie's common sense told her she must believe it. And really, there was no time for doubts and worries. A steward was waiting to show her to her cabin. Carrying Patrick, she followed him.

On the way, the steward pointed out some of the public rooms, and Maggie saw that they were every bit as impressive as Lawrence had described them, all panelled oak and thick carpet, with rich velvet drapes and carved pilasters. The thought of entering one of them was even more daunting than that of being on the ocean — Maggie wondered how she would ever be able to hold her own with the sort of people who would be her fellow passengers. But she wasn't the ignorant shop girl and miner's daughter she had once been, she reminded herself. Lawrence had taught her so much and broadened her mind. He would tell her she was their equal, and she must begin to believe it. Why, who else amongst them would be able to create a stained-glass window for a cathedral in America's largest city?

That, too, was a daunting prospect, but Maggie wasn't going to start worrying about it yet.

Her trunk had already been delivered to her cabin, which was larger than she'd imagined it would be, and a cot had been provided for Patrick beside her bunk bed. She plumped him down in it while she unpacked her skirts and a dress so that the creases would fall out before she needed to wear them. She didn't want Patrick getting into some sort of mischief that she hadn't foreseen; she would make a thorough inspection of the cabin before letting him loose.

A loud honking attracted her attention. She peeped out of the porthole to see a tug coming alongside the *Campania*, and as she realised they were about to sail, her heart thudded in her chest like the pendulum of a grandfather clock swinging against its casing. So far today she'd had little time to think about the enormity of what she was doing; now, suddenly, it rushed over her in a crushing wave. For a moment she steadied herself against the bunk, breathing deeply and trying to get the better of the sudden rush of apprehension; then,

478

anxious not to miss the moment of departure, she rescued Patrick from the cot and went back on deck with him in her arms.

The dock was a flurry of activity and Maggie lifted Patrick up so he could watch proceedings. But it did nothing to alleviate the panic she was feeling

Everything and everyone she knew and loved was here in England. Though today the weather was overcast, the skies grey and lowering and a cold wind gusting across the deck, she thought of the sights and smells and sounds of a summer morning — the swifts and swallows floating in the pale sunshine over green fields, the fresh scent of new-mown hay vying with the pungent, slightly acrid smell of coal dust, the clip-clop of a horse or pony ebbing and rising as it trotted around the bends in the road, coming ever closer. She'd miss all that; she couldn't imagine any of it in a great city like New York.

And then there were the people she was leaving behind. True, she'd lost many of those closest to her in recent times, but the ones that were left were very dear to her. And there was always someone familiar to turn to, something she'd have to forgo in New York. She'd never forget how kind Dolly Oglethorpe, her old neighbour, had been when she'd needed help nursing Lawrence, or Father O'Brien, who had put her in touch with him, or Cathy, who was soon to become her sister-in-law. Ewart had finally asked her to marry him; he'd come home cock-a-hoop one evening to tell Maggie the news.

"And about time too!" Maggie had chided him. "You should have made up your mind to come home and make an honest woman of her long ago."

"I expect you're right, Maggie," was all he had said, but he couldn't seem to stop smiling.

Maggie had been sorry she would miss the wedding, which was to take place at Christmas, but she didn't suppose they'd miss her. They would have eyes only for each other.

But most of all, of course, she was aching for Josh. She wanted him here, beside her, more than she'd ever wanted him. To feel his arm about her, strong and comforting, to rest her head against his shoulder as the ship departed, to know that he was here for her, now and always. Would he be waiting for her when — if — she came back from America? Given that she always seemed to be turning him away, it was a big ask. Really she couldn't blame him if he looked elsewhere, found himself a woman who would always put him first instead of way down her list of commitments. At the very thought, something seemed to close up inside Maggie, pinching painfully at her heart.

Was she turning her back on a chance of happiness for ever? Depriving Patrick of his real father? She'd promised Lawrence that she would make this trip, and she intended to keep her promise. But at what cost? The enormity of the sacrifice she was making threatened to undo her, and all she wanted was to rush to the gangplank with Patrick in her arms and disembark before it was too late.

480

But she wouldn't, of course. All she needed to do was steel herself for a few more minutes and then there could be no turning back.

"Look, Patrick!" In an effort to distract herself from her disturbing thoughts and emotions, she drew Patrick's attention to the activity on the quayside below them.

Seamen swarmed about amid coiled ropes and hawsers, and there were quite a few people lined up on the dock, waving or peering eagerly to catch sight of the relative or friend they had come to see off.

Copying, as he was apt to do, Patrick was waving too.

"That's right, my love, you wave!" she said, trying to smile. "It's exciting, isn't it?" Patrick ignored her. He wasn't looking at the assembled crowd, she realised; instead his attention was focused on someone approaching along the dockside. A tall, dark figure who was waving back. To Maggie's disbelieving eyes, it looked for all the world like Josh. For goodness' sake! she chided herself. Thinking about him was driving her a little crazy. Wishful thinking couldn't make him materialise like a genie from a bottle, however much she wanted it. But she couldn't take her eyes off the figure all the same. The men working on the gangway had almost completed their job and were about to move it away when the figure broke into a run.

"Wait! Wait!"

He was no longer waving to Patrick, but shouting to the dock workers, who paused, looking towards him and making no effort to disguise their impatience.

"Wait!"

Maggie's heart gave a gigantic leap.

She wasn't going crazy. It was Josh! He must have come to see her off.

"Josh!" she called, waving frantically herself with her free arm as she tried to attract his attention.

He looked up, still running along the dock far beneath her, but made no reply. To her astonishment, she saw that he was carrying a large carpet bag, and he was making for the gangway. Then he was on it, disappearing out of her sight, and the men were wheeling it away, ready for departure.

Totally confused, Maggie turned to the companionway just as Josh emerged.

"What are you doing?" she demanded, unable to think of anything else to say.

"What do you think? Coming with you."

"Oh Josh! I don't believe this . . ."

"You'd better. And you'd better not think of an excuse to send me home again either, because it's too late for that."

And then she was in his arms, a startled Patrick sandwiched between them, and his mouth was on hers, devouring her with an intensity that seemed to draw their very souls together.

The ship's siren honked loudly again, bringing them back to reality.

"We're moving!" Maggie said, her voice trembling a little from both excitement and the power of that kiss. "We're sailing!"

"For once, I timed it just right then, didn't I?" Josh said.

He took Patrick out of her arms, settling him comfortably on his shoulders. Then he put an arm round Maggie's waist, and together they watched as the *Campania* moved slowly away from the dock.

Postscript

A year later

Winter sunshine fractured through the jewel-coloured glass, so that it seemed to glow with a depth and vitality that was almost ethereal. The blue of the Madonna's gown was deeper and richer than a September sky; the halo of light encircling her head shone brighter and more luminous than the evening star. She sat there now in her proper place on one side of her beloved son, the Lord Jesus Christ, completing the triptych with St Joseph. As Maggie gazed up at her, she felt she would burst with pride. She'd done it. She'd done what Lawrence had asked of her and she'd done it unaided. Never in all her life before had she felt so fulfilled as she did now, gazing up at her achievement.

"What do you think then, Lawrence?" she asked silently. "Does it look as you intended?"

She often talked to him still, and she had sometimes felt he was there at her shoulder as she worked painstakingly to repair the damaged window. Though her life was so different now, she would never forget him, and the things he had taught her would never cease to matter. If she had a guardian angel, it might very well be him, she thought.

But in truth, of course, he had been all too human, and she was certain now that he had indeed been Billy's father. In the pocket of her coat her fingers closed over the letter from Ewart that had arrived many months ago now telling her of the will he had found in the drawer of Lawrence's desk. He'd been surprised that Maggie had not known it was there, or found it herself, but there hadn't been time for her to turn out every drawer and cubbyhole before leaving for America. And Ewart had been even more surprised by what the will contained.

It was dated a few days before he and Maggie had been married, witnessed by Father O'Brien and the monk with whom he shared the ministry of the two churches. The bulk of his estate was to go to Maggie in the event of his death, but there was another provision: "As stated in my previous will, I bequeath to William Donovan the sum of five hundred pounds, which I hope will allow him to pursue whatever course he wishes to follow in life."

Five hundred pounds! A fortune! Of course, poor Billy would never now inherit; he had already died before Lawrence breathed his last, but there had been no opportunity for the will to be changed. But the implications of the bequest were crystal clear. The will had been written before Lawrence had taken Billy under his wing, and even referred to a previous will that had also included Billy as a beneficiary. Both Ewart and Maggie had come to the same conclusion. Lawrence was making provision for his son, even though he hadn't specifically owned him as such.

Maggie wished with all her heart that he had been able to tell her himself, but she could understand that it wasn't a subject Lawrence had felt inclined to broach, and neither, of course, had Mam. But although she was slightly shocked at the thought of her mother being unfaithful to her father, she couldn't find it in herself to blame her. Dad hadn't been the most attentive of husbands, he'd seemed to care more about his gambling and drinking than he did about Mam, and all in all she'd had a hard life. If she had found some joy with a good man such as Lawrence, then Maggie could only be glad for her.

She folded her hands and bowed her head, whispering a prayer for all of them, and might almost have been back in the converted barn that was St Christopher's instead of this great cathedral on the other side of the world. The scent of incense mingled with the slight mustiness of old stone was familiar, the candles glowed on the high altar and in the votives, and though everything here was so much grander, the feeling of reverence was just the same. The window that Lawrence had created was a part of that grandeur now, part of that offering, and would be for generations to come. And she had played a small part in its completion, which made her feel humble as well as proud.

Footsteps echoing on the tiled aisle made her turn, and she saw her husband and son approaching her. Josh was holding Patrick by the hand, but the little boy was walking well now; no more waddling — he looked ready to skip and run. He was growing tall; Maggie felt a moment's regret as she thought that soon it would be time to take him out of his baby dresses and put him in a proper pair of trousers, and cut the curls that tumbled to his shoulders. But, God willing, there would be other children. Whilst she had been working on the window, she and Josh had taken care that she didn't fall pregnant again, but now that it was finished, they might well decide it was time for Patrick to have a little brother or sister.

And there were other decisions to be made, too, important ones. Would they go home, or would they stay in this wonderful land of opportunity? They hadn't yet made up their minds. But whatever happened, they would be together, that much was certain. Both Maggie and Josh were determined that nothing would keep them apart again.

Maggie bent now, opening her arms, and Patrick let go of Josh's hand and scooted down the aisle towards her. She lifted him up, pointing at the window.

"What do you think, Patrick? Isn't it splendid? And Mammy did a little bit of it, though most of the work was Lawrence's." She wanted to keep Lawrence alive in the little boy's memory; he had, after all, played such an enormous part in his early years.

"Pretty!" Patrick stretched out his hands as if he could touch the glowing shards far above his head.

"Yes, pretty," she agreed, smiling.

"Beautiful," Josh corrected her, gazing up in awe. "Do you think you'll ever do another?"

"I'd be hard pressed to do something like this from scratch," Maggie said. "Lawrence taught me a lot, but it will take years and years — if ever — before I'm able to even think of something on this scale. But I would like to do some smaller projects. If I can."

"We'll make sure of it," Josh said, putting an arm around her waist. "It would be a shame to let a talent like yours go to waste."

"I'd like that." Maggie rested her head against Josh's shoulder, thinking how lucky she was. None of what she had been through seemed important now. She would never forget those she had loved and lost, never stop loving them. But here and now, she felt she held the world in her arms.

A shaft of sunlight touched her face with the golden glow that came from the shining stained-glass halos, and Maggie knew she was truly blessed.